To David,

SHADOW DANCE

BOOK ONE OF THE OFFLINE SERIES

C. K. ANDERSSON

For the Light!

CKA ♥

Copyright © C. K. Andersson 2023

Book cover illustration © Shade of Stars 2023

Conlang created by Frederico Schroeder

ISBN: 978-1-7393539-0-2 (ebook)

ISBN: 978-1-7393539-1-9 (paperback)

ISBN: 978-1-7393539-2-6 (hardcover)

This novel is a work of fiction. The names, characters and incidents portrayed in it are the work of the author's imagination. Certain localities are mentioned, but the characters involved are wholly imaginary. Any resemblance to actual persons, living or dead, or events is entirely coincidental.

All rights reserved. No part of this publication may be reproduced, stored in a retrieval system, or transmitted, in any form or by any means, electronic, mechanical, photocopying, recording or otherwise, without the prior permission of the publisher.

CONTENT WARNINGS

Andersson's novel is aimed at adult readers and touches on dark subjects.

Graphic
Anxiety and panic attacks
Blood
Death
Depression
Hallucinations
Psychological abuse
Torture
Violence, including domestic abuse

Moderate
Bullying
PTSD

Mild
Addiction (magical substances)
Animal abuse (implied)
Animal death
Body dysmorphia (implied)
Child sexual abuse (implied)
Classism (implied)
Nudity
Racism (implied)
Sexual assault (implied)
Sexual harassment
Strong language

For my parents

CHAPTER ONE

Saga Falk

A sigh escapes my lips as my eyes open and I fumble after the cell phone next to me in bed. It's three in the morning and my dreamscapes have been empty. *He didn't wait for me in my dreams.*

This illusion has me emotionally anchored, this man whom I can't touch in real life. Someone who isn't waiting for me when I step through the door to the flat. Dwelling in the deepest, most secret nook in the chamber of my heart, he sits on his throne and bestows the nectar of comfort upon me when negative thoughts conspire to submerge my mind.

Accompanied by a hint of melancholy deep within, I dive into the gallery on my phone. *There he is, the one whose invisible kisses heal my sorrows. Kailunn Sunseeker, the prince of the high elves.*

My fingertip runs down his long white hair on the screen. The icy gaze from his grey eyes penetrates my entire being. His full lips, curled into a slight cold smile, sending a warm wave of emotion washing over me. The warmth spreads from my head to my shoulders, down my spine, across my chest, and out to my fingertips and toes. *He's truly enchanting.*

Longingly, I let out another sigh. I could lose myself in pictures of him for hours on end, but I'd better try to capture any remaining traces of sleep dust. I need the rest if I'm going to be able to go to work later today.

The smell on the bus is awful. I'm scrolling through my thoughts as well as the phone while I make my way downtown before work. The buildings in the cold concrete landscape pass by outside while raindrops patter against the window. For a moment, I lift my gaze and focus it briefly on a couple holding hands, one of them keeping a dog in a raincoat on a lead as they're walking down the street. *They look so beautiful and happy together.* During a split second, I experience a sucking sense of loneliness and my mind sneaks to Howard.

Howard, or Retsam as he's known in *Reign Online*—an MMORPG my friends and I have been playing for thirteen years—started sending me private messages shortly after we had joined an in-game guild. The atmosphere between us had been friendly. He had given me some superb advice to enhance my play style and fully utilise my priest's class abilities, and I had been flattered that one of the absolute best players in the guild was paying attention to me.

After a while, we had started to voice chat, and I noticed he showed an interest in me, asking me how my day had been. Even though it seemed rather exciting that someone was flirting with me for once, I couldn't help but feel I was somehow betraying Kailunn, which isn't logical considering Kailunn is a fictional character and Howard is a real person with thoughts, feelings, and dreams. However, Kailunn has been my security for many years. He's there when I need him. I can play his voice on repeat in my head when I need encouragement, and he doesn't have demands—unlike Howard.

I adjust the padded headphones over my ears and change the music to something a little less sentimental. Slowly sinking into the seat, I let my eyelids wander down over my eyes. Time for a brief respite from the thoughts in my head and a chance to pluck the emotional spikes from my soul.

The rain-heavy air hits me as I get off at my stop and I adjust the collar of my coat. I rush to one of the clothing stores and lightly shake my curls as I step inside and let the warmth envelop me, my gaze wandering over the clothes through the fog on my glasses. *Don't like the colours. Too modern. Too low-cut for my taste.* My fingers run over a pink jumper with a high collar and, thoughtfully, I chew on my lower lip. Normally I wouldn't choose such a colour as I tend to dress in neutral tones, but the design appears flattering, and the material feels nice against the skin.

"Saga."

Just as I'm about to make my way towards the fitting rooms, a strange voice calls my name and I look around, baffled. The other individuals in the store don't seem to be paying me any attention. With a weak shrug, I decide not to put too much thought into it. *It's probably just my imagination.*

I step into one of the fitting rooms, locking the door behind me. After hanging my coat on a hook, I take off my headphones, grey hoodie, and brown camisole. My gaze jumps between the different mirrors, and I pose at different angles, having adjusted the pink top over my butt and hips. It's a little pricey, but having felt a bit dejected lately, I could do with some cheering up.

After taking off the garment, I lightly pat the fabric, folding it gently over my arm. As I reach for my camisole, I freeze.

"Saga."

I hear it again. *That voice…*

It crawls close to me, almost whispering in nature, savouring every letter. I catch my breath, noticing how my heartbeat rushes. My ears prick up and I stand completely still; listening, waiting.

People are changing nearby. Some are talking on the phone and others are happily conversing with others standing outside, and none of them seem to be the owner of this voice.

I shake my head, closing my eyes and counting my breaths. *One. Two. Three.* Invisible, cold fingers and tentacles seem to slither over me; they caress my hair, and indistinct whispering fills my ear. I take refuge in the corner of the fitting room whilst wrapping my arms around myself. *What's going on?*

Slowly, my eyelids open as the invisible phenomenon ebbs away, allowing the warmth of the room to seep into my pores. I rush to put my clothes back on and attempt to shake off the unpleasant feeling. Out of the corner of my eye, I see something flash in one of the mirrors. I turn my head and both my hands fly up to my mouth, covering it as a weak gasp escapes my lips.

A tall man in heavy armour with golden shoulder-length hair and a scar on his right cheek looks back at me with sky-blue eyes. *He has such gravitas.* In one hand, he's holding a powerful sword, and he's extending the other palm in my direction, glowing with intense white light. His facial expression testifies to his strength, and the intense gaze grabs hold of my entire being, almost shaking me.

The light blinds me. Rubbing my eyes and glancing back again, an outline of someone else emerges in a mirror to my left. I feel like I'm about to suffocate as my heart flutters all the way up to my throat.

I must have completely lost it. These illusions are playing tricks on my mind.

SHADOW DANCE

The strings of my heart strain in an almost violent manner and it feels as if they're about to break. I lean towards the mirror, holding out my hand. Hesitantly, I touch the glass with my fingertips, and I see how Kailunn, in his towering figure of two metres, leans down on the other side. He imitates the movements of my hand before putting his palm against the surface where my hand rests, looking at me with his piercing eyes shimmering in silver. In his other hand, he's holding a pipe with a thin trail of smoke curling out of its chamber, and its aroma sneaks into my nose. *It smells just like vanilla.*

His exhalation spreads a thin mist on the glass, and I move closer, staring at him with my mouth half-open. A ripple effect spreads over the surface of the mirror where our hands meet, and I feel like I'm losing control over my thoughts. *All I can think of is him.* He's adorned in a long white and purple robe with ornate details sewn with gold thread. Sun-shaped jewellery dangles from in his earlobes and intricately detailed gold cuffs embrace the pointy parts of his ears, glimmering in the light.

A strong arm gently finds its way around my waist; silky strands of hair and a short beard tickle my neck, causing me to break out of the state of bewitchment.

"Where do you think you're going, little butterfly?" I hear a deep, soft voice utter next to my ear.

Blinking twice, I notice the other man's reflection. Once again standing in the right mirror, looking at me as he embraces me from behind, now wearing much more casual-looking clothes than the previously displayed armour. A white linen shirt with lacing in a V-shaped collar and dark brown trousers. *He seems familiar.* The clear blue eyes radiate a smile just as warm as the one decorating his lips, and when he tenderly places a kiss on my earlobe, I stifle a sudden giggle deep down in my throat. Somehow, it feels like he's connected to me. *Who are you?*

An intense shiver of pleasure courses through my entire body as the knight's fingertips playfully wander over me under the fabric of my camisole. *Why does it feel good? It's not Kailunn who's touching me.*

He looks to be slightly shorter than Kailunn and in my head I'm frantically searching for memory fragments of him. I throw a glance to the left, noticing the high elf leaning against the frame of the other mirror as he stares right into my soul and takes a puff from his pipe.

I must stop hallucinating.

Narrowing my eyes, I take a deep breath as I count to three before exhaling. *Is this some kind of spiritual experience or have I simply lost my mind?*

As I get home from work and lock the front door, I hang my coat in the hall and put down the bag containing my new jumper. A show is playing on the TV and I find Ambrosia, my childhood friend, typing on her phone whilst resting on the sofa.

"Hey, roomie," she says as I put my shoes away and greet her.

I make my way into the kitchen to wash my hands. It has been a long day and my head feels heavy with fatigue. Bringing a glass of water with me, I take a seat next to Ambrosia and sigh as she sinks into the cushion and stretches her legs over my thighs.

"How was your day?" I ask, shifting my legs a little to make myself more comfortable.

"I had an entitled customer being shitty to me, so it was pretty standard," she replies, fiddling with her nose piercing while she stares down at the phone.

I look at the TV screen, tilting my head to the side as I try to get into the action, but my mind lies elsewhere.

"Something strange happened to me."

As the words leave my mouth, I immediately regret it, but it's too late to take them back now. Ambrosia sits up and looks at me with her big green eyes. She has a clump of mascara at one inner corner of her eye and I'm trying not to be distracted by it. Nervously, I tuck wisps of hair behind my ears.

"I was in a changing room in a shop and was just about to try on some clothes when I heard a strange voice," I continue. "It felt close, as if the person was standing right next to my ear. I panicked, closed my eyes, and when I opened them again I saw... people in the mirrors. A tall, blond man with the bluest eyes I've ever seen. He was dressed like a knight. A few seconds later I saw..."

I fall silent momentarily as I notice how Ambrosia furrows her brow, her gaze clearly expressing confusion.

"I saw Kailunn." I turn my head away. "It felt real. Then I was embraced by the blond man."

"Seriously? Have you lost your mind?"

Ambrosia's statement cuts into my chest like a blunt knife, and I smile dryly.

"Forget about it," I say, standing up as I push her legs away. "I should have kept it to myself."

Quickly, she rises to her feet to grab my arm.

"I'm just worried about you. You're such a sensitive soul."

"If you care, you'd listen to what I have to say and not ask a bunch of unnecessary questions before I've even finished speaking!" I hiss, losing my temper to mask my embarrassment. Angrily, I pull away and feel tears welling up in my eyes. *This is ridiculous. I cry almost every time I get upset.*

"Why are you getting so pissed off?"

"What do you think?" I snarl. "Each time I open my mouth to talk to you, you pretend to be some sort of armchair psychologist."

"It's infuriating when you constantly get worked up over nothing!"

Ambrosia's harsh tone makes me narrow my eyes at her, and I cross my arms over my chest. A deep breath works its way through my nostrils. We stare at each other for a while saying naught. Finally, I run my fingers through my hair as I calm myself down. The voices from the TV in the background seem distant.

"Sorry," I mumble and feel my shoulders slump a little. "I don't know why I get so angry sometimes."

Arms wrap around me as Ambrosia pulls me into a hug.

"I should apologise, too," she says next to my ear. "I can be a little insensitive. It wasn't my intention to make you feel bad."

"It's fine."

Her hands stroke my back, and the hug tightens.

"Geez. You almost broke my ribs," I mutter.

"You're like a twig."

The slight teasing tone of her voice lightens the atmosphere between us. She puts her hands on my shoulders and takes a step back as she looks at me.

"You forgot to mention an important thing about the blond guy. Was he hot?"

A nervous laugh finds its way out of my throat in pure surprise.

"Being human, he obviously didn't radiate the same beauty you get with elvish features, but despite that, he was handsome."

We settle down on the sofa again, and I notice Ambrosia quickly typing on her phone. I touch my fringe and gently poke her with one of my big toes.

"What are you looking at?" I ask, sipping on my water.

She twists a fiery red curl around one of her fingers for a while without answering, before slamming the sofa's armrest excitedly with one hand.

"Yes!" she exclaims. "I've found him. Check it out!"

Surprised, I blink twice and feel curiosity take over. As she turns the screen towards me, my heart skips a beat. The memory of his lips against my skin flashes by as a tingling sensation spreads in my stomach. How is it even possible? *He's not Kailunn*. Only Kailunn makes me feel anything these days.

"This is fan art, but you get the idea." Ambrosia grins at me. "Grand Prior Garren Roseheart, highest-ranked paladin in Whitekeep, and my class leader in *Reign Online*. Maybe your mind's playing tricks on you because you need a proper man like him."

"I've probably only come across him a few times in my role as a high elven priest, and I remember little," I mutter, unable to tear my eyes from the screen. "He's handsome, though."

"Right? I wouldn't kick him out of bed."

His eyes almost branded me. I scratch my neck and sigh heavily. My gaze follows Ambrosia as she gets up and makes her way to the kitchen.

"Do you think I'm crazy?" I ask bluntly, in a slightly louder voice.

"You're eccentric, but I wouldn't say crazy," she replies, as I hear her closing the door to the freezer.

The sound of the metallic clatter of cutlery interrupts my train of thought. When she returns, she places a half-empty tub of ice cream together with two spoons on the table in front of us with a loud bang.

"Eat," she says while grabbing a spoon and scoops up a generous amount of vanilla ice cream.

"Have you forgotten I don't like other people's germs?" I grunt sourly, shooting a glare in her direction.

"You realise I won't wash two dishes just because you have a phobia?" she replies and licks the spoon prior to scooping up more ice cream. "Besides, you'll never be able to kiss anyone again if you keep doing what you're doing. Stop acting so paranoid."

"Maybe I don't want to kiss anyone."

My sentence is barely audible, and I look at the ice cream while pushing my large, thick-rimmed glasses up the bridge of my nose with one finger. Strategically, I scoop up some from one side of the tub which looks relatively untouched, telling myself Ambrosia hasn't already been digging there with her saliva-soaked spoon.

"Are you saying you wouldn't kiss Kailunn if you had the chance?"

She raises an eyebrow at me and scrunches her nose when I drop some ice cream on the floor. Grabbing a napkin left from yesterday's takeaway, I wipe it clean before I suck a little on the spoon, all the while letting my thoughts wander. *There's nothing I'd rather do.*

"But it would mean he's real, and the majority of real individuals have demands and expectations," I say, still with the spoon in my mouth as I'm avoiding answering the question.

Ambrosia shoves more ice cream into her mouth and licks her lips with the tip of her tongue.

"Focus on a casual relationship in the future, then. Just have a good time, and don't think about germs."

"It's not my thing, Ambrosia."

I can't imagine going further than hugs and kisses without a deep, emotional connection; I don't have the same need for deeper intimacy, unlike a lot of other people. She just doesn't get it.

I shrug, putting the spoon down and taking one last look at the paladin on Ambrosia's phone screen before handing it to her.

"I'm not sure I'd dare to fall in love again, so I'd rather keep to myself," I continue.

Her eyes flash as she leans towards me.

"How about you and I get together if we're still single at forty?"

I roll my eyes.

"We already live under the same roof, and I couldn't bear to be romantically involved with you. You rarely do the dishes and leave your clothes everywhere."

Ambrosia throws her head back as she laughs out loud, twirling a lock of fiery red hair between her fingers.

"And you're just like a force of unbridled fury creating angry chaos. You keep me organised though," she says, nodding. "We'd make a hot couple."

"I'm flattered, but no thanks," I answer, giving her an amused smile.

I put my feet up on the table and wiggle my toes in my thick purple socks. *Germ phobia or not—I'd love to kiss Kailunn in real life. I just don't want to admit it to her. She knows I like the elves in Reign Online and especially him, but she doesn't need to know all the details of my reveries.*

"Should we watch a movie instead?" I ask. "I'm not in the mood for whatever this show is."

Ambrosia browses the streaming service's offerings while my thoughts drum in my head with a playful beat. *Maybe I ought to learn more about the knight later tonight, should I remember it.*

Another workday at the gaming cafe. At this point, they all seem to be the same one on repeat. My colleague, Emelie, is standing at the counter scrolling on her phone. She's a tall, slim girl with shoulder-length platinum blonde hair, smooth skin, and large doe eyes in blue, who believes the entire world revolves around her. She knows she looks good, unlike me, with my long dark brown hair which appears to have a life of its own. I've never considered my appearance to be particularly striking.

So far, she has spent the day avoiding as much work as she can, and my mood is shifting in a somewhat negative direction. After brewing a cup of coffee for a guest, I wipe down the coffee machine with a cloth and turn to Emelie.

"Maybe you should play with your phone when you're on a break and go clean the tables instead," I suggest in a dry tone.

She doesn't even look up when she answers me.

"You're not my boss, bitch."

That little shit. Anger bubbles up inside me. Dispersing my thoughts quickly, I take a deep breath through my nose, telling myself it's not worth arguing with her. *Just stay calm, Saga.*

Our manager and the owner of the cafe, Haru Tanaka, has been out on errands for most of the day and he finally shows up when it's almost closing time.

"Everything all right, boss?" I ask as he walks behind the counter while I'm cutting a tuna sandwich in two for a guest.

Haru has a crease in his forehead, and I see a hint of sadness in his eyes, but when he turns to face me, he smiles and rubs his palms together, as if trying to warm himself. The shoulder-length black hair has turned grey at the temples, and wrinkles appear around the eyes now and then when he laughs or smiles.

"Yes. I'll probably never get used to this cold."

The tone of his voice is curt, despite the smile, and I decide not to say anything. Finally, Emelie puts away her phone and starts washing some cups. My gut tells me she likes our boss, but it's obvious he's not interested in his staff members.

I serve the guest the sandwich and bring some plates to the sink. Emelie is busy flipping her hair while talking in her smoothest voice to Haru and a quiet sigh falls between my lips as I reach for the dish gloves. *If I do it myself, it'll be done the right way.*

"I can close today," I say after some time, wiping my hands on my apron.

"Thanks, Saga," Haru replies and shoots me a smile. "Are you sure you're comfortable with it?" He buttons his brown coat while Emelie gets ready to leave for the day.

"No problem, boss! Maybe I'll sit down and do some gaming before I leave, if it's all right with you."

"Of course."

I feel his heavy hand on my shoulder.

"Take care of yourself. Put yourself first," he says, and I nod as I look away.

I don't want anyone to notice how I feel deep inside, especially not my boss.

I've been alone in the cafe for a while, and I took the opportunity to wipe everything down so it's sparkling clean for the next working day. Ambrosia is at home right now. Usually, she's rather loud over voice chat with the guild members prior to our weekly raid starting and I just want to take it easy for a while before they need me.

A gale seems to have brewed up out there and I don't recall hearing anything about this in the last weather report. I just might have to grab a taxi home.

The padded headset rests comfortably over my ears. I'm logged into *Reign Online*, picking flowers in a lush forest landscape belonging to the territory of the humans. Normally I'd find this activity relaxing, but not today. I completely forgot to make vials and elixirs last night, so I'll have to sort it out now.

Thoughtfully, I fiddle with my necklace, adorned with the symbol of Sunseeker's people—the same one which I also carry as my keychain—

as I open my alchemy book on the screen and read what ingredients I need. I'm unlucky with one plant. I haven't got hold of a single one and they're currently being sold for outrageous prices by other players, since it's Friday, which means raid night for most guilds on the server.

I sip on a glass of water and place it next to the keyboard, then take off my glasses and wipe them with a cleaning cloth for a moment. The room feels slightly cooler today, so I stay nestled in my coat while leaning back in my comfortable chair.

"*Saga.*"

The dark, whispering voice in my head almost has me jumping up from my chair, and I spin around in the seat so quickly I get tangled in the headset's cord. It's the same one I heard in the changing room not long ago. Icy fear rushes inside me as I tear off my headphones and scan the dim room.

"Who's there?" I ask in as steady a voice as I can muster.

I know for a fact no one else is here but me. I had made sure of it. *My brain's playing tricks on me again, just like in the fitting room.* Slightly shaken, I take three deep breaths and try to calm my racing heart before putting the headphones back on again.

The game is frozen. *Brilliant.*

ALT+F4. No response. CTRL+ALT+DEL.

Frustrated, I keep pressing the button combinations repeatedly, to no avail.

"*I see you. Your inner self, the light and the dark, trying to devour each other.*"

"What the hell is going on?" I exclaim, flinching where I'm seated and accidentally knocking the glass of water over the keyboard.

In panic, I reach for some napkins on the table. The screen turns off as I unplug the power cord from the computer, and I get most of the water out of the keyboard. With a swift movement, I take off the headset and dig my fingers into my hair, my elbows resting on the armrests of the chair. *Am I losing my mind?*

A gut-wrenching feeling of horror creeps forward through the shadows of the room, finding its way up over my shoes and legs and biting into my thighs. Quickly, I jump up from the chair and wrap my arms around myself, unsure of where to fix my flickering gaze. I'm absolutely terrified. I reach for the phone on the table, about to search through to my contacts, but my hand trembles.

"The gateways between our dimensions are aligned. Come find me."

The voice freezes the blood to ice in my veins. My hand holding the phone trembles even more, causing me to almost drop it. With difficulty, I keep my grip on it and let it slip into my coat pocket.

The storm outside shakes the roof and causes my panic to escalate. The black screen in front of me flickers and a dark purple shimmer with hints of blood-red appears, growing more intense, dazzling my eyes with a powerful glow. Invisible hands and tentacles violently grab my clothes and knock me to the floor. As a scream bursts out of my throat, I try to kick myself free, but it's no use. The shimmering light engulfs me.

Something squeezes my airways, making me unable to scream further. Gasping for air, I realise my life isn't passing by before my eyes. Is my existence so pointless I don't even have flashbacks in my very last moment?

CHAPTER TWO

Saga Falk

The sound of my coughing awakens me, and somewhere in the back of my mind, my inner voice whispers to me to focus. My eyelids flutter before they rise like a stage curtain and I'm unsure what kind of performance awaits.

My glasses are intact. My phone and keys are in my pockets, and as I take a deep breath, the fresh smell of grass fills my nostrils.

With a quiet moan, I rise to a sitting position. Trees, moss, and grass as far as the eye can see. A few twigs are stuck in my hair, and I attempt to pluck them out while I look around in horror-tinged bewilderment. I survey my clothes, and, to my great relief, I note I'm fully clothed. *Good. But where am I?*

My brain goes into overdrive as I get up on my feet, surveying what appears to be a lush forest. Some shrubs and plants look familiar, while I'm well-aware I've never encountered this flora earlier, and I can't recall reading about it in school. With tentative steps, I approach some flowers and squat down to study them. *These flowers.* My heart sinks into a cold pit in my stomach. I pinch myself on the arm. There's pain, but nothing else happens.

"All right," I hear myself utter. "This is just awesome."

Quickly, I fish the phone out of my pocket and unlock the screen. There's no signal—I suspected as much. My gaze fixes on the time and when it doesn't change, I realise it appears to have stopped. 21:12. I don't remember being in the cafe that long.

I browse the photos on my phone. At one point, I took a picture of the ingredients list from my alchemy book in *Reign Online*, and as I zoom in on it with my thumb and forefinger, it hits me. These plants are the same ones described in the book. *In a book belonging to the fictional world of Theadrath.*

"What the hell?" The words slip out of my mouth on a discreet exhale.

Am I hallucinating? Is this reality? Perhaps an alternate universe similar to Reign Online?

I keep scrolling until I come across an image from a long time ago, depicting a map showing where these flowers grow. The territory of the humans turns out to be the only place where these can be found. As I lift my gaze from the screen, I try to locate something which can give me an indication of where I am and where I should go.

Nothing. *I have to go with my gut feeling.*

I walk, trying to be as light and quiet on my feet as possible with my pricked ears taking in all the sounds and impressions from the forest. Birds chirping, the wind rustling through the treetops, and a light green lizard disappearing among the grass. After a while, my eyes fall on a large, partially buried stone tablet with signs carved on it. I'm almost certain I've seen it in-game and I pull out the map on my phone again. Indeed—it's marked as a specific landmark. If I walk for a while longer, I'll hopefully reach a country road which will lead me to the nearest village.

SHADOW DANCE

If I'm in a fantasy setting, I won't blend in with my glasses, long-sleeved pink high-collared jumper, black coat, dark grey jeans, and white gym shoes. Should I pretend I'm from a faraway kingdom and this is the height of fashion? Should I pretend I've used magic to dress up? *I'll figure it out,* I tell myself, trying to stifle a feeling of panic laced with anxiety growing stronger with each passing minute.

The battery on the phone is halfway through and I do my best to memorise key points I need from the map, before I switch it off and put it in my pocket. For a moment, I feel like a girl scout and I'm almost a little proud I'm keeping myself composed. If this is a world just like the game, I might do well, since I've played it for so many years.

In the distance, I can make out buildings, and the pace of my steps increases. The sound of an approaching vehicle fractures my train of thought, and I look around frantically. There isn't a single tree I could hide behind as far as the eye can see. I dart towards the side of the road, stopping to throw a glance over my shoulder. My heart beats faster when I notice a carriage getting closer and anxiety creeps under my skin, but I keep telling myself I have to stay focused. *Be on your guard, but don't seem afraid.*

When the carriage stops a few metres from me, I straighten my back and nervously push the glasses up over the bridge of my nose with one finger while plastering a smile on my lips.

"Hey!" I exclaim, waving with one hand.

From what I can see, it's an elderly man and woman dressed in plain clothes sitting in the front seat, and I can hear chickens and the bleating of a lamb from inside the carriage. They look like farmers. I don't remember ever coming across them. I rarely pay much attention to random, non-player characters in *Reign Online*. They keep staring at me and the old woman with the seriously wrinkled face opens her mouth to say something, but remains silent.

I might have to change my language use a little—I can't be using modern slang.

"My name's Saga Falk and I'm not from around here," I continue.

Their gazes shift from pure surprise to suspicion. *Maybe now is the time to play on their compassion instead.*

"I've been walking for a long time. I'm exhausted and would love a drop of water and a ride, if you'd be willing to show me that mercy. However, I have no money to offer to you, because a band of robbers took my coins, and I narrowly escaped them."

A moment of silence passes, and a sense of nervousness burrows its roots in my stomach, stretching them all the way up and then down to my fingertips. The old man mumbles something to the woman, and as a result, she smacks him lightly on the upper arm.

"We can't just leave the girl; it's getting dark soon!" she says. She turns her attention to me, peering kindly. "You're in safe hands with us, girlie. Climb up at the back, but be careful not to unlock any of the cages. Unfortunately, we have nothing we can offer you in the way of drinks."

With a silent cheer inside, I nod gratefully and hurry behind the cart. The wood creaks as I climb up, hoisting myself over to the other side through a fabric curtain opening in the middle. I'm greeted by a number of cages and a tied lamb, and I force back a gag as the pungent smell of animals and excrement hits me.

"Thank you so much for your kindness!" I call out to the couple, trying to make myself comfortable in the straw.

The wagon bounces in potholes as we travel over the country road and my buttocks hurt, but I tell myself this is far better than having to walk for hours.

SHADOW DANCE

In a temporary state of confusion and shock, I open my eyes as I'm brought back to reality by the carriage's sudden jerking and stopping. I must have fallen asleep, despite trying to stay alert. I lift my glasses, rub one eye to chase the sleep away, and peer out through the curtain. The evening has arrived, and it's lively out on the streets. *Wait a minute—this doesn't look like the village on the map.*

"Where are we?" I ask as the old man pulls away the fabric.

He extends one hand towards me to help me down from the carriage.

"This is Whitekeep," he replies, chewing on a straw poking out from the corner of his mouth.

Whitekeep. The capital of the humans, and not at all the village I thought we'd be travelling to.

"All right. Thanks for the ride."

After surveying my surroundings for a while, I head up the main street. During my time in *Reign Online*, I've spent quite a lot of time here, but it's a different feeling to be here in person, away from a monitor. Most of the buildings are massive, just like the white wall which surrounds the city; reaching majestically up into the sky, as if worshipping the sun by day and the moon by night. Quite a few people are out and about and there are sounds of cheers and toasts.

Two city guards in heavy, rattling armour pass me by, and I feel someone grabbing my arm. Quickly, I whirl around as I tear myself away from the grip.

"Where are you from?" one of them asks with a voice that's muffled by a helmet covering both the head and the face.

The other guard's hand finds its way to a sword hanging from his hip, and I realise I've probably reacted a little too drastically when I pulled my arm back.

"The name's Saga. Saga Falk," I answer and try to sound unmoved.

"I'm from a kingdom far away and I've just been given a ride to your city."

"Answer the question!" the first guard shouts in a demanding tone.

"Yikes, calm down, dude," I mutter as tiny drops of sweat break out on my forehead. "I'm from a kingdom called…"

My mouth goes dry, and I try to collect my swirling thoughts as quickly as I can.

"I'm from Malmö in Sweden. It's common to dress like this back home."

As my voice cracks from insecurity and my stress levels increase, I put my hands to my face, pretending to burst into tears.

"My family was murdered by a count who demanded a large amount of money, even though we paid for ourselves every month, simply because I didn't want his hand in marriage. I barely escaped after watching him stab my parents and my little sister to death. Honestly, I'm just trying to find a new place to call home and to overcome my personal tragedy."

"My deepest condolences," the first guard stammers. "Do you have somewhere to go?"

With a dramatic sniffle, I grab his armoured fist with both my hands while putting my best puppy-dog eyes to use.

"I have no money and no roof over my head. Could you two gentlemen please help me?"

"We know someone who might be able to help," he responds. "Come with us."

The city guards keep me company as we make our way through the streets of Whitekeep. For someone whose middle name is melancholy and who experiences anxiety more or less every day, I've been doing rather well so far. I just have to make sure I'm always a couple of steps ahead of everyone else until I get more clarity on why I'm actually here.

"Impressive. The gift of speech is clearly in your possession when you choose to use words rather than observing your surroundings."

SHADOW DANCE

That voice again. To my best ability, I avoid showing any signs of the fear rippling inside of me and I suck air into my lungs. The source of that voice has put me in this tricky situation. If it hadn't been for that, I would have been home by now, gaming with my guild and chatting, and most likely bickering, with Ambrosia during the breaks.

Strong, almost overpowering smells of alcohol, food, and sweat hit my face as we step into the inn. It's packed with people, making me slightly claustrophobic. I fight off the nausea when the smell of fried meat tickles my nose—as a vegan I'm sensitive to certain smells sometimes—and steel myself by quickly scanning the room.

From what I can see, the majority of guests are human. There are also dwarves, forest elves, and a woman who looks almost alien-like with her light grey, slightly silvery skin, large black eyes with silver pupils, and long snow-white hair. Her forehead is covered with runic symbols and her unusually long, pointy ears are decorated with numerous silver earrings. I'm guessing she's a frost elf, and I try not to stare, but due to her incredible beauty, I'm having a hard time taking my eyes off her. She's sitting on the lap of a heavily built woman with bushy locks of brown hair. They seem to be a couple, or maybe they're temporarily accompanying each other. Eventually, I force myself to direct my attention elsewhere.

The city guards, named Derek and Hale, with whom I chatted a little during our walk, nod towards a tall woman in a dark blue dress, in a way that suggests they are acquainted. I assume she's the hostess of this place. Her green eyes look at me curiously in silence, then she gestures with one hand for us to follow her to the bar.

As the men take off their helmets, I find myself staring again.

Whoa… when did NPCs get so handsome?

Hale's light brown hair and those honey-coloured eyes almost hypnotise me for a moment, and Derek, with his glossy dark hair and black eyes, is also quite nice to rest my gaze on.

"Good to see your familiar faces around here again, lads," says a deep voice, and I realise it's the tall man behind the counter who's chuckling roguishly at the guards.

I remember him. He's the innkeeper. I know for a fact I used to do quests for him when I was fairly new to the game. *What's his name again? Is it Anderson?*

"Give us the usual, Guy," Hale says, sitting down on one barstool as a satisfied sound leaves him.

Guy Anderson leans towards me and strokes his thick, dark beard.

"You're a peculiar-looking lass," he remarks as he pours beverages into two tankards.

I swallow hard, unable to get a single word off my tongue.

"She has travelled a long way and has been through some trouble," Derek replies, taking a big gulp of the drink Guy puts in front of him. "She needs a roof over her head, if that's anything you could help with."

"I don't have any money," I mumble, scolding myself internally for sounding so wimpish.

Girl, just keep your mouth shut.

The innkeeper throws a cloth over one shoulder and leans forward over the counter. The hair on his chest bursts out of the collar of his grey tunic, like a small forest of body hair.

"I can offer a room for free, but only for the night, simply because I know these boys."

"Thanks so much!" I chirp happily, unable to hide my excitement as I clasp my hands in front of me. "Sorry, but do you have a change of clothes I could borrow?"

"I'm sure my wife can lend you something. But considering your small frame, I don't think they'll fit you."

I do my best not to roll my eyes. *Like I haven't heard similar things being said to me a million times before.*

Anderson lets out a hearty laugh, and it's evident how much he loves his wife.

"I'm just grateful to get out of these clothes and have somewhere to sleep," I say cheerfully.

I notice him squinting at me.

"Wait," he says, suspicion lacing his words. "That necklace looks like it's made of gold. And what kind of symbol is that?"

"This?" Cold shivers start running down my spine. "It's nothing, it's not even genuine gold," I correct myself quickly.

I've messed up.

Hale stares at me wide-eyed.

"That's the high elven queen's symbol!" Derek mutters with a pale face.

"Wait," I respond, waving my hands dismissively in front of me. "I found this necklace in the woods on the way here. I haven't got a clue what it means."

It's so damn obvious I'm lying.

The men stare blankly at me, and I take a few steps back. *I have to get out of here.*

Turning around hastily in a rush, I let out a choked exclamation as I run into someone so violently, I lose my breath for a moment, my glasses falling to the floor as a result.

"Sorry!" I gasp and stagger back a few steps, my palms resting on my cheeks. "No, my glasses!"

I crouch down as I feel the wooden floor with my hands. I can barely see anything without them, especially in this dim light.

"Here."

The voice that speaks sounds dark, deep. There's a stern undertone to it and the figure squatting down in front me looks like one big blurry mix of colours.

"Don't move," it commands, and I barely dare to breathe as a pair of hands put the glasses back on my face.

Quickly, I adjust my fringe while blinking a few times to sharpen my gaze. My lips part, but no sound departs from my mouth.

The man's right cheek is decorated with a scar. Golden, half-tousled hair that goes down to his shoulders and sky-blue eyes that remind me of hot summer days when Ambrosia and I used to run on the beach, searching for seashells as kids. The gaze penetrates my entire being with an expression that looks like it has been carved in stone. A neat, short-cut beard and moustache both somehow contribute to his grim countenance.

I quickly register more details of his appearance and know in my gut I've run into him in *Reign Online* at some point. He's clad in heavy armour overlaid with gold, with pauldrons large enough to almost completely cover his neck. A long blue coat of arms with patterns in gold protrudes from under the cuirass. My attention gets stuck on the details of the chest plate for a moment—a lion's head in the centre with winding roses surrounding it. There's something vaguely familiar about his entire presence, and judging by the outfit, it's crystal clear he's a holy knight.

Congratulations, Saga, you've just run into a highly ranked paladin! If ordinary people react suspiciously to you, how do you think a possibly fanatically religious person will react?

Thoughts wander around in my head and I quickly close my hand around the pendant around my neck.

"Thanks," I say with a squeaky voice, noticing how wimpy I sound.

I'm about to get up when I see the man is up already, offering me his hand. He's tall, 1.90 metres at least at a guess, and he seems to be older than me. Carefully, I put my other hand in his and he pulls me to my feet.

Out of nowhere, there's an electric shock from the touch while my chest heats up strangely. Did the paladin notice it, too? Quickly, I pull my hand back, diverting my attention elsewhere while my brain works at full speed. *What's this strange feeling?*

Hale and Derek have risen, their heads bowed in respect.

"Grand Prior," I hear them both murmur in perfect unison at the same time.

Grand Prior Garren Roseheart, of course! I'm surprised I didn't realise it from the very beginning when I saw the detail on his armour which was so prominent in the picture Ambrosia showed me. He's the guy who trains the paladins of higher levels in *Reign Online*, with Whitekeep being his starting point where he organises advanced missions for his troops. If I remember correctly, he's subordinate only to the queen in the realm of the humans.

Abstract, blurry memories from that day in the fitting room flash before my eyes and a sense of panic and dread flutter in my stomach. *It's him. How could I repress it?*

I chase away the thoughts. *Not now, Saga. Don't think about his arms around you and his playful fingertips and his—*

Garren throws a cold glance at the tankards on the bar before turning his attention to the men.

"Is this what you engage in when you're on duty?" he asks with a harsh tone in his voice.

"No, my lord," Derek replies, staring down at the floor in front of him.

"We're on a mission," Hale hastens to fill him in. "This woman seemed rather suspicious when we encountered her. Just look at her attire! She told us a tear-jerking story. However, now we're not entirely sure it's true, and we assumed if we acted in a normal, off-duty manner, she might end up confessing."

My heart sinks into my stomach, and the words shoot out of my mouth.

"Hey!" I exclaim. "How dare you make assumptions about me?"

Sweat breaks out on my forehead under my fringe and my mouth feels unusually dry. My eyes dart around. I don't know if it's just my imagination, but it seems as if everyone in the room is looking in our direction and their glances are burning holes in me. *Panic*.

"Her necklace."

Anderson, the innkeeper, who has been watching us in silence for a while, speaks up whilst nodding at me and I almost wish my gaze could kill, or at least make him faint.

"She's in cahoots with the high elves," he continues. "Who knows what they're after, with such a queen and prince?"

A gasp escapes my lips.

"That's not true! Sure, I'm not from here, but I'm not in cahoots with anyone. I'm a human, just like you."

The air seems to leave my lungs as one of Garren's fists closes around my wrist, which belongs to the hand I'm holding the necklace with. I feel small and vulnerable in a universe I assumed I knew a lot about—until now. Anxiety roars inside of me, deafening my inner voice. *I have to stand up for myself.*

CHAPTER THREE

Garren Roseheart

The wrist in my hand seems about as strong as a twig.

"Show me the necklace, lass," I order sharply, trying to catch the woman's gaze.

She struggles, unable to move away, and the fear in her voice is palpable.

"Let go of me, Garren!"

"How do you know my name?"

I pull her closer to me, close enough to feel her warm breath on my face. Her dark brown eyes flare with anger mixed with terror and I parry her reaction as she attempts to kick me.

"Get it together!" I command sternly, having all the guests' eyes on us. "I suggest you calm down and come with me, as we have a few things to discuss."

"No!" she screams shrilly and tries to tear herself away again.

"This is going to end badly for her," a drunken man exclaims as bursts of laughter erupt in the room. "Grand Prior Roseheart is no one to be trifled with in the first place!"

"Let me go, I said!"

The panic in the woman's voice escalates and she looks around, her gaze seemingly begging for help. I've had a long day and my patience is wearing thin.

"That's enough!" I roar.

I release my grip on her wrist. Within a second, I crouch down nimbly, grab both of her legs, and lift her as I stand up. Her howling gets even louder than previously as I throw her over my shoulder. She weighs nothing.

"My glasses!" she shrieks, and I notice she has dropped them on the floor again.

With clenched fists, she furiously pounds on my armour and kicks with her feet.

"Don't make me tie you up," I growl, turning to the inept men. "You there! Pick that up and hand it to me."

The dark-haired guard stares at me, looking bewildered. I grab his collar with one hand and throw him to the floor in front of me.

"Are you deaf, lad?"

"N-no, my lord," he stammers after being scolded, holding the woman's object up to me.

I snatch it out of his hand as the woman on my shoulder continues to scream.

"How dare you touch me? This borders on sexual harassment!"

"You'll have your glasses back shortly if you can keep quiet for five minutes," I say gruffly, trying not to get even more worked up.

I don't wish to lose my temper completely and in my mind I imagine how the Light guides and warms me. *Yes, the Light is kindness, patience, and strength.*

SHADOW DANCE

A moment of welcomed silence takes over her, her will to fight seemingly simmering down.

"You better not be lying to me!" she murmurs under her breath.

Between clenched teeth, I suck air into my lungs. What an odd, hot-tempered personality she carries. I haven't decided whether I should concentrate on being offended by her sheer disrespect or allow myself to explore the tiny spark of curiosity her words ignite deep inside.

The crowd in the inn lets out cheers and wolf whistles as I turn around, making my way towards the exit. I focus on the Light entirely, shutting the perverse remarks of these fools out of my consciousness. *This most definitely isn't how I expected my day to end.*

CHAPTER FOUR

Saga Falk

"I can walk by myself, and you promised I'd get my glasses back," I mutter as I feel the chilly evening air embracing me.

Everything around us is one massive fog. My heart's pounding violently against my ribs and I'm a little dizzy. *He carries me around like I'm a feather.*

"If you're as quick on your feet as you are with your words, it's in my best interest not to let you touch the ground yet," Garren replies, stopping mid-step. "However, if it ceases your protests for a few minutes, it's worth the risk. I'm beginning to get a headache."

With a slight movement from the paladin, I slide down into his arms and then feel my shoes hit a hard surface. The blood that previously rushed down to my head returns to the other parts of my body and the dizziness slowly lifts its veil from inside my mind.

"Tell me your name," he commands, putting my glasses back on my face again.

"Saga Falk," I answer and shyly look up at him now that I can finally see, tilting my head back slightly.

Yeah, he looks tall compared to my 1.60 metres. Tall and probably muscular under that heavy armour. The prominent scar on his face makes me wonder if I can remember where he got it from, but since I've always played as a high elf in-game and don't have much information about the paladin class, I can't for the life of me remember this man's backstory.

He raises one eyebrow.

"Come with me, Falk. Don't think for a second about running away."

Nervously, I pick at my bottom lip as I walk next to him, feeling rather baffled. I thought I could get away easily with my made-up stories.

"Where are you from?"

Garren's deep voice, edged with a calculating undertone, makes me swallow hard. I hope he doesn't notice how anxious I am.

"Malmö," I speak in a low tone. "Here in Whitekeep you may not know my hometown—we have a different style from what you're used to."

I point to my attire and shrug.

"How do you know my name?"

Think quickly.

"Of course, my people know of the highest commander of the Order of the Light," I answer, my voice poised as I'm fabricating yet another thin net of lies.

As he takes his long strides, his cloak in dark blue floats behind him, and I'm finding it hard to keep up with his pace without half-running. No further words depart from his lips and now and then he throws a stern glance my way.

Now that we're outside, my attention is drawn to a heavy gold-shimmering sword tucked into a scabbard at his hip, which is richly detailed with precious stones. It appears to be heavy. A leather bag hangs at his other side, which I guess doubles as a wallet, and I note the belt he's wearing around his waist with a strap hanging down from it. Memories of my school's history lessons back in the day flash before me momentarily. *Leather belts were used as a symbol of high status and wealth.*

"Where are we going?" I ask cautiously, touching my fringe.

"To the church," he replies curtly.

"Why?"

"Ask no more questions, lass. You're under arrest."

Garren shoots me a cold gaze when he notices my jaw drop and I can sense something smug in his expression. I gasp, shocked and chilled to the core.

"What the hell am I being arrested for?"

He puts one finger to his lips and hushes.

"Don't talk until we get there."

I'm about to open my mouth again when my attention draws to some children in dirty clothes in an alley and my feet stop moving. Their hair is matted and they look hungry, sitting on the ground. When they see us, their gazes seem to shoot daggers at me, and I feel sick to my stomach while creeping anxiety knocks at the door of my soul. I shiver and pull my coat tighter around me. I don't remember this from *Reign Online. This feels uncomfortable, toxic, up close, and so incredibly sad.*

Being unable to subdue the hot tears from welling up, I find myself covering my face with my hands, trying to mask my emotional turmoil.

"I've had enough. I just want to go home now."

My low voice shatters into invisible pieces. An incipient panic attack, a feeling I know far too well, blooms deep in my stomach.

I miss my bed, computer, and my home. My job. I miss Ambrosia, Remy, and even Haru.

A violent cough erupts from my throat and I sink to the ground in a crouching position, closing my hands around my necklace as I clench my jaws tightly and tears slide down my cheeks.

"I can't breathe," I utter as the paladin's heavy shadow falls over me.

Shutting my eyes tightly, I cough again as a choked sound leaves my throat. *Help me.* The thought rides a rollercoaster in my head and one of my palms hurts. My nails are digging into it, but I can't bring myself to let go.

"Help me," I hear myself whisper, my heart pounding so hard I think I'm about to pass out.

I force my eyelids open, but see nothing but a blinding light. I gasp for air and scream as my eyeballs burn like white-hot fire and an unspeakable pain courses through my body, licking my skin and invading every nerve. My hands let go of the necklace and fly up to my face, trying to claw at my eyes.

Something closes tightly around both my wrists and I'm pushed down with my back to the ground. My breathing seems as spasmodic as before, and I cough again.

"Calm yourself, Falk."

A voice which appears to reach me from another plane; something distant. *Whose voice is that? It sounds like the paladin.* Hushed words take flight from my mouth, but their meaning eludes me. A warmth spreads in my body, slowly and soothingly, through the fingers around my wrists. Within seconds, drowsiness settles over me, my head heavy with invisible weight.

The pain in my eye sockets and body subsides and my vision returns to me, coiling like a snake. I blink a few times as I take a ragged breath, seeing Garren sitting next to me, a bright light fading from his eyes. *Am I hallucinating?*

SHADOW DANCE

I can't bear to fight back as I'm lifted off the ground and the paladin carries me in his arms.

"Am I still under arrest?" I mumble tiredly.

A sharp gaze from mirthless blue eyes bores into me. I'm met with silence, and for a reason unbeknownst to me, I'm feeling more anxious than I did prior to my strange panic attack.

Garren sets me down on the ground in front of a church. The way it has been built reminds me of the same structure of Linköping's cathedral on St. Persgatan, which my school had us visit when I was younger, only this one's white, and significantly larger. Guards stand by the steps, completely immovable, except for when they bow their necks in respectful salutes to the man beside me. Almost directly adjacent, I see barrack-like buildings on one side—I assume that's where the knights of the Order of the Light train and live—and on the other side of the church there's another building that looks like an armoury.

The strength has returned to my legs, but tiredness still lives within my bones. The little I remember of the course of events replays like a silent movie in the back of my head. I go through the archive of gaming-related memories in my brain, trying to find something I can use to my advantage.

"We're going in here," Garren announces.

With a certain familiarity in his movement, he opens the door to the armoury and extends his arm forward, gesturing at me to enter. I nod, pulling my coat tighter around me as we step inside, and I survey the new surroundings. It's a chilly, relatively bare room with a single painting on the wall and a smell of old dampness hanging in the air, like a towel which never dries. In surprise, I raise my eyebrows as the knight unbuckles the belt with the weapon and the bag. Before carefully placing them down on an old, worn wooden chair, he presses a respectful kiss on the hilt.

"Leave your weapons," he orders, observing me where I'm standing, probably looking rather nonplussed.

"I'm unarmed," I retort timidly.

"That remains to be seen. Come here."

I stare at him, overwhelmed with insecurity; afraid to move.

"Come here," he repeats.

As I meet him with silence, he runs his fingers through his hair and sighs heavily. I avert my gaze and feel worry take root inside when I hear the sound of his armour and feel his hands searching in my coat pockets. I try to back away and watch him fish out my belongings.

"Be careful," I blurt out. "I'm still paying off the phone!"

Garren's wide-eyed confusion causes me to take a deep breath, and I make a dismissive gesture.

"I can explain what a phone is," I continue. "It's not a weapon, I promise."

Nervously, I bite my bottom lip as he takes a closer look at my keychain. *Excellent, Saga. Now you're in double trouble—as if it wasn't bad enough with the necklace.*

The man in front of me places my belongings on another chair and turns to face me with his arms folded over his chest.

"You have a lot to explain," he remarks.

I say naught as he grabs my arm, pulling me through a door into the church. The tiredness dampens my will to fight back; I just want to sleep and wake up at home in my bed again.

Candles in beautifully decorated candelabras illuminate the dimness with a warm, dancing glow and I catch my breath. I've never been a believer, but there's something about this church that immediately gives me a feeling of safety and embraces my senses in an almost warming way.

SHADOW DANCE

A scent of burning candles finds its way into my nose and reinforces the sense of security.

My gaze wanders over the stained glass windows with intense colours, the decorations on the walls, and the empty benches. At the front of the nave, I see the chancel and a stone altar, illuminated by candles on top of a cloth. The scene frames a figure dressed in a long white and gold robe with a high collar, an open book resting in her hands, and as we make our way forward, the figure turns into a woman with eyes hidden by a white blindfold.

A hood partially covers her face and around her slender neck hangs a long, thin shawl with beautiful embroidery on it. Her straight white hair shimmers like glistening snow in the dim light from the small flames, creating a beautiful contrast against her dark skin. Thin fingers caress the writing in the book she's holding, and I wonder how she absorbs the contents without the power of sight.

The woman lifts her head in our direction, and Garren bows his head respectfully.

"High Priestess Astryn," he greets, his voice laced with a surprising gentleness. "Pardon our late visit."

Astryn carefully puts the book down on the altar, and I flip through my memories. I remember doing quite a few quests for her back in the day, considering she's my high elf's class leader. She looks just like when I met her last time I played. *She's absolutely stunning.*

"Please don't worry yourself, Roseheart. I knew your steps would lead you here today," she replies, turning her head in my direction. "Tell me your name, my child."

Perplexed, I stare at her in silence for a moment before parting my lips. "Saga."

I blink a few times as the high priestess puts one hand on my arm, and I can hear her drawing in air through her nostrils.

"You're lost," she says as she places her other hand on the cover of the book. "You're not from here."

I throw a discreet glance at Garren, then direct it back at Astryn. She still has her hand on my arm and reflexively I pull it away from her as an intense heat begins to spread from her palm, seeping through the fabric and tickling my skin.

"I don't like it when people touch me, which seems to happen all the time in this place," I say curtly, glaring at the paladin quickly and rubbing my arm where Astryn had her grip.

If looks could take one's life, the knight would most likely have killed me instantly. Astryn smiles softly, lowering her head slightly.

"The magic pulsates within her, slumbering. She's different," she says in a voice as beautiful as a glimmering, babbling spring brook.

"It appears the Light resides in her with great power," he replies whilst nodding and holds my gaze. "She had quite an unusual magical incident when I arrested her."

A magical incident? No, I had suffered a panic attack.

"I healed her briefly in order to get the magic under control."

They talk like you're not even here. Awesome.

I secretly pinch my arm, hoping I'll wake up from this nightmare. But alas, I'm still here in this massive church with these two individuals who seem familiar with each other. A blind priestess and a high-ranking holy knight who threw me over his shoulder and detained me without giving me an explanation as to why. And now they're talking about me possessing some kind of magical ability. *This is way too much.*

Their voices flow together and my attention sails away on an ocean of thoughts. I sweep my eyes over the dancing flames of the candelabras and the stained glass windows again, fatigue enveloping every part of my body. I could easily fall asleep where I'm standing. Closing my eyes, my thoughts drift slowly towards the moonlit shore of my mind.

"They will put you to the test."

The inner voice is back once more, a barely audible whisper that sticks to my eardrums, tapping them. I don't react, focusing entirely on my breathing and keeping the panic at bay.

"Be careful not to enrage the knight. Blinded by faith, his hands drip with blood. He would not hesitate to condemn you and extinguish your spark, should the Light beckon him to do so."

I swallow hard, cold shivers running down my spine.

"Who are you?" I formulate the question in my head and await the answer. However, I'm met with silence; the kind of inner, echoing soundlessness that frightens me more than the voice itself.

When I open my eyes again, I see Garren has collected our belongings, holding the bunch of keys and the phone in one hand. His other hand has taken hold of my arm, shaking me lightly. How long have I been in my own little world?

"Are you conscious?" he asks, and I nod quickly as I push my glasses up the bridge of my nose with one finger.

"Yeah," I stammer, trying to steady my voice.

"Come with me."

Without allowing me a moment to collect my thoughts, he pulls me with him through a door while Astryn follows us with silent footfalls, stepping into a wide hall with a long dark blue carpet that stretches across the stone floor. The hall is illuminated by candles on the walls. The moving shadows crawling around us seem to change shape, accompanied by the faces of the oil paintings melting into grotesque masques and instilling an icy dread in me. Unable to stop myself, I cling to Garren's arm while breathing faster, my feet heavy with fear.

The act of holding the doctrinal man's arm has an exorcising effect, as if something warm from his mere presence flows into me, resulting in the terrifying apparitions circling diminishing.

"Don't you see them?" I whisper, pointing next to me.

"What are you saying?" Garren says sharply, glaring at me, but stops and shoots a gaze at the wall to our left. "There's nothing there."

"I saw something," I insist, breathing out a sigh of relief.

They're gone now. The oil paintings look normal, too.

"You speak in riddles."

He breaks free from my grip, but my hand quickly grabs his.

"No, don't let go!"

The words tumble out between my lips, and I shake my head quickly.

"I don't know you, but I know what I saw and if I hold on to you, they seem to disappear. Think of it like you've arrested me and you're about to take me to the judge or whatever it is you do around here. Instead of handcuffs, we simply hold hands."

Garren raises one eyebrow and watches me in silence for a few seconds. The shadows dancing across his visage; I can barely tear my eyes from the scar on his cheek. I feel his hand squeeze mine with a slightly firmer grip and blink in surprise as he stuffs my keys and phone back into my pockets.

"Don't think about doing anything foolish," he says with a stern undertone as we continue walking through the hall in silence.

Discreetly, I glance at him and let my gaze journey over his face. It appears as if he has had a rough life. *I wonder what he looks like if he smiles for real.*

The memory of the fitting room when he smiled flashes before me, and I press my lips tightly together. *That wasn't real.*

We halt at a solid door with a small shutter at the top. At this point, my stomach is protesting for something edible, but I don't think there's any point

SHADOW DANCE

in asking for anything right now. Grand Prior Roseheart is still holding my hand and I hear the tinkling sound of a bunch of keys. Astryn unlocks the door and Garren ushers me into the room. I look around in the dim light from a couple of candles. Devoid of furniture, there's only an object in the middle of the chamber. The air feels stuffy, trapped like an invisible, forgotten prisoner.

As I turn to Garren with a puzzled expression, the touch of his hand breaks from mine. The door slams shut and locks.

"Wait!" I shout, having to stand on the tip of my toes in order to see through the latticed window.

"It's time for you to speak with the Mother of the Light," he says, and I close my fists around the metal bars, trying to dislodge them.

"Don't leave me here, please!" I scream, my voice mirroring my panic. "Small spaces make me claustrophobic!"

The hatch closes and his footsteps move away from the chamber. At this rate, it's just a waste of energy trying to get his attention. *He's pissing me off.*

One of my hands finds its way into my pocket and I grab the bunch of keys while focusing on my breathing. Counting to three repeatedly, I push away most of the panic; my pulse calming down as my anger subsides, replaced by melancholy.

Don't lose hope. Just remain calm.

Slowly, I turn and stare doubtfully towards the centre of the room. The object appears to be encased in glass, emitting a faint, pulsating glow. What is that?

I stand motionless for what seems to be an eternity. Listening to my breathing, I rake in my thoughts before deciding to approach the object. I'm careful not to touch the glass when I take a closer look. The item looks like a gilded dagger and the handle is decorated with intricate floral details. The faint shimmering luminescence shifts between white, gold, and light blue. Is this a magical relic? Why is it kept here?

A voice from across the room reaches me, pulling my tired gaze to itself. The words are indistinct, but the voice is familiar, reaching my soul within a matter of seconds.

"Who's there?" I ask softly, blinking a few times.

A scent of freshly cut grass and apple pie waltzes into my nostrils as I find myself standing outside a red cabin. I can't tell where I am, but somehow it feels like home. In a rocking chair on the porch, an old woman with a face partially covered by a hood smiles in my direction. Wearing simple clothes, several layers on top of each other, her shoulder-length grey strands of hair stick out from under the fabric. Her wrinkled face makes me think of a map of life, riddled with all its ups and downs.

"Granny, is that you?"

My tone is low, and as the sun caresses my face, I put my hand over my eyes, so I don't have to squint.

"It can't be you. You… you left us when I was ten years old. I was there at the hospital the day before you passed away. I remember mum telling me not to cry in front of you so you wouldn't feel guilty. Everyone else was crying when they saw you, except us two. Even dad shed a few tears, and your relationship over the years had been strained. It was nice to see you apologised to each other."

I realise I'm digging up buried memories, and I shift my gaze down to the grass at my bare feet. My legs are partially covered by a white dress, and my long hair is tied in two braids resting over my chest, just like I used to have it when I was a little girl.

"I take on a guise close to your heart," the old woman replies and continues to rock slowly in the chair. "You can call me granny, if you like."

"Who are you, really?"

I look up again as I slowly approach the porch with short steps. Something moist runs down one of my cheeks, but I don't pay much attention to it. My full focus is fixed on the smiling old woman who's peering at me with her dark brown eyes. She has a piece of apple pie on a small plate with a fork, which she hands to me.

"Have a bite and everything will become clear."

Her voice is kind, and she lets out a boisterous laugh. I can see her bottom row of teeth has one tooth missing, just like my actual grandmother.

I don't know if I'm in a trance right now, but I obey her without asking any additional questions. As I take a bite of the apple pie, it feels like I've just swallowed something that warms the soul from deep within, a beautifully coordinated dance in every cell of my body. My soul is floating somewhere in the cosmos, even though I'm still on the porch, the floorboards kissed by the warm rays of the sun. I sit down by the old woman's feet and continue to chew the pastry while she lovingly puts her hand on my head to stroke my hair lightly.

"My child, a part of me resides within you," she continues, and for a moment I see a blinding white light in her eyes that disappears as quickly as it first appeared.

I wipe a few crumbs from the corner of my mouth with the back of the hand holding the fork, running my tongue over my teeth to get as much of the pie off as possible before I speak.

"What do you mean when you say a part of you?"

I take another bite. Looking up at her, I feel like a little kid again. *Safe in the presence of granny.*

"My energy and its frequencies. Use it to illuminate the darkness, but don't forget even the light casts shadows."

The old woman leans forward and takes the dish from me.

"Don't eat too much at once—it'll make you feel sick. You can have more later."

And in the blink of an eye, I'm back again. This dim room. The pulsating, magical object. I'm sitting with my forehead against a cold stone wall. Raising my head, I slowly look around. The sound of a bunch of keys reaches my ears and I notice how one of my feet has fallen asleep. I must have been sitting in an awkward position.

A silhouette in the doorway steps inside, extending a hand in my direction.

"Praise the Light! You're different," I hear the man utter softly on an exhale.

I ignore the knight's hand and stand up, brushing off my pant legs and coat. Wiggling my foot, it stings for a while until the feeling returns to it.

"What do you mean? And where's that nice old lady I was talking to just now?" I ask as I rub one eye.

My body and brain are tired and can't quite keep up anymore.

"You've been speaking with the Light for several hours."

Garren looks at me oddly, and I'm almost flustered by the intensity of his blue eyes. He points to the object.

"An ordinary person who lacks the Light within them can't stay in the same room as our sacred artefact for more than a few minutes prior to suffering incomprehensible pain. Not even the high priestess has stayed here that long," he explains.

I scratch the back of my neck thoughtfully, my cheeks flushing with contained anger.

"Did you lock me in here just to see if I would get hurt?"

A moment passes between us, silence glued to our tongues before his answer reaches me.

"We had to take drastic measures, lass. For your sake, as well as ours."

CHAPTER FIVE

Garren Roseheart

I'm at a loss for words. The woman walking beside me through the halls has the Light within her to the point she has been able to stay in the same room as our most sacred artefact for hours, without any indication of pain. Her whole being and lineage is like one big question mark, but she's tired and refuses to cooperate. Perhaps some sleep will loosen her tongue and make her willing to share answers in the morning. The evening has arrived, and I wouldn't turn down a few hours of sleep, either.

High Priestess Astryn and Abbess Sylvie are waiting for us outside the church, and I nod towards them. Sylvie is a high elf who has devoted her long life to running the nunnery in Whitekeep, and at this moment in time, she looks after roughly thirty nuns of different origins and varying ages.

"This must be Miss Falk," she says, decorating her voice with a honeyed tone.

Saga looks at her in disbelief, the expression on her face seemingly mirroring hundreds of thoughts swirling in her head at once.

"Who are you?" she asks timidly, stifling a yawn with the back of one hand.

"I'm Abbess Sylvie and I'm the one who'll be looking after you. You'll be staying with my sisters tonight."

Saga nods silently, looking somewhat overwhelmed. I hear her taking a deep breath before tilting her head and turning her attention to me.

"I assumed I was under arrest, Grand Prior? You, who, without even asking for permission, threw me over your shoulder right in front of the people at the inn and dragged me out on the street."

The way she titles me, questioning and with an undertone bordering on irony, causes my heart to beat faster and I collect my thoughts quickly prior to retorting.

"You're still under arrest. However, I see no reason to lock you up in a dark basement just yet."

I rest one hand on the hilt of my sword, a posture I'm used to—one which gives me composure and keeps me grounded during tense moments.

"I'll be coming for you tomorrow morning. Be sure to be ready no later than at seven o'clock," I continue.

Saga adjusts her glasses and looks surprised.

"What? Seven in the morning?"

"That's what I said. Is this going to be problematic for you?"

"I don't even have an alarm clock," she grumbles.

"Don't worry," Sylvie smiles kindly, taking her under the arm gently.

There's almost a motherly air about the abbess and Saga turns a bewildered gaze to her, noticeably uneasy by the touch of the high elf.

"The sisters begin the day at half past five every morning, so someone will wake you up."

The strange woman's dark brown eyes seem to darken further when she glares furiously at me, reminding me of a storm out at sea at night, silence resting on her lips.

Sylvie speaks with a low tone in her ear, and I refrain from attaching my attention to what's being said. A twig sticks out from one of Saga's tresses as she walks away with her back to me, and I let my gaze journey over her short figure. She may look scrawny and suffer from panic attacks, but her meeting with the Mother of the Light has convinced me she's stronger inside than she lets on.

Once home in my own residence, in a building within the Order of the Light's precinct where those of higher rank live, I start changing after the evening ritual. Swiftly, I take off my white shirt, which I've been wearing under the armour, and lay it over the back of a chair. A hot, feverish sensation bothers me. Pensively, I fiddle with my golden necklace and settle down on the edge of the bed. With the holy scripture of the Light in my lap, I run my fingers over the pages whilst filling my heart's cup with a silent prayer.

After a while, I put the bound scripture to the side and lie on my back in bed with one hand behind my neck. Closing my eyes for a moment and feeling how the sweat breaks out on my forehead, I wipe it away with the back of my other hand. The image of the dark-haired woman clinging to my arm has etched itself behind my eyelids. For someone who claims to dislike the touch of another human, she hadn't shown hesitation in lacing her fingers in mine.

Never before have I come across such an outlandish individual. She strikes me as someone who chooses her words well, and on occasion, spits out spontaneous thoughts like a fire-breathing dragon. The use of language, the clothes she wears, those strange belongings—her entire being is foreign. She bears resemblance to a detail in an oil painting that creates confusion, rather than complementing the artwork. Earlier, she had pulled at my strings, infuriating me to a point where I hadn't been far from losing my temper completely. Concurrently, I find myself unable to chase her flaring eyes out of my mind. *The Light is incredibly powerful within her.*

CHAPTER SIX

Saga Falk

Around me, I hear the breathing, snoring, and mumbling sounds of sleeping individuals. I'm in the convent's dormitory with the nuns in Whitekeep, having been given a nightgown and some toiletries by the abbess.

My hands cling to the pendant around my neck and I'm exhausted yet unable to sleep. I try to divert my attention to thoughts about things other than what has happened, just to give myself some mental breathing space.

For a moment, I sit up sharply. Kailunn is in this universe. *I must meet him.*

I crawl back under the cover again and close my eyes tightly. *I wonder what he's like.* Does he act the same way he does in *Reign Online*? Fantasies about our first meeting build up in my head, and I pull the covers up over my nose, smiling. My heartbeat echoes in my ears and my cheeks heat up when I let my thoughts wander to his lips and how it would feel to caress his face with my fingertips.

Minutes turn into hours. Just as I'm about to doze off, I'm awoken by one of the sisters, a dwarf with short ash-blonde hair and big green eyes.

"Good morning," she whispers, and I notice her dialect is different compared to the humans and elves I've met up to this point.

With a big yawn and a stretch, I rub my tired eyes and put on the glasses I had lying next to my pillow. My phone and the bunch of keys are hidden under it.

"Morning," I mumble, slowly rising into a sitting position.

Surveying the room, I see most of the sisters are already up and busy getting ready for the day. The woman puts her finger to her lips and whispers.

"We're not supposed to talk until after our individual morning prayer."

She hands me a change of clothes and gives me a quick smile prior to carrying on with her activities. A simple grey dress, a couple of garments which I assume are underwear, a grey shawl, and something that's apparently meant to be used as a brassiere, but it looks rather uncomfortable.

The other sisters are changing in the same room, and I feel a little awkward about undressing in front of them, but I have no other choice. Their clothes are a different colour—only my dress is grey. Purely a spontaneous thought, but it gives me the impression I'll be standing out more than before.

After the morning service, I follow them as they make their way to the canteen. They're talking quietly to each other. The dress I'm wearing, with its high, somewhat tight collar, makes my skin itch. The other women have wrapped their shawls around their heads and hair, but I failed miserably at the task, and as such, I've thrown it carelessly around my neck instead. Their curious looks almost burn me, and I try to avoid looking at them. I'm well-aware I look strange, especially with my big glasses.

Once in the canteen, we each take a tray and stand in line while an elderly nun serves the food. As it's my turn to get served, I get anxious as I realise what's on the menu. Some sort of meat, potatoes, and vegetables stew. A lump in my stomach grows bigger for every second that passes by.

"Sorry," I say in a hushed tone and smile apologetically. "Do you have any other proteins? I'm vegan."

The nun stares at me coldly for what feels like an eternity as she stretches her back.

"What are you talking about?" she says, not looking too impressed that I've addressed her.

"I don't eat animals or anything that comes from them," I correct myself. "So, I'm wondering if there's another option instead of meat?"

I hear some nuns giggling and I notice myself blushing. The older woman in front of me grabs my tray and sets it aside with a loud noise that almost makes me jump.

"If the food doesn't suit you, then you'll be without," she says harshly and waves for me to go away.

"It's nothing personal," I try to explain, the words stumbling out of my mouth. "It's just that—"

"Take a seat and say a silent prayer while the others eat their morning meal," she quickly interrupts me, and I stare at her with my mouth half-open. I can't make a single sound. Baffled, I trudge away and sit down at a table, casting hungry gazes at the sisters sitting with their trays in front of them. They chat, snickering and glancing at me.

Maybe I should have kept my mouth shut and eaten the vegetables and potatoes. Tears well up in my eyes. I stare down at the table top in front of me as I count to three and take slow breaths, just like my mother taught me once upon a time. *I hate this.*

One of the older, more learned sisters reads aloud from a scripture when everyone's seated, but I don't listen. When she's done, they all start eating and I sit with my clasped hands in my lap. I'm trying to stay positive, but my thoughts return to the same subject: ice cream, crisps, cookies, mum's aubergine casserole with rice and salad on the side. I can envision in slow-motion how I pour lemon juice over the meal and bring the fork to my mouth. The aromatic basmati rice, the steam rising from the food, the scent playfully tickling my nose…

Time has lost its meaning for me in this universe, and I have no idea how long we've been in the canteen. My thoughts become slightly scattered on the surface when the murmur in the hall increases in intensity. At first, I ignore it, but then I hear footsteps. Out of the corner of my eye, I see the women smiling, some of them giggling as they whisper to each other, their eyes twinkling. As the sound of footsteps approach my table, I clench my jaws and avoid looking up. *Surely someone will start yelling at me again.*

The figure opposite sits down at the table and a somewhat familiar voice reaches my ears.

"Are the sisters chastising you already?"

Shyly, my gaze lifts. Garren Roseheart stares at me and my heart skips a beat. He's wearing a cream-coloured shirt with a long dark blue coat over it, and a necklace with a lion's head in the middle and roses around it. I can't see the rest of his outfit from where I'm sitting, but even when he's dressed so simply compared to yesterday's heavy armour, he oozes authority.

I remember why he's here and nervousness grabs hold of me.

"I don't eat anything that comes from animals because I'm a vegan, and the nun over there took offence when I mentioned it," I murmur, scratching the surface of the table with one fingernail.

Garren watches me silently for a moment as if pondering, before leaning towards me with his elbows on the table and catching my gaze again.

"Are you aware it's past seven o'clock?" he asks.

I shake my head and continue to peel away the varnish on the table top.

"I don't have a watch, so how could I possibly know that?" I mutter.

With a sigh, I run my fingers through my fringe and realise maybe I should behave better, for my own sake.

"What I should do is to apologise for keeping you waiting, but I've barely slept and haven't eaten since yesterday, so it shouldn't come as a surprise that my mood shifts."

Garren stands up, adjusting his coat while making a few subtle circular movements with his head, as if to soften his neck. The dark brown trousers and heavy leather boots he wears seem to complement the rest of the outfit and only now do I see his shirt collar is held together by a fancy-looking brooch. His hands appear strong, and I notice the belt at his waist yet again. Same as yesterday, with the same bag and weapon.

"Let's go," he says, beckoning me to come with him.

"Can I get my stuff first?" I ask.

"Certainly."

We steer our steps towards the dormitory in silence and I can feel the sisters' gazes burning my skin through my clothes. When we arrive, he leans his back against the wall next to the door, crossing his arms over his chest.

"Make haste," he says and nods respectfully to a couple of older nuns greeting him.

"Okay."

I enter the dorm and walk towards my bed. Chewing on my bottom lip thoughtfully, I look around and the lump of anxiety in my stomach just keeps growing. Three younger women, probably students, are sitting by my bed and poking at my things. One of them has my phone in her hand. The anger rises inside me, and I speak before I think.

"Don't touch my stuff!" I snarl, charging at them.

The sisters quickly get up to their feet and two of them move behind me, while the third, who's holding the phone, smiles sneeringly at me.

"You should rinse your dirty mouth," she says, waving the phone. "Here in the monastery, we share everything, so I have every right to investigate what a potential future sister hides under her pillow."

"Give it back," I growl.

She doesn't move, let alone blink. "No."

The others laugh teasingly and one of them pulls my hair while another tries to grab my glasses. With a firm movement, I force their hands away. When my gaze hits the floor and I notice they've rummaged through my clothes, which are now spread out in a sad-looking pile, I find myself close to losing my temper. I didn't expect this behaviour from nuns at all.

"These individuals are to represent the standard bearers of the Light. See how they have stolen your belongings."

The voice bouncing inside my cranium is making my head spin. How does it know what has happened?

Why do I feel numb, but also furious at the same time?

"What the hell is wrong with you?" I snap, getting myself more worked up as I notice how my voice quakes.

The girl who's holding my phone has somehow switched it on. Her eyes grow wide when she sees whose picture it is I'm using as the background on the lock screen, causing me to panic. The voice in my head is chattering away, spinning threads of incoherent thoughts into a confusing web of internal cacophony. It feels like I'm watching myself from above as I steady my feet and rush into the nun with all my might, slamming her down onto the bed before losing my balance and falling on top of her. She lets out a shrill scream, still refusing to let go of the phone.

"I asked you to give it back to me, but you didn't listen!" I clamour.

Buried memories sting my eyes and sharply I catch my breath. *I never stood up for myself against him, the one whom I shared my life with. My fear was stronger than my strength.*

"Weak."

Amidst the internal turmoil, the voice taunts me as it scrapes the walls of my cranium with its claws. My vision becomes clouded with blind rage; I see nothing. A thick veil of darkness covers my face. It creeps into my nostrils, forcing itself down into my lungs, and I taste the cold, bitter shadows on the tip of my tongue. My body feels numb, my soul shackled by shame.

"Don't hurt me!"

Her scream pierces my ears. The darkness disperses and the inner voice fades once again. I'm finding myself straddling the woman I pushed. In one of my clenched hands, some thin, frayed strands of hair poke out whilst I'm holding my phone with the other hand.

My heart is about to implode. I switch off my phone in panic as the door to the dormitory flies open and Garren rushes in with two nuns, Sylvie being one of them. Before I have time to react, he grabs my waist with one arm and tears me away from the sister.

"What has got into you, Falk?" he growls and sets me down on the floor some distance away.

"They steal things here," I whisper, staring at the three young women tremblingly embracing each other. "Look over there, on the floor. They've been touching my stuff! This person was messing with my phone and refused to give it back, and the other two tried to intimidate me and take my glasses off."

"She's possessed," stutters the woman whose hair I've pulled at without even being aware of it myself. "I could see it in her eyes! They turned as black as the night!"

"Piss off!" I shout. "What do you know about being possessed when you're the one messing with someone's personal things? That's what I call being possessed—by greed! You lot are lousy thieves pretending to be good people, hiding behind your faith."

"I've heard enough!"

Sylvie's face is contorted with anger, her voice laced with shrillness as she turns to Garren.

"I'm sorry, Grand Prior, but we can't keep the girl here. She has used violence within our sacred walls, and she behaves disrespectfully towards the sisters."

I just pushed her.

When the paladin puts his hands on my shoulders and looks at me, I feel like the air is disappearing out of my lungs, just like a deflating balloon that gets smaller and smaller as the air dissipates out of a small hole in it. I just want to curl up somewhere and be forgotten by the world.

"I shoved her," I exhale, barely audibly. "I panicked when the other two started messing with me and then… I don't know what happened after that," I continue as hot tears settle in my eyes.

For the first time, I think I see something soft in the man's gaze. He leans his face closer to mine, as if to say something, but remains silent. Instead, he wipes a tear from my cheek with one thumb in a light, caressing motion and sighs before turning to the nuns.

"I humbly thank you for your hospitality, Abbess Sylvie," he says and throws a harsh stare at the fidgeting women. "However, I suggest you hold a serious conversation with the girls and remind them of the values of the Light. They must repent their sins."

I blink away a few tears and wipe my nose with the sleeve of my dress as they exchange more sentences, which I neglect listening to. That small, almost gentle gesture amidst the chaos has thrown my emotions out of balance, and I'm not sure what to do with myself. I watch him picking up my clothes and my bunch of keys, handing them to me.

"Follow me, lass," he says, and the sternness is back, both in his voice and in his eyes.

I avoid meeting Sylvie's strict gaze as I walk behind the holy knight with my head bowed.

CHAPTER SEVEN

Saga Falk

We enter a building not far from the church which we visited yesterday. The long hall is decorated with banners, swords, and golden shields. Those we meet show their respect to Garren with bowed heads. One of them puts a hand on his shoulder, saying something that makes them both laugh. Crow's feet appear at the corner of Garren's eyes and dimples decorate his cheeks momentarily. He looks different like this. *Yeah, he looks almost human, instead of an infuriating religious warrior robot with just about no emotions other than sternness.*

The words being exchanged between them don't matter to me, and I sneak secret glances at the paladin holding me under arrest, seemingly unable to take my eyes off him. During a split second, I can make out a shimmering golden halo behind his head. *I'm probably just hallucinating due to hunger, fatigue, and shock.*

Garren motions that we're leaving by nodding at me, and I follow him through a narrow, beautifully lit side hall where oil paintings adorn the walls along with coats of arms and old, hand-written letters framed behind glass. He nods curtly to a guard standing by a solid door, then unlocks it and ushers me in.

A deep breath enters my lungs as I take a step inside. The air in the room carries a faint scent of roses, emanating from a small rose bush standing at one end of the room where it receives daylight from a stunningly detailed stained glass window. I've always thought roses do best outside, but these look like they're thriving. *Maybe magic is used to keep them in pristine health.*

A desk in what looks like solid oak stands at the other end, and behind it, with its accompanying chair, a wall bedecked with bookshelves. The aroma of the roses mixes with the smell of old books and parchments. Banners decorate the other walls, as well as a sturdy shield with a detailed rose in the centre, embellished with gold details in intricate patterns, and I catch sight of a large oil painting of a landscape overlooking a lush valley. The beauty of this chamber is close to breath-taking, reminding me of a time-bitten library as I survey the expanse of books.

Garren closes the door behind us. He pulls out a second chair and places it on the opposite side of the desk. I watch him as he hangs his coat on the back of his own chair and settles down.

"Sit," he orders, and I obey immediately.

My gaze fixes on a plate of apples standing to my left. He must have sensed how hungry I am, as he nods and speaks again.

"Help yourself."

Smiling gratefully, I sink my teeth into the juicy fruit. *So. Damn. Delicious.* The juice runs down one corner of my mouth and I wipe it away with the back of my hand before continuing to devour the rest of the apple. Garren leans his elbows on the table, putting his hands together so only the fingertips are touching, his eyes steady as he watches me for a while.

Satisfied, I wipe my mouth with the sleeve of my dress when I'm done eating and he points to a small tin bucket at the side of the table where I throw away the core.

"Thank you so much," I say in a hushed tone.

I'm still hungry, but I don't dare take another apple.

"You're welcome." The man in front of me leans back in his chair with his palms against the table top. "Do you want to go through what happened in the monastery?"

His sentence is a command clad as a polite question. Somewhat absent-mindedly, I fiddle with the clothes I've carried with me the whole way, lightly touching my keys and phone. I'm tired of thinking ten steps ahead all the time, tired of trying to come up with lies to avoid getting caught. Most of all, I'm tired of having to fear for my life and for my mental well-being.

"If I tell you everything in detail, will you promise not to overreact, no matter how odd it sounds?" I ask with caution in my voice, noticing how his eyes narrow.

Garren rubs the well-trimmed beard on his cheeks and chin with one hand, then crosses his arms. Briefly, I notice how his shirt is taut over his pecs, and my mind goes blank for a second or two.

What the hell is wrong with me? Think about Kailunn instead.

"You may proceed," he replies, and the calculating look from his blue eyes washes over me like ice-cold ocean waves.

I swallow hard and run one fingertip over my lower lip as I collect my thoughts.

"I come from Malmö. It's a real place, but you don't know it. It's not on your maps, just as Theadrath and your geography aren't shown on ours."

I scratch the back of my head, thinking about how to best phrase myself.

"Where I'm from, we have advanced technology, including items like this."

Gently, I tap my fingers on the phone.

"With this phone, I can stay in touch with family, friends, and those I love. I can also stay informed about what's happening in the rest of the world, because we have a global network everyone has access to. The network can also be used for entertainment purposes, and that's where… well, where all this stuff comes into play."

I draw in the scent of the roses through my nostrils, attempting to calm my nerves.

"Many people spend time playing games together via this global network I just mentioned. We play on consoles, computers with screens, and small portable devices. It's our way of experiencing a world we can't take part in in any other way than through games, books, movies, among other things."

I stop myself.

"Please ignore the last bit. I'll explain it all another time. Anyway—this game I've been playing for many years is more or less an exact copy of your world. I've met you there, Garren, though not the real you. That's why I knew your name when we met for the first time."

Garren stares at me with wide eyes, his emotions impossible to read. The anxiety makes me fidget and nervously touch my fringe.

"Are you okay?" I ask quietly.

I flinch as he gets out of the chair with a loud scraping sound from the chair legs against the wooden floor. He clasps his hands behind his back, keeping his eyes fixed on me.

"Go on," he orders, and I clear my throat to strengthen my voice, which feels like it's about to fail at any moment.

"Me and my closest friends have played together all these years and we've done a lot of missions for different characters. Including you, High Priestess Astryn, Kailunn…"

For a moment, my voice trails off and my head is spinning, until I muster the courage to continue speaking.

"In my world, you're all fictional. You don't exist except on our screens. Due to certain circumstances, which I'd rather not talk about, I made an active choice not to associate with men on a romantic level again. And that's where Kailunn starts painting the picture."

I take off my necklace, placing it in my lap.

"It's not even gold, because I've never had enough money for proper jewellery," I say whilst laughing softly; a hollow laugh to mask my embarrassment.

"During the course of the game, I became increasingly captivated by the fictional Kailunn. That's why I have the symbol of his people on my key ring and my necklace. I can't meet him, so I carry his symbol close to me, because it's the one thing of his I can touch."

Silence pours its wine over my tongue, and I avert my gaze, not wanting to look at Garren right now. I'm vulnerable and ashamed, while for some reason also feeling as if a weight has been lifted off my shoulders by having uttered the words out loud in front of someone else.

I switch on my phone, unlock it, and pull up the photo gallery. Quickly scrolling through the photos, I find a screenshot from *Reign Online* showing Kailunn, Garren, and Astryn, along with several other random characters in the background.

"This is you, the one who isn't real," I say in a low tone, holding the phone out to him.

Garren stands motionless for what feels like an eternity before slowly taking the phone from me, sceptically inspecting the screen. I say nothing at all, giving him some time to process the information.

"This sounds like witchcraft to my ears," he utters, and I wave my hands at him.

"No, it isn't. Check this out."

I put my belongings down, get up from the chair, and walk over to the other side of the desk where he's standing. With an apologetic look in my eyes, I take the phone from him, scroll for a while, and pull up a photo of Ambrosia and I. This one's from when we were abroad. She hugged me tightly, our heads touching, and I closed my eyes, laughing at something she had said. It was taken just minutes before a concert, and I remember it like it was yesterday.

"This is me and my best friend. We've been friends since childhood, and we play the game together."

I scroll again, finding a clip from when I was at another concert, having recorded myself singing.

"This is me again, but this time it's a video clip. No witchcraft. It's simply a part of our technology back home."

Garren stares at it and blinks a few times.

"You don't sing particularly well," he notes, and I glare sharply at him.

My god. This infuriating man.

"No one cares in such a situation," I say and switch off the phone while blushing. "It's the music that counts, and the fact the band is on stage, and you get to experience something awesome."

I shrug and run my hand through my hair.

"Now you know a little about my background."

"You didn't allude to how you ended up here."

Garren sits down and I slowly pace to and fro in the room, my thoughts following the tempo of my steps. He watches me in silence, and it takes a while before I speak again.

SHADOW DANCE

"A while ago, I heard a voice calling me on several occasions. At first, I thought it was someone who recognised me, but I could never locate the owner of the voice. Then I assumed I heard the voice because I'm not sleeping well these days and I—"

I almost mention my anxiety and halt my tongue at the last second. Quickly, I change the direction of the conversation.

"Everything turned into chaos when I was at work one evening. I was alone because I had promised to close for the day and my co-workers had already left. There was a storm outside, and I sat and played the game for a while, waiting for the weather to calm down. The voice started talking to me again, mentioning that I need to find out who's contacting me. A light blinded me, and it was like something was trying to pull me down while I was suffocating. When I regained consciousness, I realised I was here, and this place is real. The real Theadrath."

I take a deep breath and shift my attention to Garren. He shoots an intense gaze at me, burning a hole in my soul. After tucking my hair behind my ears nervously, I continue my explanation.

"At the monastery, I got angry when the women rummaged through my things. I panicked. The situation felt uncomfortable. Pious nuns shouldn't act like that, but they were being horrible. As I was getting worked up, the voice started talking to me again, saying a bunch of things I couldn't comprehend. This, combined with my rising anger and certain memories, which I guess were activated by the sound of that voice, resulted in me pulling the woman's hair out, which I honestly don't have any recollection of doing."

I sigh loudly, and more or less throw myself back into the chair while massaging my temples. The headache that has been lurking for a while is making itself known.

"I'm not an aggressive person," I say, looking embarrassed, "but that voice is messing with me. It's like it knows which buttons to push, while alerting me to upcoming events and people."

"It appears to be a herald," Garren says shortly, his voice crystal-clear. "A messenger who contacts you through what I assume is black magic."

"Maybe," I respond with a tired tone in my voice, not understanding the deeper meaning of his words.

Why would someone try to contact me? I'm not an important person.

Garren strokes his beard. "Perhaps they seek to access the Light within you," he mutters and furrows his brows.

"You have made a mistake."

I stretch my back in the chair and my eyes rush over the ceiling, the walls, and the windows.

"What do you mean?" I say, realising straight away the words have been spoken out loud.

The paladin narrows his eyes at me, closing his fingers around the large pendant with the lion's head in the centre and the jewel-encrusted roses around it.

The voice chuckles in my ears, a darkness hidden within the softness.

"Be watchful that he does not chop your little head off."

"Stop talking to me," I whisper, focusing on my breathing.

One. Two. Three.

"Your blood will flow, like the fairest of streams."

"Who are you?"

The panic expands inside, and I dig my fingernails into the armrest of the chair. I get up from the seat in a rush, but an invisible force slams my kneecaps and I fall to the floor. My hands fly up to my face and the blood in my veins feels like it's burning inside. My eyelids close tightly. I gasp for air and when I peek through my fingers, a dark field stretches out before me.

My hand finds its way down to my chest and it dawns on me I'm not

SHADOW DANCE

wearing my necklace. *Anxiety*. A deep sharp breath invades my lungs, the scent of burnt wood being carried on the back of the wind. Out of the corner of my eye, I catch a glimpse of moving figures. Turning my head in their direction, I notice some humanoid creatures heading towards me with strange, choppy movements. They're silent, terrifying. As they get closer, I see their features are completely blurred out, making them look even more horrifying.

An unspeakable terror grips me by the throat, and I throw myself backwards, trying to get to my feet so I can run, but my own shadow holds me to the ground. Desperately, I kick to break free. One of the creatures grabs my hair, pulling my head back. I boot it on the shin and hear it thump on the ground with a wailing sound.

"Don't touch me!" I scream and the same blinding light from when I had my last panic attack appears in front of my eyes again, but this time, it doesn't burn my eyeballs.

I can see through this membrane of light!

My hands, too, seem to give off a faint white radiance. Another creature grabs me, and as I clench my fist and deliver a blow to its face, the glow from my hand burns a part of the creature's blurred visage. The figure roars and writhes in pain; my terrified heart is about to implode in my chest.

I can barely breathe.

My knees are pulled up to my chest and I lean my forehead against them. Closing my eyes, I count to three in my head, over and over.

"Saga? Can you hear me?"

A voice finds its way into my ears and caresses my eardrums softly, like a dancing little invisible fairy. My eyelids flutter and open. The vision is blurry, and I realise I'm not wearing my glasses as I bring one hand up to my face. The lips feel parched and slowly I run the tip of my tongue over them to give them some moisture.

"Here," says the voice that just spoke to me, and someone grabs my hand, unfurling it and placing something in my palm.

My fingers close around the object. My glasses.

"Thank you," I mumble quietly and put them on.

I sharpen my gaze by blinking rapidly a few times, allowing it to wander around thereafter. I lie in a bed with several individuals gathered around me—Astryn being the only face I recognise among them. She's much more simply dressed today than the last time we met, apart from her blindfold being the same as before.

"You've finally woken up." Astryn smiles and puts a hand over mine. "We were worried, but the clerics have done an outstanding job of tending to you."

I try to smile, but the act of moving my facial muscles feels like an effort. I still can't comprehend how the priestess is capable of navigating where everything is, despite being blind.

"Where am I?" I ask tiredly, slowly rising to a sitting position.

"You're in the infirmary, having slept for a little over twelve hours."

One of the priests places a hand on my forehead; a slightly chilly sensation spreading from her palm, seeping into my pores. It's pleasant, and it doesn't take long for my brain to start processing the information I've just received. Twelve hours means it should be evening now.

Hunger sucks in my stomach and I throw a glance at the bedside table next to me, searching for something edible.

"What happened to me? Where's Garren?"

Astryn raises an eyebrow, and I realise I've casually referred to the paladin by name instead of his job title.

"Grand Prior Roseheart and some brothers and sisters of the Light brought you here. You caused a bit of havoc as the Light appeared within you. You punched one of the lower-ranked knights in the face and bit the grand prior's arm as he attempted to calm you down in order to perform a healing ritual."

Blushing fiercely, I look down. *Yikes, this is embarrassing.* I stare at the contours of my feet under the covers, wiggling my toes nervously.

"Are they mad at me?" I ask, my voice cracking.

"No one's angry."

Astryn gently squeezes my hand, moving thereafter as one of the clerics helps me get out of bed, leading me to the washroom. With slow, tired movements, I change into a nightgown the staff had handed to me. Staring at my pale reflection in the mirror, I attempt to fix my matted hair—my fringe has definitely acquired a life of its own.

Once back in the room, I see the priests have left and Astryn has taken a seat on the edge of the bed. Finally, I smile weakly and crawl under the blanket as the high priestess points to a tray on the bedside table. It's a stew with a mug of water and an apple next to the bowl. My stomach rumbles and I hope she doesn't hear how loudly it protests.

"What do they serve here?" I ask as I inhale the smell of the food through my nose.

"This is from the grand prior. He mentioned you're…"

She scratches her forehead thoughtfully.

"Back home, we call it being a vegan," I fill in. "I eat nothing from animals."

A weak smile dances across my lips and I quickly hide it by pressing them together tightly. *He remembered.*

"That sounds like a highly unusual way of life."

Astryn tilts her head to the side, and I shrug as I place the tray over my thighs and grab a small wooden spoon.

"I don't judge anyone who eats animals—I just choose another diet."

It feels like I'm inhaling the food, and when the first warm bites slide down the oesophagus and into my stomach, I tilt my head back a little while making a satisfied noise.

"Delicious," I chirp happily and see a smiling Astryn get up.

"I'll leave you to enjoy your meal. We'll surely meet again," she says.

"Thank you for everything so far, High Priestess."

I can't stop thinking about how beautiful she is, both inside and out, when I watch her leave the room with graceful movements. As the thoughts slowly rock back and forth in my head, I continue devouring the stew in front of me, gratefulness settling in my heart.

Satisfied, I put the tray away when I finish my food, burping quietly and wiping my mouth with the back of my hand. I'm still tired, but not quite in the same way as before, and I already feel somewhat better. I'll have to remember to thank Garren next time we see each other.

Thoughts turn into manifested thunderclouds of worry in my head. Am I still under arrest? Will he hurt me now that he knows some details about my origin, just like that voice said he's capable of doing?

Saga, you dumbass. He gave you food. But the fact remains—I bit him. And judging by Astryn's words, I seem to have possibly given one of his subordinates a blow to the face, too.

Suddenly, everything seems rather complicated.

The sound of a rooster crowing somewhere in the distance awakens me the following day and I lie here, taking in the sounds of my surroundings for a while, until a member of staff enters with breakfast on a tray.

"How are you feeling today?" he asks.

It's a young-looking guy with long, pointy ears, close-cropped dark

SHADOW DANCE

green hair which makes me think of moss, and light green eyes with some splashes of gold mixed with the shade of summer grass. A forest elf, perhaps. He has a piercing in one earlobe that looks like a little leaf, and I like him immediately, without even knowing who he is. *He gives a kind impression.*

"I'm fine, thank you," I reply, grabbing the tray from him as I fixate my hungry gaze on the bowl of steaming hot porridge.

"It's made with nuts and water," he utters. "Rumour has spread you have a different diet. It's considered madness by some."

"It's a completely normal lifestyle for me," I say quietly and spoon the porridge in my mouth. "What if I questioned other people's way of life?"

As I burn my tongue, my face contorts in a grimace. Taking a sip of water relieves most of the pain. The elf chuckles with his hands at his sides.

"It's also rumoured you're quite temperamental," he continues, seemingly having no plans of leaving the room.

Picking my words carefully, I can't help but roll my eyes.

"Do people in Whitekeep have nothing better to do than gossip about the newcomer?"

"Not when she attacks our beloved grand prior."

The slightly teasing tone of the last sentence is evident.

"What's the deal with Roseheart? Could you tell me a little about him, please?"

The elf blinks in surprise, visibly amused. *Maybe he likes to gossip as much as I do.*

"He's Queen Ariadne's right-hand man, despite Her Majesty already having an advisor," he says, thinking. "He stands in the same prominent position as Warlord Thurston and the high priestess. It's said he and Thurston rarely see eye to eye. The warlord uses brute force and controls his army with an iron fist, while the Light guides the grand prior and his paladins, and instead they are driven by their doctrine of faith and magic."

A chuckle stumbles between his lips.

"I count myself lucky I don't have to go to war with all its political intrigues, and instead, I get to look after others by using the Light."

"Where are you from?" I ask, putting away the tray with the now empty bowl on it.

"Summervale," he says, surprised I show interest in him as a person. "I belong to the forest elves. We're rather scarce due to travelling orc clans having decimated us."

"That sounds terrible," I mumble, my eyes firmly fixed on him.

He nods weakly, about to continue speaking, when the door to the infirmary opens and a woman peers in. She gives me the impression she's the headmistress around here.

"Elluin! The grand prior has arrived and wishes to speak to Miss Falk in private."

Elluin waves at me a little awkwardly.

"Thank you for the confabulation," he says as he swiftly grabs the tray and rushes out of the room.

I groan loudly and run my fingers through my hair. It makes me sick to my stomach just knowing the paladin is about to make an entrance and I'm ashamed of something I don't even remember causing him.

CHAPTER EIGHT

Garren Roseheart

Upon hearing a familiar voice allowing me to enter after knocking, my armoured hand pushes the door open to the room where Saga Falk has been resting since yesterday. The small room has little to offer in terms of decorations besides a painting on the wall. It's stuffy here, and I wonder why the keepers haven't left the window ajar so she can breathe fresh air.

She's sitting in bed with the covers pulled over her stomach, wearing a simple nightgown, and her dark hair looks more tangled than before. The dark circles I thought I saw under her eyes the last time we met seem to have intensified. She puts her hands to her cheeks, looking timidly at me.

"I'm so sorry," she says, shaking her head slowly.

"What's the reason for the apology?" I ask as I step up to the bed, keeping a respectful distance. "And how are you faring this morning?"

Her demeanour has completely changed overnight.

"I'm fine—I think I've recovered. I was told by one of the nursing staff I bit you. I have absolutely zero recollection of it."

Saga pushes the glasses up over her nose, preceding putting her hands in her lap.

"Thank you for arranging the food for me. I was starving."

Clasping my hands behind my back, I notice how I straighten up a little. "You're welcome."

She watches me in silence for a moment, visibly trying to organise her thoughts.

"You're all right, when you're not throwing me over your shoulder to arrest me and when you're not making some poor city guards soil their pants in fear," she says, giggling softly.

Laughter lines appear by her mouth, and I see a glimmer of starlight in those dark eyes I haven't noticed prior. My intensified heartbeat and the blood rushing in my ears distract me momentarily and I do my utmost not to look bothered. *This woman is pure witchcraft. Be on your guard.*

"I assume you mean that as a compliment and not ironically," I say, seemingly unaffected, and emotions hit like a sledgehammer in my heart as she nods and some hair tresses cascade over her shoulders and chest.

She's captivating.

"Where did I bite you?"

Saga's gaze sweeps over me, making me feel exposed. My lips curve into a wry smile.

"Here," I reply, removing my gauntlet and reinforcement sleeve.

"I can't see it," she says, beckoning me to come closer.

She adjusts her glasses once more, and when I move closer to the bed, she crawls towards the edge. Before I know it, she gently grabs my arm and I notice the look of shame in her eyes as she inspects the bite mark and the bruise around it. Her fingers are cold against my skin, and

I wonder if I should close my fists around her hands to warm them. Do the clerics not keep their injured warm enough in the infirmary?

"I'm so sorry," she says again and lets go of me, and I notice I've been holding my breath without realising it.

Discreetly, I exhale and steel myself.

"I've seen worse war injuries," I reply, pointing to the scar on my cheek.

Did I just use humour? By the Light, I don't behave like myself.

Saga grimaces in surprise and stares at me in silence for a moment. Suddenly, she bursts into laughter, a laugh that washes over me without inhibitions.

"Yeah, it seems like it," she giggles and clears her throat as she looks away briefly.

The colour has risen on her cheeks, and she studies me.

"May I ask how you got that scar?"

I nod.

"A clan leader of a group of orcs was in a foul mood and took it upon himself to split me in half," I begin. "Fortunately, I'm quick on my feet." I put the reinforced sleeve and gauntlet back on and adjust them carefully, taking my time before replying. "I beheaded him, resulting in his clan surrendering."

Her dainty hands fly up to cover her mouth, and the look from her dark eyes exudes horror. *Perhaps I shouldn't have answered her so truthfully.*

"I see," she breathes out upon recomposing herself.

Her gaze wanders, and I watch her collect her thoughts. When she turns to me, there is an air of uncertainty about her.

"Am I still under arrest?"

She has changed the subject. *Then I won't have to do it.*

"I see no reason for it. However, I suggest you turn to the Light to get your magic under control, and the herald's voice in your head be fully investigated," I reply, putting my hands together. "I can assist you."

I hear what I'm saying and a feeling of slight excitement blooms within. I, being grand prior, have far more important matters to attend to than training a novice to become a paladin and should delegate the responsibility fully to one of my officers. On the other hand, I may have some time a few days a week to keep her under my wing, sharing my knowledge.

Saga raises one eyebrow and purses her lips whilst pondering.

"What does that mean, exactly?" she enquires.

She hasn't rejected my proposal yet. *Praise the Light.*

"You are to receive monetary compensation, food, simple clothes, a roof over your head. In return, you train during the day with the other recruits and a few evenings a week you meet with me, in order for me to see how far you have come."

Her ears prick up.

"Compensation, you say? How much are we talking about?"

I bite my tongue to keep myself from grunting. *So, she's driven by the idea of riches instead of faith.* Maybe it's as she mentioned, that she had little to live off where she comes from.

"It varies from week to week. Most of the Order of the Light's income stems from donations. The commander to whom you're assigned is the one who evaluates your performance, and you must perform well if you wish to receive your fair share of the coins. The most important thing is to have the right faith in your heart."

The blank expression on Saga's face is evident.

"I believe in myself," she says cautiously. It's clear she chooses her words with great care, nervously scratching her elbow. "Although I'm not a heretic or whatever you'd call it."

I bow my head slightly and look down at my sabatons. Normally, I wouldn't involve myself with someone who doesn't walk on the same path of faith. I dedicate my life to the Light, but there's something peculiar about this woman. The Light courses through her veins; slumbering, powerful. She has appeared in the most unusual way, perhaps lost in time and space, and I believe it's the Light which has brought her here.

I lift my head again.

"May I take a seat?" I ask.

Saga gives me a quick, slightly doubtful glance and pulls the covers up to her chest before nodding silently. *Her heart is distrustful.*

I sit down on the creaking edge of the bed, offering her my hand.

"Put your hand in mine and imagine your inner power," I say.

"Okay," she replies, carefully placing her palm in mine.

The nightgown has come up slightly over her arm and I see how thin her pale wrist is. *Is she getting enough food?* I focus on the Light—on the love, safety, and belonging my faith gives me—and after a while, a warmth spreads from my armoured hand into hers. She flinches, but I shake my head, gesturing for her to stay still. Her eyes widen as a faint white glow shines from her fingertips and I can't stop myself from smiling. *By the Light, what a beautiful sight.*

"Imagine something, anything, that brings you joy," I say in a low voice.

Saga closes her eyes for a moment and hums softly whilst thinking. When she opens them, there is a hint of expectation hidden deep within as she stares at our hands. A bunch of shimmering, luminous butterflies fly out of my palm, circle above our heads, and land in her hair, on her arm, and shoulders. Carefully, she brings the index finger of her other hand closer to the butterfly on her arm and smiles widely as it climbs onto it. The slow movements of the wings scatter small, sparkling fragments in the air.

"I love animals, especially butterflies," she says with a dreamy tone in her voice, her eyes firmly fixed on the little creature while she remains still so as not to make any of them fly away. "Mum and I used to go looking for them in the woods when I was younger. My favourite one is the common brimstone, but as the years went by, I saw them less and less. Butterflies always calm my mind when I'm worried."

In silence, I look at Saga's face and move my gaze over every feature, etching the smallest detail in my memory. I didn't expect her to share memories, but I find it soothing to listen to her voice, with its conspicuous accent, as well as unusual use of language. In a short time frame, this woman has appeared out of nowhere, angered me on several occasions, and attacked me and my subordinates. And yet I'm fascinated, perhaps not solely because of the magic slumbering within her. Her gentle side appeals to me, and so does her inner strength. I've come to accept I'm curious about her and where she comes from.

Throughout my adult life, I have focused primarily on the love of the Light, fought and spilled blood in its name, and spread the good word about my faith during my long travels. There have been a number of individuals that caught my eye, in particular as I've climbed higher up the ranks, but I've always made an active choice not to mix with them too much—and not for too long. My discipline is something I'm proud of, and it supersedes the warmth of a temporary bedfellow. However, this woman is pure witchcraft, with the power to affect my state of mind within seconds.

The calm surface of my thoughts breaks, the ripples caused by her voice.

"No, they disappeared!"

Saga looks a little disappointed, her hand slowly pulling away from my palm. I find myself wishing she would hold it there just a little longer. A deep breath fills my lungs and I catch her gaze.

"Those butterflies were all your work—with the help of the Light," I explain.

"For real?" she mumbles as she pushes her glasses up the bridge of her nose.

I nod and rise from the bed.

"I believe there's something bigger behind your arrival than you, I, or anyone else is currently aware of," I continue. "I shall investigate the herald's voice. But I need to know if you're ready to take the leap from being a newcomer with no roots here, without a goal, to becoming a part of the Order of the Light's strength and standing by our side, no matter what shall come."

She tucks strands of hair behind one ear and looks sceptical.

"Are you sure I'm the right person to train as a paladin?" she asks. "I'm not strong physically and…"

The voice fades away before she clears her throat and continues, now in a lower voice.

"I suffer from anxiety. And sometimes I experience panic attacks, as you've noticed by now."

I nod reassuringly.

"With us you're not alone—we look out for each other. I'm convinced that paladin is the right path for you. The other option would be the clergy, but you've most likely burnt your bridges with them." A smirk finds its way across my lips, and I watch with hidden amusement how her cheeks redden. "In addition, you seem to have anger buried within you, which the clergy doesn't accept. With us, you can find inner peace in your heart and soul and learn how to use your magic."

Surprise edges her visage when she stares at me.

"How do you know…"

She doesn't finish the sentence and shakes her head as she lowers her gaze. The sunlight dancing in from the window hits her face, and she squints a little as she looks up at me again, presumably waiting for me to speak.

"The Light inside you whispers that someone has wronged you, even if you have no visible scars," I explain.

I may have gone too far in the conversation, so I stand up, take a few steps back, and let my arms hang by my sides. Giving her some distance, so our time together doesn't turn into a moment of worry for her. I turn my head away when she gets out of bed and do my utmost not to look at her from the corner of my eye.

"Can you see my memories through the power you get from the Light?" she asks.

"No, that would be witchcraft," I reply. "What I can sense is the wavelength of your magic, much like a pulse, and the potential messages it carries in that second."

I focus my attention on the solitary painting on the wall.

"Without knowing specific details, I'd like to mention that you shouldn't blame yourself for what has happened to you. Whoever has wronged you will receive his punishment from the Mother of the Light one day."

My eyes narrow, my fist clenched.

"Had that individual got in my way, I would have issued the punishment myself."

Too late, I realise I've uttered the last sentence out loud and become somewhat frustrated with myself. *Self-control and focus.* Light footsteps move across the floor and when I turn my gaze towards her again, I see her standing in front of me in that cream-coloured nightgown that reaches past her knees. Her eyes shift from wanting to ask a thousand questions to a faint warmth, as if she has found temporary comfort. I'm about to take another step back, to put distance between us.

"Wait, Garren!"

The words stumble out of her mouth, and I find myself unable, or perhaps unwilling, to move as her slender arms wrap around me.

CHAPTER NINE

Saga Falk

It strikes me that there's a strange kind of connection established between us. I'm vulnerable, spiritually exposed, and emotional. For the first time in a long time, I feel seen, and it's somewhat intimidating. It's as if I exist outside of my own little world I tend to hide away in.

I'm used to being invisible, but he sees me.

I barely know who this holy knight is, and he can be tight-lipped. And yet, he makes comments now and then that comfort me and give me hope amidst the misery and confusion. Maybe he's the key to me figuring out why I'm here, and eventually, I'll be able to go home. I miss my computer, bed, and shower. I even miss my sweatpants and my thick, oversized jumper.

"Wait, Garren!"

He stops in his tracks, and before I allow myself to overthink things, I wrap my arms around him, placing my cheek against his cuirass. Hugging someone clad in armour feels strange, almost as if I'm embracing a robot. I close my eyes tightly, a deep breath entering my lungs.

"Thank you for your words," I say in a hushed tone.

This isn't right. I need to find Kailunn.

A pang of guilt makes me hastily release my grip on Garren. He has raised his hands, as if to return the embrace, but he lets them fall to his sides and looks at me with a strange expression in his eyes. I continue to speak, changing the path of the conversation in hopes of the tension in the room releasing.

"I think I'm ready to join the Order of the Light."

I salute him like a soldier, and the strange look is replaced by a disapproving one.

"It's not Thurston's army you're joining," he mutters gruffly.

I'm cheering a little inside. The grumpy paladin is back once again, and balance has been restored.

"We're leaving," he continues curtly.

"One question," I say, fiddling with the hem of the nightgown. "Where can I grab a shower?"

Garren's eyebrow raising indicates confusion and I correct my question.

"Where can I wash myself?"

"In the bathhouse," he replies, taking a long look at my hair. "I presume I should show you how to get there."

My cheeks heat up and I bite my tongue to keep myself from saying something unpleasant to him. *I'm well-aware of how my hair looks right now.*

Someone knocks lightly on the door, and Elluin carefully pokes his head through the doorway.

"Pardon the interruption, but I have your belongings here," he stutters nervously.

I wave at him. *Perfect—I was just about to ask where my stuff was.*

"Hey, Elluin! Grand Prior was just about to leave so I can change in peace. Or does he intend to keep watch over me?"

I smile sweetly at Garren, tilting my head to the side and taking delight in hearing him grunt in annoyance. Normally, I tend to not bring myself to retaliate verbally. However, I feel embarrassed by the way he had looked at me. Besides, I'm stuck in a strange place. Maybe it's just as well to show the stern knight I'm not completely unaware of his piques.

"Make haste!" he says as he turns to face the door.

He grabs it, flinging it open with such force that Elluin stumbles through the doorway and lands right in his arms. Brusquely, he shoves the apologetic elf away and leaves us with determined steps. *Yikes, I must have hit a nerve.*

Elluin hurries to put my stuff on the bed and I see how red his cheeks are.

"Are you okay?" I ask anxiously.

"Oh yes," he says quickly, with a dreamy glint in his eyes. "He's special, our grand prior. A well-liked man for the great deeds he has performed, his deep faith and strength, and his attractive appearance."

I roll my eyes as I put my hands to my sides. The floor feels cold against my currently bare feet.

"He has his moments when he seems sensible. Other times, he's quite harsh and grumpy."

Elluin looks at me in shock with one hand over his mouth and I chew on my bottom lip for a few seconds. Maybe I overdid it a little. After all, it has been some stressful days so far and I long to go home to my mediocre life more than ever. In addition, Elluin isn't entirely wrong. Garren is nice to look at, with his chiselled cheekbones and neatly trimmed facial hair. The scar on his face enhances his attractive features.

I've never turned down a little gossip in my life, which Ambrosia usually makes sure I get plenty of. Moreover, I know very little about Garren Roseheart's backstory. I haven't played as a paladin in *Reign Online* and I forgot to read more about him that night when Ambrosia had found his picture for me.

"How old is he, and do you know if he's seeing anyone?" I ask curiously.

Elluin casts a quick glance at the door before moving closer to me, muttering, with his hand still placed over his mouth.

"He's forty-three years old, no children as far as I know. Rumours say his first love is the Mother of the Light. That he's too busy maintaining the security of our realm and planning the Order of the Light's strategic moves at the various country borders to have time to get involved with anyone. Many bards sing of the great deeds he has performed in battle, especially in his younger days."

Elluin lets out a sigh, as if daydreams veil his mind momentarily, and I raise an eyebrow. I didn't expect that from Garren. However, this elf is proving to be a decent source of information. Perhaps I can get some additional details out of him now that I seem to be here indefinitely.

"And what do you know about Prince Sunseeker?" I ask, trying to look nonplussed as I fiddle with my linen sleeve.

"Prince Sunseeker? Why do you want to know about him?"

"I'm just curious."

I shrug nonchalantly as I reach for my clothes and begin unbuttoning my nightgown. Elluin looks like a harmless person, and I'm guessing he has a certain predilection for men, so I don't feel uncomfortable with him being in the same room.

As if reading my mind, he turns the other way, clasps his hands behind his back, and rocks back and forth on his feet while I undress.

"The prince is an enigma. He's several hundred years old, so in elvish terms he's still fairly young. His mother, Queen Viessa Sunseeker, reigns over the Valley of the Sun and it's said she rules it with an iron fist. However, age is catching up with her. Her son is the one who makes all the decisions nowadays. It's common knowledge high elves are habitual users of magic, and they must always have access to a magical source, their thirst for it caused by an innate need. Moreover, they're said to excel at using magic to manipulate their enemies. Many of them therefore choose to train as mages."

Typical—I already know about this. I wish he could tell me more specifically about Kailunn as a person.

I zip up my jeans after fiddling with the button for a few seconds, fix my bra at the sides, and pull on my pink jumper before putting my glasses back on. The necklace is around my neck, hidden under my top, and the cold jewellery warms up, soon matching my body temperature. I detangle my hair as best I can with my fingers before pulling on my coat and shoes. It's great not having to wear yesterday's dress again.

I clap my hands lightly against my coat pockets to make sure I haven't forgotten to tuck away my few belongings.

"All done," I say to Elluin, giving him a thumbs up as he turns to me with a smile. "Thank you and your colleagues for taking such good care of me."

"Hearing words like these is the reason I'm in this line of work," he replies cheerfully.

We step out of the room. Garren is standing in a narrow hall, talking in a low voice with the woman who I assume is the headmistress of the infirmary. When he turns his head and meets my gaze, he doesn't look as annoyed anymore. His attention shifts to Elluin and the expression changes to sternness, but it disappears as quickly as it appeared. He reminds me of a chameleon that, instead of changing colour, switches between different, millisecond-quick emotional states depending on the situation and company. I think back to the butterflies swirling out of his palm and his twinkling eyes as he sat beside me and watched them in silence. I don't see any sign of his previously gentle state of mind right now.

For a moment, I wonder if I made the right decision in accepting his invitation to join the Order of the Light. If he's this harsh, what will his officers be like? Anxiety prepares a picnic in my stomach.

"Thank you for taking care of me," I say to the woman as I bow my head slightly. "I also want to take the opportunity to praise Elluin, who did an extraordinary job."

I give the elf a quick smile and watch his face light up. I feel good and am proud of myself. Good, because it seems like I've somehow done a good deed for someone else; proud, because I'm forcing myself to be social. In this place, I must use my words and dare to speak up in order to make it out of here and back home to Malmö.

"What's this?" I exclaim and notice how the anxious lump in my stomach grows.

Garren and I have been walking through Whitekeep and I've tried to avoid looking at people who cast suspicious glances at me. The sun warms my skin a little despite the slightly chilly wind and I've been studying the buildings, alleys, cobblestones, and market stalls. One of them sells flowers; I had laid eyes on the most beautiful light purple roses, whose petal edges almost seemed to glow in a light blue shade. I had felt compelled to walk over to smell them and the salesman had been staring, before he caught sight of the man behind me—his stare immediately being replaced by a smile. It must have been a fake one, but I smiled back at him and promised myself I'll buy myself some flowers one day if I stay here long enough.

We also passed a small shop where a seamstress sold simple clothes and I selected a couple of items, but Garren insisted I choose several of each. It dawned on me I'm going to have to wash my clothes by hand, so having spare attire will be useful. He paid for the lot. When I explained I would pay him back later, he simply shook his head.

I turn to Garren when he doesn't respond immediately.

"What's this?" I repeat, putting my hands to my sides as I stick my chin into the air.

"This is the bathhouse," he answers curtly and nods towards a large building behind a wall and an open gate.

"I'm well-aware of what this building is," I say sarcastically, trying to sharpen my somewhat shaky voice. "You didn't tell me men and women are going to the same place. I assume no one wears a bathing suit there?"

"Why would we be covering ourselves with clothing? The bathhouse is used to clean oneself, so it would be illogical."

"Do men and women bathe together, then?"

"Correct."

"Are you being serious right now? Why didn't you take me to a place where only women have admission?"

"No such place exists in Whitekeep. People bathe together."

Garren raises an eyebrow. The sun's dancing rays make his blond hair shine like gold and for a moment, I almost forget how frustrated I am. One of his hand drums on the sword hilt at his hip and he extends one hand in my direction.

"I assumed you had no problem being undressed in front of others, considering you changed in front of that elf you gave high praise to."

Good lord, I'm fuming.

A surge of anger makes my blood boil and I clench my fists as I slowly count to three and focus on my breathing. When I answer him, I choose my words carefully, wrapping them in a calm and composed veil.

"First of all, he's a healthcare professional, and a good one at that, so he has no interest in seeing me naked. He turned around as I was changing—without peeking. Secondly, he was quite smitten with you, Grand Prior, and I firmly believe his thoughts were on you and what you look like when you're undressed."

I glare defiantly as Garren stares at me, saying naught in response, the colour rising on his scarred face.

"And one more thing," I continue, tightening my grip on the bag of newly bought clothes I'm carrying. "It's not polite to assume things, no matter how long or how little you've known a person for. It's not the type of behaviour I'd expect from a high-ranking person like you, who I'm guessing meets different individuals daily from all walks of life."

A moment of silence follows, and I turn my face away from Garren as he continues looking at me intently.

"I apologise," I hear him say in a muffled voice. "It was wrong of me to speak to you in such a way."

Surprised, I focus my gaze on him again and he looks ashamed. *There it is, a genuine feeling that actually lasts more than a millisecond.* Anger pulls back its waves in my inner tide and I nod at him.

"It's fine, just don't say stuff like that again," I respond, sighing quietly as I turn towards the bathhouse.

The thought of going in there makes me feel uncomfortable. I'm aware I can't see well without my glasses, but I find it hard to relax when I know there are men in there, no matter if I can make them out or not. And let's be honest: how hygienic is a place like this?

I press the bag with the clothes against my chest and try to see the positive in the situation. To get clean, to wash my hair. Garren stands next

SHADOW DANCE

to me with his hands clasped behind his back, looking up at the sky where some white, fluffy clouds temporarily cover the sun's warming face. He closes his eyes for a moment.

"The bathhouse is a place for socialising, so everyone mixes," he explains, his eyelids slowly wandering up again and meeting my gaze. "There are private rooms where you can clean yourself, but they're reserved for politically important guests and those whose wallets weigh heavier."

"So, are there staff in the general area?" I ask, putting my hand over my eyes so I don't have to squint due to the sun deciding to peek out again.

He nods and turns so he can lean his broad back against the wall.

"Correct. They're available when the doors to the bathhouse are open. They make sure thieves don't steal people's belongings, and at a specific time each day, they only allow parents and their children to enter the building."

After handing me a few coins, he stretches before closing his eyelids again.

"This is the entrance fee. Do try not to take too long, Falk."

The rays of the sun dance with playful feet, caressing his face. Sometimes he looks like an angel who has lost his halo. Until now, I haven't thought at all about how beautiful his lips look, or paid attention to those long, dark eyelashes. His worry lines seem to be ever-present, even when his forehead isn't furrowed, but somehow it seems to solidify his handsomeness and unique features. Horrified, I realise I want to tuck away a hair tress that has fallen in front of one of his eyes and curse at myself within.

Get yourself together, damnit.

I shake my head, getting irritated with myself. Only Kailunn should get my full attention, and no one else. Anything else would be absurd. For a moment, my thoughts revolve around Retsam before quickly dispersing, much like fleeing deer into the thick winter fog. Back into the memory archive, hopefully to stay there and not be brought out again.

I take a deep breath, stretching my back. *I can handle this.* A little nudity isn't going to do me any harm, though I'm prudish. Ambrosia and Remy always make fun of that side of me, but it's not something I've chosen myself. I've always been like this.

Garren speaks to me, eyes still closed.

"Have you changed your mind?"

"This feels strange," I murmur. "The bathhouses where I come from are different and you're covered to some extent."

"Most people carry towels they cover themselves with until they get to the basins. These basins have a magical mist on the surface that prevents you from seeing everything in detail."

"But there's a risk I'll still see people when they're about to step into or get out of the pools," I interject, twisting my hands nervously around each other. "And then I haven't even started speculating about the changing rooms."

"You seem distressed, lass," he says, his voice edged with a surprising softness which almost throws me off.

I cast a quick glance at the knight, then I look at a point next to him and let my mind wander. *What if I run into some weird guy in there? What if someone touches me and no one will see it when there's a fog covering the surface of the water?*

If Ambrosia were here right now, she would have called me paranoid before taking me by the arm, and we would have walked into the bathhouse together. Ever since we found friendship in each other as kids, she has proclaimed herself my protector. She had been the only person analytical enough to see through my exterior and point out my ex wasn't good for me, telling me I should break up with him and move in with her instead.

My thoughts are dispelled when a woman bumps into me, pushing me to the side and almost making me trip. She stares at Garren with a sheepish smile on her face, barely noticing me.

"Grand Prior Roschcart, what a pleasant coincidence!" she exclaims. "I was thinking about you the other day. Have you heard anything about the reports of an orc clan to the south, setting fire to a farmhouse and stealing their livestock?"

"Such matters aren't on my desk," Garren replies, giving the woman a polite smile. "That's an assignment for one of Thurston's southern units."

I stare with my mouth wide open at the woman as she pushes up her plump bosom and squeezes in front of me to get closer to Garren. She eyes him from head to toe without hiding her obvious infatuation.

"You appear to have had little rest. Please, allow me to wash your back for you and make sure you relax properly before you start the day."

"Is this woman for real?" I exhale. Realising I've spoken out loud, I put my hand over my mouth and turn away from them.

"I humbly thank you. But I'm tasked with looking after our recruit."

I feel a hand over my shoulder and how a couple of hair strands tickle my cheek.

"Play along," Garren whispers in my ear as he makes me turn around. "We shall discuss certain matters that are important to know as a new member of the Order of the Light," he speaks again, this time with a louder voice.

With disbelief in her eyes, the woman shoots a sharp glance at me, and I blink twice before giving her a quick smile, trying to figure out what to say.

"Yeah, that's right, we're about to discuss things in the bathhouse… together."

In the corner of my eye, I think I see Garren glaring sternly at me.

"You don't look like you're from here," says the woman, and her eyes narrow slightly.

"When one's faith is right, then one's origin doesn't matter," I say, trying to sound perky.

"We must get going," Garren interjects and nods his head to the side, in the building's direction.

He smiles politely at the woman and motions for me to follow him.

"Who was that?" I ask curiously as we enter through the open gate.

I throw a quick glance over one shoulder and see her standing there, looking after us.

"One of several people who seems to have a liking for me," Garren answers monotonously.

We stand at the entrance to the bathhouse for a moment and cold shivers run down my spine.

"Did you mean it when you said we're going in here together?"

"Is she still looking at us?" he asks, and I nod. "Very well. There's your answer."

"You mustn't see me naked!" I gasp, and he waves one hand dismissively at me.

"You need not worry. For my part, I will cover myself as best I can."

My cheeks heat up, probably turning bright red, and I glare angrily at him.

"You weren't meant to join in!"

"Plans change depending on the situation. I suggest you learn to adapt. Make haste."

He walks up the steps that lead to the bathhouse, and as I stand still staring at him, he glances over his shoulder.

"You're wearing armour! It must be difficult to take it off and put it back on," I say.

I try to dissuade him, but to no avail. His cloak and coat of arms flutter behind him in the wind, and I sigh as I awkwardly follow him.

SHADOW DANCE

If Ambrosia had been here, she would have been proud of my rapid, if chaotic, evolution from being a prude to bathing with a man who will also be my new boss.

I keep the towel wrapped tightly around me where I've been hiding in a corner for a while, avoiding looking at the other women in the changing room. The walls are tiled in a faint grey shade, the same as the floor, and the cold from the tiles creeps up through the soles of my feet and up my legs. A female mage with green eyes and short pink hair watches over our belongings, which we have been told to put in different cabinets. Instead of using a door, she, or some other mage, has established a spell at the doorway that is veiled in a thin film, shifting in light blue. It's possible to see out through the magic membrane when standing inside the room, but nothing is visible from the outside.

I decide to wear my glasses temporarily until I reach the pools. I'm not keen on going out there to look for that grumpy paladin when I can't see well without them.

Politely nodding to the friendly mage, I take a deep breath and step out of the room as I survey the hall erratically. Garren paid our entrance fee to the bathhouse before we went our separate ways to our respective changing rooms. *Sigh. Now I owe him even more money.*

I see some women walking past me and begin following them at a safe distance. Old memories from when I was a child and went to swimming classes come to mind. I'll never forget that cold that seemed to be ever-present when going down to the pools.

When I step out into a large hall, I see different basins and individuals in the process of washing themselves. A group of dwarves are sitting together and laughing loudly at something, perhaps a story one of them has just told, and a little further away, a couple of elven women, one of whom is washing the other's hair. It gives me an incredibly intimate feeling, and it's almost as if I'm intruding by my mere presence.

Daylight finds its way in through large windows, which also seem to have a kind of magical film over them, similar to the doorway to the dressing room. The light walls are decorated with painted images on the tiles. Light green and orange plants of a large variety pose in pots in different places. I can't remember the names of them when I think back to my time in *Reign Online* and my eyes wander. Where is that irritating paladin?

My feet take uncertain steps. With one hand, I grip the towel tightly to keep it from sliding down and exposing me. *What a nightmare that would be.* I almost feel sick to my stomach just thinking about it. I walk past some large, tall pillars, my stress levels increasing, and feel like an alien in this environment with strangers all around me.

"Over here, Saga."

A familiar voice speaks. *He called me by my first name.* I flinch and turn around.

"Garren?" I say, seeing him standing by one of the pillars I just passed by. *Wow, okay. I'm looking respectfully.*

My brain blanks for a moment as my gaze falls on his bare torso. He's far fitter than I could have guessed, and I can make out a couple of scars running down his chest. A towel is wrapped around his waist, and I quickly look away as I find myself staring at his abs, perhaps not quite as respectfully as I'd like. *I can't possibly feel attraction to a man again, especially one who isn't Kailunn. No, it's wrong on every level.*

"Are you well?" Garren asks, crossing his arms over his chest.

Quickly nodding, I hug the towel around myself even tighter.

"Oh yes, this is fantastic and not strange at all," I blurt out, laughing nervously. "It's perfectly normal to bathe with a man I hardly know."

"You don't have to worry," he assures. "I won't look at you and I'm not interested in attempting anything inappropriate. However, it may feel safer for you to be here with someone whom most people here respect, as they will most likely leave you alone due to my presence."

My other hand nervously fiddles with my fringe and I discreetly glance at him while my brain works at full speed. He probably has a point. His gaze is fixed somewhere else but on me, and I exhale with relief.

"Okay," I nod and throw a look towards the pool a few steps behind him.

It's completely devoid of people and for a second, I wonder how clean the water will be, considering all the guests using these at the same time.

"The water is cleansed by our magicians who work in shifts," Garren says, as if he has read my mind. "They work this way because using magic drains their life energy and they have to recover before they can use magic again."

"I didn't know that," I blurt out in surprise. "Do you also use life energy?"

"Both light and dark magic use it," he replies. "There's also magic that uses other types of energy sources."

I nod silently. *So that means I, too, will use life energy once I learn to harness my magical power. Scary.* I walk up to the pool and look down at the surface of the water. Indeed, there's a pale blue mist over the surface that seems to rise above the edge of the pool until it finally disappears somewhere into thin air. Cautiously, I crouch down, careful to keep a tight grip on the towel around my body and stick my hand down into the mist. When I touch it with my fingertips, some of the magic cloud swirls up over my hand, finds its way up to my elbow, and then slowly dissipates.

I glance over my shoulder at Garren.

"Could you please get in first?"

His face takes on a surprised look whilst he nods. I put my hand over my eyes and hear him stepping into the pool.

"Is it common to be shy where you're from?" he asks, and I can't tell if he's trying to be funny or mean by his tone—or maybe he's simply curious.

Discreetly, I peek out between my fingers and can make out the towel is at the edge of the pool and Garren is largely covered by the magical, swirling cloud. *Good.* He points to a small ladder some distance away I wouldn't have noticed otherwise.

"I'm not sure," I say tonelessly, as I shrug and blush all the way down to my neck. "Could you turn around, please?"

Once again, he obeys without objection. My gaze pauses on his back, and I swallow hard. It's covered with a myriad of scars reminiscent of lashes from a whip, creating a bizarre body painting on the skin. I wonder what has happened to him as I look around to make sure no one's watching me before I start to climb down the ladder. I put the towel down as I feel warm water caress my toes. Swiftly I climb down until I feel the floor against my feet and cheer inside. *Hopefully, nobody noticed me take off the towel.*

I lightly splash the water with my hands and make sure I'm covered in mist before moving to the other side of the pool. When I reach the wall, I feel something by my knees. It's a ledge I can sit on while the water and magic still cover my body.

Feeling my face getting a little hot from the warm water against my skin, I take off my glasses and place them on the edge of the pool.

"Can I turn around now?" the paladin asks from his corner, raising his voice so I can hear him over all the murmuring of the other bathing guests and the sound of the pools.

"Yeah."

I squint my eyes. Everything further away merges into a haze of different colours and the only things I can see relatively well are my own hands as I bring them closer to my face to rub my cheeks and forehead in circular motions. It feels good to feel the warmth of the water against my skin and all my major worries about the bathhouse seem to escape.

"Please excuse me if I look at you strangely, but I can't see well without my glasses," I explain, wiggling my toes playfully.

"I can't hear you," Garren says loudly, making me sigh heavily.

I have absolutely no desire to try to make myself heard by almost screaming over the sounds in the building.

"Come closer, then," I say in an even louder voice, beckoning the haze further away.

The water laps soothingly against my arms as the paladin moves towards my side of the pool and I continue to squint until his outline becomes clearer and I can make out most of him, albeit in a slightly blurrier format. Instinctively, I pull my arms up over my chest as if to cover myself, before clearing my throat and telling myself deep within I'm being silly; the magic does a good job as is.

I notice he still isn't looking at me and find myself staring at his upper arms. The muscles are well-defined and the water droplets in his hair and on his skin glisten in the daylight streaming in through the windows. He pulls his hands through his hair and closes his eyes as he splashes water on his face and washes himself. Tilting his head back, he runs his fingers along his neck and throat, then massages one shoulder. I finally tear my eyes away from him, annoyed with myself for blushing.

"Don't they have any soap or shampoo here?" I ask, trying to shatter my own distracted thoughts.

"Shampoo?"

Garren opens his eyes and looks at me before he averts his gaze in an apologetic manner.

"Something to wash your hair with," I explain, glancing at him. "You can look at me while we talk, but only at my face."

He bursts into a short, surprisingly soft laugh, and my stomach tingles.

A dagger of nervousness stabs me, and I catch my breath.

Get it together, Saga. It's bad enough that you're naked in a bathhouse with someone who isn't Kailunn.

Garren cups his hand around some of the magical mist above the surface, lifts it, and twists it around his index finger with circular motions in the air.

"The same kind of magic which cleans the water is used to cleanse our bodies," he replies, waving the cloud away from his hand. "That's the reason they charge an entry fee to these premises."

"This sounds like witchcraft to my ears," I say, chuckling to myself and smirking teasingly.

He mirrors my smirk. "Do you have magic where you're from?"

I shrug as I rinse my hair with the water and shake the fringe out of my eyes.

"No. Everything's modern and advanced, but we can't purify anything in this manner. Had we had this possibility, then we would probably have been able to offer water to our most needy countries that live in drought and poverty." I avoid mixing politics into my statement. "You know a bit about my background now, so I feel it's only right that I get to know a little more about you. You may be about to become my boss, but knowing more about the person I'll be working for would make me feel more at ease."

The fact of the matter is I'm curious and I have nothing better to do than feed that curiosity while I'm in this strange situation. *Maybe it'll be easier to relax.*

Garren clasps his hands behind his neck as he leans against the pool wall, chaining my gaze with those intense blue eyes.

"By all means, but we'll do it my way. You ask your questions, then I ask mine."

For a moment, I look at him in silence, before deciding to accept the terms.

SHADOW DANCE

"Fine. Have you been a holy knight for long?"

"Yes. My training to be one began when I was ten years old."

"That's early," I note, lifting an eyebrow in surprise. "You were still a child."

A weak smile stretches across Garren's lips.

"I was the youngest in my department. The Light has guided the Roseheart family through generations and the magic bloomed in me at a young age."

"How was it, being the youngest?"

I find myself leaning closer to him as I prick up my ears in curiosity.

"You can probably guess what it was like to be the youngest, thinnest boy and yet be the one with the most Light magic in his blood. It wasn't always looked upon favourably."

Garren brings his hands down and looks at his palms.

"I took a lot of beating before I grew stronger."

"That's terrible!" I exclaim in horror. "Did you tell an adult about what was going on?"

His mouth curves into another smile, and I think I sense something sad in his expression.

"Everything was different back then," he replies. "It was a harsher, more brutal climate. I guarantee it won't be like that when you become a recruit in my order."

I caress my fingertips on the surface of the water under the mist.

"How can you be certain about it? I had the misfortune of encountering several rather unpleasant nuns before. Nuns are supposed to be pure saints, they say."

"Rotten individuals can be found all around us, but now you're under my protection."

The look from his eyes goes right into me and I gaze at him. The way he emphasised the last sentence causes a tingling heat to spread in my chest and I try to fight off the feeling.

"What question do you have for me?" I ask in an effort to break free from the heat's mental effect on me.

"What made you take a liking to the prince in the game you're playing?"

Garren doesn't take his eyes off me, and I'm caught off guard by his direct approach. Spending a moment looking at a blurry point somewhere in the distance, I answer him upon collecting my thoughts.

"I have an image of him always controlling his emotions, having a gentle side, and being loyal. That he's calm and thinks before he speaks or acts. Being calm is a good quality to have."

I shrug my shoulders slightly, realising how stupid I sound. Applying attributes to a fictional character that may not correspond at all to the real Kailunn—it's truly ridiculous.

"Lass," Garren says with a soft tone in his voice, and it makes me irritated, cutting right through me like a knife in butter.

"Don't you dare speak condescendingly to me!" I mutter before I can stop myself, regretting my statement. "Sorry. It's complicated and I don't want to talk about it."

Leaning against the pool wall behind me, I close my eyes tightly. Refusing to let tears appear in front of the paladin, I focus on my breathing. *One, two, three.*

I flinch when I feel a pair of warm fingertips against my cheek, and my eyes fly open. Garren has withdrawn his hand with a peculiar expression decorating his face. Under any other circumstance, I most likely would have screamed at him, but his touch is comforting and gentle. My skin is lapping up the remnants of his body heat.

"Would you like to know more about Prince Sunseeker?" he asks in a low voice, and I nod enthusiastically in response.

He sighs heavily and sits in silence for a moment, as if he's flipping through his vocabulary.

"I've met him a number of times when we discussed the security of our respective kingdoms. He carries himself with elegance, his movements similar to those of a feline, and often throws in alluring words the few times he speaks with his tongue contrary to using telepathy. He prefers to mix with his own people and is on a constant quest to quench their thirst for magic. But don't be fooled by his gentle demeanour. He's far more bloodthirsty and cunning than he lets on. It's rumoured Queen Sunseeker sends him on missions to capture magical creatures, which they drain of magic and thus life."

I'm unsure how to deal with this new information. *Bloodthirsty, Kailunn? Capturing living creatures? He's so incredibly beautiful in every way. No, I'll have to form my own opinion when we meet. I'm convinced he wouldn't hurt anyone on purpose. The high elves are peaceful and have magical stones and plants with which they can quench their thirst.*

The paladin interrupts my thoughts with another question, in a voice so low I must strain to hear him.

"What was your perception when you met the fictional Garren Roseheart?"

"I didn't get to meet him that often, since I play a priest who's a high elf," I admit, clearing my throat nervously. There's a strange atmosphere between us and I don't know how to react. "The few times I did missions for him, he was demanding, strict, and didn't talk nonsense for several minutes, which many others seem to do in the game. In fact, my best friend Ambrosia has a thing for your character. She plays a human paladin."

I try to lighten the mood and lightly splash my hands in the water, smiling to myself.

"I think she'd be jealous knowing I'm here with you. I clearly remember her saying she wouldn't kick you out of bed."

Garren appears distracted as I fall silent, and my gaze traces his face. His attention is fixed on a point far away and he runs one hand through his wet hair and scratches the beard on his cheek.

"There seem to be quite a few people with a similar opinion," he mutters under his breath.

The sunlight from the window dances across his grim features.

"Where I come from, many people would want to be in your shoes," I say, my smile turning sarcastic. "No commitments and new partners all the time so they can keep the excitement in life."

I grunt in disapproval and think back to that time Ambrosia made me install a dating app on my phone. The experience can only be described as a digital meat market. *Never again.*

"Temporary bedfellows are low on my priority list with regards to spending what little rest I have."

"How do you spend your free time, then?" I ask, trying not to sound too curious.

A long moment of silence passes, and Garren looks thoughtful. The mirthless expression breaks into a faint smile lighting up his face.

"Over the course of the years, I've come to appreciate the art of music and I find it soothing to play the violin."

The answer surprises me. As I look at his fingers, I imagine how they move across the stringed instrument, creating beautiful music; how the notes find their way through the atmosphere like invisible butterflies. My heart skips a beat, causing a ripple effect that creates a tingling sensation in my stomach, but I force myself not to put too much importance on it. I would never have guessed the stern paladin has a musical streak.

"I like music, too." I nod and lightly play with my fingertips in the magical mist, as if I'm playing an instrument. "Dad signed me up for piano classes when I was seven years old. Unfortunately, I was bad at it. I could sit for hours and practise at home, but when it came down to it and I was on stage, I would forget everything. It was embarrassing when all eyes were on me, sitting on the piano stool and not being able to remember a single note."

My hands cup and I lift some of the magical mist into my palms.

"Once I even turned to the audience with my hand over my mouth, exclaiming I had forgotten how to play. They laughed, mostly because they probably thought twelve-year-old me was cute. In the end, I played the song too quickly, with a bunch of mistakes, and my piano teacher looked like she wanted to sink down into the earth. I stood up, thanked the audience, and ran off the stage. Afterwards, I stopped playing the piano, much to my father's frustration."

I slowly shake my head. Smiling wistfully at the memory, I stare intently at my knees, pulled up to my chest, when they occasionally peek out of the pale blue mist. *I miss you, dad.*

Garren watches me in silence, and I can't interpret what his expression is trying to tell me.

"You certainly did your best," he says and nods meaningfully. "Sometimes we're faced with situations, ones that make us feel ashamed, that we simply have to get out of in the best way possible and ultimately, they make us grow as individuals."

I interlace my fingers and place them on top of my knees as I lean my chin against them and listen to the sounds of the basins, the guests talking and laughing, and my heartbeat.

"Yeah," I answer, running the tip of my tongue over my lips for a second.

It feels good to talk to someone, for once. Someone who isn't a therapist and doesn't seem to judge me, either. I continue my story.

"After I stopped that, I started taking a self-defence class. Mum thought it was important for a girl to defend herself. That, too, I was terrible at. I've got some rather impressive sticks for arms, as you've probably noticed, unlike you."

I raise my head as I point to my upper arm. Garren's mouth mirrors the smile on my lips, and he raises one arm out of the water and mist as he looks at it. I move a little closer to him while being careful not to accidentally expose myself and put mine next to his, as if to compare them. I truly don't have any muscles to brag about, despite taking dance classes and using my arms quite often.

"However, it's not always the muscle mass that determines how strong a person is," he says, winking at me. "I'm convinced you are stronger than you think. If I may…"

With a slow movement, he runs his fingertip lightly across my wrist and a warm white light appears momentarily over the skin.

"Do you see how the Light seems to awaken by coming into contact with my inner magic?" he says, nodding contentedly. "It slumbers within you. You must learn how to use it and bend it to your will, so it doesn't do more harm than good."

My hurried heartbeat keeps spinning, causing me to border on vertigo. I loathe it when other people touch me and the thoughts bounce back to how I shouted at Garren the first time we met. And now I'm here, letting him touch my wrist. While we're naked. *I must have lost my mind.*

"It's a good thing my training is about to start," I blurt out and let out a shrill, nervous laugh.

Quickly turning around, I reach for the edge of the pool as I fumble for my glasses.

"Are you looking for these?" an unfamiliar voice asks, and my heart almost stops.

A hand grabs mine, stuffing something in it.

"What the hell?" I whisper.

Quickly, I put on my glasses and blink repeatedly. I freeze when I see a man crouched down in a towel, making me stagger back a couple of steps. A gasp leaves my lips as I try to get the sight of his private parts out of my head, quickly covering my face with my hands.

"What are you doing here, Cináed?" I hear Garren mutter coldly. "I assumed robbers and murderers sleep at this time of day."

Stress is making my stomach ache, and I sneak a peek between my fingers. The unknown man is muscular, covered in tattoos from his neck down to his legs, and his long, dark hair tied up in a bun with the sides of the head shaved. He, too, has a moustache and beard, but the facial hair is thicker and considerably longer than Garren's. A septum ring decorates his nose, and so do piercings at his eyebrows and in his ears. His green eyes are firmly fixed on me, his beard parted by a foul smile. He looks unfazed by the paladin's icy treatment.

"Rumours on the street whisper a damsel has arrived from distant lands and her magic differs from what we're used to seeing. Do you mind if I accompany you?"

With a swift movement he tears off the towel and jumps into the pool.

"Make yourself scarce," Garren warns steadily, the muscles in his arms tensing.

"Don't be so sensitive, Grand Prior," Cináed says in a silky voice. "Under normal circumstances, I wouldn't mind wrestling you at all, should the opportunity present itself. The idea is quite exciting." He tilts his head to the side and turns his attention back to me. "What's your name, girl?"

My brain is racing. It's probably better to come up with a fake name.

"Maria," I say as I wrap my arms around myself and look around to see if I can make eye contact with any of the staff.

A hushed, amused chuckle leaves Cináed's lips. Before I have time to react, he has moved behind me, closing his fingers around my shoulders.

"The path led me here this morning because I wanted to see you with my own eyes, to make sure the rumours are true," he whispers in my ear, seeming to savour every word. "And I already know your name, Saga Falk."

"Don't touch me!" I shout.

I tear myself away, but he grabs my wrist and pulls me in again.

"Can I get a little taste of your magic?" he teases.

I hear Garren take a deep, ragged breath. Reflexively, I raise my other hand and smack Cináed across the face, causing him to let go of me as he staggers.

"Piss off!" I snap.

With a piercing stare, I shake my head angrily at Cináed and clench my jaws. He rubs his cheek with one hand and pouts—a fake display of emotion, as an amused twinkle appears in his eyes.

"Well, well, aren't you a feisty one? I wish you no harm, though I prefer to stay informed about who comes and goes in my city."

I hear Garren grunt loudly.

"Your city?" he says coldly. "You're a thief and a murderer, and you would do everyone a favour by leaving Whitekeep for good."

"As prickly as ever, Roseheart. You excite me, but it hurts when you spread lies. There's no evidence of my being a murderer."

"So, you admit to being a thief. That's enough grounds for you to rot in a dungeon."

"What are you going to do, Grand Prior? Are you going to handcuff me? Tie me up, perhaps?"

Being on my guard, I take another step back without taking my eyes off Cináed as they argue. He's not as tall as Garren and doesn't have as much muscle mass, despite being fit. *Is he a murderer?* I remember running into him in *Reign Online* on a few occasions. Isn't he the guy who usually hangs out by the harbour in one of the shabbier inns? *Yeah, I remember now.* Remy and I did quests for him some years ago, and once we finished the questline, I had looked up Cináed's backstory.

"I don't think he's a murderer," I say quietly, bringing my hands up to my neck and face as I automatically cover myself. "He may be dishonest, but I don't think he has taken the life of an innocent person on purpose."

I flip through the archive in my head, and immediately it dawns on me.

"I also know your full name, Cináed Dasterian. You're an orphan and have a sister you haven't seen in years. You prefer to use daggers as weapons, and you don't shy away from using poison when the need calls for it."

Cináed's lips part slightly, and I see his chest rise as he sucks air into his lungs.

"What do we have here, then? A little witch?" he mumbles, and it takes a little while for the confident smile to reappear.

"No," I say firmly and brush a couple of damp strands of hair out of my eyes. "I'm—"

"What's the real reason that brings you here, Cináed? My patience is wearing thin."

Garren interrupts my sentence before I can finish it and steps in front of me. The tattooed man narrows his eyes at the paladin and leans towards him.

"I wanted to speak to you in private, without your subordinates being present."

A quick glance is thrown in my direction; then, a shrug. This time, his voice is even lower.

"Disturbing information from the Highlands has reached me via my sources. Dark energies have begun seeping out of the earth—controlling individuals' minds and eventually their bodies, twisting and turning them. Rumours have it one of them uttered the damsel's name after being killed by the soldiers, and heralds have appeared in various places. They're preparing dark rituals."

"No," I stutter, shaking my head furiously. "No, it can't be true. I'm not someone special."

Cináed shrugs again.

"Something's special about you, for certain. And Roseheart, I suggest you review your maps and expeditions. Enlist the help of Thurston and his Silver Wardens."

With one swift movement, he jumps out of the pool without using the ladder, and I cover my eyes again as I glimpse his toned rear.

"You know where to find me, Grand Prior. As for you, fiery girl? I'll be seeing you later!"

My head is spinning, and I feel dizzy. *Can't I have a single day where nothing dramatic happens, so I can start thinking about what I'm going to do and how I'm going to get home?*

The warm water splashes with a playful sound as Garren turns around.

"He has disappeared," he announces curtly.

When I take my hands off my face and open my eyes, tiredness from everything that has happened to me in the past few days settles in my bones. It's early morning and I already want to go to bed, sleep for ten days, and wallow in my loneliness.

"Are you well?" he asks in a low voice edged with softness.

"Everything's great. Super."

I just want to go home and sleep in my bed, go to work, and avoid all this. A lachrymose feeling takes over in my heart and I shake my head, trying to regain my composure. Grabbing my towel at the edge of the pool, I wrap myself in it as the fabric soaks up the water. Using one hand, I climb up the small step while holding the towel with the other and cast a timid glance at him.

"I'm off to the dressing room. See you outside."

CHAPTER TEN

Garren Roseheart

Total self-control, guided by the Mother of the Light through life.

I'm standing outside the bathhouse, polishing one of my gauntlets with the inside of my cloak and letting my thoughts focus on the hour that has just passed. Cináed's foreboding message lingers in the air, his words repeating in my head. *Black magic, death*. I have a bad feeling and ponder what my next move should be. In addition to mapping out where this black magic invasion originates from, I should also inform the high priestess, Thurston, and Her Majesty Queen Ariadne as soon as possible.

Saga Falk. I need more details about why the woman's name is rumoured to have been mentioned in connection with these atrocities. Does it have anything to do with the voice in her head?

Total self-control. For a moment, I put the gloomy thoughts to rest, shifting my attention to Saga. The way she moved in the water, how her dark brown eyes studied me, her damp skin against my fingertips. I put a hand to my chest, sending a silent prayer to the Light. Her wet fringe that had stuck to her forehead and how she adjusted it now and then by shaking her head, her damp eyelashes, and a hint of feminine forms I caught glimpses of through the magical mist above the surface of the water.

When that thief had grabbed her wrist, it took a great deal of self-control not to lose my temper, but to my surprise, she had put him in place herself, without me having to lift a finger. To see the display of her courage; truly amazing.

This woman is causing a certain turbulence in my world.

However, there's a somewhat bitter aftertaste on my tongue. Saga appears to know details about Cináed from her game, but she barely knows anything about my fictional self, and therefore not about my real self, either. She has said she embodies a high elf, but despite this she knows Cináed's full name, as well as some of his background by heart—and he's human, just like me. I find myself getting somewhat irked. Not at Saga, but at Cináed, and most definitely at that pointy-eared prince.

Apart from wealth, I fail to understand what else the elven prince has to offer. He has good looks on his side, but there's more hidden below the elf's usually placid surface than he lets on. Didn't she get to experience his hidden side in her game? Could it be because the game is merely an image of the reality we live in here, and the people in her universe use the image for entertainment, being deprived of the deeper details?

Jealousy has no place in a heart filled with the Light and its warmth. Still, it bothers me that at first, she knew my name and professional status only—nothing more. Where she's from, it appears as if it never occurred to her to learn more about Garren Roseheart.

"Hello?"

I hear a familiar voice, and my thoughts dissipate. Saga stands next to me with slightly damp hair. I haven't noticed her, due to being utterly preoccupied in my mind.

She's wearing one of the cream-coloured blouses I bought for her earlier during the day and, although somewhat baggy, it complements her stature. The blouse is being worn under a short brown coat that doesn't look as thick in material as the one she was wearing when we first met. The brown linen pants have a relatively skin-tight fit and I discreetly sweep my eyes over her defined hips, taking a silent breath. She may have clad herself in attire similar to that of a stable boy, save for the unusual shoes and glasses, but she's truly stunning.

"Are you ready?"

My mouth feels dry. It's a foolish question to ask, considering the fact she's standing next to me with the bag of clothes in one hand.

"Yeah," she says and shakes her head lightly so the fringe falls into place. "Do I blend in better now?"

"Without a doubt," I reply, finding myself smiling as she looks down at her shoes. "Perhaps you could use some new boots."

"No, these cost far too much for me not to use them. Besides, my feet will hurt if I use other shoes, because the insoles in these are specially adapted."

She wiggles one foot.

"If need be, I'll dye them so they won't stand out as much."

I raise one eyebrow and look at her from head to toe.

"You're a problem solver," I hear myself uttering, unable to hide my surprise.

"I've got it in my blood from my dad's side of the family."

A proud smile dances on her lips and she brushes off her blouse with her free hand.

"These clothes are fairly comfortable. Thanks for getting them for me."

I bite my tongue so as not to say anything impulsively straight from my curious heart. Instead, I clear my throat and speak.

"We're going back to the headquarters," I say, nodding politely at a couple of guards patrolling past us.

"Okay. I'm ready to start the day properly, preferably without any more shocking surprises."

Saga takes a couple of steps in front of me, and I get annoyed with myself when I glance at her figure. *Self-control and discipline.* It has been a while since I allowed myself to associate with someone—I prefer to focus on my faith to the fullest extent. This thing with Saga is of a purely formal nature, although she arouses a tickling curiosity in me.

"Don't worry yourself with that cursed thief's words," I say, taking a long stride forward so we're walking side by side, thus suppressing the temptation to catch a glimpse of her hips again. "I shall look into it."

"I'm not special—I'm not even from here. The thought of those poor individuals putting my name forward in such a context makes me upset."

She glances at me and squints because of the sunlight. Thoughtfully, I scratch the back of my neck and rest one hand on the hilt of my sword as we stroll through the streets. Some playing children hoot and wave at me and I wave back. Saga stops in her tracks when one of the little girls runs forward, grabs my cloak with a puny hand, and asks if I can lift her up. The girl's father rushes forward while apologising profusely, and I smile kindly at him.

"Don't worry," I assure him and turn to the girl. "What's your name?"

"Ari," she answers and wipes her nose with her other hand.

"She looks up to the grand prior," her father explains and tries to lift her up, but she resists and bursts out in loud whining. "She always wants to hear about your great deeds before bedtime."

The girl holds her hands up to me.

"May I?" I ask the man.

Her father looks at me, eyes wide. A relieved smile replaces his

SHADOW DANCE

somewhat apologetic expression as he nods.

Ari laughs in delight as I pick her up in my arms, rocking her from side to side. Out of the corner of my eye, I notice a group of women with baskets in their arms whispering to each other as they watch us.

"Ari. Promise me you'll listen to your father," I say after a while, and she nods.

"When I grow up, I'm going to be a paladin too," she says, determinedly sticking her little nose in the air. "And then I'll marry the grand prior."

"Ari!" the man exclaims, a horrified expression on his face, and I shake my head.

"When you grow up, you'll have plenty of time to decide who you want to marry, but don't forget you don't have to get married at all if you don't want to," I say. "The choice is yours."

With one fingertip, I poke her playfully on the tip of her nose. She giggles and I hand her over to the father, nodding farewell.

"May the Light guide you, always."

I turn to Saga, who has been silent until now, to see what state she's in and my heart skips a beat when I see her surveying me with a surprised smile. The gaze that flows towards me is unfathomable, to the point that I feel like I'm mere seconds from drowning.

"Get moving," I tell her curtly.

I quickly turn away and nod politely to the women with the baskets who greet me.

"Grand Prior, you're a real enigma," Saga coos, trying to catch my eye as we head off.

"I'm getting a headache," I mutter, running my fingers through my hair.

"That was so cute," she continues and smiles to herself, and out of the corner of my eye I see her turning her attention to a point in the distance. "I would have wanted to know more about you if you were like this in my game."

Keep focusing. Don't read too much into it. It requires great effort not to smile as I listen to her sentence repeatedly in my head.

"How old are you?"

Her question penetrates my eardrums, and I throw a glance at her.

"Forty-three."

"Elluin was right," she mumbles, fiddling with one of her hair tresses.

"I beg your pardon?"

I try to get her attention, and she waves her hands dismissively. Had she asked questions about me?

"It's nothing," she interjects quickly and changes the hand holding the linen bag with the clothes in. "Do you like children?"

I put my hand to my forehead and groan.

"By the Light, lass. You don't let me think in peace."

"You seem to be good with children, so how come you don't have any of your own?"

She jumps forward a couple of steps in front of us and turns to face me as she walks backwards. A short moment later, a look of embarrassment pulls its veil over her face.

"Sorry, that was insensitive of me."

My feet stop moving, and I give her a steady look.

"Being my queen's right hand is more than a full-time job," I say succinctly. "My life is dedicated to the Light and to maintaining this kingdom together with Thurston. I'm not left with much time for other things."

"Maybe you just haven't found the right person yet," Saga counters, shrugging slightly. "But once love knocks on your door, it would be rather silly not to let it in just because of your career choice. At least that's my opinion on the matter."

She looks pleased with her own statement as she turns her back to me and picks up the pace of her steps a little. *By the Light*. She has put a binding rope around my chest, and I say naught. Rarely do I find it difficult to make my case, but now, my tongue is glued in place.

With my head weighing heavy with thoughts, I follow the woman, taking the liberty of caressing her hair and shoulders with my discreet gaze.

"And what of your age, Saga?" I ask, trying not to sound too curious.

"I just turned twenty-nine," she replies and smiles widely. "On my birthday, I baked a cake I shared with Ambrosia and our mutual friend Remy. I also brought a few pieces to my colleagues at work." She sighs dreamily. "That cake was delicious."

"If you'll excuse me for mentioning this: you don't look a day over twenty-three," I point out, finding myself even more captivated by her as she flips her hair.

"It must be all the green tea I've drunk over the years. I barely drink any alcohol because I get drunk easily and I dislike the idea of losing control of my own thoughts and words. Instead, I consume copious amounts of tea. It wouldn't surprise me if I'm going to experience caffeine withdrawal soon."

She speaks of unfamiliar subjects, and yet I want to hear more.

She chuckles to herself, playfully swinging the linen bag in her hand. We turn onto a smaller street, a shortcut to the order's quarters, which isn't as busy with pedestrians and horses. Soon we'll arrive at our destination and from there I won't have the opportunity to talk to her privately anymore for a while. I collect my thoughts and take a quiet, deep breath.

"You mentioned you don't accompany men anymore."

"Yeah," she says, looking up at me with astonishment in her eyes.

"May I ask the reason for it?"

"Is this another interrogation?" she hisses, before looking apologetic. "I've had bad experiences because of my former boyfriend."

I swallow soundlessly, unable to halt my tongue from speaking again.

"Were you together for long?"

A moment of silence follows. And then, her soft voice reaches my ears.

"Yeah, you could say that. He was my first boyfriend. A couple of years younger than me, which I guess I should have thought of before we became an item. In hindsight, I made a downright idiotic choice when I agreed to move in with him. I guess I was tired of being alone and not knowing what it felt like to be with someone, because I had never had a boyfriend before."

The words seep out from between her lips while she's frowning. A loud sigh falls from her mouth, and she runs her hand through her hair.

"After I broke things off with him, I decided not to see anyone again. It's less complicated that way."

"What did he do to you?"

Biting my tongue, I realise my mistake. *I shouldn't be asking these questions, nor should it matter to me.*

"I apologise. It's none of my business," I say quickly.

Saga's gaze locks into mine, as if she's trying to determine if I'm trustworthy or not. The dark brown eyes look glossy. She shrugs and looks down, keeping her attention on her shoes as we walk next to each other.

"He hurt me," she mutters. "I guess the mental and physical abuse were among the kindest things he did. Moreover, he hurt my dog when she was still alive, and I can never forgive him for it."

A strong sympathy seizes me whilst a low-key anger simmers inside. I stop in the middle of a step and call to her softly.

"It wasn't my intention to upset you, lass."

Her feet mirror mine and stop moving, but she avoids looking at me, her face turned to the side. When I take a step closer to her, she stays still, and I notice her eyes are shut. The hand holding the bag trembles a little, her knuckles turning white. My fingertips lightly caress her upper arm and without uttering a single word, her eyelids open. She watches me silently, a hint of timidity and a thousand questions falling like stars in her eyes.

"I apologise," I say in an even lower voice and gently touch her shoulder. "And I'm sorry you and your pet were treated so badly."

"It's fine," she mumbles, and I can see she's fighting the tears. "I was weak and couldn't stand up to him when he used violence to get what he wanted. My mother was right—I should've continued to take self-defence classes when I was a kid and worked on becoming stronger and braver. Maybe I could have defended myself and Greta better. My dog, that is."

She shakes her head.

"I get anxious talking about this. I'm not good with words that concern myself."

My armoured hand that touched her shoulder lightly caresses her cheek and she's still staying as still as before. I say nothing at first, letting the meaning of the words sink in as I look into her eyes.

"You're brave," I say softly after a while. "You're in a foreign place and yet you show strength, and you dare to speak. That takes courage. And you're not weak because you couldn't protect yourself and Greta. Look at how you defended yourself in the bathhouse and when I was about to arrest you the other day."

You also corrected me when I spat out foolish comments earlier.

A faint sound reaches my ears as the woman releases the linen bag which falls to the ground. One of her hands finds its way up to my fist I've just touched her cheek with, and she continues to stare at me as she cups her hand over my gauntlet. She takes a step closer to me, her other hand running one fingertip lightly over the family crest on my cuirass. I sincerely hope she doesn't notice how hard my heart is pounding. *Witchcraft.*

"Your last name suits you," she says in a barely audible whisper. "You may have thorns on the outside, but you're hiding a heart of roses within, and I would never have guessed it from sitting at home in my room, gaming."

The spell from those dark eyes washes over me and I'm lost. With her words, she burns my heart with such force I can hardly breathe. I blink to sharpen my gaze and place my free hand on her other cheek. The colour rises on her face and a fierce longing to kiss her lips whispers in my head, but the voice of my heart makes me restrain myself. *By the Light! Have I become spellbound?* I barely know this woman except for the details which she has shared and the fact that the sacred magic flows within her.

Saga stutters something nervously, words I can't make out in my bewitched state, and she slowly pulls away from my grip.

"Gosh, what a mess," she stutters and adjusts her glasses in a manoeuvre to hide her bright red face with the help of her hands. "Let's pretend this didn't happen."

How can I forget when my heart is now sealed by you, stamped with your sigil?

I break the tension between us by bending down, picking up her bag and handing it to her.

"It has been a few peculiar days," I say, and she accepts the bag as a nervous smile spreads across her face.

"Yeah, definitely."

She still stutters and the words seem to stumble over each other.

We walk in silence the rest of the way, except for when I greet soldiers and city guards. From time to time, I throw glances her way, catching glimpses of the pensive lines around her eyes and her tense jaws. When we proceed through the gate to our destination, I adjust my coat of arms with one hand.

SHADOW DANCE

"You're assigned to one of my officers," I say firmly, ignoring my pounding heart. "She'll meet us here shortly."

"Grand Prior Roschcart!"

A familiar voice seeks my attention and I look away from Saga to meet one of my subordinates.

"Feremir," I greet back and nod politely. "How's the eye?"

Owain Feremir removes his helmet and shakes volume into his auburn, shoulder-length locks. He is half-elf—the love child of a human and an elf—and the slightly elongated, honey-coloured eyes find their way to my protégé.

"I certainly got myself bruised up in battle," he laughs, extending his hand towards Saga. "Nice to meet you again, beautiful Miss Falk. Please, you may call me Owain."

Saga shakes his hand as she studies his face closely.

"Hi, Owain," she murmurs, taking a breath as she stares at his bruised eye. "Is that something I caused?"

"I've told people I got it from a vegan." Owain grins, stretching his back. "A new adventurer at the inn exclaimed that a vegan is a woman who can turn into a fire-breathing dragon depending on the sun's position in the sky, and another was certain he had almost been killed by a vegan once. I scored quite a lot of points from the ladies."

Saga groans and puts her hands over her face for a moment, shaking her head.

"Sorry," she says, a faint smile appearing on her visage. "But something good came out of this situation—I can now claim to be a fire-breathing dragon if someone bothers me, and you came out a winner, too."

"Feremir, chasing the ladies as per usual," I say dryly.

The half-elf grins at me.

"It does one good to enjoy the company of beautiful women, just like the purest balm for both heart and soul. I can recommend it to the Grand Prior."

He chuckles and looks back at Saga.

"Today's tasks are calling my name, but it was wonderful meeting you in a calmer state. Please seek me out should you want to socialise in a more relaxed context."

He grabs her hand again, placing a light kiss on it and winking at her with his good eye. With a nervous laugh, she pulls it back and tucks a few strands of hair behind her ears.

"See you!" she replies shrilly and waves at him after he nods at me and takes his leave. "What a player," she then mumbles and glances at me.

I raise one eyebrow and look at her searchingly.

"That's what we usually call such types where I come from," she mutters. "The type of person who flirts all the time, even if he were to be in a relationship. I can't comprehend how he had the audacity to hit on me in front of his boss."

The charged atmosphere between us from before has released its grip. *Thank the Light.*

I can't help but smile faintly at her scrunched-up nose as she explains what the word means and how she looks disapprovingly at Feremir, who's disappearing further and further away.

"You seem offended," I say, trying not to show my inner satisfaction that she has just rejected the man's advances.

Saga looks at me and something alluring appears in her gaze, but it seems to disappear as quickly as a shooting star.

"Well, he's definitely not the kind of man I'd go to the bathhouse with," she says in a coy voice that tickles my eardrums playfully.

I avert my gaze, sending a silent prayer to the Light and trying to control my increasingly rapid pulse. Is she sending me mixed signals, or have I simply become bewitched yet again? People might communicate in this manner where she's from, without necessarily including a hidden message. Yes, it could certainly be the case. It means nothing. She has already mentioned she doesn't wish to mix with men again. *Except possibly Prince Sunseeker?*

As I catch sight of Commander Ahriele Darby making a beeline for us, I forcefully suppress my rising disappointment and put my conflicted emotions on the shelf.

CHAPTER ELEVEN

Saga Falk

I'm in a mediaeval classroom of the Order of the Light, at the back of a hall with white stone walls decorated with coats of arms. Mosaic windows in various light tones drape the playful daylight in beautiful colours. The air in here is cool and in my quiet mind I wonder how cold it would be to sit here on a winter's day.

The paladin Ahriele, to whom Garren has entrusted me, is a tall woman with long, thick blonde hair, and her large brown eyes seem to hold a constant hint of hardness. She moves with fluid yet determined movements, as if her every move is foreordained, and I find myself getting a little jealous of how pretty she is. She looks to be in her forties, and yet she has some of the smoothest skin I've ever seen. Her bosom is full under the coat of arms she wears over a yellow robe, and she oozes authority and raw strength. I don't think she's someone to joke around with.

When Ahriele had introduced herself and started leading me towards the sleeping quarters to show me where my bed is, I glanced over my shoulder, but Garren had already taken his leave. My thoughts slowly turned to him and the conversations we had had during the morning while listening to Ahriele's instructions. She handed me a few clothes, toiletries, and a thick book, which I assume is their holy scripture, before leading me to this specific room and announcing I'll be starting my studies right away.

I assumed I would get some time alone with her so she could explain things in more detail, but we had arrived when about ten other students were already seated at their desks, and I avoided looking at them as I settled into a chair at the back. I keep having flashbacks from when I was a teenager in high school and getting increasingly more stressed from the other students' eyes on me.

"Recruits, we have a new face among us. I expect you to welcome her as you should," says Ahriele in a steady voice. "Introduce yourself."

A creeping stomach ache forms within. I swallow hard as I slowly get up from the chair. Uncertainly, I let my gaze wander across the room and feel ice-cold anxiety rush down my spine. I wish I was home.

Nervously, I push the glasses up the bridge of my nose with one finger and smile.

"Hey. My name's Saga Falk. I'm twenty-nine years old and I'm from Malmö. I know I both talk and act differently, but I hope we can get along."

I look down, not sure what else to mention.

"Short and concise. Take a seat," says Ahriele.

I quickly obey and try to pull the chair behind me as quietly as possible while she orders us to open our books. Quickly scrolling to the page the commander mentions, I squint. *This is mediaeval cursive.* I'm not used to these frills supposed to represent text.

"Falk, read the first paragraph aloud," Ahriele orders.

SHADOW DANCE

My heart jumps up into the pit of my throat where it gets stuck, and I notice the sweat breaking out on my forehead and upper lip. My mouth feels dry, and I can't get a word out for several excruciatingly long seconds. I see Ahriele's lips move as she glares at me, but can't make out what she's saying. *The stress is killing me.* The words are mixed up in a jumble, and I notice how tense my shoulders and neck are.

"I can't read this," I mutter, as my face is awash with embarrassment. "The letters look different to what I'm used to."

How does she expect me to jump into a lesson, which is completely foreign to me, and read this?

Ahriele gestures for me to come forward. Slowly, I stand up and my feet feel leaden.

"Study the book tonight," she says coldly as I stand in front of her, before pointing to the floor by her shoes. "Give me ten push-ups."

I stop and stare at her with wide eyes.

"Are you serious?" I mutter before I have time to think.

"You do as I say. No one gets a free pass here, regardless of background, and no one speaks against me."

This is bullshit. With clenched jaws, I lay down on the floor and prepare myself both mentally and physically for the upcoming effort. The floor feels cold against my palms, and I close my eyes tightly, the weight of eyes heavy on my shoulders as I'm silently judged by the rest of the class. Is this what the Grand Prior meant by them taking care of each other in the Order of the Light? *Such laughable words.*

One... two... three... four...

I'm well-aware of how weak my body is, despite my years of taking dance classes. I barely manage five push-ups before I grimace, open my eyes and timidly look up at Ahriele.

"I can't take it anymore," I mumble with my heart pounding hard against the bars of my chest.

Her boot against my back pushes me down.

"Keep going!" she says sternly. "No one will show you mercy on the battlefield."

What the hell is she talking about? What battlefield?

It hurts and I'm unable to stand up. After moments that feel like an eternity have passed, she removes her foot and rudely waves for me to go and sit down again. She puts her hands to her sides, turning her attention to a guy sitting a few benches away.

"Does this amuse you, Eric?"

She almost roars out the words and I sink into my chair with my face turned to the table top. *Embarrassing.*

The grin on the guy's face washes away, his cheeks turning pale.

"No, Commander," he replies.

Ahriele walks over to his seat, leans towards him with her hands on the sides of the bench, and stares at him.

"Give me fifteen, recruit!"

Out of the corner of my eye, I see Eric get down and do push-ups with her boot on his back, seemingly with no problems, and I stare at the book in front of me. How did I think joining the Order of the Light and training to be a paladin was a good idea? I don't have the physical strength required, can't read their cursive writing, and just minutes into the class, I've already been scolded, punished, and humiliated. I'll never be able to recover from this damn spectacle.

The morning continues with scripture study—fortunately without involving me—and judging by the hunger pangs in my stomach, it's getting close to lunchtime. I just want to get out of here and away from these people for a while to gather my thoughts.

As the cluster of recruits heads towards the mess hall, I follow them at a distance so I don't have to hear what they're going on about. Ambrosia would probably call me paranoid, but I'm certain some of them are talking about me.

It smells good in the canteen. Expectantly, I look ahead in the queue, watching the staff ladling food onto the platters. My stomach protests and my mouth waters when it's my turn.

"Are you Miss Falk?" asks the woman who's about to serve me.

I smile uncertainly at her and nod. Carefully she takes the tray from me, grabs another ladle, and the food she puts on my plate looks different from the one served to the others.

"Lentil stew, but without the added meat," she says with a smile and hands the tray to me again. "Water is on the table," she continues, pointing to a row of carafes.

"Thank you so much," I murmur gratefully and smile from ear to ear.

That man must have arranged this. My lousy day suddenly seems a little brighter.

Hesitantly, I look around and consider where to sit, while trying to avoid paying attention to all the eyes that seem to be turned in my direction. *Word of the stranger has spread quickly.* I sigh quietly and find an empty table.

Thoughtfully, I sip on my glass of water and open the book while running a fingertip over the writing. Perhaps I should write the letters down on a piece of paper and try to connect them with the style I'm used to reading.

My thoughts drift away when I pop a bite in my mouth, twirling around the image of the man with gold in his hair. *This food is scrumptious.* I wipe my mouth with a napkin and think back to when his hands gripped my face and the smouldering gaze from those blue eyes. *No, I shouldn't focus on that.* Shaking my head, I try to chase the thoughts away. It was just a strange moment. My brain builds up fantasies about Kailunn instead, his soft lips and his narrow elf eyes with the beautiful eyelashes, but the thought pattern breaks at the memory of my teasing glance and the words which the wind had carried away, causing the paladin to avert his gaze.

Well, he's definitely not the kind of man I'd go to the bathhouse with.

It dawns on me that I've openly flirted with the man who runs the Order of the Light. I let go of the spoon, putting my hands to my temples and letting out a frustrated grunt. Both Ambrosia and Remy have mentioned how bad I am at flirting, and I agree. Still, I feel much like a moth drawn to the light. As soon as I get the chance, I seem to blurt out a suggestive comment to the grumpy paladin. *Fuck's sake.*

With Retsam, I had felt unfaithful to the fictional Kailunn, and now that Kailunn exists here, I'm unsure about how I feel. Shame? No, I don't think so, simply because I haven't met him yet. If that angelic man with his missing halo suggested we take a bath together again, I'd probably go along with it, just to get to know him better. I work for him, so having more information is beneficial to me. The fact that he's handsome, displays a sensible, gentle side, and can take well-placed criticism where it's needed are bonus points in my books.

The corners of my mouth twitch and I smile faintly as I think back to Garren's expression when the butterflies had appeared. He had seemed so carefree and there was something about his look at that moment I can't get out of my head. And as his fingertips had touched my wrist, our energies had intertwined and created that white light together. *Warm, safe, and not scary at all.*

The act of two female recruits from my class settling down before me

SHADOW DANCE

with their trays causes my thoughts to dispel. One of them is a muscular dwarf with close-cropped black hair, freckles, curious dark eyes, and a pointy nose. Piercings of various sizes cover her ears. The other is a dark-blonde human with wavy hair that goes down to her chin, full lips, round face, and hazel eyes. Her dark eyelashes are so long, they remind me of gorgeous eyelash extensions.

The dwarf smiles at me.

"May we keep you company?"

"You've already sat down, so there's no point in asking," I say and shrug.

I grab my spoon with an unusually tight grip, feeling uncomfortable when all I want is to be left alone.

"My name's Helga, and this here is Gwen."

The dwarf points with her thumb at the woman next to her, tilting her head.

"We'd like to get to know you better."

"Why?" I say bluntly, with evident scepticism in my voice.

Gwen rubs her palms together as she peers at me, curiosity sparkling in her eyes.

"We've never heard of Malmö before. It sounds so exciting!"

"It might be easier for you to learn the ropes if you have friends by your side," the other interjects, beaming with genuine happiness.

I fidget where I sit. The food is tasteless to my tongue.

"I'm not social," I reply, shrugging again. "All this is new to me, and I need to process it before I can start making new friendships."

"We don't want you to feel any pressure."

Helga waves her hands apologetically, and Gwen puts her hands to her face as she smiles sweetly at me. I sigh quietly, forcing myself to mirror their smiles. *Maybe it wouldn't hurt to be more outgoing.* Thoughtfully, I poke the food with my spoon.

"Fine. Malmö is a distant place. I live together with one of my best friends. During the day I work in a cafe and in the evenings… I don't do much in the evenings."

"Do you have a sweetheart?" Gwen asks, curiously leaning forward a little over the table top.

Quickly, I shake my head.

"No, I've been alone for quite some time. I used to have a boyfriend. However, I broke up with him because he wasn't good for me."

Helga chews on a piece of chicken and peruses me.

"Sometimes you have to take the bull by the horns and get rid of a person who weighs you down," she says as Gwen nods in agreement. "Isn't that right, Gwen?"

"Certainly," the other woman agrees. "My parents wanted me to marry a nice man, but I found him to be a bore. I saw no future with him, so I chose to be recruited here instead and focus on my faith. With some luck, maybe I'll meet my future marriage partner here."

Helga grins and takes a big gulp of water.

"Grand Prior Roseheart has caught the eyes and hearts of many, in particular within the Order of the Light."

Amiably, she nudges the other woman in the side with her elbow. The colour rises on Gwen's cheeks, and I notice a cold little lump in my stomach.

"One time, I mustered up the courage to ask the Grand Prior if he wanted to meet with me, but he politely declined. He's special and charming—our very own hero of Whitekeep. Many have asked him, but so far, he has refused."

Gwen twirls a strand of hair between her fingers and something dreamy appears in her eyes. I clear my throat discreetly, nervousness grabbing hold of my heart.

"So, he rarely meets with his subordinates?" I almost whisper as I push my tray and book to the side and bring my face closer to Gwen.

SHADOW DANCE

"Correct."

Helga moves closer to Gwen, as if the three of us are part of a special gossip clique.

"He doesn't even go to the bathhouse with his closest brothers and sisters of the Light," she adds to the conversation, curiosity playing a clear melody in her voice.

Uh-oh. I put one hand to my chest, feeling my heart beating fast. The heartbeats are almost deafening. I try to stabilise my voice.

"Does he have private lessons with his recruits at all?" I ask, feeling how the nervousness in my stomach sends signals through my body.

"We've never heard of that, have we, Gwen?"

Gwen agrees with Helga, and I see they've already finished eating, while I still have about half of my portion left. It's probably cold now, but I can't eat when, without knowing why, I'm nervous.

"I wish he did. I would have given up part of my salary to train with him," Gwen sighs dreamily, almost hypnotising me with her fluttering eyelashes.

"There are probably many people who would reason in a similar vein," Helga remarks and looks at me again. "Your face is quite pale. Are you well?"

"Yeah. I'm simply trying to process all the information."

My voice is unusually shrill, and I smile nervously while glancing around.

"We have to get moving so we may gain decent seats for the training session," continues Helga as they stand up with the trays in their hands.

I blink in surprise. "Sorry, what training session?"

"We have no more studies today, and as such, we usually observe the training sessions of those with a higher rank. There were talks in the hallway the grand prior will be there, which is quite unusual. These days, he's usually preoccupied with other tasks than sparring with the other, lower-ranked paladins."

I take a deep breath through my nose. *Of course, I'll be seeing him again.* A tingling sensation spreads in my stomach and I firmly force the nervousness away. It'll be interesting to see how he trains, just to get a clearer picture of him.

Within the walls of the Order of the Light there's a larger, screened-off area with training dummies and items likely used to measure strength with and to practise close combat. The area is lined with several benches where we manage to get seats in the front row before the rest of the audience arrives. I'm sandwiched between Helga and Gwen who behave as if I'm their newfound friend. I let my mind wander back to Remy and Ambrosia, wondering how they're doing; the weight of the book of the holy scripture resting atop my thighs. *I miss them so much.* In fact, I miss Haru too, even though he's my boss and I depend on him for my monthly payslip. Anxiety creeps around the soles of my feet. At this rate, I've probably lost my job.

The paladins partaking in the sparring put on their helmets, and I recognise one of them. Owain waves at me, shooting me a charming smile before covering his head and face, and Helga raises her eyebrows in surprise.

"Do you know him?" she whispers curiously, and I shrug.

"I met him briefly earlier today," I answer, keeping the explanation short.

My gaze searches expectantly around the area and the nervousness makes itself known again. *I shouldn't even care.*

"There he is!" Gwen whispers excitedly, grabbing my arm as she bounces up and down in her seat. I wince and grimace in disapproval, about to tear myself away from her, when my gaze catches on a tall figure clad in golden armour with a blue coat of arms. A helmet covers his head and face, adorned with a blue plume at the back, and the way he moves is unmistakable. *The strength and self-confidence of a lion.*

I didn't recognise him in this armour at first. Perhaps he has several sets he uses on different occasions. He's carrying a war club attached to a leather sling on his back, instead of that sword I'm used to seeing resting at his hip.

As he advances towards the paladins, they quickly stand in a straight line, each with one hand on their hearts. He stops with his sabatons firmly on the ground, giving them a curt nod as he unstraps the weapon. His booming voice fills the training grounds.

"Get ready!" he bellows, the war club resting in both hands. "Four of you are about to face me."

"Yes, Grand Prior!"

The knights call out in chorus before the straight line disperses into pairs. It looks rehearsed. I lean forward a bit, my gaze glued to Garren. The sun makes his armour glisten in the light, in an almost blinding way, and the plume sways hypnotically with every movement.

"This is beyond exciting," Gwen whispers as she sits close to me.

Her breath is warm, practically moist, and I'm slightly disgusted by the sensation in my ear. I mumble something indistinct and nod, unable to stop looking at that man. The other knights all carry a shield, so why isn't he using one? What if he gets hurt? A million different worrisome questions erupt in a cascade in my brain, and my stomach hurts.

"For the Light!"

Garren's authoritative, deep roar reminds me of a lion, and I draw a sharp breath. The strength of the voice penetrates me right into the bone marrow, shaking me to the core. A powerful white glow appears behind him as a pair of enormous wings edged with shimmering gold. My hands flying up to my mouth stifle the surprised scream that escapes my lips. The giddily exuberant crowd bursts into even louder cheers, and

Gwen squeals in sheer delight. *What a fangirl.* Helga seems to be the only one who's relatively calm, and judging by her facial expression, she's watching what's unfolding before us for purely educational purposes.

Four paladins Garren quickly points out as the chosen ones take off and charge at him with their shields and weapons drawn. War club at full swing, he parries two of them, slamming his weapon into their shields with such force and speed the others stumble backwards, losing both their balance and their swords.

"Train harder!" he roars.

On light feet, he flings himself to the side as the third knight attempts to strike at him with full force. He rams her in the side with his body, causing her to lose her footing and violently tumbling to the ground.

"Disappointing performance! You can do better than that!"

Swinging his weapon, he smacks at knight number four who has just raised his sword at him. The war club hits the opponent in the wooden shield and breaks it in half with a loud cracking sound. With tremendous strength in his movements, he pries his weapon free from the shield. As the opponent attempts to land a blow to his helmet, a light appears around him momentarily. The sword fails to break through the magical barrier, and the light disappears. The opponent lets out a frustrated roar as he tosses his sword aside, his hands glowing in white. Meanwhile, the large wings of light behind Garren are fading.

"Good, call on the Light!" Garren shouts, moving nimbly with a sweeping motion to the left as the opponent lunges at him. "But you should know better than throwing your weapon in anger!"

It looks like he's dancing around the knight who's trying to hit him repeatedly. I shake my head as I'm watching what's happening, my palms sweating. How is this an appropriate form of training? What if someone gets seriously hurt?

SHADOW DANCE

The other knight grabs Garren's leather sling where he had his weapon attached before and puts a stranglehold on his neck from behind. My heart flies up into the pit of my throat and I lose control of my tongue.

"Let go of him!" I scream with a shrill tone, my words drowned out by the clamour surrounding us.

The war club falls out of Garren's fist as his hands rush up to his opponent's arm. He bends his knees, arches his back forward and puts one foot behind the man's sabaton. With a 180-degree turn of his body, he throws the other guy to the ground with a loud thud as he swiftly grabs the war club, slamming it down just a few centimetres from the knight's head.

The audience cheers wildly, and I feel my heart pounding in panic. Garren helps the knights to their feet and when all four are standing next to each other, the recruits take off their helmets, while Garren leaves his on. The knight he defeated last is Owain, who's smiling just as charmingly as before, but I can sense the disappointment in his handsome features.

"What a magnificent display!" Gwen chirps and gets up while pulling on my arm, forcing me to rise. "Let us go and speak to the grand prior! He usually allows the recruits to talk to him the few times he graces us with his presence in training."

My heart still beats as hard against the grating of my chest as I let myself be led away by Gwen and Helga. A large group has already gathered around Garren, and I try to pull out of Gwen's grip, but to no avail. Several minutes pass and the women talk to me now and then, but I don't listen. My brain is too tired from everything. I'm a withdrawn person, even though I choose to be social sometimes—in this case only to survive in Theadrath—and most of all, I just want to be surrounded by silence.

When it's our turn, I say naught as Gwen more or less clings to the paladin and coos a series of sentences I can't bear to register in my mind. Garren still has his helmet on, and I catch glimpses of blue eyes through the visor. I look down at the ground, feeling as though I'm lost in the cluster of people and finding it hard to breathe. Helga, too, asks questions and he answers them both politely.

Finally, I get out of Gwen's arm hook and rub my upper arm lightly. "Falk."

I hear Garren's voice through the bevor and lift my gaze to meet him. He takes off his helmet, runs his fingers through his golden locks, and I swallow hard as I ogle him. His face is a little shiny with sweat, which doesn't surprise me at all after watching that show.

"Grand Prior," I mutter awkwardly. Unsure what to do with my hands, I hug the book with the holy scripture tightly in my arms, pressing it against my chest.

"Take a walk with me," he says curtly with his helmet under one arm.

Politely nodding to the others, he bids them farewell, despite their disappointed looks. He turns around and starts taking his leave. Gwen stares at me, her gaze carving into me like daggers.

Garren glances at me over his shoulder as he continues walking.

"Make haste!"

The voice is stern, and I lower my head slightly as I jog to catch up with him. I open my mouth to retort, but he puts a finger to his lips, urging me to be quiet. I hold my breath, wondering why he wants to meet with me again after only half a day of training.

We enter a botanical garden. There are some individuals carefully tending to the plants and flowers. Perhaps they're alchemists working with elixirs, while belonging to the Order of the Light because of their faith—or maybe they're gardeners.

The garden is lush, full of greenery, and soothing; a timeless corner in a city bustling with life. The atmosphere chases away most of my anxiety and worry which have built up during the day. My gaze sweeps over the various shrubs and I recognise the violet roses I saw at the florist earlier. A little further on, a white gazebo nestled in a somewhat secluded corner and plants climbing up the timber with small dark green leaves. Garren steers his steps towards the building with me a few paces behind him, and after unbuckling the leather sling holding his weapon on his back, sits down on one of the two benches. Uncertainty has taken root within, and I don't know which of the two to choose, but I decide to sit down next to him, with enough distance between us so it doesn't feel too intimate.

"I've been told of your rather subpar performance today," Garren says in a much softer tone than before and puts his helmet down on the bench.

Irritated, I purse my lips and choose my words well.

"The commander is to blame for it," I say in a low voice, looking around to make sure Ahriele isn't around. "She asked me to read from this book and I explained I can't read the writing, resulting in her punishing me in front of the class. And that's not the end of it! When I couldn't do all the push-ups, she became more stubborn and pushed me to the floor with her foot. It hurt!"

Garren smirks and I blink in surprise when he chuckles.

"Ahriele is tough, but not impossible to work for. She wants to ensure the long-term well-being of her students."

"Yeah, sure she does."

I roll my eyes and lean against the back of the bench, still clutching the book in my arms. Garren's gaze seeks the book.

"Show me what part of the scripture she asked you to read, lass."

I nod and open the book as I clear my throat silently, pointing to the writing with one finger.

"The first paragraph on page 113," I answer, shrugging. "I can't, for the life of me, make out the letters."

Without looking at the book, the man to my right turns his

attention to me, his pupils dilating. As he utters the words straight from his memory, I watch him and try not to linger too long on his lips. *I can't stop looking at him.* His entire being emits some kind of invisible pulsating energy, as if he's one massive energy field. A sudden urge to feel his golden hair against my fingers and tuck it behind his ears makes my fingertips itch. *What the hell am I thinking?*

"Thank you," I say in a low tone and scratch the back of my neck. "I should write the letters side by side the way I'm used to reading, so I can learn. It's like going to school all over again and dealing with homework."

Carefully, I close the book and place it next to me on the bench. Giving Garren a long look, I try to force myself to speak, but his radiance up close leaves me speechless for a while. He seems to notice my mood and wipes his forehead with the back of his gauntlet.

"It's getting hot in the armour," he says as he smiles and tilts his head a little to the side. "How did you find the display?"

My heart takes a leap in my chest and nervousness bounces around in my stomach.

"I liked your wings. They were awesome," I say sincerely and catch my breath as I blush fiercely.

You're embarrassing yourself. Shush.

When Garren chuckles again, the blushing on my cheeks deepens and I don't know what to make of myself, so I turn my face away, pretending I'm looking at a flower further away. He moves in closer to me. His deep voice shifts into a low whisper that dances across my eardrums.

"I saw the worried frown on your face when Feremir gave the impression of having the upper hand."

I'm used to being invisible, and somehow, he sees me. I barely dare to breathe and wonder if I should rise to break this mysterious, charged atmosphere between us, but I find myself fixed in my seat. As I collect my thoughts to respond to his statement, I avoid looking at him.

"I didn't want anyone to get hurt," I say, noticing how nervous I am.

"Saga."

It sounds like he's almost tasting the letters with the tip of his tongue as he utters my name, gently placing it on a breeze, and I get annoyed with myself when I notice the tone of his voice causing goosebumps over my arms. *How can he affect me? What the hell is wrong with me?*

"Saga," he repeats, taking off one of his gauntlets. "It's perfectly normal to feel confused." He falls silent for a moment and takes a long, audible breath before speaking again. "Admittedly, I share your confusion."

I blink a few times, slowly turning my face back so I can meet his gaze.

"What do you mean?"

Acutely aware of my voice breaking, I clear my throat prior to straightening my back as I try to regain control of the thoughts ballet dancing in my head.

"You're peculiar," he says as his gaze locks onto mine. "You move in like a storm and create chaos all around you, and in the storm's eye you sit in stillness and watch the world, unaware of the rings you have created on the surface of the water."

"Wow, all right," I blurt out without thinking, my brain working at high speed to analyse the words floating in the air between us. "I could have never guessed knights could be so poetic."

When his warm fingertips touch my cheek, our energies flow together, and I catch my breath. Slowly, I lift one hand and place it over his, feeling something heat in the back of my chest. I close my eyes as I'm blinded by the white light pouring out of them. When I open them again, I see right through the glow and notice Garren's eyes, too, shine with the same intensity.

"What's happening?" I say with wonder in my voice.

"Something magnificent," he replies, his voice caressing me. "By the Light, you're special. Presumably, this is the reason for your arrival. I'm convinced your purpose is something greater than you realise. We'll know anon."

He lifts his hand from my cheek as I slowly withdraw my own and the white glow around my eyes fades away. My vision has returned to normal, and I see his intense blue eyes are back, carefully studying my face.

I should pay more attention to what he just said, but I simply can't ignore his earlier statement. It's mind-numbing and practically makes me sick with nervousness.

"You never answered my question," I murmur, placing my clenched hands in my lap. "Why are you confused?"

"Because of you, lass."

The paladin's direct answer catches me off guard. Before I start to frantically over-analyse his words, he puts his hand inside a small leather pouch at his waist and pulls out a pocket watch on a chain, then placing it in my palm.

"Meet me here at half past nine this evening, and I'll help you decipher the scriptures. Arrangements will be made for the night guards to let you in. Don't be late."

"T-thank you," I stutter, touching the surface of the pocket watch carefully with one fingertip.

I think back to the conversation I had with Gwen and Helga earlier today and can't stop my burning curiosity from expressing itself in the next question.

"Hey. Why are you helping me?"

Garren gets up from the bench with his helmet under his arm and pulls his gauntlet back on.

"Had I ended up in a place where everything was foreign to me, I

SHADOW DANCE

would have wished for someone to help me."

He smiles and attaches the weapon to the sling that goes on his back.

He looks so powerful in his heavy armour. I hang the chain of the pocket watch around my neck and tuck it under my blouse so it rests against my bare skin, protected from prying eyes. As I stand up, I grab my book.

"Yes, of course," I nod in agreement. "I appreciate you taking the time, Garren. Thank you."

I fix my fringe as best I can without a mirror as we walk towards the exit of the garden. He's a good person, despite his grumpy temperament.

"You're welcome," he replies.

His voice is unusually deep in a way that makes me sweat a little, and I feel that enervating tingle in my stomach. After a couple of seconds of silence, my gaze rushes to the war club.

"That looks heavy," I say, just to break the charged atmosphere between us with a neutral topic.

With a practised hand, he unholsters the weapon again, stops walking, and points it at me.

"Here. Try it."

Grabbing it with both hands, I feel its full weight as he releases his grip. I can barely hold it up. I snort in annoyance and lift it with trembling arms, wondering how on earth he makes it look so easy.

Garren smirks wryly, causing me to glare defiantly at him.

"It's about as heavy as you," he says, a teasing glint edging his eyes. "There's no surprise you barely weighed anything to me when I carried you in my arms."

"Whatever."

I set the war club down at my feet with a loud thud, hiding a faint smile by turning my face away.

"If I had a weapon that was suitable for my size, I guarantee I could swing it around as theatrically as you do."

He grabs it from me, and when I look at him once more, the smirk is still present.

"Pay attention to the commander. Learn from her, and eventually you, too, will use a weapon correctly."

"Ahriele's and my chemistry don't go together," I grunt sourly, scrunching up my nose disapprovingly.

"Would you rather I teach you?"

A moment of silence passes between us as I collect my thoughts.

"Yeah, because we can talk to each other without one wanting to strangle the other after two seconds," I mutter quietly in response and shrug.

"My training methods are rather rigorous. I'm certain I'd wear you out within minutes," he says, his smirk growing wider.

I blush profusely and shake my head, cursing myself inwardly for letting my imagination wander in a direction I absolutely don't want to think about. My gaze shoots cold arrows at him.

"Hey! Don't flatter yourself. I take dance classes, so I have some fitness. Perhaps not much strength to boast about, but if I can dance for almost a full hour with nothing more than a couple of breaks to drink water, I'm sure I can handle five minutes with you. I guarantee you wouldn't be able to handle my routine."

Garren chuckles and puts on his helmet.

"Hot-tempered and full of surprises," I hear him say through the bevor. "If you can make it through a week with the commander, I might start thinking about training with you a few times a week, since the magic within you differs from the other recruits."

I rub my hands together triumphantly with the book under my arm.

"All right then! It's a deal!"

To his obvious surprise, judging by his body language, I grab his armoured hand, shaking it as firmly as I can and decorating my lips with my cutest smile. *This time, it's me who has the upper hand.*

"See you tonight then, Grand Prior! Please bring me a pen and paper."

I spend the rest of the day trying to decipher the handwriting in the book. I'm feeling quite proud of myself when I finally read part of a paragraph, whilst sitting on a bench inside the walls of the Order of the Light and the last rays of the day caressing my face. *I've been sitting here for so long; some sunscreen would be good right about now.* I'm chewing on an apple as I'm studying the book. The fruit here tastes much better than back home. I had dinner not too long ago, but I remember my mother's words—that I should eat healthier stuff—and I don't want to disappoint her, even though I'm so far away.

Out of the corner of my eye, I glimpse someone waving at me, and when I look up, I see it's Gwen and Helga. I smile with uncertainty and wave back. They approach and settle down next to me, and I can almost feel the charged curiosity floating in the air.

"How did matters go with the grand prior?" Helga asks while fiddling with one of her earrings, twirling it back and forth between her fingers.

"It was all right," I say as neutrally as I can muster, forcing my smile to look more confident.

Gwen leans into me and I pull myself to the side a little so the tip of her nose doesn't touch my cheek.

"What did you discuss?" she asks, and I'm unsure if it's wonder or something rather poisonous that edges her voice.

"He announced I must behave better and listen to the commander."

I throw my head back and chuckle at my statement. It's not a lie, not even a white one.

"I should probably listen to him if I want to earn a living," I continue.

"Speaking of the weekly salary—we've just received ours," says Helga, looking pleased. "It's not much, but it's better than nothing. Will you be accompanying us to the inn?"

"I don't have any money yet," I answer.

"We'll buy you an ale," Gwen remarks, taking me under the arm.

I grimace apologetically.

"Thanks, but I'd rather not drink. I'm tired today. Maybe I can tag along next time?"

"Very well."

Helga waves to Gwen and both get up almost at the same time.

"See you tomorrow, Saga. Have a pleasant evening!"

A sigh of relief stumbles out between my lips as I say goodbye to the women, watching them disappear further and further away. I can't stand their company right now. Gwen's character is intense, and Helga gives off a calculating impression. I don't think I'll ever be able to fully trust them, certainly not in the way I trust Ambrosia and Remy. I wonder how they're doing at home. Do they miss me? I'd give anything to bicker with Ambrosia right now, even though she has a hard time admitting she's wrong, and it gets on my nerves sometimes.

With a melancholic smile playing on my lips, I take the pocket watch out of my blouse collar and open its lid. Close to eight o'clock. *It's almost time.*

Absent-mindedly, I grab my phone out of my trouser pocket and switch it on. 21:12. The battery has stayed at the same level as the day I arrived here, which surprises me. At this point, the battery would have been partially depleted at home, but here it doesn't seem to have moved at all. Maybe this is something I can use to my advantage.

I quickly scroll through the gallery, glancing around to make sure no one's snooping, thereafter pulling up a photo of Kailunn. *I've missed seeing your face.* Stretching my back where I sit on the bench, I feel how excitement grabs my toes, making them wiggle. Since the battery hasn't died yet, I can start documenting the environment. It might come in handy someday.

With the book open in front of me and the phone resting in the middle of it so as not to draw attention to me, I stand up and lead my steps towards the garden. I know what I'll be doing in the next few hours before my meeting with the paladin.

CHAPTER TWELVE

Garren Roseheart

Dusk draws its mantle over the canopy of the firmament and the last rays of sunlight sneak through a window in my study, where I'm leaning over maps, hand-written letters, and documents from Her Majesty Queen Ariadne. The candle on the desk flickers as it spreads a faint glow around it, shadows moving across the face of an elf mage and Ahriele standing next to her. Both have bowed their heads slightly in my presence.

"Grand Prior. Prince Sunseeker requests an audience," Thalanil says in a crystal-clear voice.

She's an elf with dark skin, icy silver eyes, and a faint shade of shimmering blue in her long, dark locks. In her hands she's holding a black and red communication gem and she looks at me blankly, awaiting an answer.

A long sigh escapes my lips and I run a hand through my hair. Straightening my back against the back of the chair, I adjust the lacing at the collar of my white shirt and shoot a sharp gaze at her. *What does that pesky elf want at this time of day that he can't discuss with my queen instead?*

"Proceed," I reply dryly.

Preoccupied with a phantasm of eyes as deep as the darkest night, I fiddle with the jewellery hanging around my neck with one hand and drum with the fingers of the other on the armrest. Thalanil whispers something in a foreign language and lifts the hand resting on the communication jewel. A crackling light blue glow radiates from her palms and the jewel floats in the air between them. A circular, pulsating blue light appears from one shoulder to the other behind her head and a moving image of the elven prince appears at my desk.

"Well met, Prince Sunseeker," I greet coldly yet politely, throwing a quick glance at a pocket watch on the table. *Twenty past nine.* "What prompts this meeting?"

I see how the prince moves his head slightly, pushing his chin up.

"Grand Prior Roseheart," he begins in a voice as soft as the finest silk, clasping his hands behind his back.

His tall palace guards stand beside him, completely motionless in full regalia, and their faces covered by helmets. It's quite remarkable that the prince, who's two metres tall, has guards even taller. *The high elves seem to find pleasure in making others feel insignificant and small.*

The prince's long white hair with its silver shimmer is straight as nails and not a single strand is out of place, unlike my half-tousled hair with curls that seem to have lives of their own. He hasn't aged a single day, which shouldn't come as a surprise given the longevity of his people.

"The magical girl carrying my people's symbol around her neck is said to be with you," he continues.

The intensity of the gaze from the silvery eyes is palpable, despite the physical distance between us. I let go of my jewellery, leaning my elbow on the armrest and my cheek against my clenched fist as I survey him.

"Rumours about the stranger seem to spread faster than the usual Whitekeep gossip," I say.

The elven prince watches me for a moment. Motionless, cold, cunning.

"The last of the star thistles is always the most succulent."

These elvish idioms—pure riddles.

"What's your aim, Prince Sunseeker?" I find myself sounding aggressive, bordering on threatening. "Is it her magic you're after? Is it tempting you to quench your own thirst? She has no connection to you other than a piece of jewellery."

"Know your place, *sulsair*. Your position carries no weight with me."

The elven prince's shoulders seem tense, yet he remains immovable. The silky-smooth voice drips with venom, tainting my ears with its bitterness.

"She will meet with me. Or perhaps you intend to cause dramatic consequences based on your own selfish beliefs? Your order has no ownership of her magic."

I see Ahriele's expression contorting in anger, but I raise one hand, gesturing for her to calm down.

"Naturally, it's better our kingdoms work together, given the reports that have landed on my desk of the use of black magic in the Highlands, which in turn could affect both of our realms if it was to spread."

The tone of my voice is dry, and I force myself to bow my head politely. *He's royalty, after all—and always as haughty, that pointy-eared, magic-devouring snake.*

"We should discuss this. The Valley of the Sun is within the border of the Highlands, so this topic should certainly concern you."

"Of course. We will head for Whitekeep tomorrow and should arrive within the next few days," the prince says, and I can see a slight smile on his lips. "We shall keep in touch. I look forward to meeting the little star thistle."

The connection between our communication jewels breaks, and I grimace in disapproval. Thalanil's magic fades and she returns to holding the stone with both hands. Irritated, I wave her away and Ahriele puts her hands on my desk. She leans forward and her eyes bore into me as the door to the room closes.

"What's the matter, Garren?"

Her gaze is stern, creating a stark contrast to the softness in her voice.

"It's nothing."

"You're a lousy liar and always have been."

She's right. I am. We know each other better than anyone and it doesn't surprise me in the least she has picked up on the fact that I'm not acting entirely like myself lately.

"I need to be somewhere," I announce, and take another look at the pocket watch.

I'm two minutes late.

"Why in such a hurry?" Ahriele asks.

I reach for a couple of sheets of paper, a quill, and an inkhorn as I stand up. There's a lantern by the gazebo, meaning I don't need to bring my own. Ahriele grabs me by the arm.

"Ahriele," I mutter evasively. "Now isn't the time."

With a disappointed expression in her eyes, she lets go of me and crosses her arms over her chest.

"Don't let the night's whispers turn you into a fool," she admonishes.

I usher her out of the study, locking the door behind us.

"I've got a sharp head on my shoulders," I answer curtly and swiftly steer my steps towards one of the side exits.

Wait for me, Saga.

SHADOW DANCE

CHAPTER THIRTEEN

Saga Falk

The boss is late.

The last few hours I've spent taking photos of things I came across in the garden and to my great joy, the battery doesn't get drained. I had taken selfies with some of the most beautiful roses I could find and snapped a picture of a pink caterpillar munching on a leaf. As darkness began to fall, I sat down on the bench and scrolled through the phone's photo gallery again, dreaming myself back to my room at home and various thoughts about Kailunn. It's getting a little chilly and I wish I had brought my pink jumper with me.

Upon settling down next to me, I notice Garren is breathing quickly, as if he has been in a hurry.

"Is everything okay?" I ask.

"Yes," he replies and hands me writing materials. "Apologies for keeping you waiting."

"It's only a matter of a few minutes, so no worries." For a second or two, I look at the quill in my hand. "I've never written with one of these before. I feel sorry for the bird that may have had to die for me to write with this."

Quickly, I clear my throat and grimace.

"Sometimes I think out loud," I say in an apologetic tone.

Garren smirks and shakes his head.

"Don't worry yourself."

Looking down at the sheets of paper, I run one finger lightly over my lower lip while my thoughts wander. I get up from the bench, sit down on the wooden planks, and put the inkhorn down next to my book on top of the bench, using the bench as a writing pad. I assume writing on top of the book would be disrespectful, so I endure the uncomfortable position, but at least I can make notes.

The light from a lantern spreads a warm light over us and a moth seeks it with fluttering wings. The crickets' symphony tells a story of a summer coming to an end.

"Garren, could you write all the letters of the alphabet from beginning to end in a similar style as in the book, please?" I ask.

I point to the paper, showing I want them written from the top to bottom.

"Certainly."

The paladin settles down next to me, grabs the quill, and carefully opens the inkhorn. His thigh brushes against my knee and shyness blooms within me, but I fight off the tingle that flutters around aimlessly in my stomach. My gaze follows his movements across the paper, and I can't help but linger on his fingers. Short-cut nails, hands that have borne witness to hard physical work over the years. *I wonder how good he is at playing the violin.* I imagine his fingers moving along the strings and feel the skin on my arms tingle as goosebumps appear.

SHADOW DANCE

I stare at his lips as he leans over the sheet of paper and blows lightly on it to make the ink dry faster. *It's as if he has cast a spell on me.* His invisible crackling energy field, the holy aura surrounding him, seems to sweep over me and I can almost touch it. This is getting emotionally messy, and yet I can't stop myself from getting closer to him.

"It's done," he says after a short while, looking at his work with satisfaction in his eyes.

"Thank you," I mumble.

He hands me the quill and I dip it into the container of ink.

"You overdid it," he remarks, shaking his head. "Scrape the excess ink off the side of the inkhorn."

I follow his instructions before putting the quill against the paper, but all I get is a single smudge.

"But why? I don't understand what I'm doing wrong."

"Allow me."

Garren places his hand over mine and immediately I'm somewhat giddy with nervousness as our energies mix with each other. He, on the other hand, looks unfazed as he brings our hands to the inkhorn and dips the quill into it.

"All right, now we're getting somewhere," I exhale when he lets go of my hand and I write sensible-looking letters on the paper.

His perusing gaze traces over my handwriting and he nods slowly.

"One's handwriting says a lot about one's personality," he says with a low tone and glances at me.

I stretch my back and roll my shoulders. It hurts to sit like this.

"Oh? What does the expert think mine says about me?" I ask, biting my tongue as I realise how I sound.

Nope, I'm not attempting to flirt. I have more important things to think about.

Giving me a long look, Garren's expression is inscrutable. For a moment, he tilts his head to look up at the sky where the stars are appearing, closing his eyes for a few seconds, before turning his attention back to me.

"Yours shows you're hot-tempered and stubborn. Right here."

He points to how I have bent the letter K.

"Is that all?" I ask, unable to mask the disappointed tone in my voice as I glare at him.

"No." Nodding, he points to the letter S. "The way you write these curves speaks of passion, courage, and strength. The first letter of your name."

My mouth feels parched in an instant, and I put down the quill, closing the cap on the inkhorn. The atmosphere between us is charged, the borders between our souls blurred, and I hold my breath as I'm grasping for an answer.

"Maybe so," I say softly and direct my attention to his writing. "And what does yours say about you?"

Garren gives me a wry smile.

"Have a guess."

I press my lips together prior to beginning my evaluation.

"Okay. Your squiggly letters, like these S's, make me think of infinity. Infinite faith. Your T's give an indication of courage and loyalty—they remind me of crosses—while your W's look sharp. Firmness of principle—you may not always find it easy to compromise. Stubbornness. Strength of character."

Shyly, I glance at him to see his reaction to my interpretation. He sits with his elbow on the backrest of the bench and his cheek propped in one palm as he watches me in silence. His eyes are twinkling, making me think back to the starry sky back home I always look up at when I walk home from work, or when I sit in my room and look out the window while my mind wanders freely. *Yes, I always find solace in the pearls of the universe.*

"You're skilled," he says, giving the appearance of being impressed.

SHADOW DANCE

"Thank you," I say, smiling to myself.

Slowly, I rise from my seat, turning my back to him and wrapping my arms around myself as I look up at the sky. The constellations are unfamiliar to me and within mere seconds, I feel like I'm the loneliest person in the world. Quietly, I exhale and fix my eyes on one star shining the brightest, whilst sending a thought to the cosmos to somehow make my parents understand I'm doing fine.

My ears pick up the sound of Garren standing up, and I flinch slightly as something is placed over my shoulders. *His coat. He put his coat over my shoulders.* I don't know where to go with my thoughts and find myself getting a little emotional deep inside.

"Autumn is coming, and you should dress accordingly, otherwise you might catch a cold."

His hands are still resting atop the coat, and I should pull away, but my heart keeps my feet still. *His touch doesn't scare me.*

"Could you please explain the Light to me?" I ask upon composing myself from my inner emotional turmoil. "I'm aware I should read the scriptures to get a deeper insight, but I read slowly and think maybe it can be explained in short terms."

"The Mother of the Light lavishes us with her warmth and love. She teaches us empathy and patience. Gives us strength and guides us when we're lost in the dark. She's infinite love, understanding, and the gateway to something greater. Through the Light, we grow perceptive of the world around us and gain insight into something beyond our ordinary senses."

"That was indeed short and concise, but I think I get the gist of it."

I continue to stare at the same star and take a couple of deep breaths, focusing on my breathing. *One, two, three.*

"Aren't you freezing?" I say timidly.

"The cold has no grip over me when I'm in your presence, lass."

I slowly turn around as Garren lifts his hands, glaring at him.

"Why do you say things that confuse me?" My question is blunt, and I pull his coat tighter around my body.

"Does it affect you positively or negatively?"

The words leave his lips as he settles down on the bench and moves my book, the inkhorn, and the sheet of paper to the side.

He's making room for me. I swallow the nervousness that has formed a lump in my throat, and upon gathering my courage, I take a seat next to him. Keeping my eyes fixed on my knees; wishing I could hide away in that big coat resting over my shoulders. I know what the answer leans towards, but I don't want to think about it. I hear the wind in the treetops and the distant murmur of the members of the Order of the Light. The crickets are still playing their melodies somewhere among the grass and bushes. *I can't be feeling this way—I haven't even met the real Kailunn yet.*

"I don't know how to answer that right now," I say quietly, realising how immature I sound for my age.

I get fed up with myself sometimes.

As some moments pass in silence, an idea to avoid answering his question strikes me out of the blue.

"Hold your hand out, please."

With an enigmatic look in his eyes, he obeys without uttering a word. His palm is facing me, and I lift my hand and slowly bring it closer to his. I focus on the energy in my body, from my toes all the way up to my head. When our palms are a couple of centimetres apart, I feel warmth in my chest and under my skin. A faint glow emerges from my fingertips as I gasp. Garren's fist glows with a strong brilliance and he seems unfazed by our energies entwining.

"Is it common for magic to manifest like this as soon as two people are close to each other?" I mumble and blink a few times.

SHADOW DANCE

"It's unusual. You summon the Light as you sit close, and I barely have to put any effort in. In fact, you amplify my power."

Garren's fingers slowly intertwine with mine and he keeps his gaze fixed on me, as if silently asking for permission. The heat from his magical energy tickles my skin, moving up my wrist and arm. When the sensation reaches my shoulder and neck, I fail to stifle a giggle, causing him to smile.

"Right now, I'm giving you a part of myself, my inner power," he says softly, his free hand reaching for mine and radiating the same strong glow as our fingers touch. "When you become more comfortable with your own energy and have learned to manage it, you'll be able to do the same of your own free will."

His eyes give off a soft white light, and I notice how my vision has changed.

"However, there are other ways magic can travel between two bodies, one in particular being highly effective," he continues.

"How?"

"Through a kiss."

Uh-oh.

My heartbeat spins rapidly in my chest as Garren lets go of my hands and our magics slowly fade away, seeping back into our own bodies. I feel awkward and the sensation of his light magic caressing my back lingers for a while. The pain in my body seems to have subsided. Did he just heal me?

I clear my throat, unable to stop thinking about what he said earlier today.

"You mentioned you're confused. Because of me, apparently."

Garren turns his face away and stares at a point somewhere else, causing a pang of guilt in my chest. Perhaps this is a question I should have kept to myself.

"Sorry, that was stupid of me," I apologise.

He quickly turns to me, his blue eyes hiding a glow within them that catches me off guard.

"You have nestled yourself among my thoughts, Saga." He furrows his brows and runs his hand through his hair. "You're not the first individual to catch my eye, but you're the one that lingers. It's meaningless to chase you out of my mind when you keep occupying it."

It takes but a mere second for embarrassment to settle on his features and he carefully fiddles with the heavy piece of jewellery hanging around his neck.

"I'm well-aware of the inappropriate nature of mentioning this, considering you're not familiar with our ways around here, we hardly know each other, and because you…"

His voice trails off into silence and he looks down at his palms. For some reason, melancholy takes a grip on me when I see the crow's feet around his eyes and how shadows sweep across the scar on his cheek. He, who until now has always radiated strength and is described as the hero of Whitekeep, is sitting on a bench next to me; vulnerable, emotionally exposed. It tugs at my heart.

"I'm sorry I make you feel this way," I mumble barely audibly.

"Don't say that."

Garren waves one hand dismissively, his face mirthless, cold.

"Prince Sunseeker and his retinue will arrive in Whitekeep in a number of days. It should be in your best interest to be vigilant around him."

"What are you saying? Is Kailunn coming here?"

Putting my hands over my mouth, I try to dampen the shrillness to my voice. Quickly, I fly up from the bench and almost drop Garren's coat due to the hasty movement.

"I'm not ready for this at all," I mutter out loud to myself. "I thought I was, but I was wrong."

My breathing is stressed as I fish my phone out of my pocket and scroll through the files on the memory card. Garren watches me in silence and eventually I sink down onto the bench next to him as I open a document

SHADOW DANCE

I saved from the web years ago while pulling the coat tighter around my body. *Kailunn Vairmilenne. He's known as Kailunn Sunseeker in the language of the humans, which is the most commonly spoken language in this universe.*

"There's only brief information here."

Frustrated, I sigh at the document on the phone, putting my hand to my forehead and trying to calm myself down. It's crystal clear I know more about Garren at this point than I do about Kailunn, despite my careful research over the years, and this worries me. How can I have feelings for someone when I don't know what he's like?

"Prince Sunseeker is cunning," Garren says in a low voice, his eyelids drifting down halfway over his pupils. "The high elves have a complicated history throughout the ages and have had to sacrifice a lot during the wars. It shouldn't come as a surprise he's crafty, but I find it hard to accept he'll possibly use his cunning to get at you inappropriately."

With a raised eyebrow, I quickly analyse his spoken words.

"I'm a big girl, Garren. I don't need anyone protecting me regarding men and what their intentions are," I mumble, pursing my lips.

His eyelids open completely, and he forces me to look him deep in the eyes with his determined gaze. "Saga. He's manipulative, and he'll do anything to get more magic in his possession, even if it means exploiting a gentle soul. It's rumoured the high elves devour the magic of living creatures, leaving them to wither and die once they're finished with them. This goes against their own traditions."

"No, I refuse to believe he's evil!" I shake my head and close the document on my phone. "They're peaceful people and they would never intentionally harm anyone for their own gain. That much I know."

"I'm not applying malicious attributes to his character—I'm merely advising you to be on your guard. Don't be blinded by your heart. Addiction to anything, including magic, is a dangerous thing and a driving force behind less-than-honourable actions."

We sit in silence, and I shift my focus to the night sky above us with its shimmering night pearls. Slowly, I moisten my lips with the tip of my tongue and take a deep breath, calming my chaotic thoughts.

"Thank you for keeping an eye out for me. I appreciate it. You're doing it even though you don't have to."

My voice is a little unsteady and sadness digs holes in my soul. What if everything I've built up in my head about Kailunn over the years, even before I fell in love with his fictional image, is the exact opposite?

Garren nods without saying a word and I desperately try to think of a way to lighten the mood.

"Check this out."

After browsing the phone for a while, I find the photo album I created a couple of years ago. Me, Ambrosia, and Remy were cosplaying our characters from *Reign Online* for a convention abroad, and we took a group photo of ourselves outside the building where the event was held.

"Here I am, dressed as the male elven priest I usually play. I was so excited I had found a pair of high-quality elven ears, but I lost one. It must have looked silly, me walking around with one long and one short ear."

I can't help but chuckle at the memory, and Garren's stern look is replaced with amusement. *A genuine smi*le.

"Who's the young man?" he asks as he studies Remy's outfit.

"That's Remy, our mutual friend. He's a warrior in-game and wanted to dress as him."

"The details of the armour are impressive."

"Yeah, and the suit isn't nearly as heavy as it looks. He designed it himself and it took him about six months to finish it."

Garren's gaze lingers on the picture.

"I apologise if I come across as brusque. Generally, I prefer women to

SHADOW DANCE

men, but your attractiveness as a male elf with a single ear is undeniable."

I grimace in surprise and a muffled giggle finds its way from between my lips as he keeps smiling at me. The atmosphere between us feels much better already. I bring up the picture of the fuzzy little caterpillar from today instead and try not to smile too widely. *He's not that scary to spend time with, after all.*

"I took this in the garden today."

Garren nods at the phone in my hand.

"How do you use this item to capture your subjects?"

I tap on the camera app, switching it to selfie mode and holding it up in front of us.

"The camera lens is here," I explain while pointing at it. "And you can see yourself on the screen."

Garren seems perplexed when he watches himself, eyes wide, and I can't help but laugh.

"Sorry, but you're so funny," I say, shaking my head a little. "Keep looking over here and I'll snap a picture of us."

Garren leans forward towards the phone, and I glance at him.

"If you move, the picture will turn out blurry."

"What do you need me to do?" he asks.

"Just sit still." I grin as I try to get the angle right. "You're so broad-shouldered I have to move closer to you."

I feel my thigh brush against his as I shift.

"Bring your head closer to mine," I say, and he moves a little, but it still seems off when I'm about to take a picture. My glasses keep reflecting the little available light, but I don't like my appearance without them, which is why I keep them on.

"No, this won't work. Is it all right if I come closer?"

He nods and I try to make the picture look reasonable by leaning into him, but I end up grimacing in displeasure.

"I have a suggestion. Come here," I hear him say.

Garren's arm slips around my waistline and he pulls me to him so I'm resting in his arms. I gasp at the same time as my surprise paints my cheeks red. *I need to remain calm.*

"Let's try again," he says, seemingly unfazed by the fact I'm sitting on him.

The heat from his body feels comforting and my soul soaks it up hungrily. The other arm finds its way around me and before I know it, I'm in the middle of an embrace. *His arms are so strong.* I pick up the phone again, tilt my head slightly to the side, and try to strike a pose. Garren leans his head against mine as he hugs me a little tighter and I hold my breath.

"You and your friend," he utters softly and the voice dances into my ears playfully. "You held your heads close similarly in that picture."

"Yeah," I stammer and finally take a silent, deep breath. "All right, are you ready?"

"Yes," he replies, smiling wryly as he looks at the camera. "Your face is serious. Imagine some confused soul finding your poor lost ear."

I laugh, press the shutter button on the screen, and hear the click. The picture is quite nice. I show it to him, nodding approvingly.

"And that's how you take pictures with a phone. It's cool, right?"

"It's truly fascinating."

Garren is still embracing me. I lower the hand holding the phone and hear him sigh quietly next to my ear.

"You disappear in my arms," he murmurs. "Make sure you eat properly, even if the food isn't comparable to what you're used to."

I swallow hard and close my eyes as I let the thoughts circulate freely in my head. *Why am I allowing this to happen?* This feels like a secret mediaeval date. The tingling in my stomach pulses, sending out signals in my body. Ones I didn't think I would be capable of experiencing anymore after my breakup with my ex—at least not with someone else other than my fictional image of Kailunn. It's unusual, strange, and perhaps a little exciting. *Sheesh, what a mess.*

Carefully, I loosen his arms' grip on me as I shift myself back to the bench.

"I'm eating properly," I respond timidly, putting the phone in my pocket.

I want to say something more—thank him for the help with the writing—but the words stick in my throat. Sorting the sheets of paper on top of my book, I hand him the inkhorn, coat, and quill, trying to maintain a neutral look. Upon grabbing the items, he locks his gaze on mine again as we stand up.

"You truly are a little butterfly," he utters. "If it flutters its thin wings in search of the attractive light that draws the butterfly to it, it's only because it doesn't know the fire can devour it. Remember that, lass."

He turns away from me, taking strides towards the exit of the garden while I stand and watch him with my mouth open.

"Hey! Wait!" I exclaim, rushing after him. "Speak clearly, please!"

The chilly night air creeps in through my blouse. His facial expression as he turns to face me is peculiar, and he raises an eyebrow in surprise.

"Do I have to explain all things in detail?"

"In this case, the answer is a resounding yes. No one speaks in riddles at home!"

I glare at him. Pushing the glasses up the bridge of my nose, I hear him grunt in displeasure.

"Stubborn lass," he mutters under his breath.

He stuffs the inkhorn and the now dry quill into one of the pockets of the coat he has folded over one arm.

"You may have a dream castle built inside your head, but take care the debris doesn't injure you on the day it all comes crashing down."

Great, another conundrum. My gut tells me he's talking about Kailunn, and I stick my chin defiantly into the air with my hands at my sides.

"Is that so? Then let me tell you something. I may have a dream castle I hide in, but at least I dare to stand by it. And I don't judge anyone until they show their true personality." I take a deep breath before I continue speaking, noticing how I'm getting annoyed. "Where I come from, they say kisses can tell a lot about a person's heart and intentions, about their personality, and you have to kiss a lot of frogs before you find the right one."

The holy knight strokes his beard thoughtfully and tilts his head to the side.

"That's remarkable. How many have you kissed thus far?"

"It's none of your business and neither is it my point," I snap, masking my fluttering heart with frustration in my voice. "That's about as relevant as me asking you how many you've had, which has no bearing in this regard and nothing I need or want to know."

I've completely lost track of my argument and I'm scratching my chin as I realise I've probably got angry over nothing again. There's nothing wrong with being curious about someone else. And why did I talk about kissing frogs? *I'm such a mess.*

"Maybe I got a little upset and I apologise for that," I mutter and roll my eyes. "And perhaps I started talking about stuff that wasn't relevant to the subject at hand."

Garren fiddles with the jewellery around his neck as he watches me in silence for a moment that feels like an eternity. He lifts it, brings it to his forehead as he closes his eyes, before kissing it softly and letting it rest against his chest once more. My heart skips a beat, and my stomach tingles. I think back to all the movies I've watched and all the games I've played over the years, silently admitting to myself I've always been particularly drawn to characters who share his doctrinal traits, even though I'm not a believer myself.

"Saga," he says, and the stern expression on his face softens. "I'll do my utmost not to pry too much into your background when you're not comfortable sharing it."

I look down for a moment as I kick a small rock with one foot, watching it fly away. Kailunn will show up soon, which I'm not prepared for, and I'm clearly attracted to this other man, too. *Would it be wrong to explore the feeling I'm experiencing?* After all, I'm single and Ambrosia always says I shouldn't give up feelings completely, despite having had a hell of a relationship with my ex. Feelings scare me, but it might be useful to act on them so long as no one gets hurt. I'm twenty-nine years old and a little more experience in the kissing department wouldn't hurt.

Perhaps I should feel shame towards the elven prince, like I did when I was involved with Retsam. However, as it stands right now, I don't. He's no longer the fictitious elf, the one who lives in my imaginary castle and who makes no demands of me. Everything that was once fictional is now reality. Yes, it's messy, but it somehow doesn't feel quite as emotionally dangerous to act on feelings here, unlike the world I'm from, and right now I'm curious about the paladin. *It doesn't mean I've forgotten about Kailunn, whom I haven't even met yet.*

"Okay," I say, looking up at the man in front of me. "What you mentioned before, regarding magic and how it travels through different bodies."

Garren raises one eyebrow, studying me with steady eyes.

"What of it?" he asks, his voice studded with surprise.

"Well, now that we've touched on the subject of kisses, we might as well test the theory, right?" I continue, firmly straightening my back and doing my utmost to seem calm. "I need to learn how to use my power, and you could be my teacher."

With a dismayed expression on his face, he stares at me. A lump of anxiety shoots straight down into my stomach from my throat.

"Never mind!" I say quickly, almost tripping over the words with my tongue.

I'm so dumb. It's idiotic to even mention this after such a short time, regardless of the level of attraction. I turn away from him and wipe my nose discreetly with one sleeve, telling myself that everything's fine, despite this moment of utter fail. *Making a fool of myself seems to be my signature move ever since I disappeared from Malmö.* In a hurry, I walk away with the book and the sheets of paper tightly pressed to my chest.

"See you later, boss!"

A hand grabs one of my arms and I drop the stuff I'm carrying with a thud. Garren makes me turn to face him again, pulling me close. His coat falls to the ground at our feet. He places his palms against my cheeks, gently running his thumbs over my skin as our eyes meet.

I'm dumbstruck as I watch his pupils dilate. My eyelids wander down while my cheeks flush and I hold my breath momentarily when soft lips press against my mouth in a gentle yet determined kiss. The sound of my heartbeat echoes in my ears, the blood rushes to my head, and dizziness swirls inside my cranium. This doesn't feel like an ordinary kiss, and it doesn't take experience with many frogs to establish that opinion. His moustache and beard tickle me a little. That strange warmth that appears in my chest from time to time spreads its roots throughout my body with tremendous force and I feel weightless. My hands sneak up to Garren's neck and the silky strands of hair caress my fingers. *They're so soft.*

There's an intense heat behind my eyes and a faint sound appears in my throat that causes Garren to break the dance of our lips.

"By the Light," he utters in a breath and a strange note in his voice makes my eyelids flutter for a second before I open them.

I blink several times as I notice how brightly shining golden butterflies swirl around me. Some grab my clothes with their thin legs, flapping their wings at ultra-fast speeds, and I hover slightly above the ground. My palms glow with the same strong light as the butterflies. Waving my feet, I can almost touch the ground with my big toes.

Garren sinks to his knees, his fingers tightly furled around his pendant with both hands, and I hear him mumble something, unable to make out his words. His usually clear blue eyes light up and I stare at him with parted lips as a pattern of burning gold appears on his forehead. A gasping sound escapes me as I remember something I've read online. *The third eye.*

The magic courses through me, accompanied by a dullness that pulls my eyelids shut. My head leans down towards my chest, and dizziness consumes me.

CHAPTER FOURTEEN

Garren Roseheart

The throbbing in my forehead is subsiding and I find myself clutching the pendant around my neck so tightly that it has left a temporary imprint in one of my palms once I let go of it. This hasn't occurred to me previously, not even when I spoke to the Mother in the artefact room during my initiation into the Order of the Light in Whitekeep.

This experience has rattled me to the core; something I would call pure witchcraft. Sparkling stars and otherworldly phenomena I can't comprehend, or perhaps fully accept, had appeared before my eyes and through the glittering curtain I had been able to catch sight of Saga.

She had her back turned to me with a number of blurred, shimmering figures around her—one of which, a taller one, touched her left upper arm with caressing movements. When she turned to me, her face had been adorned with a loving smile. As she extended a hand to me, I saw the centre of her forehead pulse with a white glow.

My brain whispers to me she's dangerous, this woman who has collapsed into a little heap on the ground. Had she been someone else, another individual belonging to another realm, she would have been considered a danger, not solely to Whitekeep but to nearby areas as well. The Order of the Light would most likely, under my directive, have equipped their best knights to eliminate the threat. And here she is before me; vulnerable, a few bright butterflies in her hair that vanish into the night.

Silently, I crawl in her direction. My eyes search the garden to make sure we haven't attracted attention and I'm met with calm, except for faint sounds in the distance and the chirping of crickets. The same serene atmosphere as before. My brain continues to whisper to me, but is soon drowned out by the muffled song of my heart as I gently grasp her slender shoulders, turning her towards me and pulling her into my arms.

I take her glasses off and set them aside on the ground as I brush a few strands of hair out of her face. Her breaths are steady, and a sigh of relief leaves my lips. With one hand, I remove my necklace. I offer a prayer to the Mother to protect her child before pressing my lips against the pendant, subsequently putting it around Saga's neck.

My eyes take in every detail. Long, dark eyelashes, small silver streaks hiding in the dark brown fringe, and dark circles under her eyes. My thumbs caress her cheeks lightly while I'm gripped by enormous compassion. She appears to be tired deep inside. *If only she knew how strong she is, to hold her head high in a world that's unfamiliar to her.*

After a few minutes pass, Saga catches her breath, coughing. Her eyelids open slowly, and I try to catch her gaze with my own.

"Saga," I say in a gentle voice, touching her shoulder lightly with one thumb.

The gaze expresses confusion until it locks onto me.

SHADOW DANCE

"Hey," she says, smiling weakly. "How about we don't do that again?"

I can't help but mirror her smile despite a twinge of disappointment deep inside, and I watch her as she lifts herself up into a sitting position, reaching for her glasses.

"Are you hurting anywhere?" I ask, unable to mask the worry in my voice.

Her fingers touch her fringe for a moment as she collects her thoughts.

"I think I'm okay," she smiles apologetically. "What happened?"

Running my fingers through my hair, I shake my head slowly.

"Something that cannot be explained in simple words." I rise to my feet upon replying and offer her my hand. "Some time is needed to evaluate this."

"Agreed," she murmurs as she gets up, staring into my eyes while saying naught.

The cold from her fingers spreads into my pores and I squeeze her hand gently. Her perusing gaze sweeps over my features, fragments of a thousand thoughts painted in her eyes. Slowly, she withdraws her hand, and I can still feel the warmth of her lips lingering on mine.

We walk side by side through the garden, our steps languid. I've put on my coat, and she hugs the book and the sheets of paper in her arms. Her feet cease their movements as she touches the chain around her neck with one hand, her eyes widening as she studies it.

"This is…" she begins, her voice trailing off.

"Yours," I interject, giving her a smile.

"T-thank you," she stammers, bringing it closer to her face as she twists and turns it. "Wow, this looks expensive. I can't accept this."

Quickly, I shake my head.

"It's for protection. I own one more."

For a moment, I bite my tongue. It's certainly true I have another in my possession, but this particular one is blessed and has been in my family for several generations, while the other is more recent and doesn't carry quite the same sentimental value. I may need to arrange a meeting with the high priestess and ask for a second blessing, should she deem me worthy in my current faithfulness.

Fortunately, my explanation seems to be satisfactory, and she nods. A tender twinkle appears in her eyes, and she hesitantly takes a step closer to me. Reflexively, I lean down a little when she tiptoes as if trying to reach up to me. Placing one hand over my mouth, she plants a kiss on top of the back of her hand.

"Thank you, Garren," she whispers and takes a step back again while shyly lowering her gaze.

"You're most welcome," I reply, doing my utmost to sound steady.

A longing to kiss her lips once more tugs at my soul, despite what happened before. To hear her whisper words of tenderness in my ear, allowing her to submerge my heart in the baptismal font of newfound love. Instead, we wish each other good night, nodding politely at one another.

I watch in silence as the shadows embrace her and make her disappear out of my sight, finding myself envying the pillow that gets to caress her dreams and dark locks tonight.

CHAPTER FIFTEEN

Saga Falk

I sit in bed in the dormitory with two other empty beds and stare at the pendant in my hand in front of me. It's decorated with swirling roses, a lion's head, and embedded red gems to represent the petals. Gently, I run one thumb over it, turning it over as I examine the back. Engraved in small, squiggly letters, I can make out the name Roseheart. *Do I have a family heirloom in my hand?*

I blink a few times and look at the front of it again, resting my gaze on the lion. The motif suits the paladin well and I feel unworthy, almost ashamed, to be wearing it. Why had he given it to me? *For protection, he said.* Still, the question hangs like an invisible helium balloon in the air, and I think back to how it felt when his facial hair tickled my skin as we kissed, before everything had ended in chaos. I still can't believe I plucked up the courage to pretend-kiss him with my hand over his mouth when we were about to say goodbye. *Apparently, I'm now playing a kissing game with a lion. He might devour me if I'm not careful.*

Despite this thought, I can't help but smile and crawl under the covers as I let the jewellery rest across my chest. It's quite heavy, but the weight has a relaxing effect and I feel sleep take hold of every cell in my body and slowly envelop me in its fog.

I don't know how long I've rested, but I'm groggy with sleep and grumpy when I'm startled by noises outside the door. Helga and Gwen barge into the bedroom, clearly drunk, and slam the door shut with a loud bang. *Damnit, not these two again.*

"I'm trying to sleep," I whine, pulling the blanket up over my head and turning my back on them.

The bed creaks as Gwen sits down, pulling the fabric from my face.

"Saga! How nice to have you as our roommate!"

"Just wonderful," I growl and glare at her. "Can we sleep now?"

"Not just yet," she says and lies down next to me on her stomach, pouting with her lips in disappointment.

Ugh, she reeks of alcohol. Helga has already gone to bed and her loud breathing fills the room. Gwen waves her legs in the air behind her, shooting me a goofy smile.

"You're cute," she chuckles and pokes me on the tip of my nose with one finger.

"Stop it, Gwen!"

I sit up sharply while trying to pull the covers up to my neck, but the weight of her body makes it difficult, nigh impossible. She points to the pendant resting against my chest.

"I recognise that," she murmurs and crawls closer to me.

"Back off," I warn.

"Where did you get it?" she asks, and the smell of alcohol on her

SHADOW DANCE

breath wafts over my face.

I forcefully push back a gag and grab her shoulders as I try to shove her away.

"Go to bed."

"Let's sleep together," she murmurs softly, placing one hand over my stomach.

"I said go to bed!"

My voice snaps with anger. With a solid kick under the covers, I force Gwen away and push her to the floor with a loud thud. She gasps, a look of embarrassment settling on her smooth face.

"Sorry," she mumbles with a slurred tone.

"Go to bed," I say a third time, trying to calm my stressed breathing. "We'll talk tomorrow."

It sounds like I'm instructing a dog.

My eyes follow Gwen as she slowly rises to her feet, making her way to the other side of the small room. She crawls into bed, and it doesn't take long before sleep takes her over and I lie staring at the ceiling with my hand around the pendant. *I just want to go home.*

"You have acquired a taste for a thorny rose. How exquisite."

Not now, not again. My heart panics as the voice continues to whisper in my head while my gaze flits over the bedroom and the shadows on the walls circulate, creating nightmarish shadowy figures. I pull the covers up over my head and squint, but the voice keeps getting louder, until it feels like someone's standing beside me, talking into my ear.

"How was it to taste his lips? Were you intoxicated by his power? Did you want it for yourself?"

I toss and turn in bed, putting my hands over my ears.

"What do you want from me?"

I focus on the question in my head, counting to three while slowly breathing in and out.

"I want you in your magical wholeness. In due time, you will give me what I seek. With you by my side, I shall complete my life's work."

"Who are you? Why do you hide behind a voice without a face?"

I take a deep breath as an icy feeling rolls over me and when I exhale, my eyelids fly open. Black gravel under my bare feet makes the soles of my feet ache; a smell of decay; a blood-red crescent moon that casts an eerie hazy light on a firmament, one so different from the gorgeous starry sky that I saw earlier tonight.

"Where am I?" I say out loud.

Panic takes over when I see how my shadow moves strangely before detaching itself from me, slinking away across the ground. Without hesitating for a single second, I chase it with my breath in my throat, trying to reach it with my toes, but it's coiling away like a snake. My feet hurt even more as I trip over the gravel, but I get back up and look around. My gaze lands on my shadow, swirling around a tall, black-clad figure with a face partially hidden by a hood. I can make out pale skin and thin lips.

"Hey! Is it you who speaks to me?" I shout.

I grab the pendant around my neck with one hand, holding it out in front of me.

The man's mouth moves.

"No, I am simply a tool for a greater purpose."

"What's that supposed to mean?"

I take a couple of steps closer, the soles of my feet stinging, and wipe my eyes with the back of my hand. The foul stench in the air causes me to cough. I notice I don't have my glasses on, but I'm able to see everything clearly. In passing, I remember Garren mentioning something about a herald. *Is this him?*

"Who do you work for?" I ask, trying to keep my voice steady.

SHADOW DANCE

"All will be revealed in due time."

"No, I demand to know right now!"

The energy and power within me make my chest and stomach heat up. My mind goes blank, silent. I rush towards the figure while a shrill scream finds its way out of my throat. The air leaves my lungs as I slam into him, and he staggers to the ground. I fall on top of the figure, quickly grabbing him by the collar while shaking him.

"Answer me!" I yell as I push one knee over his chest and blink when I hear him chuckle softly.

Anger bubbles up deep inside—a bitter, poisonous emotion. Forcefully, I tear his hood from his face and gasp as the blood freezes in my veins. Horrified, I throw myself to the side and crawl backwards, lifting the pendant in front of me with a trembling hand.

"Why the shocked face, lass? Did you swallow your newfound courage?"

The man's eyes are sewn shut and yet he directs his face straight at me, as if he knows my exact position. *How can he see what my face looks like?* When he smirks with his lips parted, a pair of long fangs are on display, and flashbacks rumble in my mind. *There are vampires in the upcoming patch for Reign Online, right? Vampires, a new continent, new areas to explore, and a brand-new raid boss said to be the hardest yet. Is this guy a random enemy used as a herald by the boss?*

"Don't come any closer!" I warn, desperately masking the fear in my voice with anger.

With terror in a pounding heart, I gasp again as the man rises with unnatural agility and lunges at me. His long nails almost dig into my shoulders and a scream breaks free from my mouth as I struggle to keep his fangs away from my throat. I push the jewellery against his face and hear him roar as the smell of burnt flesh stings my nostrils. When his hands fly up to his face and the roar turns to a pitiful hissing, I swing the arm holding the necklace and smack him in the temple, knocking him off balance and sending him falling to the side.

Filled with fear edged with fury, I get to my feet, and while the man is crouched on the ground, I deliver a powerful kick to his crotch, grimacing in pain as I pull my foot back. The sound of the air leaving his lungs and the pain he appears to be experiencing stir my anger. *This isn't like me at all. I'm not a violent person.*

"Who do you work for?" I scream.

"He is my messenger."

A strange distant voice reaches my ears and I whirl around to see who's speaking. A man with long raven-black hair in a ponytail and shaved sides watches us. The eyes are intensely red, and he wears a monocle on his right side with an accompanying chain attached to a piercing in his earlobe. Wearing a white poet's shirt with a high collar, a dark waistcoat, and a black coat with white details over it, he gives an aristocratic impression. Heavy boots cover his feet. As I hastily register his features, I see he has somewhat pointy ears, heavily defined cheekbones and jawline, and the gorgeous, androgynous features of a half-elf. *Perhaps he's a half-elf-turned-vampire?*

"Who the hell are you?" I growl, knuckles turning white as I hold the piece of jewellery in front of me.

"Little Saga. I can smell your fear—there is no need to pretend in front of me."

I take a few steps to the side as he speaks to me, preventing the herald on the ground from grabbing hold of my feet should he regain his strength, and putting more distance between me and this other stranger. *Maybe I've read about him online if he mentions who he is.*

"You know my name since you call to me now and then," I say, glaring at him. "Why don't you introduce yourself so we can get to know each other better?"

SHADOW DANCE

"Your presumptuousness is a rarity in my neck of the woods."

The man is holding a staff in one hand that appears to have a magical stone on top of the hilt that glows with a dark purple glow.

"My name is Lysander. It is a pleasure to meet you and not just speak to you through my subordinate. Now that we are touching on the subject of messengers, there is something I must do."

Lysander takes a couple of quick steps towards his crony. He sticks his hand inside a pocket and my eyes follow the moonlight reflecting on the blade of a black dagger. With a swift movement, he plunges it violently into the herald's chest as a soft smile dances across his lips.

Horrified, I take several steps back with my hand over my mouth. Lysander lifts his head from crouching over his writhing, dying messenger, the smile still present.

"He was under strict orders not to touch you. Evidently, it was difficult for him to follow simple instructions. Misconduct must always be punished, without exception."

He stands up and makes a straight line for me whilst extending his hand in my direction. I can see he's wearing all-white gloves, which for some reason feels incredibly bizarre, given what I've just witnessed.

"I will not hurt you, dearie. I could cause you some damage via telepathy, but I believe it would be far more delightful to meet you face to face and enjoy your company to the fullest. That is why I sought you out when you were still at home. Yes, I look forward to seeing your full potential once you have learned to harness the power within. Take the help of the leader of the Order of the Light, he who is their main weapon, and become strong enough that you may give me your gift later."

Do the game's characters have lives of their own? Are they advanced A.I.s? Am I even in Reign Online or in an alternate universe similar to the game?

Confused, I take several steps back.

"S-stay away or I'll burn you with my necklace," I stutter.

"You cannot hurt me with that," Lysander replies, smiling with visible fangs. "I have a little something for you."

"Keep it to yourself! I'm not the least bit interested in being in your debt."

"Ungrateful girl!"

Lysander roars, and cold shivers run down my spine. The red eyes and sclerae turn pitch black, and writhing tentacles with leech-like mouths and wildly flailing eyes tear open his flesh, skin, and to some extent his clothing before surrounding him.

I hear myself shriek as two of the tentacles latch onto my legs under the nightgown, causing me to lose my balance. I kick wildly with my feet to free myself, but to no avail.

"Why do you wish to anger me?" Lysander asks, now with the same calmness in his voice as before, standing astride me as he juggles the staff.

He's close enough for me to see he has a septum piercing, in the design of a small raven skull in his nose.

"You're hurting me!" I scream as tears well up in my eyes.

Panic claws at me and I can feel the foul, cold breath of the other tentacles against my skin. My airways feel tight, and I can't breathe. *Help me.*

The biting tentacles release their grip, withdrawing from me. Lysander closes his eyes and takes a deep breath between gritted teeth as a heavy black mist washes over him for a moment, and when he opens his eyelids, the red gaze is back. Strangely enough, his body and clothes have no signs of damage anymore.

"Please accept my apologies for losing my temper. This truly was not how I expected our first meeting to turn out," he says, crouching next to me. "But perhaps now you are willing to accept my gift."

My legs and feet hurt, and I try to pull away, but the man shakes his head at me. My shadow is back, attached to my body, and I feel whole again.

SHADOW DANCE

One of his hands finds its way up my leg and I panic.

"Leave me alone!" I scream, unable to lift myself from the ground.

"You are bleeding, dearie," he exhales softly and gives me a gentle look. "You must have angered me a great deal. I would advise you not to be so fierce, for your own sake. It can be quite provocative for someone like me, who does not carry themselves with a lot of patience."

I continue to scream as more tears well up in my eyes, terrified of what I fear is about to happen. Lysander lifts my nightgown, drawing circles with the tip of his finger around one of the bite marks on my thigh. He brings his face closer to the wound and my muscles tense in sheer panic as he runs his tongue over it in slow, licking motions.

"It will heal faster now," Lysander explains, seemingly unfazed by my horror. "I must confess you taste absolutely delicious. The spice of magic in your veins truly enhances the flavour profile. Indeed, I wish I could drink more from you. But not yet. Good things come to those who wait."

I fall silent when I feel the tip of his tongue against the other wound and notice how my body trembles. One hand holds the jewellery so tightly it hurts my palm and fingers. I feel exposed, humiliated, and small. A paralysing mix of emotions I know far too well from previous experiences in life.

Lysander pulls the nightgown back down over my legs, before leaning over me. I close my eyes tightly and fight the urge to cry as I turn my face away from him.

"The morning has arrived," he says in a low tone, playing with my fringe with his fingertips. "You probably have important things lined up that require your attention. Until next time, my dear. Be a good lass and get your magic in order and shed no more tears."

In an instant, I'm back in my bed. My breaths are short, rapid, panicked. Slowly, my muscles relax as I realise where I am. The sound of birdsong outside the window and the welcoming rays of the morning sun filter in through the curtains. My forehead is furrowed as I anxiously look down at my feet and check my shoulders. *No wounds. Good.* Slowly pulling up the nightgown, I become cold to the core as I see the bite marks. They're sealed and no longer bleed. *I don't want them on my body. They make me feel dirty.*

My gaze finds its way to the beds on the other side of the room. Helga and Gwen are still asleep, and I glance at the pocket watch on the bedside table. Half past five.

Sleeplessness weighs on my head, and I take a deep breath, looking down at one palm. I'm squinting as I try to summon the magic within. It takes a while, but finally a faint white glow displays from my fingertips, and I nod triumphantly. Carefully, I put my hand to one wound, imagining how heat and positive energy flow from my cells to my leg. The feeling when the wound decreases in size is indescribable. Maybe it's a mixture of pride, strength, and the realisation I can handle things on my own when I set my mind to it.

After the first wound heals, I continue to heal bite mark number two, but tiredness settles in my bones. Halfway through the healing, I pull my hand away. That's enough for now—I can continue later after I've had some food and rest.

Keeping the sounds to a minimum, I get out of bed and prepare to change and get ready for the day. With the book and the sheet of paper from yesterday in my arms, I try to wake Helga after a while, but she mumbles something while Gwen pulls the duvet up over her head and turns herself away. I shrug, closing the door to the room as I leave it and leading my steps towards the canteen, my stomach grumbling loudly. I can't be responsible for anyone but myself right now.

SHADOW DANCE

Days go by and I'm getting used to not having access to the modernities I'm familiar with. With the help of my notes, I've been able to follow the readings Ahriele usually gives, as well as being able to conduct self-studies.

The book describes the history surrounding the humans, the wars they fought, and how the Light guided them to victory. Some pages are covered with detailed, symbolic illustrations. I find myself wanting to learn more, since I've never played a human in *Reign Online*, and make a mental note to study the scripture more closely tonight. Momentarily, my thoughts dance around Garren. I haven't seen him since we kissed that night, and I want to see him again. The thought makes me nervous, although not unpleasantly so.

I can't quite get the image of Lysander out of my mind, and I've been having anxious dreams—though still not quite as terrifying as when he made his telepathic entrance. I'm flipping through the memory bank in my brain to see if I remember reading anything about him. I don't have the faintest idea who he is, and that's unusual, as I study the notes released prior to each patch going live. Did I miss them this time?

Can I even trust the information if this is an alternate universe parallel to the game? Maybe I've just been lucky so far and some of the things I'm familiar with from the game may not be accurate here.

After lunch, all the recruits gather outside in the training grounds together with Ahriele. Everyone has their own armoured shirts in the correct size, while I've been given one that's slightly too big for me. I tug at the leather strap of the helmet as I adjust it on my head and look at the wooden sword at my feet. Bending down to pick it up, feeling its weight in my hand. *It's not terribly heavy.*

Gwen, who has barely spoken to me since the drunken incident several days ago, leans into me as she wearily swings her metal sword, giving me a contrite look.

"Saga, I want to apologise," she mumbles. "I got drunk a while ago and I think I may have acted inappropriately."

"It's fine," I say, giving her a well-meaning smile. "Sorry if you got hurt when I kicked you off the bed."

"What did I miss?" Helga asks with raised eyebrows, and I wave one hand dismissively at her.

"Nothing important," I interject.

Gwen gives me a quick, grateful look and I turn my attention to Ahriele as I hear her speak loudly over the murmur of the students.

"Recruits! Grab your weapons!"

She looks incredibly powerful in her armour with large pauldrons. The blue coat of arms sticks out from under the breastplate and the heavy, shiny gauntlets enhance her already authoritative aura. *She's gorgeous.*

Helga and Gwen choose two training dummies next to each other, and I have a gander around. I spot one next to the guy who was grinning at me a while ago. *Sigh.* I swallow the small lump of anxiety in my throat and stand in front of the training dummy some distance away from him, pretending he doesn't exist.

"Aren't you too old to just begin your training with the Order of the Light, Saga?" I hear him ask sarcastically.

I grip the hilt of the sword and swing it at the training dummy a few times without answering him. In the corner of my eye, I see Eric's ironic smile.

"Twenty-nine years old, unmarried, and fighting with a wooden sword meant for the very youngest."

I turn to face him, telling myself over and over not to get mad. Tilting my head to the side, I give him a sweet smile and put my free hand on my hip.

"I don't know who taught you sense and etiquette, but you need a crash course in it," I say. "You, too, appear to be unmarried, and I can guarantee you no individual would want to touch you with that attitude, even if you were the last person alive."

"How dare you talk to me in such a manner?" he stutters, his cheeks reddening.

I wave the sword playfully, my smile growing wider.

"That's an easy one. It's because you never seem to shut up."

I take a step closer to him, almost leaning into him.

"Where I'm from, I eat rude guys like you for breakfast. So, my recommendation is that you take care of yourself and don't address me again, unless the commander wants us to work together. Understood, little man?"

Eric blinks several times and doesn't make a sound.

"I interpret your silence as a yes," I say boldly.

I turn away from him, taking a deep breath and trying to calm my hands from trembling in anger. *Good job. You don't have to be anxious about standing up for yourself against stupid people.*

From a distance I see Ahriele leading her steps towards us, and mentally, I prepare myself for what she's about to say.

"You two! You don't get paid to stand and talk," she says sternly as she stops in front of us with her hands clasped behind her back.

"My apologies, Commander, but the new recruit creates constant distractions," Eric says, glancing at me. "She appears to be infatuated with me."

I snort in a mocking, short laugh.

"Don't flatter yourself, kid."

"Silence, both of you!"

Ahriele's gaze stops over my chest and for a moment I wonder what she's looking at. Then it dawns on me like the clearest day.

"Falk, come with me," she says briefly, then raises her voice. "The rest of you, keep training while I'm gone."

"Yes, Commander!" the recruits shout in chorus.

Ahriele gives me a stern look and I follow her, my heart pounding wildly.

"Where did you get the necklace?"

Ahriele and I are in a lush courtyard inside the Order of the Light's compound and her voice is brimming with anger.

"It's a gift," I say, doing my best to keep a cool head.

"Impossible," she says, narrowing her eyes at me.

I try to make my voice sound as steady as I possibly can.

"I'm speaking the truth! Why would I lie?"

"Because you're a thief."

"Stop accusing me, Ahriele! You don't know me at all."

For the first time, I mention her name in her presence and she stares at me, the type of look that would strangle one if it could.

"Know your place," she warns in a low tone.

"Whatever."

I don't care about the way she looks down at me right now. Putting my hands to my sides, I step up to her.

"If you don't believe me, why don't we ask the person in question whether or not I stole their necklace?"

"Then let us go."

Ahriele grabs my arm, but I pull away and wag my index finger at her.

"I can walk by myself," I say dryly.

We continue with an invisible taut chain between us and reach the building where the higher-ranking members of the Order of the Light have their offices. For a moment, I glance up at the roof of the building and catch my breath. It's truly massive and seems to rise to the skies, as if to worship a divine power.

I follow Ahriele as she strides confidently through the halls,

SHADOW DANCE

eventually stopping outside Garren's office. A broad-shouldered man in armour with his back against the wall nods at us.

"We're applying for an audience with the grand prior," says Ahriele and gets a nod in response.

The man knocks on the closed door, and I hear a familiar voice.

"Come in."

Ahriele bows her head slightly to the knight, thereafter opening the door and ushering me in unkindly.

Garren appears to be deeply engrossed in various documents in front of him on his desk, including a large map with several strategically placed figures across it. When he looks up and catches sight of me, he appears a little surprised and I think I see something warm in his features.

Ahriele gives me an icy stare prior to pointing at me.

"Grand Prior, pardon the intrusion. But this girl is a thief."

"That's not true at all!" I say defiantly, trying to take my helmet off as I'm sweating, but the leather strap won't cooperate with me.

Garren gets up from his chair and his outfit immediately draws my attention to itself. A white and gold shirt with intricate gusset details at the collar and sleeves, tucked into black pants and a heavy belt hanging at the waist. His feet, protected by a pair of sturdy boots. I find myself unable to tear my eyes from him as he walks up to us and makes my heart flutter faster with his piercing gaze.

"Why does trouble follow you when I'm elsewhere, Falk?" he says softly, his fingers closing around the leather strap under my chin.

Discreetly, I hold my breath as he takes off my helmet and hands it to me while sighing loudly. He turns his attention to Ahriele, and I exhale. He takes a step back to lean against the edge of the desk, grabbing it with both hands.

"She stole nothing," he says curtly. "I offered it to her, and she accepted it."

Ahriele clenches her fists and I see the skin tighten over her jawbones.

"You give away an heirloom that has been in the Roseheart family for generations to this inept girl?" she says angrily. "What's the reason for this?"

"I'm quite good at some things," I mutter, somewhat offended by her remark.

"Nobody told you to speak!"

Ahriele snarls at me over her shoulder and I bite my tongue to keep myself from saying something impulsive.

A dark streak crosses Garren's face as he stares steadily at Ahriele.

"She needed protection, and I provided it to her."

His deep voice causes my mind to go blank for a second. *I'm not even mad at Ahriele anymore.*

"That's not your responsibility, Garren!"

It occurs to me that those two seem to know each other well, at least well enough to dispense with titles and polite phrases altogether. *Classic popcorn moment. If this was happening at home, I would have sent Ambrosia a GIF—ordinary words just won't do.*

"Ahriele, you're in no position to give me orders."

Garren's voice is cold thus far, and the worry lines look menacing.

Ahriele grabs his hand and narrows her eyes at him.

"Are you afflicted by witchcraft? As your childhood friend, I worry about you."

Uh-oh. They've known each other for a long time.

He gives her a slight smile as he frees himself from her grip and then looks straight at me.

"Come here," he says, beckoning to me.

Unsure of what to do, I fiddle with the helmet in my hands and bounce my gaze like a ping-pong ball between them. He tilts his head to the side and extends a hand.

SHADOW DANCE

"Come here, lass."

Hesitantly, I walk up to him. Placing my hand in his, I immediately feel our energies intertwine intensely, almost as if they've been missing each other for the past few days. The white light appears in our palms, and I take a deep breath to steady my thoughts and gain control of the magic flowing within.

"There's no witchcraft involved. Our magics are connected," Garren says, perusing Ahriele's puzzled face. "She may be an outlander, but by the Light, I believe she's here for a reason and I've sworn an oath to protect her for as long as she allows."

Ahriele straightens her back, her features softening.

"Are you smitten with her?" she asks in a low tone.

"That's irrelevant," he replies and lets go of my hand, causing the Light between us to fade away. "It's imperative she's safe with the Order of the Light, and we figure out how the power in her can be used."

Confused, I blink a few times and a stitch of disappointment puts its teeth in me. *What's he talking about? Am I just a magical vessel to be used by them, for their own benefit?* My gaze searches over the spines of the expanse of books on the bookshelf behind Garren and their voices merge into a single jumble. I don't listen anymore. My mind drifts off to mum for some reason. *My beautiful and wise mother; she always has something sensible to say. I could do with some of her wisdom right now.*

I flinch, brought back to reality from my thoughts as Ahriele turns on her heel and walks out of the study. Hesitantly, I start to follow her, but Garren puts a hand on my shoulder.

"One moment, Saga."

"I have to go train with the other students," I mumble anxiously and see how Ahriele closes the door behind her, leaving us alone.

"You can go shortly. I want to talk to you in private."

"Okay," I reply, taking a step back so he doesn't have his hand on me anymore.

Garren watches me while stroking the back of his neck with one hand.

"You appear to be distracted," he says, as if seeing right through me.

I avert my gaze, directing my attention at my shoes while wiggling one big toe.

"No, I'm just tired. I haven't slept well the last few nights."

"Did my words to Ahriele bother you?"

"What do you mean?" I ask, drawing an invisible pattern on the floor with one foot in front of me while holding my helmet under my arm.

"That I merely seek to exploit you for the Order of the Light's gain."

I shrug weakly and avoid looking at him.

"It sounded like that's what you were saying, and I can't say I appreciate it," I say curtly. "I'm fed up with being here. Everyone seems to speak in riddles. You have titles I constantly have to address, and no one speaks a plain language at all. It's confusing."

Frustrated, I clench my jaws and take a deep breath before speaking again.

"I'm the roommate of two ladies who get completely wasted at the inn, and then barge into the room in the middle of the night when I'm trying to sleep. One of them crawled into my bed and almost molested me. And that's not all of it!"

I draw another deep breath and turn my back on Garren. My shoulders feel stiff.

"When I was finally about to get some shut-eye after our last meeting, the voice started speaking to me again. It wouldn't let me sleep. As I confronted it in my head, I found myself in an imaginary place. The herald appeared—it was a vampire. After he attacked me and I hit him with your necklace, his boss showed up. I'm sure you can guess how well that went."

I feel Garren's hand on my shoulder again.

SHADOW DANCE

"I apologise. I didn't ask for your permission to touch you," he murmurs in a feathery voice.

My shoulders become less tense. The touch feels comforting, and I don't mind it.

"It's okay," I mutter, noticing how my thoughts are becoming distracted by his aura.

"What happened when the other one appeared?"

"He told me his name. Lysander. I don't know who he is and don't think I've read about him anywhere. He stabbed his herald to death right before my eyes, before getting chatty. Unfortunately for me, he didn't care much for my attitude."

My voice trails away and Garren's grip on my shoulder tightens a bit.

"Did he hurt you?"

I nod slowly.

"A little. His anger turned him into a monster. Disgusting tentacles with eyes and mouths shot out of his body. I'm not sure how it happened—I was in a state of panic. He knocked me over and two of his tentacles bit my legs. When I expressed my fear, he seemed to repent and reverted to his original form again."

I take a deep breath and steel myself.

"He lifted my nightgown, licked the bite marks, and mentioned I tasted delicious. In other words, he's a vampire, too."

I hear Garren's breathing quicken and he makes me turn to meet his gaze.

"Show me the wounds," he says in a low tone, anger flaring in his eyes.

My heart pounds like a panicked sparrow as I bend down and pull my pant legs up.

"I healed one of the wounds the next morning on my own," I say, barely audibly. "I forgot to heal the other one because my mind was occupied with a million things."

I stand motionless as Garren crouches down before me and touches my thigh with his fingertips. The warmth of his healing energy seeps into my body, causing a calmness to spread as a ripple effect in my mind.

"I'm impressed with your healing abilities, but next time I'd suggest you come to me or seek out one of the priests if you can't reach me," he says as he carefully pulls my pant legs back down.

He looks up at my face, and I desperately try to hold back my emotions.

You haven't contacted me in days, and I don't want to chase you.

"I don't dare to sleep," I say, trying not to show any signs of my state of mind. "Do you have any magic potions that can keep me awake while my body recovers and rests?"

He shakes his golden tresses.

"No. You need actual sleep."

I wipe one eye with the back of one hand and continue.

"Lysander said he didn't want to hurt me much, but this was proof of him and what he's capable of doing. Imagine what he'll do next time he shows up."

We look at each other in silence before I break its surface with my words.

"Are you going to see to it that I remain unharmed, Garren?"

I hang my words in the air to dry as the herald's words of warning regarding the paladin come to mind.

"As long as you allow it, I shall do my utmost." His voice cracks at the edges. "You say you're in love with an image you've created around the elven prince, but you still get closer to me every time we see each other, lass. You never stop dancing in my thoughts, and I meant it when I said I swore an oath to protect you."

I bite my bottom lip for a moment, saying naught.

I must meet Kailunn as soon as possible, somehow. This is getting too messy.

Garren slowly gets up and brushes off his pant legs. His countenance is unreadable and I can't analyse what he's thinking.

"I'm alone," I continue quickly, changing the track of the conversation. "Having roommates doesn't help with diminishing the feeling of loneliness. And now I can't sleep and tell myself I'm home again."

Garren grabs the helmet from me and sets it aside on the desk. With his back to the desk, he grips the top of it and gives me a long look.

"Would you like to spend the night with me?" he asks.

Shocked, I gasp and glare at him.

"What are you saying?" I protest loudly and force myself to lower my voice. "What do you take me for?"

"There's no inappropriate agenda involved," the paladin assures, drumming his fingers against the desk. "As you've probably noticed by now, I'm an honourable man. I presume since the Light flows within both of us and we easily awaken each other's powers, that my energy could offer you peacefulness while you sleep."

"Oh," I mumble sheepishly, feeling stupid that I allowed my thoughts to race. "If I accept your offer, how do I get past the guards without arousing suspicion?"

Garren crosses his arms over his chest.

"Show them your necklace," he replies, nodding towards it. "They won't ask questions."

"That sounds simple."

"Indeed. Things don't have to be more complicated than that."

I nod thoughtfully and can't help but glance at his map on the desk. Memories from *Reign Online* pop into my head and I remember the different country borders. A curiosity about the figures on top of the map sparks inside of me, but I shake my head. There are other things that require my full attention.

It's to my advantage if I accept his offer, both in terms of security and the fact I don't mind his company. Rumours may start to abound, but I don't have time to think about that right now.

"Okay, boss. I accept your generous offer," I say, watching a faint smile spread across Garren's lips. "But don't forget what you mentioned before. No cheeky ideas, or I'll kick you where it hurts."

Garren puts one hand over his chest.

"You have nothing to worry about," he replies, and I think I see a smile in his gaze.

"All right. But I need to get back to my class before I miss too much."

As I turn to leave, his fingers gently close around one of my upper arms.

"Haven't you forgotten something, lass?" he says with a mischievous glint in his eyes as I turn to him again with confusion painted across my face.

He puts the helmet back on my head and places one finger under my chin, forcing me to look up at him as he tightens the leather strap.

"Does that feel good?"

"Yeah," I answer timidly.

"Good. I don't wish to be too rough with you."

Smiling wryly, he gives me a light pat on the helmet, and I glare at him sourly, noticing how my cheeks flush with embarrassment. He knows what to say to get my thoughts—as well as that annoying tingling feeling in my stomach—racing, and it frustrates me. I'm starting to find it enjoyable. *Think about Kailunn, damnit.*

"I shall see you tonight after eight o'clock, recruit," he murmurs in my ear.

My heart skips a beat as his warm breath caresses my eardrum, and he opens the door for me.

CHAPTER SIXTEEN

Ahriele Darby

You're sitting next to me in the inn with some of the other commanders, and yet, you're incredibly far away. Your eyes look at me from time to time, but their gazes are restrained, and I can't read what you're thinking. Why are you so distant?

You and I have always been able to converse with each other ever since we were little. When my brother died, you took his place, always holding my hand whenever I cried until my tears dried. When I was five years old and my beloved dog got killed by the wolves in the area, it was you who donned an old, rickety tin helmet, armed yourself with a flimsy wooden sword, and patrolled our yard with a sheet tied around your neck for a cloak, all while your personal guard, hired by your family, stood at a distance, keeping a watchful eye on you. You were only eight years old and even then, I could see the roses in your heart and sense your lion-like courage.

You come from a wealthy, reputable family in trade and warfare in the name of the Order of the Light, and yet you spent time with me and my mother, we who lived on the outskirts of Riverside. The girl without a father, and with a mother with an illness that made her bedridden. An illness which wasn't visible on the outside of the body, but which took all the strength from her when my brother had left us. I was the girl who picked flowers and berries in the forest from morning to night, selling them to support my mother and I. She who washed people's clothes in the river, mucked in stables and fields, and worked as a seamstress when she was only ten years old. I don't know where I'd be today without our ties of friendship.

I raise my mug to my mouth and sip on its contents while politely pretending to listen to one of the paladins telling a story. The past few days have been demanding and the new recruit has been testing my patience greatly. One second, she's clumsy and inept, and the next she does something which surprises me and gives me a glimpse of the power hidden within her—when she's not bickering with Eric, that is.

One of my hands is placed on my forehead as I sigh silently. Garren gives me a light pat on the shoulder and tilts his head to the side, giving me a scrutinising look.

"Is there something on your mind?"

"It's nothing," I reply as I give him a curt smile.

I see him nod at me before he pulls out his pocket watch and casts a glance at it.

It's unusual for Garren to spend time with a larger group of people after work. Judging by his poor appetite and the fact he has barely touched his wine, I'm assuming he's distracted, and he's only here out of politeness.

"And what occupies your mind?" I ask.

"Absolutely nothing. Everything's in order," he says and winks at me while taking a small bite of the food in front of him.

SHADOW DANCE

"As I mentioned before—you're a lousy liar," I mumble and can't help but smile again when he grins.

It's wonderful to see him carry a genuine display of emotion on his visage; these days he doesn't often have such a smile. The weight of responsibility that rests on his shoulders must outweigh any true display of joy.

A bard and her companions play music with swirling notes that find their way into my ears with playful, invisible feet. The bard's voice reminds me of a bird singing beautifully, one which awakens curiosity, joy, and sadness within. She uses my heart as her most tender instrument and I lose myself in her singing for a few minutes while watching her in silence. She certainly is as beautiful as her passionate singing voice.

As I sip on my ale once more, three figures enter the inn. Immediately, I recognise Helga and Gwen, along with a third individual. When the figure lowers its hood, I see it's my troublesome recruit. Saga exudes uncertainty as she walks next to the other two women. Gwen, holding her arm, pulls her close and whispers something in her ear and Saga nods silently as they make their way to the bar. Out of the corner of my eye, I can see Garren has caught sight of them and is straightening his back a little. He avoids staring, but throws glances in their direction at regular intervals. An expression rests in his eyes I don't recognise. It reminds me of a lion hiding in the grass whilst spying on something, but not to kill it.

The bard finishes her song, turning her attention to the recruit. Saga catches sight of her as she beckons her over, but she doesn't move from her spot; a steady, nervous smile on her lips can be seen from a distance. She's holding a mug of water she's sipping from while the other two are busy imbibing alcohol. As the bard and her entourage rise and lead their steps towards the party, I notice Garren's jaws clenching.

Saga's uncertainty seems to be reinforced when another woman from the bard's group leans forward and speaks to her. I prick up my ears curiously, fervently wishing I could hear the words being exchanged between them. The bard puts an arm around Saga's shoulders and judging by the hand movements, she's in the middle of enthusiastically describing something, while the newcomer seems visibly bothered by the touch. Finally, I see Saga burst out laughing while shaking her head with one hand over her mouth and putting the mug down. She says something to the bard, then gives her both thumbs up. *What words are they sharing?*

My new student shoots them a wide smile as she slips out of the woman's grasp when they bid farewell. She finds an empty chair in a corner and sits down on it, lightly shuffling her feet a few times and appearing to look at her shoes while Gwen and Helga laugh out loud at something a female dwarf next to them just uttered.

An indescribable feeling spreads inside me when I look at Saga and see how lost she is, even though she's dressed like almost anyone. Pity, perhaps? Remembrance of when I was new to Whitekeep in my younger days?

I see how her fingers fiddle with the chain around her neck, the pendant hidden under her blouse. A dark-clad figure approaches her, causing her eyes to widen. Garren takes a deep breath and puts his cutlery away, but before he gets up to his feet, I stretch my hand towards him, resting it over his arm and forcing him to look me in the eye.

"Wait," I say quietly, doing my utmost to avoid catching the attention of the other knights.

His gaze is stern, but he sinks back into his seat, jaws still clenched. I glance at Saga again and see her lifting herself up from the seat. She appears confused as she starts following the hooded figure, hurrying out of the inn together.

"Has no one taught the lass not to accompany strangers?" Garren murmurs in a dangerously low tone.

"I'll handle this," I say softly and give him a reassuring pat on the arm. "Don't worry, brother."

Stepping out of the inn and being embraced by the chilly night air, I pull my coat tightly around me. My gaze sweeps around the area, noticing an alley I don't usually fixate on. On silent feet, I walk in its direction, taking care to not reveal myself as I hide and listen.

"Cut the bullshit. You sought me out at the inn, so what do you want from me?" I hear Saga say with defiance in her voice. "Don't think for a second you scare me."

Peeking out from my hiding spot, I see her face to face with Cináed. Or rather, her tiptoeing and glaring up at him with her arms crossed over her chest.

"I'm not here to scare you. However, I have a proposal."

Cináed looks at her with a dark smile and puts his hands to his sides. Saga's eyes seem to catch fire.

"What are you talking about?"

"You need to do something for me."

"I'll kick you between the legs," she warns. "And I'll scream if you try anything."

"My goodness. Calm down, lassie."

He leans forward towards Saga, so close the tips of their noses almost touch. Her eyes narrow as she takes a step back.

"Xerxi Arrowsong, twin brother of Xanjou. They work for the warlord, Vincent Thurston. Xerxi caught my eye many moons ago and I can read what's written in his heart; my beloved forest elf is capricious. It doesn't matter how much I try to make him purr. Sometimes he comes to me and often he keeps his distance, just to tease. I can't stand it anymore."

"That's not my problem," I hear Saga say, and I can't help but smirk momentarily. "You're an adult. Deal with it yourself."

"I have a distinct feeling the Order of the Light and Thurston's Silver

Wardens will need to work together to defeat the black magic that's ravaging the Highlands before it can spread," Cináed continues, ignoring her spiteful tone. "Most certainly, they will have to make use of you, as you're magically charged, otherwise you wouldn't be kept under their wing."

"I'm not a weapon," she says bluntly, pushing her chin into the air.

"They'll use you no matter how much you fight back, lassie. Do you think the grand prior visits the bathhouse with you due to boredom? He's a busy man."

I swallow hard and let the new information sink in. *Oh, Garren. You have lost yourself and become ensnared.*

"He does it out of kindness," replies Saga, turning her back on Cináed.

"You should learn how to read signals. That lion with the roses around your neck you try to hide—that's his, is it not?"

Saga turns to Cináed again, glaring angrily at him.

"So what?"

"He expects you to help the Order of the Light, which is the reason why you have his protection. The day you turn your back on him, you haven't only denied his feelings but also denied his faith, and he won't look upon it kindly. Believe me when I say the man's married to his faith."

A moment of silence passes and I can hear my rapid heartbeat in my ears.

"Tell me what you want," hisses Saga, but her hard expression has softened.

"I want you to influence the grand prior so I can accompany you on the expedition to the Highlands. You can use my cunning and my daggers in good conscience. In return, I finally get to spend time with my beloved in the Silver Wardens."

"What would happen if I refused to comply?"

Cináed produces a dagger seemingly out of nowhere, grabs Saga's shoulder, and forcefully pushes her into a wall as he presses himself against her, putting the sharp edge of the dagger to her throat.

"Listen, lassie. My trusty weapon here hasn't tasted blood in a while. But your blood is magical, and I could get a pretty penny to bleed you. Repeatedly. You have no family here that would miss you."

"I can't influence the grand prior—I'm not that kind of person."

Saga's voice is edged with panic. *Should I step in?*

"Little, innocent Saga. You have some external beauty and he's most likely not going to be entirely blind to it, considering he doesn't belong to the clergy. If you dress in something cheeky, I'm certain he'll see the Light more clearly in you before he has time to finish his evening prayer."

"No, it's not right," she stutters, her shoulders trembling. "I can only talk to him and hope he listens."

"Be sure to do it as quickly as possible."

Cináed quickly puts the dagger back and gives her a light pat on the cheek.

"We shall meet again anon. Don't disappoint me, girlie."

Cináed melts into the shadows, and a heavy atmosphere settles over the alley. I hear Saga's short, quick breaths as I hide in the darkness and notice she stays motionless for quite some time after the man has disappeared. Slowly, her hand finds its way up to her throat, trembling as she gently rubs where the edge of the dagger kissed her skin. She sinks down into a crouching position with her face buried in her hands. For a moment, I want to approach her when I hear her crying, but I reconsider and stay hidden. I don't know her well enough yet and am unsure how she would react if she finds out someone has been eavesdropping on a private conversation.

"It'll work out," I hear her mumble shakily to herself. "I just have to play it cool."

She takes several deep breaths. The act of controlled breathing seems to calm her down and after a while, she wipes her eyes with her sleeve and gets up on her feet.

She doesn't notice me as she walks past my hiding place. I find myself feeling somewhat sorry for her. She appears vulnerable and the weight on her shoulders seems like it could tear her apart.

Following her on silent feet, I see her walking up the street in the direction of the Order of the Light's headquarters rather than going back to the inn; head bowed, eyes fixed on the ground. She has her arms wrapped around herself; perhaps a soothing embrace.

My heartbeat quickens as I note a familiar tall figure joining her. She turns to the other in surprise, and I see him gently touching her upper arm with his fingertips. She doesn't shy away. They walk next to each other. Discreetly, she moves closer to him, almost as if seeking comfort, and I smile sadly to myself as Garren gives her a deep look.

You and I have always been able to converse with each other, my brother. But now you have chosen to close the door to your soul.

CHAPTER SEVENTEEN

Saga Falk

"Thanks for letting me stay here," I say as the paladin unlocks the front door of a mediaeval-style townhouse and lets me inside. "It feels safe knowing someone else is with me if, or rather when, Lysander shows up again."

We're in another part of the headquarters, somewhere I haven't been before. The buildings are within high walls, and had I not known we're still within the Order of the Light's territory, I would have probably guessed it's a separate place.

"You're welcome," Garren replies with a curt nod.

He locks the door behind us. I see nothing in the darkness where I stand with my few possessions in my arms. A rustling sound finds its way into my ears as he reaches for something, and a small dancing flame spreads a faint warm light around him when he ignites a match. When he brings the candle flame to an oil lamp, the lit-up home is suddenly much more homely. While he goes off to light another, I put my things down on a small wooden bench next to one wall and take off my shoes and coat.

My eyes begin to take in all the details. This townhouse is one big room with what looks like a kitchenette and fireplace on the left side of the entrance. It is ascetically furnished—a simple dining table with two chairs, a desk with an accompanying chair, and a bed on the right side with two bedside tables. There's no carpet on the cold wooden floor. At the end of the bed, I notice an instrument case. *His violin.*

"Make yourself at home," Garren says, pointing to a door behind him. "The washroom is over there."

"Thank you," I say softly.

Uncertainty is taking me over. Seeing another closed door next to the other, I don't give it much thought. I select some of my clothes, bringing them with me into the washroom.

Leaning my back against the closed door, I draw air into my lungs to the point it seems as if they're about to expand permanently before exhaling again. Cináed's words ring in my head while I wonder if I was right to accept Garren's offer to stay here. *He's a man, and I have a hard time trusting them.* I shake my head, getting annoyed with myself. It's not right to tar all men with the same brush, and I don't want to delve into sad memories. I must focus on surviving and getting home safe and sound.

I look at myself in the tall mirror. Thoughtfully, I play with my fringe a little and adjust the glasses over the bridge of my nose. My skin looks pale and tired, and I think back to the Korean skin care routine I used to indulge in when I had enough energy—and enough money—to do so. For a second, I hold my breath, feeling ice-cold inside. I'm going to meet Kailunn looking like this. *Shit.* I have to wash my hair beforehand and make it look reasonable once it dries. It's too bad I didn't bring my make-up with me when I ended up here.

SHADOW DANCE

With a silent sigh, I change and look at myself again. It's chilly in this residence, so I wear my pink jumper over the nightgown and necklace. It might look slightly odd being dressed in this fashion, but I prefer to be warm and comfortable.

Cautiously, I open the bathroom door and cast a quick glance through the crack before stepping out. A faint warmth spreads through the room from the lit fireplace. Garren has changed into more casual attire and is sitting at the dining table, set with two platters. There's a bowl of fruit in the middle of it and my mouth waters when I see something similar to yellow grapes.

He looks up and shoots me a smile.

"Are you hungry?" he asks.

Settling on the other chair and nodding, I place my palms expectantly against the table top and drum on it with my fingertips.

"It looks good," I say, pointing to the yellow fruit. "Are these grapes?"

"Sunberries. They're quite unusual at this time of year—the farmers must have had a good harvest."

He takes a bite of an apple, which he has cut into pieces, and I pull off one of the round sunberries. Lifting it to my nose, I turn and twist it, trying to guess what it smells like, but it has no scent. Garren chuckles after I pop the fruit into my mouth and scrunch up my face.

"You could have mentioned it's sour," I say, glaring coldly at him.

"It may be, but it's said to be good for the body and the mind," he replies and tilts his head to the side.

I mutter something indistinct and take another one. It's moreish, despite the sour taste.

We continue to eat for a while without exchanging more sentences while the pleasant warmth rises in the room. Eventually I sweat, so I pull the jumper over my head, hang it over the back of my chair, and adjust my nightgown and necklace. Garren's gaze sweeps over me and lingers on my face. I can't tell what he's thinking and feel flustered, so I clear my throat and decide to break the silence.

"Garren, you'll never guess what happened at the inn," I begin.

Curiously, he raises an eyebrow and I continue.

"A bard approached me, telling me she has heard rumours about the mysterious and potentially fire-breathing vegan who has joined the Order of the Light. She mentioned she might write a song about me!"

"You've already gained admirers."

He smiles and wipes his mouth with a napkin. A mysterious streak appears in his eyes.

"When I met you earlier tonight, had you been crying?"

I look down at my plate and shrug weakly.

"Maybe."

"Did someone upset you?"

I take a deep breath and fiddle with the chain around my neck.

"Do you remember the guy who came up to us in the bathhouse?"

"The foul-mouthed Cináed? Yes, unfortunately. He leaves such a negative impression that it's difficult to forget about his squalid existence."

"He sought me out, asking to travel with us on an expedition to the Highlands, as he believes the Order of the Light and the Silver Wardens will need to join forces against the dark magic which runs rampant there."

"What's the reasoning behind it?"

I run my fingers through my hair.

"Apparently, Cináed has a boyfriend in the army. He wants to spend more time with him, since the guy's a bit too aloof for his taste."

"The Order of the Light will not be working with a thief," Garren remarks firmly.

I clear my throat again and scratch the back of my neck nervously.

"He asks to join us," I say again, thinking about how best to phrase myself. "He claims he has useful abilities in battle, and it would be beneficial for us to make use of his skill set."

The paladin stares at me. However, he's submerged in his own thoughts, and his gaze runs straight through my body. His silence worries me, and I rub my hands together nervously.

"Please, Garren," I say, doing my best to catch his attention.

I get up from the chair, walk over to him, and he swims out of his thoughts, breaking the surface of the thought pattern. Carefully, I put a hand over his arm.

"Please," I say again. "You know I've met him, or rather his fictitious self, before. I think he might be useful."

Garren's hand slips over mine, and a white glow appears between them for a brief moment. His gaze draws me down into its depths.

"I reluctantly agree," he says. "If he falls in battle, I won't have to see his face again."

Sighing in relief, I decorate my lips with a smile, keeping myself from focusing on his last sentence. *I'm being more selfish than I'm comfortable with right now, but I must think about myself. I must survive.*

I should withdraw my hand. Instead, I continue standing there, finding myself enjoying the warmth from his touch as he runs his thumb over the back of my hand.

"To imagine these dainty hands hide such power," he says, smiling softly. "You truly are an enigma, Saga."

"I'm happy as long as no one thinks I'm a witch and burns me at the stake," I answer and let out a nervous laugh.

Garren looks concerned.

"Is that a standard procedure where you come from?" he asks, and I can almost taste the disgust in his tone.

"Not now. Many of our philosophers and those who shaped our now modern worldview were mocked, tortured, and then punished with death in the most brutal ways you can imagine. All this simply because they had a different view of what the world looked like. I feel so terribly sad when I think of them, of how they were tormented by other people who accused them of being heretics."

A melancholy smile appears on my lips, and I fall silent for a moment while my thoughts gather. Garren continues to caress my hand and I wipe my eye with one sleeve.

"And what is your worldview?" he asks, curiosity edging his voice.

I feel my shoulders tense up.

"I believe it's significantly different from yours," I answer and laugh nervously as I lower my gaze and slowly pull my hand to me. "We don't need to touch on that subject."

"I'm keen to learn more about you."

Garren leans in to me as he looks up at my face. Screaming internally in surprise by the intensity with which he stares at me, I cling to a mental image of Kailunn, lest I reach out and tuck back one of the paladin's hair tresses.

"I saw something peculiar after we shared a kiss," he continues.

My ears perk up and curiosity wins me over.

"What was it?" I ask as the knight stands up and motions for me to follow.

"Take a seat over there."

A little hesitantly, I settle down on the bed. The mattress is soft, and the bedspread caresses my legs pleasantly. I wiggle my toes, watching Garren pull the chair out from his desk and straddle it with his arms over the back of it, before he meets my gaze once more.

"I'm a man of faith," he says, thoughtfully scratching the beard on one cheek. "My life is devoted to the Light. However, what I saw at our meeting…"

He falls silent for a moment, and I feel worry gnawing inside, causing me to press my lips together.

SHADOW DANCE

"I saw things I should reject. My faith demands it. At the same time, I can't deny my eyes rested on you as you were surrounded by figures which I presume were human, at least visually. I have seen nothing quite like it before. Everything around you glittered as stars and crystals of the night, and it appeared as if I watched you through a cracked barrier of some description."

I take a deep breath and run my hand through my hair.

"So, you're curious about my worldview," I say quietly. "All right, then. I've done deep dives into the larger religions where I come from, both in school and as an adult, and over the years I've come to understand I believe in a higher plane—I believe in the universe. Those figures you saw? I call them my guardian angels without wings, for lack of a better word. I saw them for the first time when I was a little girl. They were at the end of my bed one night when I woke up, and it didn't terrify me. I simply looked back at them calmly and when they disappeared, I went back to sleep, as if what I had got a glimpse of was the most normal thing in the world."

I can't help but smile weakly.

"Now you've seen them too. It feels strange, as if you've experienced something for my eyes only. It's amazing they followed me here."

Garren gives me a long look in silence. The light and shadows dance across his features and I can see his brain working at full speed, processing what I've just shared with him.

"One of them touched your arm," he says softly, raising one eyebrow as I give him a wide smile.

"Yeah, the one with blond hair. He shows up from time to time. And I have to admit that I, too, saw something after our kiss."

Nervousness surfs in my stomach, but the sentence has been spoken, lingering in the air between us, and I can't take the words back. I lightly pat the mattress in front of me and watch him get up straight away. The wooden legs of the chair make a loud scraping sound as he pushes it back against the desk, before taking his seat where I just had my hand. As the thoughts swirl in my head, I take a deep breath, pointing to his forehead.

"You had another eye, shining in gold, on your forehead and I saw you sink down to the ground. Those who believe in it call it the third eye. Others might call it weird."

A moment of silence passes between us, and my eyes trace his cheekbones and lips as discreetly as I can.

"Shall we put the theory to the test again?" he asks as he stretches his back a little.

"What do you mean?"

"I seek more clarity," he elaborates and my gaze catches on his beautiful, long eyelashes as he looks away from me. "In my prayers, I have asked the Light for an answer to what I witnessed, but I haven't received one as of yet. Mayhaps the reason is that you're not from here, even though you have, within you, the same magical energy I carry."

I'm well-aware I shouldn't listen to the tingling sensation in my stomach; I should keep clinging to the image of Kailunn in my head until I get to meet him. Still, I find myself placing my hands in Garren's, feeling the warmth of his skin against my fingertips and palms and the magic sensation in my chest spreading its heat like wildfire throughout my body. I blink as my eyes begin to glow and see him turn his gaze towards me, the same glow in his. Shyly, I lean forward and press a gentle kiss on the corner of his mouth, watching the extra eye appear on his forehead.

Then he emerges before me, my guardian angel. The one I come to think of in difficult times, the one who often comforts me when I need the most support, when even thoughts of Kailunn don't help. He caresses my left cheek, and without hearing a voice, I'm certain he's talking to me. I listen with my heart as Garren turns his head, looking straight at the nameless one.

It feels like an eternity has passed, but in reality, it's most likely a

SHADOW DANCE

matter of seconds. The light around us pulses and fades away, disappearing into the shadows of the room. The guardian angel has taken his leave and I suck air into my lungs as I lift my glasses and rub my eyes. Garren sits with his hand on his head, his eyes closed. He gives the impression of being in pain. I focus on trying to keep my energy in check and not activate it as I gather my courage and place my hands against his cheeks.

"Are you all right?" I worry, my conscience weighing heavy with guilt.

I'm the one who caused this. *It's my fault.*

Garren opens his eyes and shoots me a weak smile.

"I'll recover quickly. I must confess you're the first individual who has had this effect on me."

"It doesn't sound like something positive," I mutter, lifting my hands away, but he puts his palms over them and places them on his cheeks again.

"I saw him," he says, stroking me with his thumbs. "He spoke to me without using a voice. It was akin to when the Light communicates with me."

I shouldn't ask, but the curiosity is too strong.

"What did he say?"

Garren shakes his head as I pull my hands back, and he smiles wryly.

"It would be a sin to reveal the words," he replies, chuckling when I glare at him. "The conversation was private in nature."

"You tease," I mutter, finding myself leaning closer to him. "Watch out so I don't smooch you again. Who knows what other visions you might get next?"

Congratulations, Saga. What an absolute mess you've got yourself into.

The pupils in Garren's eyes dilate, the heat from his gaze washing over me. For some reason unbeknownst to me, I like having this effect on him.

"I'd welcome them with open arms if it means you're close to me," he says softly as he cups my face with his hands.

"You speak as if you're falling in love," I mutter unsteadily.

"I won't deny the fact that I'm drawn to you. You fascinate me."

"You barely know me," I counter wittily. "The flame which burns twice as bright, burns half as long."

"And you don't know Prince Sunseeker. Despite this, you feel the need to be faithful to him."

Garren gently touches my fringe with his fingertips. *He has a point.*

"But it's not the same thing," I say, just to have something to say and not think about the fact that I enjoy his touch and the attention he's giving me.

"Correct," he replies, smiling softly. "It certainly isn't the same thing. I'm not a fantasy created by your imagination."

This man has a way with words. I sigh quietly and close my eyes as the thoughts scratch inside my cranium. My brain says one thing and the heart wants something else. I'm not used to this.

"Would you like me to move?" I hear him ask.

"No, stay." I shake my head, my skin drinking the warmth of his fingertips as he gently touches my cheek.

"I have no bold plans," he continues as I slowly open my eyes. "And if you want me to stop touching you, you just need to say so."

"You may continue," I mutter, feeling pleasantly dull.

Garren puts his fingertips to my forehead and for a moment the white light appears in his eyes, before disappearing as quickly as it first appeared. An unusual sense of calm spreads through me.

"Hey," I murmur. "The thing you mentioned about us being drawn to each other. There's nothing wrong with it, right?"

"I see nothing wrong with it. Despite sharing the same faith as the clergy, I'm not bound by their shackles," he replies and smirks wryly. "If you worry about the smallest thing, you'll get deep worry lines, just like mine."

His tone is gentle, and I can't help but giggle at his words.

"Your wrinkles give you character," I profess.

SHADOW DANCE

I watch Garren in the dim light of the oil lamps and the small fireplace as he enters my soul with his gaze. My heart is pounding; the blood is rushing in my ears as I slowly lie down with my head against the pillow and give him a shy look. A feeling of awkwardness makes me more timid when he gives me a weak smile.

"Not to worry, Saga. I won't hurt you or let anyone else do so," he says.

Carefully, he takes off my glasses and places them on the bedside table. My stomach tingles when his fingertips touch me.

"It looked uncomfortable."

"You sure are observant," I mumble.

Both of our energies seem to be under control. No third eyes.

He surveys me, as if to make sure I'm comfortable. As my nervousness shapeshifts into a shy smile, his somewhat concerned expression lights up.

"I want to take this opportunity to let you know I didn't offer for you to sleep in my abode due to selfishness," he explains. "I aim to protect you for as long as you feel you need it."

"I know," I answer. *This, however, is a bonus.*

I gather the courage to rest my hand against his chest, feeling his fast heartbeat against my palm. *Maybe it's not just me who's nervous.* With my heart fluttering at the same rapid pace as his, I crawl a little closer, shutting my eyes as he strokes my hair lightly. I miss my life in Malmö, but it seems I've found some comfort amidst the misery of getting lost in time and space. A whisper leaves my lips.

"Good night, Garren."

"Sleep well, lass."

CHAPTER EIGHTEEN

Ahriele Darby

I know it's late, but I must talk to him. Pulling my coat tighter around me, I knock on the familiar front door. The curtains are drawn, and I can't hear anything. Has he gone to bed?

A faint clicking sound finds its way into my ears. I take a step back when I hear the lock open and see Garren's drowsy face peering at me. His hair is tousled.

"Sister? What's occurring?" he asks, his worry lines deepening.

"We need to talk," I say quickly and push my way in under his arm.

"There's something you should know," he whispers, locking behind us.

"Why are you talking so quietly?"

I take off my shoes and set them aside. My eyes fall on the bed and worry creates knots in my stomach. A small figure with the covers pulled almost completely over her head, and I recognise those dark brown strands of hair sticking out. Quickly, I turn my head to meet Garren's gaze.

"Brother, what's the meaning of this?" I ask with my arms crossed over my chest.

"Sit down, but keep the tone of the conversation low. She's finally sleeping."

As we settle down at the dining table, I clench my hands and hiss my next words.

"Has she ensnared you to the point where you take her to your bed?"

"Ahriele!" Garren's voice is low but stern, making me lean back a little in my chair. "To calm your misguided concerns, Saga and I aren't involved in such a way. And if we were, it would have been no one's concern but ours."

I put one hand over the table top and lean towards him.

"She's like a charged magic weapon, completely out of control," I say. "Furthermore, have you forgotten your position in the Order of the Light? People will speak ill about the two of you."

"It doesn't bother me in the slightest," he replies curtly, and the shadows dancing over his face enhance his mirthless expression. "She's in contact with whoever I believe summons black magic in the Highlands. He forces his way into her consciousness."

His sternness seems to lose its leaves, and rosehips of softness appear in his eyes.

"She's afraid of sleeping alone. If you were in the same position, you, too, would have offered her help."

He puts his palm over the back of my hand, locking his eyes onto mine.

"Your heart is kind, sister. I can understand why you're suspicious, but please control your emotions. Constant nightmares haunt her. Truth be told, she needs to be taught how to control the Light, lest she hurts herself or others."

When a faint whimpering sound from the bed reaches my ears,

SHADOW DANCE

Garren gets up quickly and rushes away from me. I watch him lean over her as he strokes her hair.

"Saga," he says, his voice lowered to a hush.

One of his hands gleams with a white glow, and carefully, he turns her over. He puts his hand to her forehead, whispering a silent prayer with his eyes closed.

"Her place should be with the priests," I say as I stand up and walk over to them.

"That's out of the question. She has expressed that she wishes to stay with me."

Garren opens his eyes and his hand ceases to glow as Saga coughs.

"I can't breathe," she says in a choked voice, and Garren pulls her into his arms as he strokes her hair again.

"Don't be afraid," he says gently, and her laboured breathing returns to normal.

"What's the matter with her?" I ask.

Saga's worried gaze flits around the room for a while before it lands on me, while her hands cling to Garren's nightshirt.

"Hey, Ahriele," she stammers and gives me a forced smile. "Sorry—Commander."

"How are you faring, Falk?"

I settle down opposite them and watch her blush as she lets go of Garren, shifting herself to the side and adding some distance between the three of us.

"It was just a nightmare," she replies, before smiling confusedly. "I'm okay now. What brings you here at this time of day?"

"I saw you with Cináed and I thought I should convey this to the grand prior."

I quickly bite my tongue, feeling callous. I didn't even give her a minute to recover from whatever was going on inside her.

"Is that so?" she says, her cheeks turning even redder. "Did you spy on me?"

"No, I have better things to spend my time with. But I know Cináed's rough around the collar."

Out of the corner of my eye, I see Garren giving me a grim look and Saga nervously fiddles with my brother's family heirloom around her neck.

"Did you hear our conversation?"

It's clear she's trying to steady her voice.

"Yes," I answer as neutrally as I can, noting how tense my shoulders are.

"If you must know, I already told the grand prior of my meeting with him."

She falls silent for a moment, her gaze sharp upon glaring at me with renewed courage.

"Then you must have heard I won't plan on taking advantage of him, which seems to be something that's playing on your mind."

I clasp my hands at my sides.

"You seem to have found your tongue again, for you're not afraid to speak to your superior in this brazen way," I say.

"This isn't brazen at all," she murmurs, her upset voice sinking into my bones. "What's rude is you implying I use my body to get what I want. Women should support each other and not drag their fellow sisters down."

"Calm yourselves." Garren interjects quickly, and I see how he gently places his hand over Saga's bare knee. "The commander worries about you."

"Obviously, all she cares about is you and your reputation, like I'd tarnish it somehow," she mutters, opening her mouth again, but is silenced when Garren strokes her knee with one thumb.

We stare at each other for what feels like an eternity, my recruit and I.

"Are you in love with Garren?" she asks.

A sneering laugh finds its way out of my throat.

SHADOW DANCE

"Such a ridiculous question!" I stifle the rest of the laughter and shake my head as Garren groans with his hand to his forehead. *Foolish girl. Only women appeal to me.* "He and I are practically siblings, and thus I care about who he spends his time with."

Saga leans forward towards me, her eyes dark like thunderclouds.

"First of all, he can make his own sensible choices, given that he's an adult. Secondly, he makes me feel safe."

"Ladies," Garren mumbles, and I notice the colour has risen in his cheeks. "No need to bicker."

"She actually made me forget about my nightmare for a short while by arguing with me. Maybe I should thank her instead," she mutters.

I note how Saga's fingers find their way to his hand on her knee and intertwine with his, seemingly unconsciously. I stand up, shooting a sharp gaze at Garren as I cross my arms over my chest.

"This is an utterly foolish idea," I say curtly, pointing at them. "She's too different. Brash, behaves strangely, and has proven to be inept at most things so far. Her heart isn't in the right place to walk the path of the Light. Your age difference is evident in the way she behaves, and it's clear you're on two completely different levels."

"Ahriele, what has got into your mind?"

Garren sighs as he looks at me with tiredness overlaid in his eyes, and a pang of guilt hits my soul.

"What do you know about my heart?" Saga says firmly whilst slowly standing up. "Yeah, I'm lousy when it comes to physical strength. I may not share your faith, but I believe in what lives within me. This thing which you call the Light; where I come from, I would probably call it something else if we had something similar."

She pats herself on the chest.

"Just because I haven't quite adjusted to your life yet doesn't mean I'm completely useless. If you had come to my world with all its technology—the cars, bikes, aeroplanes, and the lights from neon signs—would you still have the same opinion about someone who's different? Or would you rather have an honest, caring person show you understanding and security, as Garren does? He has shown me what a true gentleman he is."

Saga gestures at him for a second with her hand, her eyes fixed on him, and I can't tell what's hiding in her expression. Garren's eyes widen slightly.

"I'm drawn to him, the one you call your brother," she says as she turns her face to me again. "If you demand an explanation from me, I can't give you one. My heart is split right now, but the fact remains, I feel good around Garren in a way I've never experienced before. He has watched over me all evening, without a thought of taking advantage of someone who's vulnerable. When anxiety and panic took hold of my whole being, he was there and took care of me. He did it without questioning why I was acting strange or why I snapped at him. In fact, he reminds me of a lighthouse which spreads light in the night, guiding the lost and making sure they don't collide with anything."

Her dark brown eyes take on a melancholy veil.

"So, Commander. As you can see, you know nothing about my heart. I suggest you be humbler the next time you talk to someone you don't know, because you have no idea what their background is or what feelings are hiding in the corners of their hearts. Now, if you two will excuse me, I need to be by myself for a few minutes."

My mouth is dry as the deserts in the south. I'm not sure what to say when Saga makes her way past me on silent feet and shuts the door to the washroom behind her.

"Perhaps we should wait with the proper continuation of our conversation until tomorrow," Garren says, his gaze firmly fixed on the closed door.

SHADOW DANCE

"You're probably right," I mutter, feeling awkward—something I don't normally experience.

A sigh escapes Garren's lips and when he looks at me, his wrinkles seem to have deepened further. I want to wrap my arms around him, the way we always used to hug each other when we were little, and hear his comforting words. However, it's plain as day his thoughts are with someone else.

"Ahriele, I appreciate you showing concern. But I prefer you don't speak harshly to Saga, especially when off duty. She isn't well."

Garren's voice is hushed, and he gives me a weak smile.

"She won't take your place, my sister."

He gets up and walks towards me. When he pulls me into his arms, it appears my brother is back again, the little boy who patrolled the yard wearing his helmet and a sheet for a cloak.

I sigh quietly and wrap my arms around him tightly while hiding a tear which has appeared in the corner of my eye. Relief washes over me, and with it submerges the rage and anxiety that previously threatened to consume me.

CHAPTER NINETEEN

Garren Roseheart

No sounds are heard from inside the washroom when I put my ear to the door. Carefully, I knock and call her name as softly as I can.

"Saga. You can come out now."

I lean my back against the wall next to the door frame, waiting. A moment passes in silence, until I hear a faint rustling sound and light footsteps approaching the door. It creaks slightly as it opens slowly and Saga's eyes peek at me through the crack. Crying has made them red. Seeing her like this tugs at my heartstrings.

"Ahriele left a while ago," I announce.

Saga shuts the door behind her as she steps out. She wipes her eyes with one sleeve and fiddles with the hem of her nightgown.

"I'm tired," she says, and the sigh which stumbles over her lips is lined with hidden tears. "Lysander will surely visit me again as soon as

I try to sleep. He probably has nothing better to do than to haunt me."

I can't stand seeing her like this. I open my arms welcomingly in her direction and nod at her.

"Come here," I say gently.

When she shyly puts her arms around my neck, my emotions multiply and intensify. I want to kiss her tears away and hold her close all night, to keep her safe. I gently stroke her hair, neck, and back with my fingertips and notice how her tense body appears to relax.

She presses her lips together as she allows herself to be lifted into my arms and I guide my steps towards the bed. Nervously, she pulls the nightgown down over her bare legs as I lay her down and I lean over her with my hands on either side of her.

"I'll watch over you," I say in a hushed voice, diving deep into her dark brown eyes. "Here by your side, just like before."

"Okay," she nods.

I lie down next to her at a reasonable distance so as to not make her uncomfortable. She crawls under the covers, turns on her side, and pulls them up so only her eyes peek out, her gaze running over me.

I smile at her, her previously spoken words ringing in my head. *Her heart is split, but she feels safe with me.* Perhaps it's too early to extinguish my newfound hope.

"Can you come a little closer, please?" she asks after a moment of silence and pulls the blanket down far enough so her nose, mouth, and chin show.

"Okay," I reply, giving her an amused grin when she looks surprised. "I'm getting used to your expressions."

"You're so silly."

One of her hands finds its way to my face and one fingertip gently strokes my forehead.

"You seem to have a lot on your mind," she murmurs thoughtfully as she touches my worry lines.

"We all worry about different things in life," I reply, attempting to uproot the sombre undertone in my voice. "Some, perhaps more than others. I feel privileged to live my life this way, despite the responsibility on my shoulders."

"I'm sorry if I cause more work for you."

Saga gives me an apologetic look and I chuckle.

"You're like a breath of fresh air, despite your at times somewhat irritable temperament," I say with a crooked smile, and she glares at me.

"You're not easy to deal with either," she mutters. "I get annoyed with you."

Her fingertips trace down my scarred cheek and she looks at me with such probing intensity that I feel goosebumps spreading over my arms.

"You're trouble," she continues, stroking my bottom lip with her index finger. "Stubborn, strict, and almost impossible to compromise with. Still, you can be quite charming now and then."

"What a compliment," I respond, trying not to be affected by her touch.

The best course of action would be to mention that we should try to catch some sleep, considering what an eventful evening we've had so far, but I remain silent for a while. She fidgets with the collar of my nightshirt, as if she's resting in deep thoughts while her fingers take on a life of their own and I end up gently grabbing her wrist.

"Isn't it time to rest your eyes, lass?"

"Soon. I want to try something first."

Her palm begins to glow faintly, and she looks both surprised and pleased as she conjures the magic of her own accord, without my intervention. I release her, holding my breath as she places her hand against my chest. The warmth is pleasurable in a way I haven't experienced before, not even during healing performed by priests and other paladins.

"Are you done?" I ask, embarrassment overlaying my voice as I notice how I sound strained.

She lifts her hand and gives me a puzzled look.

"Sorry, doesn't it feel good?" she asks as I place my hand over my eyes. "I tried to activate my inner power on my own, because it seems like I'm stronger now after hanging out with you for a while."

"It's outstanding," I say hoarsely and tense my jaws to collect my thoughts rushing around like a tourney is taking place in my head. *By the Light, she's enchanting.*

I rise to a sitting position with my back to her, whispering a silent prayer to calm my heart and pulse, only to be interrupted by her fingertips dancing across my back.

"Hey. I meant what I said before," she says in a low voice. "I feel safe in your presence. Perhaps our energies are connected to each other. Back home in Malmö, I probably wouldn't have let anyone near me again, but there's something about you, Garren."

"There was a mention of your heart being split," I say thoughtfully.

"Perhaps I'm just testing the waters currently, but I like your company. Are you comfortable in mine?"

My lips curve into a smile. Goosebumps spread as her fingertips touch the back of my neck and I steel my thoughts.

"Of course. However, you should sleep," I utter, turning to her.

"But I have trouble sleeping right now," she mumbles as she lies down in bed on top of the covers, wiggling her toes slightly while looking at me. Something mysterious, perhaps even exploratory, hides below the surface of her gaze.

I stare at her wide-eyed and feel how dry my mouth is. With a conflicted heart in my possession, I try to collect myself so that I don't drown in the storm of emotions I'm experiencing. For a moment, I part my mouth to speak, but the words seem to have become lost somewhere. Never have I been awkward in the company of another individual before—before she danced into my life.

"Your heart may be indecisive, but mine's not."

The words finally make their way out to freedom, and I watch her look at me like she's analysing each syllable, and my thoughts roam.

The thought of possibly seeing you with the prince makes my heart sink, but at the end of the day, no matter how I feel about you, the choice is yours, and I'll respect that. Regardless of your decision, I'll do everything in my power to protect you for as long as you allow it.

A weak smile settles on my lips, and I drum my fingertips against the soft blanket. *Postulate that Lysander is eliminated, the black magic of the Highlands crushed before it reaches us here, and Saga no longer needs my protection. Will she stay with me? Will she accompany the elven prince, or will she disappear, as if she never existed in this world?*

I avert my gaze as a silent prayer appears in my soul.

Beloved Mother of the Light, hallowed be thy name. I offer to thee my devotion and unwavering faith. Forgive me my sins and debts; grant me your patience and strength when I need it the most. Shine your light upon the path I walk for thee.

I repeat the prayer in my mind and only when Saga lifts herself up into a sitting position across from me do I raise my gaze. Those dark, long eyelashes ensnaring my every heartbeat.

"You look down," she mutters sadly, placing her hands over my arms. "Should we feel sad together, so we might feel better after a while?"

Amidst the gloomy state of mind, I can't help but smile. I lean against the headboard with my back while, to my delight, Saga sneaks closer and lets me wrap my arms around her. She settles down with her cheek against one of my collarbones and her curls tickle my skin playfully.

"The more I get to know you, the more I seem to ponder," she exhales, then sighing softly. "Imagine if I had met you in Malmö. I think my life would have been different."

"Saga," I say gently, caressing her hair and back. "Gaze forward instead of backward, so you don't get entangled in yesterday's net."

"You're right. It truly shows you have life experience."

She lifts her head and looks me deep in the eyes. *Her mouth, the fairest of all roses.* Once again, I lose myself in the brilliance of a thousand stars in her gaze, and her eyelids wander down as her lips part to meet me in a comforting kiss.

CHAPTER TWENTY

Saga Falk

My eyelashes flutter as faint sounds find their way into my consciousness, and I'm jolted out of abstract dream patterns. Chasing the sleep away by rubbing my eyes, I open them, blinking and yawning while my gaze adjusts to the dimness in the room. Slowly, I lift myself up into a sitting position.

"Garren?" I say in a hushed tone.

My hand finds its way to his pillow, fingertips tracing over it. The fabric feels cold; he must have left the bed a while ago. The noises that woke me seem to come from outside; people are talking nearby. My thoughts bounce back to the night before, my cheeks flushing as if a fever takes me over.

I'm sure I was the one initiating the kiss, and he had returned it—tentatively at first, like he was analysing the situation, then with a hunger which had caught me off guard. Respectfully, he had kept his hands in check and only touched my face, hair, and neck. I, on the other hand, had slipped mine under his shirt and let my fingertips dance exploratively along his body. *Oh god, this is embarrassing.* Why can't I pay attention to just Kailunn? What if the prince is just as I have imagined him, and he finds me interesting at first sight?

Shaking my head quickly, I put on my glasses. *It's nothing serious—just a little kissing game. Garren is aware of the set of rules and has accepted the terms.*

After a while I had fallen back asleep as he stroked my hair, and luckily, both the unpleasant shadows and Lysander had stayed away. Thoughtfully, I run one fingertip over my lower lip, wondering if the calm in the dreams had been affected by being so close to the knight and by having kissed him. But where is he now?

I rise and make the bed, sensing the cold of the wooden floor against my bare feet. The warmth of the flickering flames from last night is replaced with a chill as the fireplace slumbers. A thin streak of light finds its way in through a curtain and swirling little dust grains dance in the air, chasing one another.

"Garren?" I repeat.

No answer. A small lump of anxiety forms in my stomach. I hesitate for a minute or two before I pull back the curtain, allowing the daylight to flow in freely.

My eyes adjust once more to the changed light conditions. I turn around, making my way to the washroom and knock, just to make sure I'm alone. Curiously, I eye the other closed door, putting my ear to it whilst holding my breath. Complete silence. I put my hand over the knob, noticing to my immense disappointment that it's locked.

After spending some time in the washroom, I hear someone unlock the front door. My heart flies up into the pit of my throat. I know deep down who it should be who has access to this home, and yet I panic momentarily. Cautiously, I peek out through the crack of the door before exhaling in relief.

"Hey, boss," I say with a shy smile as I open the door fully and lean against the doorframe with my arms crossed over my chest.

Garren is clad in armour adorned with gold, a dark blue cloak and coat of arms in the same shade, and a sword at his side. For a second, my jaw almost drops when I see his face light up, stunned by his mere presence. *Men in armour are nice to look at, in particular this one.*

"Good morning, lass," he replies with a smile decorating his lips.

He places a small bowl on the dining table, pulls out both chairs, and waits for me to approach the table before gesturing for me to sit down.

"I brought you breakfast."

Delighted, I rub my palms together as I settle down, watching him sit down shortly after. When I take the first bite of the porridge, I can't help but let out a guttural sound caused by the taste sensation.

"This is delicious," I chirp after swallowing the bite, giving the paladin a grateful look. "Thank you, Garren."

"You're welcome," he replies, and the smile expands. "There's certainly nothing wrong with your appetite."

"I love food and cooking is actually a hobby of mine," I say, noticing I'm doing a discreet dance whilst being seated. I wave one hand in front of me in embarrassment as he stares at me. "Sorry. Sometimes I do an odd little dance when I enjoy my food; it's something I've done since I was a kid."

"You truly are the most beautiful flower in any field," he murmurs, wide-eyed.

I can't help but chuckle.

"Sudden flattery seems to be your thing when you're not grumpy," I grin. "I wonder how many individuals you've had falling head over heels for you?"

Garren raises one eyebrow, shooting another smile my way.

"Enough for me to know when I've found a rose I wish to pick and care for."

I blush and collect my thoughts, stirring the porridge with the spoon.

"How poetic," I say, tilting my head. "But a rose has thorns, and if you pick it too eagerly, you might get sores on your hands. Or perhaps it's not ready to be picked yet and then it'll wither, no matter how well you look after it."

"That could be true." Garren leans one elbow on the table top and strokes the beard on his chin before continuing. "Weeds may ensnare it. Once properly cleared away, giving the rose space to breathe, it may bloom stronger for when the time is right."

My eyes widen as I carefully put the spoon away. Opening my mouth to retort, a sudden silence overlays my tongue. Instead, I continue to watch him. *Crikey. I wish Ambrosia was here. I need to talk to her.*

"Have you had breakfast yet?" I finally ask, attempting to break the charged atmosphere between us.

"Yes, a couple of hours ago. It's almost seven o'clock."

"You're an early riser," I mutter, stifling a yawn. "I guess I should prepare myself mentally to face Ahriele today after yesterday's fiasco."

"I spoke to her last night. You'll be accompanying me today."

"How come?"

Garren glances at one hand for a moment, as if studying his nails. Seriousness takes over his gaze as he lifts it to meet mine.

"We've been called to have a meeting with the queen and a number of others, including the high elven prince."

I almost choke on the last spoon of porridge and cough violently, my eyes watering. On nimble feet, Garren gets up and pats my back lightly.

"Oh my god," I gasp and pat myself on the chest with one palm to steady my voice. "Why didn't I find this out sooner?"

I don't know how to talk to royalty! Frustrated, I get out of my chair and start pacing the room while massaging my temples. *My hair looks terrible, and nothing can hide the bags under my eyes.*

Garren's gaze follows me steadily. As he stretches his back and shoots his chin into the air with a raised eyebrow, I stop and stare at him.

"How can you be so calm right now?" I ask, my voice overlaid with irritation.

"I've been in contact with both my queen and Prince Sunseeker, and I knew of the elves' company arriving today," he replies, drumming on his sword hilt with one hand.

A loud groan falls from my lips.

"That's not helpful to me," I say accusingly. "How am I supposed to show up before two royals looking like this?"

Angrily, I point to my fringe, trying to convey the seriousness of the situation.

"I see nothing wrong with the way you look," Garren says, locking his gaze into mine.

I sigh and put my hands to my sides. "You're doing it again."

"Do elaborate."

I pick my words carefully from my vocabulary.

"You're looking at me like that. Eyes twinkling. Like you fancy me."

Garren's soft chuckling intensifies my annoyance, and I frown as I glare at him.

"You're distracting me so you can avoid answering my first question."

"Perhaps you allow yourself to be distracted since you enjoy it, without wanting to admit it to yourself," he counters, and my irritation turns to a tingle in my stomach as he winks at me.

He's right, though. I enjoy it.

"Whatever." I cross my arms over my chest and turn my gaze to the window, focusing my attention on the dancing rays of light and swirling dust grains, chasing and playing with each other. "All of this, being here—frankly, it's a little exhausting."

My mood softens when I feel Garren's fingertips caress my upper arm.

"You must be scared and confused," he says with a hushed tone, and I close my eyes as he gently pulls me close to him. "However, I can see the courage in your heart reflected in your eyes."

"I'm not brave at all," I sigh, relaxing my shoulders a little. "My entire self is a nervous wreck. I'm chaotic."

When Garren brings his lips to my forehead and whispers a prayer before giving me a feathery kiss, it feels like I'm about to melt into a puddle of emotions.

"I apologise," he says. "I didn't ask for your permission."

"It's fine," I answer, opening my eyes.

I fiddle with a hair tress and twist it around one finger while smiling to myself. *The closer I am to him, the more control I gain over my newfound magic. I like it. Perhaps this kissing game wasn't such a bad idea, after all.*

The warm gaze from the paladin flows towards me in invisible waves and I clear my throat before speaking again.

"Hey," I say, moistening my lips with the tip of my tongue. "You're doing that twinkling eye thing again."

"Is it a problem?" he asks mildly.

"How have you planned to be discreet when we're in the company of others? You're like an open book."

"We aren't in the company of others at the present time."

He always knows what to say. Blushing, and my heartbeat increasing its pace, I give him a shy smile.

"I suppose you're right."

Maybe being close to him once more would do my nerves good.

"At this rate, I'm going to get a crick in my neck since you're so tall,"

SHADOW DANCE

I grin whilst looking up at him.

Resolutely, I pull a chair to me and step onto it, triumphantly putting my hands on my sides and posing like a winner. "How does it feel to be the one looking up at me for once?"

Garren smiles wryly and nods, the light from the window playing in his golden locks.

"I appreciate this angle," he replies, tasting the words with the tip of his tongue. "A strong woman whose inner light dazzles my eyes when I look up at her."

His smouldering gaze caresses me respectfully as it traces over my hips for a brief moment. I feel desirable for the first time in aeons, despite my currently unruly fringe.

"Such a teasing knight," I say, taking his hand as he helps me down from the chair.

I notice he, too, has a necklace of winding roses and a lion's head around his neck. *Look at that. We're jewellery twins now.*

"I'd rather spend this day differently. However, duty calls," Garren says while stretching a bit, and the playful tone in his voice is palpable.

"Wait," I say, beckoning to him. "I have to tell you something."

"What is it?"

He leans forward so he's about the same eye level as me. I quickly put my hands to his cheeks, pulling him closer and giving him a quick kiss on the cheek as the magic inside me warms my chest. *This feeling's nice.* Satisfied with my own actions, I notice how he catches his breath, and when I take a step back, I shoot him my most adorable smile.

"Now our energies are mixed again. For the Light, and all that."

My cheeks hurt a little from smiling widely. *He looks cute when he's confused.* Garren blinks and stares at me as I pull out the pocket watch to check the time. *I can't believe I'm finally going to meet Kailunn.*

CHAPTER TWENTY-ONE

Kailunn Sunseeker

The imposing white castle before me has my eyes searching up to the celestial sphere as it desperately reaches towards the fluffy clouds. Sunbeams find their way down through the cloud covers, giving a hint of warmth to the slightly chilly breeze that catches my strands of hair as I sit in the saddle of my mount, Daerisa.

My party of five soldiers dismount from their gryphons. One of them grabs Daerisa's halter as she gives me a hand, helping me get down from the saddle. I caress my faithful companion across the beak and neck, speaking to her via telepathy. She makes a soft snorting sound and gently pushes her head against the palm of my hand while her bright green eyes look at me lovingly, her tail loosely wrapping around one of my thighs. She shakes her feathers in various dark and light shades of blue and iridescent white which cover most of the scales on her body, except for her claws and face.

I give her a reassuring scratch on the neck, and her tail's grip on my leg releases. My eyes journey with her briefly as she and the other gryphons leap high into the air, taking their leave on steady wings.

I glance over my shoulder and telepathically order my party to stay close to the castle walls. As their quiet, synchronised voices breathe momentarily in my head, I turn my attention to the castle guards. Their watchful eyes are fixed on me through the visors, and I stretch my back.

"I have arrived," I announce. The strength of my voice surprises me, as I rarely use spoken words, in particular when communicating with my people.

A guard nods in welcome. "Well met, Prince Sunseeker."

My countenance is immovable as I make my way up the stairs to the castle and a pair of guards in heavy armour allow me entry in through a massive, dark wooden door.

Since my last meeting in this kingdom a number of years ago, nothing has changed significantly. Oil paintings of various royalty throughout the times and significant personalities in the history of the humans cover the snow-white walls.

For a moment, my steps cease. My eyes explore a large painting depicting a brutal scene with bodies in the background, displaying a knight in the foreground with one of his heavy sabatons over the chest of a fallen troll. The knight points towards the sky with a heavy, bloodied sword, overlaid with gold details and a set red jewel, and in his other hand he carries the severed head of the troll. The troll's tongue hangs out of its mouth, a grotesque display of demise. A radiant light, similar in hue to his golden, blood-spattered locks of hair, illuminates the knight from behind and from the firmament above. From the scar on his face, there is no mistaking who the celebrated hero in the painting is.

A faint grimace of disgust leaves temporary footprints on my face. The humans seem inclined to glorify violence when they want to highlight their historically important moments, as if violence were a measure not only of the strength of the person, but also of the kingdom. *A disgusting demonstration, not entirely unexpected from the thinking and attitude of these simple people in regard to their surroundings.*

An attendant approaches with a bowed head, asking if they may take care of my outer garment. Leisurely, I take off the thick dark green coat which I wear over my white and purple garb in order to protect me from the cold during my journey.

"Shall I show Your Highness to the throne room?" he asks as he takes the garment from me and expressionlessly, I nod at him.

These grating humans and their ineptitude at using telepathy.

As the doors to the throne room open before and close behind me, my gaze wanders to a number of figures further away. Queen Claudia Ariadne, a woman with obvious poise in her stance, seated on her throne. Clad in a long, stately dress in red, gold, and white, further accentuating her dark skin tone, and resting on her head, a gold crown inlaid with jewels, glittering in various shades. Black curls spill over her shoulders and chest, and her full lips, painted in red, curve into a polite smile when she catches sight of me. Her chestnut-brown eyes squint contentedly and one hand gestures for me to come closer.

"*A Illenneihe;* the great Queen," I greet politely, bowing slightly. "I am grateful Whitekeep welcomes me and my party."

"Your step is always welcome at my door, Prince Sunseeker," she replies, and I force myself to give her a curt smile out of politeness.

Throwing a glance at the advisor standing by the throne, I notice it is the same thin man as before. Significantly older than last we met, the journey towards the end of his life clearly visible in his furrowed face and grey hair. *Regardless of many of them being uncouth heathens, human ageing and their short lifespans fascinate me.*

On the queen's left, some distance from the throne, Garren Roseheart watches me grimly. He gives me a nod and I return it politely, thereafter turning my attention to the figure standing next to him.

A thin woman of short stature dressed in plain-coloured clothing only fit for an ostler. Despite her simple appearance, I cannot help but notice the gold chain and the elaborate pendant around her neck, causing me to glance at the paladin before diverting my attention back to her. Her almond-shaped dark brown eyes stare intently at me, and I can almost touch the electric charge from the magic she hides within. *Intriguing.*

When she notices my gaze, her cheeks turn pale, and she takes a hesitant step back. Throwing her a quick glance, the knight grabs her arm with a swift movement, pulling her to him. She fiddles nervously with one shirt sleeve while avoiding meeting my eyes.

"So, this is the stranger who carries the symbol of my people," I say with a neutral tone in my voice, clasping my hands behind my back. "Saga Falk."

Saga fidgets and looks shyly at me. Her lips part as if to retort, but her words seem to lose their way, and she puts her hands to her cheeks as she turns away.

"Saga!" Roseheart mutters sternly, placing his hands on her shoulders. "Pull yourself together, lass."

"I can't do it," she whispers. "I've never met royalty before, let alone two at the same time."

"She hasn't been particularly talkative so far. Please don't take it personally, Prince Sunseeker," says the queen, giving the woman a brief look. "Her behaviour doesn't reflect the rest of us."

"You can handle this," Roseheart mumbles, and I raise one eyebrow slightly when I see how his thumbs stroke her slender shoulders.

I nod politely to the queen in response. Roseheart makes Saga turn to me again. She bows her head politely in a greeting and I can feel the subtle caress of her glances as they move stealthily over me. When I take a short, silent step towards her, her face turns bright red.

"This stunning man blesses my eyes."

I am pleasantly surprised when I hear her with such crystal clarity in my head. She seems unaware I can hear her thoughts and averts her gaze from me when the knight speaks to her.

"Are you well?" he asks, and she nods quickly.

"Does it look like I'm well? I'm losing my damn mind."

I continue to watch the young woman as I telepathically call to her as soothingly as I can.

"Saga. Can you hear me?"

Her eyes widen and her gaze lifts to meet mine.

"Prince Kailunn?"

The whispering voice enters my mind like a dancing, refreshing spring breeze. A faint smile curves my lips. *The human calls me by my first name.*

"Intriguing. You are different from the others present."

"I can't believe I'm talking to you like this."

She chews her lower lip for a second before sucking air into her lungs and closing her eyes tightly. One hand keeps a firm grip on the pendant, the knuckles turning white, and the other, kept in her pants pocket.

The eyes of the others are fixed on me as I walk around the woman on the right to get closer to her. On nimble feet, Roseheart steps between us and I look him straight in the eyes. Despite being slightly shorter than me, he carries himself with a strength of character that could intimidate most. Nevertheless, his presence cannot subdue me.

"Prince Sunseeker. I'd like to ask you not to use your magic on my recruit," he says, the outstretched claws of a lion resting in the tone of his voice.

"We're just talking," the woman mumbles and when she opens her eyes and turns to us, her gaze is glossy. She lowers her voice further as she releases her grip around the pendant. "Surely you must have noticed by now I'm not good at expressing myself with words sometimes, Grand Prior."

I smile discreetly as her eyes gleam with a faint white glow when she touches the paladin's arm with her fingertips, causing my heart to beat a little faster. A charged, magical sensation sinks into my bones from her aura and the familiar, ever-present hunger deep within my chest extends its invisible ramifications beneath my skin. *Such a powerful energy field.*

The energy seems different from the holy knight's. It appears as if the magic whispering in her is constantly pulsating, healing, and powerful; ready to be harnessed by someone who truly knows how to conduct it.

I long to imbibe more magic, and for a moment, my thoughts wander to my small box encrusted with gemstones in one of my pockets, containing magic dust.

The broad-shouldered man standing before me looks grim, but he allows no more words to drip between his lips. Saga glances at him, uncertainty manifesting in her eyes. I ignore the knight by taking a step to the side so I may capture her gaze. Again, I whisper to her telepathically, with a softness like a rippling spring brook just thawed out of winter's grasp.

"We must speak in private. My questions need answers."

Saga's wide-eyed look expresses pure surprise.

"Hang on, Kailunn—just you and me, and not the others?" she mutters, crossing her hands over her mouth as she realises what she just said and turns her head away. "I'm so sorry. That was rude of me."

"I shouldn't say his name without a title attached to it."

"What's the meaning of this?" asks the queen sternly.

"It seems Prince Sunseeker and my recruit are holding a private conversation," Roseheart announces, his rock-hard axe of a gaze slashing at me.

Saga pushes her glasses up the bridge of her nose, all whilst I pick up her shards of thoughts.

"Concentrate. You got this."

She clears her throat, smiling apologetically at the queen and her advisor. For a moment she considers the line of silent guards standing further away, ready to protect their leader until their very last breath.

"Prince Sunseeker has a point in what he mentioned to me via telepathy; we should speak in private. I don't know how to explain everything in words, but if I let him search through my thoughts, maybe it'll all become clearer to him. Your Majesty and the grand prior already know my background and how I came to be here, but the prince is sure to have more questions, given I bear the symbol of the high elves."

She gives me a nod as she speaks.

"But I have one wish, and it's that the grand prior is in the room with us. He's the one who has helped me the most up to this point. If I feel safe, then I'm sure I'll provide you with better answers."

Out of the corner of my eye, I see the knight's stern gaze softening and she moves discreetly a little closer to him, keeping her eyes fixed on me as she tucks her long, dark brown hair behind her ears. I stretch my back, putting my fingertips together in front of me.

"Very well. I agree to these terms," I say.

The queen, who has been conversing in a low tone with her advisor, nods at us.

"It sounds like a brilliant plan. Grand Prior, meet with me later tonight."

She extends a hand in his direction. Lowering his head slightly, he grabs it gently and places the back of her hand against his forehead as he whispers a prayer to the Light, before pressing a kiss on it.

When she turns her attention to Saga and holds out her hand

to her, the young woman stares at the royalty, a look of awkwardness settling on her features.

"Kiss Her Majesty's hand," the paladin murmurs to her.

With eyes veiled by surprise, she stares at him.

"Are you being serious?"

"When standing before the royalty of Whitekeep, you follow the customs," the queen responds.

A smile adorns her words, but below the surface lurks another emotion. Saga looks stunned, a thousand thoughts fluttering in her mind, one of which echoes in my head.

"I don't know if her hands are clean. I don't want to do this."

As darkness rolls in like thundering clouds in the queen's gaze, I take the opportunity to seek for her hand with my fingers and wrap them around it. With astonishment in her eyes, she turns her attention to me.

"*A lirenri Illenneihe*, Claudia Ariadne."

I translate the polite phrase from Qyarallin, my mother tongue, into the language of these simple people.

"Claudia Ariadne, the most beautiful queen."

A hint of a smile on my lips, combined with a gentle kiss on her hand, makes her face bloom in pure glee.

"You're a delight, Prince Sunseeker," she says, savouring my name with the tip of her tongue and causing my skin to crawl. "You're welcome to visit me in my private chamber later, if you wish to discuss matters concerning our people."

Bowing my head slightly, I force myself to retain my smile.

"Thank you for your invitation, Your Majesty. However, I have several errands which I must attend to."

Even if she were the last woman alive, I would continue to spend my life in celibacy.

SHADOW DANCE

Saga's discreet thought splashes against my mind.

"The tone of his language makes me think of a narrow, rippling stream winding its way through a forest on a hot summer's day. Simply mesmerising."

The three of us step out into a corridor and the paladin leads us towards the egress. I adjust my coat, fetched for me by the attendant, and fold it over my arm.

"We can talk in my study," the knight says curtly, and I see how he glances at the young woman strolling between us.

"Crikey," Saga breathes out and looks around before continuing in a hushed tone. "What's the deal with the queen?"

I cover my mouth furtively, hiding a smirk, and a veil of irritation sets in the knight's eyes.

"That's enough," he sighs.

"She seems rather keen to be worshipped, especially by the opposite sex," she says, clasping her hands behind her back.

He groans and runs his hand through his shoulder-length hair.

"How can you possibly know this from meeting Her Majesty one time?" he says dryly, glaring at her.

"It was obvious."

Noisily he sucks air into his lungs while Saga continues to look at him.

"I'm developing a headache." He taps on his sword hilt with his fingertips.

"She truly is intense for being small in size," I say with a smile.

Saga turns her head to meet my gaze, and the colour rises in her cheeks.

"Hot-tempered and stubborn," the paladin continues, and for once, he surveys me without coldness in his eyes, in agreement with my statement.

Saga opens her mouth to retort. However, I am quick-witted and catch her attention with telepathy before she can utter the words.

"You speak to the watchful lion who walks on your left without fear, but while your gaze rests on me, nervousness holds you in its grip."

Saga swallows hard and tries to look neutral as we leave the castle, and the knight politely exchanges words with a number of guards.

"He's not scary once you get to know him. And yes. It's true. You make me nervous."

Her unspoken answer finds its way into my innermost thoughts, allowing itself to be rocked by them.

"What is the reason for this?"

Discreetly, the woman takes a breath and her eyelashes cast thin shadows across her face as her gaze falls to the ground.

"Where I'm from, you're a fictional character in a made-up world similar to this one. It may be that I've built an idea about you, and I don't know if it corresponds to reality or not. It makes me a little anxious. And these thoughts are why I wear your symbol, because in my world, I favour you and your people."

I adjust my robe as we head towards the headquarters of the holy knight, glancing at the ground ahead. *How awfully dirty compared to my realm—and it does not surprise me these people are as filthy as their streets.*

However, I am genuinely interested in this human's magical energy, and I do my utmost not to show distaste for these people's capital, as well as their general hygiene, or lack thereof.

"What is your idea of me, anchored in your fictional image?"

Bluntly, I apply the question to an unspoken whisper after some moments of silence, noticing how she blushes again. The colour rising on her pale skin, just like the sun kisses the sky in the morning.

"It's nothing."

She catches her breath, then closes herself inwardly. I could easily start digging into her mind without her permission, but that is strictly against my moral compass.

"You've been silent for over five minutes. Have you swallowed your tongue, Falk?" Roseheart asks, giving her a wry smile. "Do you need help with finding it?"

I consider how the tall man looks at the woman. *The lion seems to have a weak point.*

"No, I certainly don't!" she responds and glares at him, her words clad in embarrassment. "You're the one hinting that I'm giving you a headache."

"There was never any mention of you specifically causing it."

I listen to their half-hearted bickering while we walk and notice in the corner of my eye how Saga throws furtive glances at me at regular intervals. Taking a silent breath, I can almost smell the magic in her veins and the hungry roots within impale me with their cold icicles of invisible, sharp fingers. *Her magical essence. Exquisite.*

CHAPTER TWENTY-TWO

Saga Falk

Garren leans against the bookshelf in the rose-scented study with his arms crossed over his chest, surveying the elven prince with a hard stare. Kailunn, in turn, is a short distance away from me, and I'm nervously rubbing my palms together.

"Okay," I say in an upbeat tone to lighten the oppressive atmosphere. "I'm ready to answer your questions, Kailunn."

My heart beats faster against my ribs as the tall, slender elf swiftly turns his grey eyes to me. His long, straight hair shimmers like a waterfall of diamonds in the afternoon light filtering in through the window.

"Your pronunciation of my name is fascinating," he says with a faint smile on his lips, something enigmatic taking root in his gaze. "Few dare to speak to me in this informal way."

Crap. I forgot to call him by his title.

"Being nervous and forgetting titles isn't the same as being intimidated," I say before I can stop myself and Garren gives me a sharp look. "If I'm not afraid of the grand prior, then I shouldn't have any reason to fear you, right? Your demeanour seems much more balanced than most individuals I've encountered here. Besides, I'm not used to expressing myself formally, so my apologies if I speak strangely and not quite as formally as you're used to."

"Interesting. Despite this, you expressed a desire for the knight to be present."

Kailunn moves towards me with light footsteps, like a graceful wildcat, and a nervous laugh flows out of my mouth until I stifle it.

"I'm new here and the grand prior looks out for me," I say, attempting to stabilise my somewhat fluttering voice.

His voice and the way he moves… seductive.

I freeze as Kailunn's figure moves around me, close enough to almost touch each other, like a writhing snake about to hug its prey. I turn my head, throwing a look over my shoulder as he ceases his steps behind me and I focus on breathing calmly. *Was he this calculating and cunning in Reign Online?*

As he leans down with his face right next to my ear, I feel the caress of his hair against my cheek and his voice swirling inside my head.

"Are you aware of the power, the raw magic, which breathes into your soul?"

"Y-yeah," I answer out loud, my tongue stumbling over the words.

"Prince Sunseeker," Garren warns as he takes a step closer to us.

I lift one hand and try to calm the paladin by smiling at him.

"It's all right," I say in a low tone. My heart flutters like butterfly wings when I feel Kailunn's hands close around my shoulders.

He's touching me. What should I do?

Momentarily, I consider tearing myself away as I feel my magical energy slowly, gently, being sucked out of my body, but I find myself unable to move. Instead, I close my eyes tightly.

SHADOW DANCE

"What do you know about me, Saga?"

"According to what I know from your fictional personality, you're at least eight hundred years old," I answer bluntly when I hear his voice in my head. "Your people are genetically addicted to magic, unlike the other elves who inhabit this universe. Your favourite season is winter, and you would rather spend time with other high elves than integrate with the other species. Not to be mistaken for arrogance. Rather, it's because you find calm in silence; you prefer to communicate via telepathy with those around you who speak the same way. Did I answer your question?"

"Your answer is satisfactory," he replies, exhaling next to my ear.

"I don't think I can respond to the rest of your questions in words," I mumble, shivering with pleasure when I feel his warm breath sneak into my ear.

I've been daydreaming of having him close for so long, but something seems off.

I open my eyelids while taking a deep breath. Garren stares at us with fierce flames in his eyes, and a knot of anxiety forms deep down in my stomach.

"I don't like being touched by those I haven't gotten to know," I say weakly and reach out to Garren, who takes my hand in his, pulling me close to him so vehemently I stumble straight into his arms. Some of my magic has been taken from me and tiredness has settled in my bones.

"Sit down, lass," he orders, pushing me down into a chair.

He then continues to scold the prince, and I can tell his entire being radiates concern. *Is he worried about me?*

"What's the meaning of this, Prince Sunseeker? What did you do to her?"

"It's all right," I say again, placing my hand over Garren's arm as I look up at him. "I'm just a little overwhelmed. Prince Sunseeker did nothing wrong."

Kailunn leans forward at us, his gaze firmly stitched on Garren and his palms resting on the top of the desk. Something menacing and dark appears in his eyes.

"Cease your incessant barking and remember your place, Roseheart. Not even the Light can save you should you stir my anger," he says in a low voice shrouded with invisible ice, causing me to hold my breath whilst staring at him.

Never have I imagined what the high elf would sound like when in a state of anger, and the hushed voice scares me more than I perhaps want to admit to myself.

"Hey," I say and quickly interlace my fingers in one of Garren's fists. "Shouldn't we concentrate on my answers? After all, it's the reason we're here."

The paladin tears his eyes from the other man and looks at me sternly, before his features soften. Calmingly, I stroke his armoured palm with one thumb and notice how his anger and worry seem to subside.

"The lass has a point," he says, still holding my hand in his. "It's simply useless for us to bicker, Prince Sunseeker."

Kailunn watches me intently, and his rippling sound fills my mind.

"You seem to have tamed the wild lion. It is truly a feat."

I shake my head, focusing on my telepathic response.

"It's nothing like that. He's just teaching me how to use my magic."

The icy smile on the elf's lips is incredulous, and, flustered, I pry my hand out of Garren's grasp.

"Okay," I say, putting my hands on the armrests of the chair. "Shall we begin?"

My gaze drifts over Kailunn as his hand reaches into a hidden pocket and he pulls out a small box with jewels on it. The gems sparkle in the daylight, and I part my lips slightly as I stare at the box, almost mesmerised by it.

"What do you have there?" Garren asks suspiciously, the skin taut over his cheekbones.

SHADOW DANCE

Soundlessly, Kailunn moves towards us, as if he's floating across the floor. His eyes glitter with a silver hue when he carefully opens the box, and he closes his eyelids for a moment as a deep breath fills his lungs.

"This is called Shimmer in the human tongue," he answers with a velvety tone, and his gaze almost swallows the dust in his palm when he opens his eyes again. "The source is a pulverised magical stone. In order to preserve the magic in it to its fullest, the powder has not been treated, and the body can absorb it with no ill effects."

I get out of my chair and lean forward, peeking curiously. The powder shimmers in a faint pale pink shade with purple tinges, and a faint aroma finds its way into my nostrils. The name suits it.

"The scent reminds me of vanilla," I murmur, drawing in air through my nostrils.

"Don't be fooled by it." Garren's voice is chilly when he utters the words, pushing out his chest somewhat as he stretches his back. "It's an intoxicant, favoured among those who use magic, particularly in the high elven society."

Puzzled, I raise my eyebrows and glance at the prince. "Is it true?"

I know the high elves deal with magic stones, but I didn't know they're considered drugs.

"Do not speak in such preposterous terms, *sulsair*. You worry the girl." Kailunn's smooth face paints a picture of displeasure. "Shimmer is used to enhance the magic of my people's mages. It is also used during interrogation of prisoners as it is possible for the person performing the ritual to step into another individual's thoughts and memories, to extract the information needed without the use of torture."

"It doesn't sound too bad," I say, rubbing my hands together. "Peaceful methods are good! After all, I have nothing to hide."

Cold shivers run down my spine, and I freeze. *How much digging into my mind is Kailunn going to do? Will he be able to see my thoughts and memories in pictures, as a collage or maybe even as short film sequences?*

"Two questions," I say hastily. "How does the ritual work? Will you be able to see my memories unfold before you?"

The high elf looks at me coldly, his gaze reminding me of a sky with a glistening veil of stars resting over a silent winter landscape. *Whoa… his beauty is otherworldly.*

"The powder shall be on our tongues, shared between us with a kiss. And thus, I will see the memories with the naked eye."

"That's out of the question!" Garren says gruffly.

"Wait a minute!" I blurt out and wave my hands in front of me upon stabilising my unusually shrill voice. "Is it necessary to consume it like that?"

"I would not let my tongue near a human's mouth," Kailunn says, unmoved. "However, this is the most effective way for the ritual to be performed, as long as there is assent between both parties."

My brain is in overdrive mode, processing the information as I try not to seem hurt by his statement. *His aversion to me is clear as day. He has no interest in a human and seems a little arrogant. I just have to let go of my silly, made-up fantasies about him and move on, even if it takes time. But he's so terribly handsome…*

I turn to Garren, looking up at his grim face.

"It's what you mentioned before," I mumble and tilt my head to the side. "Magic shared through a kiss."

Kailunn smiles coldly at Garren, who continues to shoot daggers at him with his gaze.

"I, too, wish to see these recollections with my own eyes," says the knight.

"It will only work if you allow me to enter your mind while visiting Saga's memories," Kailunn replies, giving me a quick glance as I put my hands to my sides.

SHADOW DANCE

"My life isn't some entertainment show which you two can watch however you want," I mutter bitterly.

Garren pierces me with his stern, sky-blue eyes.

"It seems to slip your mind that I'm your superior, Falk. For the Order of the Light, it's important to have background information regarding all recruits."

I sigh quietly and fiddle with my fringe. There's no use arguing. *It doesn't matter how many times we kiss. At the end of the day, I'll always be a subordinate...*

"Please promise me you won't dig too deep, Prince Kailunn," I say before I sink too deeply into my depressive thought pattern.

He leans down towards me, and I blush as I take a small step back, so I don't accidentally touch the tip of his nose with mine.

"You mentioned you have nothing to hide," he says, his voice like the softest cotton.

"Some stuff is private," I stammer, my blushing becoming deeper. "Do your research until you get your answers, but no more, please."

The prince gestures for me to take a seat. I sink down in the chair once more and feel the tingle in my stomach, a mixture of nervousness and anxiety. I'm unsure which feeling is the stronger of the two. A deep breath finds its way into my lungs, and I fight off the feeling of panic which nibbles at my toes, trying to make me run away.

Kailunn puts his finger under my chin as he tilts my head up to bore his cold gaze into mine. My heart feels as if it's about to implode in my chest.

"Open your mouth," he says.

"This reminds me of when I was at the doctor's a few years ago," I blurt out nervously and squirm in my chair. "She put a stick in my mouth when she was going to examine my throat and it didn't taste nice at all."

My fingers drum rapidly on the armrests, and I close my eyes, unable to bring myself to look at the elf. My heart beats hard and the blood rushes in my ears in an almost deafening way. *He's so close, so handsome.*

"Open your mouth," he orders again, this time in an even smoother voice.

"What does Shimmer taste like?" I ask, hearing Garren grunt.

"The taste is highly personal," the elven prince replies, and I think I sense amusement in his tone.

Hesitantly, I open my eyes a little and see how Kailunn dabs lightly with one fingertip in the dust. *His fingers are long, slender, and beautiful. He seems clean, so I probably don't have to worry about germs.* He gives me a piercing look and I swallow hard before opening my mouth and sticking out my tongue. When he swipes the powder over the tip of my tongue, I shiver, and my eyelids blink a few times. A pleasant, slightly chilly feeling spreads on the tongue.

"Vanilla ice cream," I smile as it slides back into my mouth. "Yummy."

I catch my breath, dizziness spreading in my mind. It feels like candy floss has replaced my brain, and the now familiar, magical warmth in my chest spreads like a bullet train through my entire body. I speak without being able to control myself and open a few buttons on my blouse.

"It's getting hot in here," I hear myself say.

Out of the corner of my eye, I notice Garren looking at me with wide eyes. Kailunn continues dabbing the powder on his own tongue. He takes a deep breath with his eyes closed, and when he opens them, they gleam like beautiful, freshly polished silver jewellery.

I lean back against the backrest, directing my attention to trying to pick the tiny, twinkling stars which have appeared before me with my glowing fingertips.

CHAPTER TWENTY-THREE

Garren Roseheart

I hold my breath as the elven prince bends down towards Saga, who's clearly under the hallucinogenic spell of Shimmer, forcing her hands down onto the armrest.

"Be still," he says in his distinctly silky voice.

My mind tells me to roar at him to go somewhere even the Light can't reach, but I bite my tongue and restrain myself, instead listening to the words my heart weaves with every beat. *I swore an oath to protect her, even if it means having to put up with this pointy-eared snake.*

"You're a work of art walking on two legs," Saga murmurs as she looks at him and laughs, a rippling laughter I've never heard leave her throat prior to this moment. "Your elegance catches my attention."

A feeling of hopelessness takes root within. She puts one finger to his lips before she catches sight of me, as if she has repressed the fact that I'm in the vicinity. Her eyes widen, a smile adorning her features as she waves at me.

"Come here," she says, gesturing for the remarkably patient elven prince to wait.

The powder must have given her temporary courage, or perhaps she's being foolhardy.

I advance to the chair. Her hand grabs hold of my coat of arms, pulling it so I lean down.

"Listen, boss," she whispers, stifling a giggle, and her dark brown eyes are flecked with shimmering silver. "You awaken my curiosity and confusion. You're making me feel things—scary, exciting things—and somehow, I'm okay with it."

My heart hammers against my ribs as she utters the words with such raw honesty, her voice causing my soul to incinerate. *Witchcraft.*

She throws her hands in the air as she stares up at the ceiling.

"Ambrosia! If you could hear me now, you'd realise I'm not the least bit prude," she says aloud, humming to herself as she closes her eyes and dances in the seat.

"What's occurring?" I ask, glaring at Sunseeker.

"She is deeply under the influence of Shimmer," he replies. "Her reaction is quite unusual compared to my people, doubtlessly due to her being a simple human with associated simple thoughts."

"My Prince," Saga murmurs with a smile and starts picking her fingers in the air again. "The word you're looking for is multi-faceted, not simple."

"Sheathe your tongue," Kailunn says firmly, cupping her face with his hands.

One of my fists clenches tightly as he kisses Saga deeply and I can hear her moan softly against his lips. The elf breaks the kiss as she sinks back into the chair with her eyes closed, breathing slowly, as if asleep. He turns to me, wiping his mouth with a handkerchief swiftly pulled out of a hidden pocket, before throwing me an icy glance from those shining, silvery eyes.

"It is time," he says. "I have given her a slightly higher dose of Shimmer. Regardless of that, considering how much magic flows within her, there is no guarantee this amount will last for long. It is unusual for an individual, in particular a human, to be as magically charged as she is."

I draw in air through my nostrils and push out my rib cage slightly before exhaling, giving him a curt nod. My hand closes around my necklace. *May the Light be with me and forgive me for my sin.*

Kailunn utters phrases in Qyarallin as he puts one hand to Saga's forehead and draws lightning-fast, luminous patterns with his fingertips in the air in front of him, his gaze fixed on me as he does so. He beckons me to step forward, and when I'm close enough, he places his other hand on my forehead as he continues to mumble in his native language. My eyelids flutter and the air leaves my lungs as an intense light fills my study and I feel how I fall backwards, despite my feet being firmly on the floor.

When I open my eyes, I find myself somewhere else, with the elven prince standing beside me. The room is airy. Leaning back against a light grey couch, I can see a curvy young woman with curly, fiery red hair, a bowl sitting in her lap. She picks out of it at regular intervals, bringing the contents to her mouth and chewing loudly.

"Saga!" she calls out, her eyes fixed on a wide, loud device displaying moving images. "Hurry up!"

She speaks a different language, and yet I can understand what she's saying.

"In a minute," I hear a voice in the distance. "I just have to pick some more flowers."

"Quit *Reign Online* and come here or I'll eat all the crisps!"

My heart starts to beat fast when I hear quick, light footsteps, and a door flies open. Saga rushes into the room and throws herself down on the couch next to the other woman. Dressed in a waist-length, sleeveless chemise with thin straps, and trousers where the legs are so short, they barely cover her behind and undergarment, I gawk at her. Her dark brown hair is pulled back into a thick, messy ponytail, and she rubs one eye as she adjusts her glasses over the bridge of her nose.

"I want some, too," she says in a childish voice and reaches for the bowl. "You're so greedy, Ambrosia."

"She who's greedy survives," Ambrosia replies, placing the bowl between them on the cushion. "Shut up, they're about to start."

"I bought these," Saga mutters and looks down at the contents disappointedly. "You've already eaten half of them, and the show has barely started."

Ambrosia elbows her lightly on the side and grunts as she chews.

"Shut up," she says again. "If you want to talk, just text me."

Saga purses her mouth disapprovingly before picking up a handful of the treats.

"Retsam sent me a video again," she says, completely ignoring what Ambrosia has said. "He's pissing me off. He may be hot, but I don't want to see his… thing. He keeps asking me for nudes, but I don't want to send him any."

"Wait, what?"

Ambrosia almost chokes and grabs Saga's arm while glaring at her.

"What do you mean when you say his 'thing'?"

Saga rolls her eyes and blushes.

"His… well. You know."

"Grow up," the friend snorts. "You're an adult. Show it to me."

"I deleted it," Saga replies, trying to focus on the moving images in front of her. "I don't want nasty shit on my phone. In fact, I didn't even watch the whole thing as soon as I knew what was up."

"Fucking hell. Haven't you downloaded tonnes of dirty fan art of the elven prince you're obsessing over?"

Saga looks genuinely offended.

"Hell no!" she blurts out. "What's wrong with you?"

Ambrosia grins widely.

"I believe you. You're excessively prude, on the verge of being a bore."

"Whatever. Can we focus on the fact I don't want the guy to send me shit like that? He seems to think he's a gift to every woman on the planet just because he has some abs and he's constantly nagging me about sending him nudes."

"Tell him to go to hell," says Ambrosia, putting her arm around Saga's shoulders. "No one's forcing my girl to do anything which makes her uncomfortable."

"I should break up with him." Saga nods thoughtfully.

Ambrosia pulls one of Saga's strands of hair behind her ear.

"You're not even dating, so don't overcomplicate things in your brain."

Kailunn takes a step closer to the couch and I hear his low, soft voice call her name. She directs her gaze at him as she swallows a crisp, leaning back against the back of the sofa.

"Allow us entry into your memories," he says, glancing at me over his shoulder. "Roseheart, try not to communicate too much with her."

"Is she able to see us?" I ask in a hushed tone, caressing Saga's slender shoulders with my gaze.

"She can sense our energies. However, seeing as how I am performing the ritual, I do not wish for her to be influenced by you."

Saga gets up and walks towards the kitchen. Her trousers make me stare at her as if I'm bewitched and silently, I curse at myself. *I'm truly shameless.* When she returns with a glass of water in hand, her eyes linger on the high elf. Slowly, she sips the liquid and gives me a long look over the edge of the glass.

"Saga," Kailunn says yet again. "What made you attach yourself to my fictional self in your world?"

"Men in real life are horrible," replies Saga tonelessly. "Not all of them; just the ones I've had the misfortune of meeting."

She adjusts a strap on the chemise which has slipped down over her shoulder and looks at the device in front of her. Ambrosia talks to her, but I fixate solely on Saga's presence and shut the other woman out of my consciousness.

"Show us what you mean," the prince urges.

The scene before us changes in the space of a second, and as I inhale, a fresh scent of grass and damp moss creeps into my nostrils. We survey what appears to be the edge of a forest grove on a summer day, the warmth of the rays of daylight dancing across my visage. A faint sound of sobbing makes me turn around.

Hidden behind a couple of large boulders, I notice a little girl, who appears to be no more than seven years old, sitting with her knees pulled up to her chest and her arms wrapped tightly around herself. Tears roll down her round cheeks and her dark hair resting in two braids looks dishevelled. The white dress she's wearing is soiled. Red shoes and light blue socks cover her feet.

Kailunn crouches in front of the girl.

"Saga," he says softly.

My heart is pounding against my ribs, and my jaws tense as I settle down next to the girl, unable to keep myself from gently stroking her hair for a second.

Saga hiccups as she cries. She lifts her head and looks me straight in the eyes.

"Mum will be angry," she sobs with a trembling lower lip.

SHADOW DANCE

I part my lips to speak. However, Kailunn is quicker.

"Why is that?"

"She bought the dress for me. It's dirty and she'll get angry."

"Did someone hurt you?" Kailunn asks, his expression immovable.

"They told me I could see the puppy, but it was dark."

For a moment, the image of a shed flashes before my eyes, with four men hurriedly leading Saga in its direction, the memory fading as quickly as it had appeared. I take a deep breath and do my utmost to stabilise the anger rising inside me, causing my temples to throb violently.

"Change the scenery," I say firmly to the prince. "Now."

"I wanted to see the puppy," she sobs and buries her face in her knees.

"Go to the next memory, Saga," Kailunn urges softly after throwing me a hasty glance.

We're walking side by side with Saga through a corridor with tall metal cabinets lined up on both sides of us. My gaze seeks her. She's young, much younger than I'm used to seeing her. Large, round glasses decorate her face and she's clad in black from head to toe. On her back she carries a pack with cat and butterfly motifs on it, and tightly pressed against her chest in her arms, a number of books.

"Where are we?" I ask her in a low voice, ignoring Kailunn's frosty glare.

"My school," she answers, nervously picking at her lower lip while lowering her eyes to the floor as a group of boisterous young people pass by.

"Look! It's the nerd," someone cackles, pushing her so violently that she stumbles into a cabinet and drops her books.

A sheet of paper falls out from between the pages, and I glance over it. It's a sketch of an elf whose appearance is eerily analogous to the prince standing beside me. *Has he lived in her heart and mind for that long?*

Saga clenches her jaws and bends down to pick them up, but one of the youths slaps her on the behind. Quickly, she spins around, clasping her hands as she walks towards him.

"Don't touch me!" she snarls, tears tinted with anger welling up in her eyes as the obnoxious group continues to laugh.

"Don't you like it, bitch?" asks the guy who slapped her, grinning. "Everyone knows you're sleeping with the teachers, so they give you good grades."

"Shut up!" she hisses. "It's not true!"

"And what if I won't? What are you going to do about it?"

Saga's hands tremble, and she breathes rapidly.

"You're a waste of air," she sneers. "Your friends are only around because you have rich parents who pay for everything."

The guy shoves her into a corner among the lockers and grabs her inappropriately, while his friends cheer him on. She screams, trying to wriggle free, and elbows him between the ribs.

"You bitch!" he hisses between clenched teeth and takes a couple of steps backwards as distant voices in the corridor reach us.

With a nod to the rest of his gang, the boys scurry away. Saga takes a deep breath and kicks one of the metal cabinets furiously, denting it.

"Dickheads!" I hear her panting before she crouches down and rubs her eyes with one sleeve.

My heart is heavy as I watch her crawl to her books on all fours. One of her hands finds its way to the sheet of paper. When she picks it up, she tenderly brushes her fingertips over its surface, her melancholic gaze tracing the sketch. After a moment of silence, she grabs the books and lifts herself off the floor.

My pulse is roaring in my ears and despite the anger inside, I wish to take the girl's hand in mine; tell her she mustn't lose her faith and hope with the world. However, my hands weigh heavy, motionless, as Saga walks past me with her blank stare attached to the floor.

Kailunn follows her on silent feet, attaching a flowing whisper to her

SHADOW DANCE

ear, which makes her glance over her shoulder, giving him a nod.

My eyelids flutter as the environment shifts anew. I blink a few times, running my fingers through my hair and adjusting my sight to the surroundings.

Saga, now an adult, is seated at a white dining table with a beige tablecloth over it. Her gaze is empty when she stares down at a plate in front of her. Across from her sits a youth chewing loudly, and I take in a few superficial details about him. Dark hair, green eyes, and rather broad shoulders.

"You're like a dead fish in bed," he sneers.

Without looking at her, he turns his attention to an item similar to Saga's phone lying next to his plate. His gaze creeps hungrily over a picture of a young-looking blond woman.

"You hurt me," she says in a tired voice and sighs quietly. "And you don't listen to me when I ask you to stop."

"It's your fault if I decide to cheat on you," the young man continues, throwing a sneering glance in her direction. "It wouldn't hurt if you do what I ask you sometimes. As a man, I have certain needs."

"I don't like what you ask me to do," she mutters, her shoulders slumping.

"And I don't like to ask you for sex, but I won't get it otherwise. It's just as well I go to the pub with the boys."

"It's over between us if you're unfaithful, so you might as well do whatever you feel like since I can't satisfy your needs," Saga shrugs, poking her food slowly with a fork. Her eyes seek mine, looking straight at me as she whispers. "I wish he would cheat on me so I can be free again. He won't let me go."

The young man across from Saga stares at her with a menacing gaze.

"Don't you start again," he mutters. "You don't want to make me cross."

I hear Saga take a deep breath with her eyes closed before throwing her fork to the side and standing up.

"Listen, Sam. I don't give a damn if you get mad or not," she says out loud. "I've had enough of this. Just go. Neither of us is happy in this relationship. Sleep around all you want. I want to break up."

The man wipes his mouth with the back of his hand. Quickly, he gets up from his chair and steps towards her.

"Don't get lippy with me!" he shouts, grabs her arm, and shakes her violently. "I'm the one who decides when this relationship is over. Do you get it? How the fuck do you think you'll manage without me?"

"Why do you care? This is my apartment, and I want you to leave! Go, or I'll call the police!"

Kailunn swiftly extends his arm in front of me as I step closer to the man, about to grab him by the throat. The elf shakes his head at me, and his usually smooth face seems to have gained lines of worry at his brows.

"These are fragments of her memories," he says, looking away from the escalating scenes unfolding before us. "We must not get overly involved or we might cause a permanent fracture to her mind."

My mouth feels dry and a silent prayer to the Light is born in my heart, begging the Mother of the Light to calm my nerves. Essentially, I want to crush the memory man's skull with my bare hands as I watch him throw Saga against a wall and grab her neck with both hands.

Once again, the environment changes and when the blinding light disappears and my eyes have adjusted to the lighting conditions, I see Saga sitting at a desk in front of a device that plays moving images.

"What are we looking at?" Kailunn asks in a honeyed voice.

We stand behind her chair.

"I'm playing *Reign Online*," she replies, smiling with her entire face as she glances at the elf. "You're there on the screen, both of you. Your fictional personalities."

I lean forward, catching my breath.

"By the Light," I exhale, noting out of the corner of my eye how the elven prince stares at his made-up self.

"The elves are so beautiful," Saga mutters dreamily and leans her head back against the headrest of the chair. "All the glitter, the magic, and their cute pointy ears."

Kailunn puts his hand on the table top as he leans down towards her, his gaze glittering intensely in silver.

"Tell me more," he urges in a hushed voice.

Saga taps her fingers on the armrests before touching her bottom lip thoughtfully with one fingertip.

"Fictional characters make no demands," she says, her eyes fixed on the screen. "They don't hurt me, and I can like them without having to worry about how they'll react if I'm having a bad day. They're there in my head and I can shape them as I want."

"What influenced your choice when you picked me, besides your affinity for my people?"

"What relevance does this have, Prince Sunseeker?" I ask bluntly.

This pointy-eared snake irks me to no end.

"It is one of my questions," he replies and gives me a polite smile, his head slightly tilted. "The girl is significantly more entrancing than I had previously anticipated, and as such, spontaneous questions will arise."

Saga reaches for a large porcelain cup on the table before I have time to answer the elf and sips on its contents whilst pondering.

"I've been playing a high elf since the beginning," she replies and nods. "It's how I came to meet your fictional self thirteen years ago, Prince Kailunn. You're charismatic, alluring. But had I played as a human, I probably would have encountered Garren sooner. Below his gruff exterior, he's caring, generous, and respectful."

My ears perk up, the pulse increasing in my body.

"Would you have made a different choice if you had met me first?"

I ask a little too enthusiastically and I attempt to regain my calm composure from before.

"Roseheart," Kailunn warns, glaring at me. "You may not mix her present-day memories with her old ones."

"Do calm yourself, Prince Sunseeker. She mentioned my name herself before I asked," I state sternly and direct my eyes at Saga again. "Answer me, lass."

Saga puts the cup down and slowly pushes the chair out. She gives us each a fleeting glance before she walks over to her bed, settling down on the edge. Playfully, she waves her feet in front of her.

"I'm fumbling a little emotionally right now," she says and blinks. "In your world, it seems safer to have feelings than where I'm from."

Slowly, she rubs her eyes as she yawns, and Kailunn quickly turns to me.

"She is waking up," he says with a silky voice. "Shut your eyes."

I dislike taking directives from the elven prince, but decide to put aside my stubbornness and obey him without saying a word.

The air seems to leave my lungs again, and this time I find myself coughing. When my eyelids open, we're back in my familiar study. Kailunn utters something in his native language before pulling his hands back from our foreheads. My eyes dart to the chair.

Saga has taken off her glasses, still rubbing her eyes, and a hushed moan leaves her lips.

"Saga," I exhale and feel my chest fill with an enormous warmth edged with compassion.

Placing her glasses back on her face, she blinks a few times before looking up at our faces, smiling nervously.

"I must have fallen asleep," she mumbles, her voice slightly hoarse. "Did you get your answers?"

"I thank you for allowing us entry into your innermost thoughts,"

SHADOW DANCE

Kailunn replies, bestowing her a polite smile. "My questions were adequately answered."

"Great!" she says and gives him both thumbs up, something I've only seen her do once previously at the inn.

I crouch before her, incapable of getting a word out. My gaze locks into hers and I run my hand through my hair.

Saga's anxious smile paints a picture of incipient worry on her beautiful face.

"Are you all right?" she asks cautiously.

Slowly I shake my head, some of my hair tresses falling in front of my eyes, and I let my gaze sweep over her legs, knees, dainty hands, and face. *You have such strength in you, without you being aware of it yourself. You strong, brave woman.*

"Don't worry," I reply upon giving her a smile and standing up. "Prince Sunseeker, thank you for your service."

Kailunn gives me a polite, frosty smirk. He brushes off his robe with one hand and stretches his back.

"It was nothing. For now, I must depart—I need to follow up on the whereabouts of my retinue. Roseheart, I would like to have a word with you later this evening."

I nod before bowing my head slightly. He turns to Saga and a small lump of ice forms in my stomach as his curved lips smile wider, causing the colour to rise in her cheeks and her to mirror his smile. *Is he speaking to her telepathically again?*

The door shuts behind the prince, and I extend a hand to Saga.

"Are you well?" I ask at the same time as my gaze drifts over her cheeks, the tip of her nose, and her eyelids, becoming helplessly stuck somewhere between her long, dark eyelashes.

"I'm fine, thanks," she replies upon standing up, massaging her neck with one hand. "I remember nothing after I took Shimmer, but it was nice to sleep for a while without being stalked by Lysander."

"Did Prince Sunseeker say anything to you before he left?" I ask, avoiding giving the appearance of my curiosity.

Saga averts her attention from me, smiling to herself.

"He thanked me for the kiss," she says, turning her face away while playing nervously with her fringe. "He can be polite, despite his obvious arrogance."

My skin is taut over my cheekbones, my heart sinking into my stomach, and coldness spreading in my bone marrow. Sunseeker had mentioned there were other ways to perform the ritual, and this was the most effective way. I'm convinced his ulterior motive had been to access Saga's magic through physical contact and my attention had been far too fixed on her to realise what he was doing. And now she walks beside me, the woman with the Light in her soul, smiling at the thought of someone else; someone who lives in her mind and heart, albeit another man keeps her safe at night.

Perhaps she has already made her choice and I'll have to accept that maybe she'll no longer behave the same way with me.

CHAPTER TWENTY-FOUR

Saga Falk

I sit in Garren's bed, watching him in silence. He has settled down at the dining table with a grim expression deeply set in his wrinkles, cutting an apple into small pieces. During the short walk from the Order of the Light to his residence, he had barely said a word, and my anxiety ripples around in my stomach like an ocean with restless waves riding on it.

"Garren? Is everything okay?"

With a hint of hesitation, I call for his attention and he, in turn, directs his attention to me. I swallow hard, take a deep breath, and run my fingertips over the bedspread as I wait for him to answer.

"Yes," he replies, wiping the knife in his hand with a napkin.

He picks up the plate of apple slices, brings it to the bed.

"Have some if you're hungry."

He settles down across from me, looking at me with a strange hint in his eyes. I wipe my mouth with the napkin which he has placed next to the plate after a while, averting my gaze down at my knees.

"You're unusually quiet," I whisper upon collecting my thoughts.

"Did I say something wrong?"

The anxiety in my stomach grows bigger and bigger when a moment of silence passes between us, and I scratch with one of my fingernails on the bedspread.

"Saga," I hear him say with a warm voice, yet bearing a melancholic undertone. "You have said nothing inappropriate. No, you are truly astonishing the way you are and how you speak."

"Gosh, now you're saying stuff like that again." I smile, leaning my back against the headboard.

In an instant, the atmosphere between us seems to have shifted—Garren's visage being visibly less grim than mere seconds ago. We peruse each other for a while.

"Don't you get hot when wearing that indoors?" I ask, nodding at his armour.

"Quite," he admits, smiling back. "However, my queen and the elven prince expect my presence anon."

"Can't you wear other work clothes while still remaining professional? In fact, do you even get to rest properly? It seems like your paperwork never ends and you're constantly meeting with people."

Thoughtfully, I wiggle my toes and slide my glasses up the bridge of my nose. *My feet hurt a little.*

Garren smirks after having chewed and swallowed a piece of apple.

"My professional position involves much work," he replies, winking at me. "These days, I bring some of it home with me."

Throwing a glare his way, I pout at him.

"I'm not that troublesome," I grumble, crossing my arms over my chest.

"But you are, lass," he replies with a teasing look and leans closer to me. "It matters not. You can be how you want to be, as long as you feel comfortable in my presence."

"My goodness, some of the stuff you say is unbelievable."

I stifle a laugh. He slowly takes off his gloves and sets them aside. My heart flutters as I watch his movements, staring at those strong hands of his. He gently takes hold of my feet and starts massaging them while glancing at me, as if to make sure I allow him to touch me.

"How do you know my feet hurt?" I ask in surprise, relaxing a little, and the anxiety in my stomach keeps shrinking.

"Mayhaps it's due to the Light interlacing us," he replies and gives me a smile which warms my chest, just behind my ribcage.

"Maybe," I mutter shyly.

I notice how Garren seems to gather his thoughts.

"What's on your mind?" I ask after a while, sinking comfortably into the bed so I can rest my head on the pillow. *He gives a great massage.*

"The prince dug rather deep into your consciousness," he says, focusing his attention on my feet as he continues to touch them. "I wish to remind you you're a strong woman, no matter what has happened to you in your past."

An icy core rushes down my spine and my body tenses. *I asked Kailunn not to do it.* My hands find their way to my stomach, and I grab my blouse in an almost convulsive way.

"I don't know if I agree," I stammer unsteadily. "Maybe I'm used to being stepped on like a doormat, and that's why I make idiotic choices in life. Or because I'm twenty-nine years old, with zero meaningful life experiences."

Shadows creep across Garren's attractive features.

"Saga. I'd like to share something with you."

A wistful smile plays a melody on his lips as he lowers his gaze. Slowly, he shakes his bowed head and some strands of hair fall in front of his face, like a golden curtain. Perhaps he seeks respite from my eyes.

When he turns his attention to me again, something dark rests in those blue windows to the soul. The voice which reaches my ears is steady, but hushed.

"I'm a murderer."

CHAPTER TWENTY-FIVE

Garren Roseheart

The gaze flowing from Saga's large, scrutinising eyes weighs on my shoulders and I feel as if I'm being suffocated by the ring collar on my armour. I let go of her feet as she gets into a sitting position. She rests her hands on either side of her against the mattress, as if supporting herself to stay upright. Her cheeks are unusually pale, and her radiance tells a story of an incipient fear.

"W-what are you saying?"

Her unsteady voice reminds me of a moth's thin, fluttering wings. Air fills my lungs and I turn my head away.

"I was fifteen years old. At that point, I had been training hard with the Order of the Light for years and I had grown considerably stronger than when I had first joined. I was quite comfortable with my life, convinced I was in the right environment to focus on my faith to the fullest."

Thoughtfully, I run the fingers of one hand through my hair, finding myself staring at the instrument case at the end of the bed. The deafening pounding of my heart as it tries to break out of my chest distracts me at first, but I shake my head firmly and rake in my lost thoughts slipping on the wet cobblestones of my mind in the rain.

"I had finished for the day and was taking a walk through the forest before I was supposed to meet with Ahriele," I continue, looking down at my palms. "She, too, had joined the Order of the Light in Whitekeep and we studied the holy scripture together in the evenings. Our commanders regarded us highly, as we were two of their most promising disciples. However, it was during this stroll through the woods I came to witness a heinous crime."

My mouth feels dry, and I lift myself out of bed. One of my hands taps on the sword hilt as I walk over to the small dining table. Grabbing a large mug, I quickly rinse the water down. *Now would have been a good time to moisten my throat with some ale.*

Out of the corner of my eye, I see Saga standing at the end of the bed with her gaze firmly fixed on me, distress weighing her shoulders down.

"What happened?" she asks quietly.

Nausea is dangerously close to making my stomach turn. When I speak, my voice is treacherously hoarse, and I do my utmost to keep my emotions under control.

"She was lying there. Undressed, terrified. She caught sight of me. I remember the sound which came over her quivering lips and the horror-tinged shame in her eyes."

I take another deep breath, closing my eyelids and putting my hands to my temples. A headache is spreading.

"Two older boys noticed my presence," I continue in a monotone voice. "A burning rage took over my heart and soul. I charged forward, grabbing one of them by the collar. He couldn't defend himself. By swiftly putting my arm around his throat from behind, I was squeezing and tearing until his neck broke. The sound of the air leaving his lungs still haunts me to this day, despite the abhorrent crime he and his friend had committed."

I swallow hard, avoiding opening my eyes. *I can't bring myself to see Saga's expression.* The blood rushes in my ears, sharp memories etched behind my eyelids.

"His friend attacked me with a rock, but I've always been quick on my feet. I punched him, knocking him flat to the ground, and the object fell from his hands. I pinned him down by putting one foot over his wrist and kicked him in the chest, causing him to lose his breath. Getting hold of what he had been planning to use as a weapon, I dealt blow after blow to his face and head. It took a while before it dawned on me that I had committed a grave sin."

The last sentence echoes hollowly. My hands move to my neck and clasp there as I tilt my head back slightly. My temples throb and I can perceive the smell of grass and soil stinging my nose, just like it had done back then. The heat and metallic taste of blood splattered across my features, the way it ran between my fingers, and lifeless eyes in a disfigured face which stared up at me.

"Through the generations, the house of Roseheart has always been influential due to our faith in the Light and our financial assets. We control much of the trade in various goods, which take place both within our own realm and across the borders. Normally, the crime I had committed would be punished with death. However, as I'm a Roseheart and I was one of the best disciples in the Order of the Light at that time, the event was hushed up. The boys' victim never received an official settlement."

I lower my head a little, crossing my arms over my chest and letting my eyelids drift up, but I avoid looking at Saga.

"The count in my hometown saw to it that I was flogged. Fifteen whippings later, I stopped counting them. He watched with wicked amusement as I received the punishment, and I didn't allow myself to shed any tears. I didn't want to give him the satisfaction of seeing me tormented more than what was necessary to keep him pleased and not cause a heavier beating. At times, I experience the pain again; some nights my brain plays tricks on me."

My hands fall to my sides, and I clench them tightly, the nails painfully digging into my palms. *I would have liked to redecorate his mocking face and paint it red with my fists.* I continue my story after taking a deep breath upon silently asking the Mother of the Light for forgiveness for my sinful thought.

"After receiving my full sentence and spending my recovery time in our family home, my father arranged for me to apply to the Order of the Light in Whitekeep. They welcomed me with open arms after my initiation, thanks in large part to my past achievements as a disciple, and here I stand. The grand prior of Whitekeep, a man whose closest ones are harbouring a dark family secret they will take with them to the grave."

Finally, I bring myself to look in Saga's direction. She has taken a couple of steps closer to me, her hands clasped close to her chest.

"Are you afraid of me now?" I ask, feeling my heart sink into a cold, dark sea of hopelessness.

Her arms reach for me, and I hold my breath.

CHAPTER TWENTY-SIX

Saga Falk

My heart is fluttering wildly, like a caged canary desperately trying to break free. The knight's confession rushes around in my head, making me dizzy. He looks so vulnerable, the man standing across from me with slumped shoulders. It's hard to imagine he has taken life—outside of battle, that is. My gaze finds its way to his hands and lingers there for a while. The same hands have healed me, held me, and chased away my nightmares. Hands which have caressed me and given warmth to my weary soul.

A faint smile plays a song of sadness on Garren's lips.

"Are you afraid of me now?"

My inner barriers are torn down by a strong sense of compassion. Blinking the tears away, I see cascades of colour wash over Garren, and with it the realisation life doesn't seem as grey as before. I reach towards him, gently brushing away the hair in front of his eyes. *The softness of the hair caresses my fingers.*

"No," I whisper, shaking my head slowly. "You may have made a life-changing mistake, but you didn't commit the act out of malice. You just wanted to protect the girl."

Those piercing blue eyes are so beautiful. Expressive. I'm not the least bit afraid of him anymore.

"I don't wish to influence you," he utters, a soft tone glazing his voice. "I'm well-aware of what's happening in your heart regarding Prince Sunseeker, and you may feel torn. Despite all of this, I wanted to tell my story, so you feel less vulnerable."

Kailunn is fascinating and elegant. An enigma I've built a throne for in my heart, where I keep him and myself safe from the outside world. However, when he touched my shoulders, it felt like my energy was taken from me, unlike Garren. He gives, without taking. They're so different from each other. This knight is like a light source I can't stop being drawn to.

"Can't we just focus on the here and now?" I say. "For most of my life, I've always been ten steps ahead in my mind, and to be honest, I'm mentally drained from it."

With a sigh crawling over my lips, I let my eyes wander across the room. My shoulders feel a little tense, tiredness resting in every part of my body. A lot has happened at once today.

Garren's hands find their way to mine and almost automatically, I intertwine my fingers in his. *I like the calming effect he has on me.*

"Rest with me and know I'll do my utmost to keep you safe," he says, catching my eye. "I make no demands of you. Be kind to yourself and your heart will make the right choice."

I give him a grateful look.

"Thank you for sharing your experiences, Garren."

I'm not as anxious anymore. He knows details about my past, and I of his.

SHADOW DANCE

As I seek his comforting embrace, he pulls me close, stroking my hair. A silent sigh leaves me. *You're a good person.*

After a while, he takes my hand and leads me to the bed. Without saying a word, he nods, and, slightly confused, I sit down on the edge. I study him as he picks up his instrument case to take out an old, beautiful violin made from light wood. The surface of the violin is adorned with detailed illustrations in black of roses, a tree with leafless branches, and a lion.

"It's so beautiful," I whisper in fascination.

"I've never played an instrument whilst wearing heavy armour," he says, smiling apologetically.

When he rests his chin on the chin rest, closes his eyes, and draws the bow over the strings, I simply can't take my eyes off him. The music spreading in the room is emotional, intense, and passionate. His fingers dance over the instrument and every so often, he moves from one side to the other. The notes penetrate my ears, unlocking the gates to the innermost rooms of my soul, and my feet tap softly, matching the notes.

His eyelids slowly drift up as I rise. He follows my movements while continuing to create art. My dance expresses my unspoken words and I move my body without letting myself be limited by time and space. I breathe in the present moment and feel the chains that have held me down, keeping me imprisoned in the past, loosen as I breathe out again.

After a while, I sink down on the edge of the bed, panting and wiping my face with one sleeve. Garren puts the violin down, giving me a deep look which almost takes my breath away, and I shoot a surprised smile in his direction.

"Much like the beautiful dance of a colourful butterfly in a summer meadow," he exhales as he closes his eyes, his tongue becoming overlaid with a hushed prayer.

CHAPTER TWENTY-SEVEN

Amarion Starling

The castle is under attack. The screams from the castle grounds are somewhat drowned out by the deafening roars of an army of towering, broad-shouldered, monstrous creatures pounding their fists and stout wooden logs into the walls until they give way under their force. Catapults swinging large rocks at the buildings. The ground shakes as my fallen compatriots rise again, and from the window I can clearly see their free will is no longer theirs. Someone revives them using black magic.

I quickly turn to meet my advisor's horrified expression and three red eyes, one of them in the middle of his forehead. His long, coily dark hair, decorated with thin gold chains and small red jewels, looks slightly tousled and the lit candles in the room make his dark skin shimmer faintly.

"We were not prepared, my lord," he announces, and his left hand is clutching a long staff with a black stone on top. "The enemies seem to have appeared from the shadows, as if from the void, before we could react. Someone is using dark arts. We have no reports regarding this from our messengers."

For a second, I glance at a snow-white raven perched on my arm. She is my fastest messenger, the one who delivers notes between nearby villages and towns when time is of the essence, but now is not the time to formulate a letter. Tenderly, I caress her over the head and beak before opening a window ajar, allowing her to spread her wings and fly. *Save yourself, my faithful friend.*

"Sandro," I say, turning around. "We must send word of the attack to the humans."

Sandro blinks with all eyes at once.

"They will not assist us! Have you repressed the memories of the war a thousand years ago, my lord? How they marched under the banner of the Order of the Light and watered our soil with blood?"

I put one hand to my head and my ears twitch as the ground shakes again and a porcelain vase on my bedside table falls and shatters.

"We have a peace agreement with them," I say, letting the tip of my tongue caress my pointed fangs as I rapidly collect my thoughts.

Sandro may look like a youngster in his early twenties, but he has lived far longer in his immortal form than I have. He has stood by the vampire royalties as their faithful advisor through the ages for as far as I can recall. I continue to speak.

"The high elven court cannot be trusted. The other elves have no collective strength, and the dwarves rarely go to war unless it is adjacent to their own territories. We must act quickly."

Sandro shakes his head, his forehead furrowed.

"I shall not leave your side, Your Grace," he says, straightening his back firmly. "What if nothing remains when I return? No, I simply refuse."

SHADOW DANCE

I grasp his shoulder lightly with one hand, with just enough force to remind him who wears the crown.

"Your loyalty knows no bounds," I retort, "but you must make your way to Whitekeep with haste. The humans are our only chance and I do not want whoever is attacking us to get hold of you."

My hand swiftly travels down his body, stopping as it reaches his stomach. I can feel the outline of the object against my palm through the fabric, and Sandro's rebellious gaze penetrates mine. *The monster slumbers.*

"What you carry inside must not end up in the wrong hands. Go now. I will not repeat myself."

A resigned sigh finds its way from between his full lips, and he closes two of his eyes while the third stares at me. The black stone atop the staff shimmers, similar to a night sky with its distant stars. Within seconds, he has transformed into a three-eyed bat.

"Keep your distance from the holy knights and their magic," I remind him telepathically, watching as he disappears into the darkness.

Grabbing my two longswords resting at my sides, I ready myself for battle.

Swinging my weapons, I remove the head of a tall, broad-shouldered man nearly twice my height with a clean cut. Blood spurts as he thumps down on the stone floor, and I lick the drops splashing over my lips. It has been a long time since I tasted life itself. I throw my head back for a moment, noticing the heat from the liquid spreading throughout my body as I close my eyes and a low growl emerges in my throat.

Like a mist, I float nimbly through the halls. The giant I slew has butchered my servants. Their torn limbs and deformed bodies scattered here and there, painting a picture of chaos. The floor is slippery from entrails and blood. *I hope someone is alive, somewhere.*

Anger boils inside as a wall in the hall falls with a deafening sound. My grip on the weapons tightens.

"Who dares enter my home?" I roar.

Two giants appear through the hole in the wall, and as they stand aside, I see a spider-like creature with tentacles and wildly flailing fire-coloured eyes over its body. On the spider's back in a saddle sits a rider, protected by armour black as the deepest night, his head and face hidden under a helmet. As the figure slides down from the saddle, I notice the knee-high boots with heavy, pointed metal details. Metal guards cover the arms and elbows and they, too, have long, sharp details protruding from them.

"Amarion Starling. My name is Lysander Duleon, and I am here to lay claim to your throne."

The tone of his voice is snide and for a moment, the figure's hands envelop in a black mist, before turning into what I can liken to spears.

"Meet me in battle without the use of tainted magic, you wretch!" I exclaim.

"Why would I do that? Hundreds of years I have spent immersing myself in the dark arts, and it would be foolish not to utilise my acquired knowledge."

I crouch and roll as a spear whizzes past me. Swinging my weapons, a roar breaks free from my throat as I chop off a part of the intruder's arm, smiling in satisfaction as he staggers. Glowing red eyes stare at me through the visor of the helmet.

"Lysander Duleon," I say and stick my chin in the air, pointing one weapon at him. "You invade my home and intend to take over my crown. It is unacceptable."

"Is it right to deprive your people of their natural freedom?"

Lysander's severed arm and his other, uninjured hand are enveloped in the dark mist and in the blink of an eye, his normal hands have been recreated. The damage I just inflicted on him does not seem to have affected him in the slightest. With nimble fingers he takes off his helmet, casting it aside with a loud noise and his eyes burning with rage.

"Is it right to let your people starve, not to quench their thirst?" he continues, and the red pupils turn black.

"The people have access to food," I point out as I prepare myself mentally for the enemy's next move. "No one goes hungry under my banner."

Lysander cackles maniacally.

"Cold blood substitute made with magic—do you honestly believe it quenches hunger the same way blood from a pulsating heart does? We are allocated what your regime gives us. You, on the other hand, look rather well-nourished."

My eyes narrow as I replay his sentence in my head. *The audacity to insinuate I take more than I give.* There has been a drought on the blood substitute front from time to time, but creating it is time-consuming and the demand has increased.

"My rule is constantly focused on replenishing the magical reservoir," I announce sharply.

"Your so-called efforts are clearly not enough," Lysander replies, his voice distorted into something more monstrous. "The throne shall be mine, and blood will flow."

His feet leave the ground as he levitates, the black mist swirling around him at an increasing pace.

"My people do not wish for war with the other kingdoms by breaking agreements!" I roar furiously, taking a step forward. "I give you two choices: go into exile, or receive your sentence here, by my hands."

A dark smile appears on the intruder's lips, and for the first time in hundreds of years, I notice an icy feeling creeping up my spine like little spiders.

Lysander's two soldiers rush towards me with long strides, roaring loudly. In a flash, I throw a sword at one of them, penetrating her throat and causing her to collapse into a heap on the floor. Her voice fades away and my white marble floor is stained with a deep shade of red. I grasp my other sword with both hands, quickly noting a weak point in the other giant's armour. When he's close enough, I thrust my weapon forcefully into his abdomen, ripping his stomach open before he can swing his club at me. My fingers grip his hair as he sinks to his knees, and I stab my fangs into his carotid artery. The hot liquid fills my mouth and a dizziness rushes through my head momentarily.

This seductive taste of life. The blood substitute truly is incomparable.

With a bellowing roar, I snap his neck with both hands before grabbing my sword once more, pulling some of his entrails out with it.

Lysander applauds enthusiastically as he floats in the air, whistling in amusement at me when I turn my attention to him.

"You are much more entertaining than I expected," he smiles mildly, putting his hands on his sides. "Your enthusiasm rubs off on me. Yes, I look forward to slicing off your limbs bit by bit and hearing you beg me to spare you."

"You are nothing and I will never beg!" my voice thunders. "I shall make an example out of you; breaking every bone in your body, gouging your eyes out, and tearing out your heart like a trophy for everyone to behold before consuming it. Nobody overthrows me, certainly not scum who solely rely on black arts."

The man tilts his head, looking at me for a second with his now completely pitch-black eyes.

"A trophy, you say? What a marvellous idea. I believe I will gift you to my shimmering little butterfly."

"I have grown tired of the verbal garbage which spouts out of your mouth, Lysander. You have wasted enough of my time!"

The fist in which I hold the weapon hardens, locking its grip around the hilt. I raise my free hand and focus my entire being on a point of energy located somewhere behind my ribs. In an instant, I shift into a large raven with razor-sharp claws and beak. Quickly, I flap at the man in front of me and I see how he recoils in the air while I violently peck at his eyes and claw at him. His hands try to catch me as he shouts, but I dodge them and circle above him before diving back down. I grab his hair, striking with the sharp tip of my beak against his skull.

"Wretched swine!" he growls in a voice edged with pain.

Swiftly I fly away, and a short moment later I have returned to my normal guise. With the sword at full swing, I thrust it at Lysander, but he parries it and I can almost smell his wrath as the mist swirling around him seems to merge with his body. I raise my eyebrows and lose my steady focus as tentacles and monstrous eyes erupt from his flesh with a loud squelch. At once, I realise the man in front of me is no ordinary necromancer.

He is infected, just like my advisor.

I fought hard, but I lost the battle against the vile necromancer. My people. I have abandoned my people. They rely on my protection. What will happen to them?

Blood tears of pain run down my cheeks where I am chained by black magic to a cold stone wall in the castle. *My home, home to both myself and those who work for me. Those who gave their lives to stand by my side until the last drop.*

Lysander stands before me in his humanoid form, juggling my royal crown between his hands.

"You are witnessing a shift in power," he says with a smile in the corners of his eyes, and puts on the crown as he takes a dramatic breath. "Now I am your lord, and you shall raise your gaze in respect to meet mine."

"I will never show respect to a cad who uses dirty tricks as a weapon to achieve his goal," I hiss between gritted teeth. "The responsibility of my crown weighs too heavy for your neck, and it will break under that weight."

I blink to sharpen my sight in an attempt to clear some of the bloody, clouding tears from my vision.

"It is evident you do not know when to hold your tongue. Let me teach you the first rule of respect: a fear of experiencing pain."

Lysander snaps his fingers, and one of my resurrected soldiers grabs me by the throat.

"You do not intimidate me, you plague-sore," I say hoarsely. "My people will never follow you by choice."

"Then I simply have to slaughter them and bring them back again," he replies, his lips curved into a crooked smile.

From one of his pockets, he pulls out a black dagger, gazing intently at its tip before returning his attention to me.

"First, I will cut off your tongue. I will have one of your former human workers cook it and eat it in front of you, before slitting their throat and drinking their blood as you watch. Afterwards, I shall return to slicing off the rest of your limbs, as promised earlier, and I intend to keep you alive. What kind of man would I be if I did not keep my word?"

My tongue is pulled out of my mouth by force. I decide not to give him the satisfaction of hearing me audibly agonise as the dagger works its way through my flesh, directing my thoughts entirely to my people and to my faithful advisor with the jewels in his dark locks. *I hope he survives his journey.*

CHAPTER TWENTY-EIGHT

Saga Falk

It has been several weeks since I met with Kailunn and the days seem to merge; each second lengthening into minutes and hours, just like the sun rises every morning and shadows grow with the arrival of each night. I'm feeling detached from the memories of my old life; they feel distant, and I desperately cling to them, so they don't blur somewhere in the fog of my brain. Garren has been in touch with the higher authorities in Whitekeep, and without knowing what I'm about to face, I've become an integral part of the Order of the Light.

It has been decided that I, along with knights of the order and warriors of the Silver Wardens, will head towards the Highlands to deal with the black magic which is ravaging the lands. On the way there, we'll bring additional reinforcements from the high elves, as their realm borders the infected areas. *Will it be weird to see Kailunn again? He dug deep into my memories.*

My thoughts often wander to my friends and family back home. As I sit, absent-mindedly watching the dancing flames of a small fire where we have camped for the night, I wiggle my toes and sigh quietly. We have been on foot for several days, although we have horses with us—which no one uses, except to carry packs—and have only stopped on a few daily occasions to eat, drink, and sleep. My energy levels are waning, and I feel tired to my core as my thoughts bounce against the walls of my skull. I've barely been able to talk to Garren in private, and out of the corner of my eye I can make out monstrous dancing shadows at frequent intervals. However, there are no opportunities to seek reassurance from the hard-working paladin, especially now that there are a larger number of individuals in the party, including Ahriele, who keeps a constant eye on me.

A hollow feeling echoes inside, and I lightly kick the ground with one foot. My body hurts to have gone so long with little rest. The one positive thing about sleeping under the open sky, when I don't want to spend the night in the same tent as some other snoring individuals, has been looking up at the stars and reflecting in silence when I don't dare to sleep due to nightmares and whispering voices in my head.

I may be part of a party, one marching towards the same goal, but I feel incredibly lonely and alienated in this environment. *Everyone looks at me so strangely.*

My gaze wanders unobtrusively and settles on Garren some distance away. He's discussing matters with Vincent Thurston, the warlord of Whitekeep. Vincent, who leads the non-religious army, is an older, taller man with close-cropped grey hair, dark bushy eyebrows, light brown eyes, and a grey beard. I remember him from *Reign Online*. I used to help Remy do harder missions for him when he needed a priest's healing touch.

Vincent radiates an impenetrable sternness, one bearing witness to

SHADOW DANCE

life experience and countless bloody battles out in the field. He's older than Garren, and it shows in the occasionally condescending manner in which he speaks to the paladin. Both of them seem to be equally stubborn, and I push my glasses up the bridge of my nose, wondering what they're talking about.

The bard I met at the inn earlier is travelling with us, entertaining us with stories, songs, and music. Tonight, she's on the other side of the campfire, enthusiastically telling Ahriele a story. Ahriele's star-veiled gaze embraces her as she intensely follows every movement the elven woman makes. A faint smile appears on my lips, and I slowly drum on one knee with one hand. *She looks completely smitten with her. It's kind of cute.* The elf she's conversing with looks beautiful with her round face, narrow dark eyes, and long hair in a shade of turquoise, of which a few thin braids peek out.

Slowly, I stand up, brushing off my pants and stretching my arms over my head. Somewhere in the party, I see Cináed and Xerxi, an elf with long fiery red hair and a patch over his right eye, sitting next to each other. The human whispers something in his ear which leaves an impression of amusement on his face. A couple of days ago I watched them briefly as they went off to a forest grove together. They seem to enjoy each other's company a lot.

Until yesterday, I had tried to stay away from Cináed as much as possible. However, he had pleasantly surprised me when he sat down and shared a piece of bread with me, as I had found myself some distance from the others with hidden tears in my eyes during a moment of intense homesickness.

We had eaten together without uttering a single word. His simple act had somehow comforted me, and I had fought back the tears. Maybe he's not a rotten person, even though he had put a knife to my throat and threatened to drain me of my blood if he didn't get his way.

Xerxi's twin brother named Xanjou, sitting opposite the two men and gazing with his light green eyes at some women, has the same fiery red hair as his brother and the same handsome, fit build. Unlike Xerxi, who uses a bow and whose hairstyle is long and often in a ponytail, he's a short-haired soldier who wields two powerful battle axes. Earlier in the day, I noticed him watching me and when he saw I caught his eye, he had given me a confident smile, which had instantly made me turn my face away. He seems to be a womaniser and I'm not interested in anything more than a superficial acquaintance.

I decide to go for a walk and stretch my legs. It's getting dark, so I borrow a lantern and direct my steps towards another part of the forest grove. In any other circumstance, I would have been terrified of going into the woods alone, but I have to get out of here, even if it's just for a few minutes. *I can barely breathe.*

The voices from the camp turn into a faint murmur before trailing off and my feet don't stop until I arrive at a clearing where I hear the babbling of a small brook, sparkling mysteriously in the gloom. Carefully, I set the lantern down, tapping my fingertips against the scabbard at my left hip where a relatively lightweight longsword is tucked in. I still haven't gotten used to having it by my side. Slowly pulling it out, I carefully stroke the blade with one fingertip.

Weapons this close make me anxious. When I had initially objected to carrying one, Vincent verbally reprimanded me, then proceeded berating Garren for choosing a lousy recruit who's a burden to the entire party, regardless of how strong my magic is.

A sigh stumbles out between my lips, and I swing the sword slowly from one side to the other, watching the light reflect on the edge. Air fills my lungs through my nose as I focus on the energy within and I can't help but cheer triumphantly as I see a white glow appear at my hands, finding its way down the side of the weapon. *If only Vincent could see me now—I'm not useless at all!*

The glow disappears after a while, leaving me a little tired. It still takes some effort to try to master what they call the Light, especially when I'm exhausted to begin with. Nevertheless, I still practise in secret every day and notice how I'm getting better and better at it, without outside help.

Outside help. Like from Garren, for example.

I force myself to swing the sword a little harder this time, pretending to parry a blow, doing a little pirouette, and dancing with the sword, like I've seen people do online—though probably not quite as elegantly—while focusing on my breathing.

My mind pulls in different directions while I perform the movements. I imagine Kailunn's tall, elegant stature in the beautiful white and purple robe with its gold details, remembering his telepathic voice in my head and his fingers closing around my shoulders. My stomach tingles at the thought of him kissing me, even though I can't remember the sequence of the events. The tingling intensifies when another familiar figure of tall stature appears among the thoughts. He sweeps aside heavy stage curtains containing images of the prince, and my memories of the holy knight cupping my face with his hands and kissing me in the garden make my heart sing faintly.

Sighing silently, I fix my gaze on the weapon I'm holding in front of me with one hand. I miss his presence, voice, and touch. I even miss his teasing comments, the sternness of his gaze, and how it softens in a matter of seconds.

With my other free hand, I fish the phone out of my trouser pocket, looking down at the screen. 21:12. A few days ago, I had changed the lock screen to a picture of a butterfly I had photographed in the Order of the Light's garden, after discovering I don't think about Kailunn in quite the same way as before. My knees do get weak when I think about how handsome he is, but there's something about him that's enigmatic—perhaps slightly too shrouded in mystery. Moreover, I reason in a more logical way. Not only is he a stranger, but he's at least eight hundred years old. *Eight hundred*. At the age of twenty-nine, I already feel old and cranky. Surely, I wouldn't be able to date elves who live for thousands of years? Perhaps it's just as well I admire him from a distance, as if he were a work of art in a museum. *Look, but don't touch.*

Date. My lips curl into a faint, melancholy smile. All these fictional 2D men who are now real, and I've already started thinking about it in this context. Me, who didn't want to date when I was at home and had all the comforts of the world within reach. Who has time for romance when there's war going on? Will I even survive this journey? *I can't do anything. Not well enough, anyway.*

Slowly, I put the sword back in its scabbard and click on the recording app on my phone. Recording audio acts as a diary for me. A way to document my thoughts, and to cheer myself up in times of need with words of encouragement. Silently, I clear my throat and prepare myself.

"Dear diary. I haven't got a clue what day it is, but currently it's evening. My body hurts all over, from head to toe. I'm afraid I'll wear out my sneakers and I'm unsure if I can use my insoles in mediaeval boots. They look super uncomfortable."

I pause, gather my thoughts, and continue speaking.

"I've been thinking about Kailunn a lot and I've come to the conclusion I need to be on my guard. He's handsome and charismatic, but there's something slightly off about him, as if he's constantly searching for something. After all, looks aren't everything, and my daydreams about him may not match reality. I'm aware I've been rambling about the same subject for the past few days, but I think this is it. I don't intend to get involved with him beyond casual acquaintanceship, even if, against all odds, he would show interest and I might be tempted. He said it himself—he's not into humans."

Drawing a long breath, I pace back and forth slowly, speaking again with my gaze fixed on an invisible point somewhere in the gloom spreading out in front of me.

"Ever since meeting Kailunn, it feels like Garren's distancing himself from me. First, I was confused, then angry, sad, and now I'm tired. The confusion is exhaustive. Maybe the problem lies with me? I'm not used to others noticing me and I probably behave immaturely sometimes. Perhaps I hesitate or fumble too much when I get attention. Frustration and indecisiveness, caused by anxiety. Sometimes I don't want to feel anything at all."

A long, drawn-out sigh stumbles out between my lips.

"I should ask Lysander to rip out my heart the next time he shows up, so this ends once and for all—I'll never be able to get home. I'll never see my parents again or sleep in my bed. Haru must have already sacked me. Unpaid bills piling up. Everyone will think I've disappeared without a trace or died in a ditch somewhere. That I've become one of the many people who disappear, an unknown number in some dark crime statistic."

I settle down by the creek with my knees pulled up to my chest and rest my forehead against them, trying to fight back the tears welling up in my eyes. Sucking air into my lungs, I count to three and exhale slowly. I lift my head and end the recording.

"Well, this was pure garbage," I mutter. "My mind's all over the place."

A small frog hiding in the damp grass by the brook catches my attention. Blinking away the remaining tears, I bring my phone closer to it, hoping I can get a picture for my collection. It has blue eyes, a light purple body with yellow dots, and makes a faint croaking sound.

"Your life must be so good, not having to worry about every little thing," I say in a hushed tone and snap a photo before it jumps away, disappearing into the darkness.

I scroll through the photo gallery, finding the picture of me and Garren and looking at it in silence. *Would I have allowed myself to date you if I were back home, despite my inner demons and flaws? Would you have seen me, or chosen someone else who's more out-going, and less complicated? Someone with less emotional damage?*

Slowly, I stand up, putting my phone back in my pocket. Gently, I massage the backs of my knees before stretching my back and adjusting the chain around my neck. The pendant rests under the fabric of my blouse, hidden from prying eyes. It's getting chilly and I should head back to the camp.

When I turn around, a gasp escapes me, and I almost drop the lantern in my hand.

"W-what are you doing here?" I stutter, overwhelmed by a wave of nervousness.

"I could ask you the same thing, lass."

Garren splits the darkness as he emerges, the light from the lantern sweeping its bright blanket over his face.

Good lord, he's so handsome. I swallow hard, trying to look neutral.

"How long have you been standing there?"

"Long enough to witness your conversation with yourself," he replies, and I can't read what his expression is saying.

I take a deep breath, masking my embarrassment with shrill words.

"What the hell, Garren! I was recording something private!"

"I apologise. It was clearly not my intention to pry. You didn't notice my presence and I'm not one to step in between a person and their soul searching, or interrupt it by trying to remove myself."

He bows his head and closes his eyes for a second, then directs an intense look at me.

"We need to talk."

My hand holding the lantern trembles and I draw air into my lungs as I silently count to three.

"And what is it you want to discuss?"

I glare defiantly at the paladin and can't help but feel my pulse increase. *Foolish heart. Behave.*

"Us. This invisible, lassoing rope which you have placed around my heart."

I tilt my head and do my utmost not to blush.

"What a dramatic metaphor! You've more or less distanced yourself from me," I mutter incredulously, and focus on calming my breathing. "There's no 'us'."

"I gave you space so you could gather your thoughts without my interference."

Irony laces my voice when I retort.

"How incredibly caring. It's so nice of you to decide when and how I best gather my own thoughts."

"Saga, calm yourself. I did my utmost to stay away from you, for your own sake, because you expressed you were torn."

Garren's low, stern voice penetrates my entire being and I look away from him as he takes a step towards me. *He has a point. I also know I get angry easily sometimes from over-analysing everything, and he did in fact mention a while ago he doesn't want to influence my judgement.*

"All right," I mumble and shrug nonchalantly. "Start talking, then."

I glance at Garren, seeing him raise one eyebrow as he looks at me.

"Let us speak in my tent," he says, surprised as I shake my head.

"Absolutely not," I reply. "I don't intend to give the wrong impression to the others by going with you. It wouldn't be fair to them if they think I'm being treated differently—I'm a stranger and don't fit into your template as it currently stands."

"I respect your choice."

Garren takes the lantern from me, settles on the ground, and puts it down by his side. He pats the grass in front of him with one hand, and I take a seat while tucking a few strands of hair behind my ears.

"Are you sleeping properly?" he asks.

What do you think? I refrain from rolling my eyes and shake my head again.

"No, I'm not. Ever since you distanced yourself from me, I've started seeing visions and strange, shadowy figures. It affects me a lot."

Garren furrows his brow and mutters something indistinct while looking grim.

"Always wear the necklace," he says after a while. "Speaking of something entirely different. I saw when you danced with your weapon. It was a feast for weary eyes."

The stern expression in his gaze blossoms into softness.

"It's nothing special. I was just improvising," I mumble, as a warmth envelopes my heart and counteracts my frustration.

I've missed your flattery.

"I couldn't take my eyes off you," he continues enthusiastically, and I notice the colour rise in his face. "It was among the most beautiful things I've ever laid eyes on."

"You're exaggerating," I chuckle.

Without putting much thought into it, I place one hand over his arm. The air in my lungs seems to leave my body for a moment, and my fingertips glow. Garren's eyes mirror the intense, shining light and he smiles widely.

"The Light has longed to travel between our bodies," he says softly, grabbing my hands with his. "How I've missed you, Saga. Allow me to take care of you for a while."

My face lights up in a surprised smile and I let myself get pulled into

SHADOW DANCE

his arms. His fingertips caress my forehead and cheeks as he says a prayer to the Light. A magical warmth spreads from his luminous hand into my skin, dancing throughout my body.

"It's nice," I smile, my voice veiled with a comfortable tiredness.

My head spins and it feels like I'm falling through time and space as I close my eyes tightly. Strong arms keep holding me and fingertips continue to caress my face. I lose my breath again before my breathing slows down. My mind tries to drift off into a deep slumber, but I fight the feeling, wanting to stay awake.

"Calm your worries and let me heal you," says Garren, as if he's far away in the distance.

My eyelids flutter. The pleasurable heat wraps around me, diving in and out of the pores of my skin, and I can't stop a low moaning sound from stumbling out from between my lips. It feels like I'm being embraced by the cosmos itself, somewhere far away from war, intrigue, and unhinged, bloodthirsty vampires.

"What a trip," I mutter with my eyes still closed, smiling. "Who needs sex and drugs when you can experience this?"

The vertigo begins to subside slowly. It's like I've been asleep whilst talking out loud, for how long I'm unsure. The feeling of a beautiful, star-studded cosmos fades away and I stretch out my hands in front of me. Something velvety brushes against my palms and my eyelids slowly rise. I blink a few times to sharpen my gaze and am met by Garren's intense sky-blue eyes looking back at me. My one hand is on his right cheek and the other has wrapped some of his curls between my fingers. Slowly, I pull my hands to me, my face painted with an expression of confusion.

"Saga." His voice is a little hoarse, and he clears his throat. "I healed you to relieve the pain and fatigue in your body. In the process, your own power awakened, and it affected your state of mind."

"Did I say anything weird while I was under the influence?" I mumble, worried about what I'm about to hear, a bad feeling ticking in my stomach like an emotional bomb.

"Saga," he says again.

"Garren, please. I need to know what I said, or I won't be able to look you in the eye."

He seems to collect his thoughts.

"When an individual is healed, the ritual can also cleanse the soul of sin—those committed by, or against, oneself. At times, these sins are enunciated aloud."

"Okay, but what did I say?" The panic and the feeling of shame make me squirm, and a sense of guilt puts its claws in me. *He used his own energy and life force to heal me, which he didn't have to do.* "Sorry, I don't mean to sound annoyed," I mutter, rubbing one eye as I sit up in front of him.

Slowly Garren grabs the chain around my neck, carefully pulling the jewellery out of my blouse and running his thumb over it as he seems to gather his thoughts once more.

"You spoke of your previous lover."

He releases his grip on the pendant and directs his gaze at me. I scrunch up my nose in disdain.

"It was the guy I lived with in Malmö for eight years, which I mentioned to you briefly before. I've moved past those experiences."

"It's an incredibly long time to live with someone who doesn't show you the respect you deserve."

I'm about to retort, but as fire flares up in his eyes I find myself submerged in silence. Carefully, he places one hand against my cheek and firmly I tell myself I mustn't surrender to my inner emotional turmoil.

"The things which happened weren't your fault," he continues in a honeyed voice, and I clench my jaws to chase away the tears which are dangerously close to welling up in my eyes. "It can't have been easy being in that situation."

"So, you know what happened?"

What a dumb question. It's plain as day he knows it.

"I assume the things you mentioned are a fraction of everything you've experienced. Moreover, I caught glimpses of your memories before, along with Prince Sunseeker."

Covered in invisible shame, I lower my gaze and let it follow the dancing shadows the lantern's light casts on the tree trunks. *I knew it. They've probably seen fragments of the worst things.*

"Did I mention anything else?" I ask quietly.

I wish he'd keep his hand on my cheek. Instead, he moves it to adjust his coat of arms.

"You spoke in tongues and mentioned something about the healing being better than, and I quote verbatim: 'sex and drugs'."

Garren's lips shift in an amused smile, and I glare at him, embarrassed to my core.

"I've never done drugs," I say in my defence. "The closest I've come in contact with them is what Kailunn gave me, if what you mentioned is true. Besides, sex isn't a necessity for me, and I could easily live without it."

Folding my arms over my chest, I turn my head away. *These details about myself are way too private, and I'm sharing them with this man. Haven't I shared enough about myself as it is?*

"Anyway, thanks for healing me," I say softly. "The pain's more or less gone now."

"You're welcome." He puts a finger under my chin, leaning his face closer to mine. "I want you to know I don't go around healing others anyhow, unless they're in need. To heal another person and touch their soul, without them being injured in a life-threatening way, is an intimate act, both for the person who performs it and the person on the receiving end. It's not only physical intimacy which brings deep closeness between two people, but also magic and faith."

"Right," I stutter and quickly get to my feet while offering him my hand.

After rising, he pulls me close in an embrace, stroking my hair gently and tenderly pressing me against his chest.

"Are you certain you don't wish to sleep in my presence tonight?" he asks with a hushed tone in my ear, causing goosebumps to cover my arms. "There's much I would like to discuss beyond the prying eyes and ears of the others."

I want to, but I just can't. People will judge me.

"It wouldn't be fair to the others," I whisper, taking in his scent, body heat, and the feeling of being close to him. *Safety and inner peace.*

Garren locks his gaze into mine and slowly strokes my shoulders with his thumbs.

"I appreciate your sincerity and sense of duty. However, I want you to come and look for me if you're afraid or find yourself unable to fall asleep."

I nod in response and adjust my fringe with my fingers as I try to gather my thoughts.

"Garren," I say softly, lowering my glance as I search for the right words, "I've missed you."

The paladin places his hands on my cheeks, making me look up at him. His gaze glistens like an ocean under the summer sun, and the streaks of joy at the corners of his eyes make my heart clench.

"It's only you I see behind my eyelids," he mutters in a voice edged with heat and caresses my cheeks with his thumbs. "The Light reflected in your smiles, your courage, and your fiery glances."

Upon drawing a deep breath, I exhale silently and look up at his face. "You're doing that thing with your eyes again, and that's okay. I like you, too."

SHADOW DANCE

The tingling in my stomach spreads throughout my body, rushing to my head. *I can't take the words back. These words I never thought I'd want to share with another real person again.* A warm feeling blossoms in my chest and my heartbeat echoes in my ears.

Before I know it, he wraps one arm around my waist. Pulling me even closer, he moves his other hand behind my neck. A warmth engulfs my singing heart when he leans me back in a deep kiss laced with hungry passion, and golden shimmering butterflies swirl around us.

CHAPTER TWENTY-NINE

Sandro Oyemi

My nostrils pick up the warming scent of humans nearby as I hang upside down from a tree branch. I do not need to breathe, but the delicious aroma tickles my nose and I suck air into my lungs while my ears prick up, pointing in different directions. I should continue my journey towards Whitekeep, but something holds me back—something magical, familiar.

My feet let go of the branch and with quick wing beats, I flutter in the direction of the scents. Once hidden behind a tree, I shapeshift into my usual guise and adjust my clothes with one hand and holding my staff with the other.

Cautiously, I peer from my hiding spot and sharpen my gaze when I spot a short woman holding the hand of a tall knight. She stands on her tiptoes, leaning into him with an adorable expression on her face. The man strokes her hair and cheek with his fingertips before leaning down to taste her lips. Jolting as I realise who he is, I break a twig under one of my boots. *Now I know why the magic seems familiar; I have stood eye to eye with his ancestors.*

The woman turns her head in my direction, flinching when she catches sight of me.

"The three-eyed vampire," she gasps. "I've seen him before!"

Have we met? It does not matter. It is useless to try to hide.

"Have no fear," I say as I step out of my hiding place.

The words stumble out of my mouth at a furious pace. With eyes wide, I wave the staff and the other hand dismissively in front of me, while the paladin steps towards me with a powerful sword at the ready. *I am not a fighter!*

"Begone, beast!" he roars, and the sword begins to glow in bright white.

"Wait!" I exclaim in an unusually shrill voice.

On swift feet I move to the side, avoiding being cleft in half. The Light is deadly to my kind, and I must maintain a safe distance between us.

"I wish you no harm! It is you I seek, Roseheart. I must speak to you regarding an urgent matter!"

With lightning speed, the man points the tip of the sword just centimetres away from my throat, causing me to back away from the magic heating my skin instantly. An ominous, ancient, and all-too-familiar feeling of violence which is not my own begins to spread in my stomach, but I fight it off with my inner strength. *You do not control me.*

"So, you know who I am and what I'm capable of doing. I'll give you a moment before I raise my sword anew," he says with a menacing darkness in his eyes.

The woman standing behind him looks at me with her mouth half-open.

"I think I know him," she says, taking a small step closer and staring

SHADOW DANCE

at me. "He's not dangerous. I've read about him online."

I do not have time to speculate about what the woman is talking about. The knight extends his arm in front of her.

"Stay there, Saga. We may have peace with the vampires, but one of them is in our territory now. He has broken the agreement between our realms, and we don't know how bloodthirsty he is."

"He probably wouldn't come here on his own and stand before a holy knight if he was bloodthirsty," she says, glancing at him. "Just look at him, Garren. He seems harmless. He said he wants to talk and you're intimidating him."

"True words have been spoken," I interject quickly and seize the opportunity to spin the thread of the woman's words. "I have flown a long way to converse with you, Roseheart. You are the one who can help us."

The paladin raises one eyebrow.

"Who are you referring to when you say 'us'?"

I lower my head, averting two of my eyes to the ground and keeping the third firmly locked on him.

"I am a royal advisor. My lord and our entire kingdom are in danger," I reply in a low voice. "We were attacked and could not repel the army. When our comrades fell, they were revived, their minds and actions controlled by a necromancer. We need the help of your people before the entire realm falls, and the enemy spreads their foul magic to the other kingdoms."

"It's Lysander, I'm sure of it!" the woman gasps, grabbing the paladin's arm as she looks up at him. "That's probably why he hasn't talked to me properly in a while. He has been busy overthrowing the leader of the vampires."

She puts her hands to her temples and shakes her head.

"This is terrible," she continues, visibly distraught. "There's too much happening at once. Dark forces in the Highlands, death, and Lysander acquiring a seat where he can exercise his power. He's a menace."

She looks at the man again.

"Do you have a map of the countries, Garren?"

The sword in the knight's hand stops glowing, and he pushes it back in its scabbard.

"Yes," he replies while nodding.

"I'd like to have a look at it to see where we are."

She runs one fingertip over her lower lip, before fixing her attention on me again, seemingly analysing me.

"You're Sandro Oyemi."

"How do you know my name?" I ask, blinking all three eyes at the same time. "I do not recall us meeting before."

"No, we haven't. But don't ask me how I know it. It's a long story and we don't have time for it right now."

She crosses her arms over her chest and studies me from head to toe.

"You're an advisor to… Sorry, I don't remember their name."

"My lord's name is Amarion Starling," I answer with melancholy in my voice, adjusting my long curls with my fingers.

"Amarion," she murmurs in an exhale.

Her expression mirrors her dipping in and out of her thoughts. She takes another step closer to me, opening her arms in my direction.

"I want to help you. Lysander has caused me a lot of trouble, too. He tore me from my family, my home, and my life. He torments me when I try to sleep."

A deep compassion replaces her slightly defiant look, and when she takes my hand in hers, hot magic rushes through my body.

With a loud wheezing sound, I pull away, coughing loudly. My knees shake and I sink to the ground while holding the staff with both hands. My body is on fire internally, invisibly, and an excruciating pain courses through every part of me. The dark force down in my stomach taunts me in my head, teasing me for refusing to use its strength to empower myself.

"I'm so sorry!" I hear her exclaim. "What just happened?"

As I gasp for air and squint at her with blood streaming down my eyes, she puts her hands over her mouth, staggering backwards.

"Do something, Garren!" she shrieks, desperation and fear invading her voice.

"Do not be afraid," I groan quietly, raising a hand in a reassuring gesture.

I have more to utter, but the gurgling sounds crawling out of my throat drown the words out. The paladin crouches down before me. With a shaky hand, I pull a small bottle out of the leather pouch hanging from a belt around my waist, dropping it on the ground as a violent cough shakes my body. Between the tears of blood, I can see how the knight closes his fingers around the bottle and lifts it up, eyeing it in disbelief.

"It is magical, synthetic blood," I wheeze through gritted teeth.

My head sinks to my chest and I draw a ragged breath. My ears prick up with the sound of the bottle being opened, the smell of the liquid wafting into my nostrils enticing me.

"Drink."

He tilts my head up by putting his hand under my chin. For a split second, fatal thoughts play out in my head of his touch killing me, much like the damage the woman has caused. However, to my relief, nothing catastrophic occurs. He puts the bottle to my lips and as I thirstily devour the drink, the burning sensation inside subsides and my eyes cease to bleed.

"Thank you, Roseheart," I speak in a hoarse voice.

The woman looks at me, her features veiled with worry. She grabs one of her blouse sleeves and rips a piece off with a faint grunting sound. Nimbly, she bends down and wets the fabric in a stream a few steps from us.

"What are you doing?" the man in front of me asks in surprise as he turns his attention to her.

"Here," she says softly and hands him the piece of cloth. "It's for him to clean his face with. I'm afraid what my touch would do to him again."

When I wipe myself with the cloth, the faint scent of the human, stuck in the fibres, finds its way into my nose and I take a silent breath. She is a charged, magical vessel, unlike the knight who has his power under control. Standing up, I reach for the remaining potion being handed to me by the man.

"Soon I will have recovered fully," I say, tucking the bottle into the leather pouch and glancing at the woman, but she has turned her face away to hide her shame.

"Let's head back to the camp," says the knight, giving me a curt nod to follow them. "We must speak to Thurston, or his soldiers will flay you on the spot."

"Fools. They cannot kill us. I will keep you alive. You will rip their throats open and sacrifice their blood to me."

"Silence! You have no say in my actions."

Pushing the voice back into the darkest corner of my mind, I follow them with silent footfalls, and hear the woman murmur to him.

"My power isn't for harming others. I need your help to learn how to handle it, Garren. And I want to check the map to see where we are."

The paladin gives her a deep look and nods. He caresses her neck with one hand, then lets it travel down her body to rest against her lower back. She moves closer to him and wraps one arm around his waist. As I keep a short distance to them, I listen to their heartbeats composing a warm melody with playful notes in sync with each other. For the first time, I wonder what it feels like to have such genuinely human, yet fragile, emotions in one's possession.

CHAPTER THIRTY

Saga Falk

"Crikey! Vincent is quite dramatic, isn't he?"

Drawing a long and audible sigh, I sit down some distance from the vampire hiding in the shadows. We've chosen to leave the others for a while in order to be undisturbed. His red eyes glow in the gloom and a chill runs down my spine as I see him blink with his three eyelids concurrently. I tell myself he can be trusted. Surely, he wouldn't cross the line and attack me when we're not too far from the camp we've set up for the night?

"I cannot blame him," Sandro replies with a slightly cracked voice. "Humans draw parallels between vampires and monsters."

"But it's obvious you're here asking for help," I continue, pulling the coat tighter around my body. "Anyone can see it, even if you're not a seasoned warlord."

"Persistence is a powerful blindfold. Fortunately, Roseheart has the gift of speech, and the discourse went well, despite the warlord's initial objections."

When Sandro tilts his head and looks at me, I can see his features better in the dim light from the lantern I brought. A few freckles dotting his face give him a rather adorable impression.

I fidget with the jewellery around my neck and give him a nod. My mind goes back to the map I had looked at earlier. At least now I have an idea of where we are, and I feel less lost.

"My presence does not seem to frighten you," he says, his pointy, long fangs showing as he smiles at me.

Four fangs, instead of just two, on the upper row of teeth. That's odd.

"No, you look quite harmless and young," I smile back, pushing the glasses up the bridge of my nose.

He shifts to where it's a bit brighter, sitting with his back against a tree trunk and perusing me with steady eyes.

"How old do you think I am?" he asks, tapping lightly with one fingertip on the rock atop his staff.

"You look to be no more than twenty-three and your voice is youthful," I answer truthfully, scrolling through the memories in my brain. "But I'm guessing you're at least a couple of hundred years old."

The light from the lantern makes the shadows under his eyes look even deeper and he touches some of his curls, which are decorated with gold chains and sparkling red stones.

"Three thousand years. That is my age."

His answer causes surprise to sweep over my features. "I'm twenty-nine and I already feel tired and worn out, so I dread to think what it's like for you."

A muffled laugh from the vampire's throat catches in the shadows as he closes two of his eyes and the third on his forehead looks at me, half-closed. *He's oddly cute, in a rather bizarre way. I wonder what his life was like before he became a vampire.*

"Sorry about what happened earlier," I say apologetically, tucking a few strands of hair behind my ears. "I haven't learned how to control my magic yet. Where I'm from, we don't have these powers."

"Not to worry. I recover quickly if I have my healing potion." He smiles widely, giving me a long look. "It shows you are not from here. You both behave and look different." He bites his lower lip, his fangs sticking out. "Pardon my disrespect."

"None taken," I reply. "I'm used to looking a little different compared to others around me."

It's comforting to share my thoughts with someone who knows what it's like to be judged by others. Leaning my head against the tree behind me, I lightly tap my fingers against my thigh and continue.

"I changed my name because the one my parents gave me was considered too odd and difficult to pronounce. So, as a result, I changed both my first and last name when I turned eighteen."

Sandro's intense gaze drills right into my bone marrow.

"Your real name," he says in a hushed tone and leans forward. "It translates to 'star' in your parents' native language. Stars are the most beautiful things in the night sky, so it is sad you felt the need to change it."

My jaw drops and I crawl a little closer on all fours.

"How do you know it?" I ask curiously. "And how do you know about my parents' language?"

"It is woven into your heart rate and the vibrations it creates in the air, so I need not know the language in order to understand it."

"That's amazing!" I mutter and move a little closer, but Sandro shifts and puts a small distance between us.

"I do not wish to repeat the previous event," he excuses himself, slightly waving one hand.

Whilst blushing profusely, I pull back, glancing at him. I've always enjoyed reading about vampires in books, and I'd like to get to know this one better. *Reign Online*'s patch notes gave little information about him other than him being an advisor to Amarion, and that he's friendly.

"I know a few things about you," I say, adjusting my fringe. "Please don't ask me how. It's hard to explain it in short terms. But I would like to know more about you, since we'll be travelling together for a while."

The gemstones in the vampire's hair glisten in the dim light, and I can't stop staring at the third eye in his forehead. It's both terrifying and fascinating.

"You wonder why I have an extra eye," Sandro says in a hushed voice carried on a cool night breeze, and he smiles when he sees me blushing even deeper. "As far as I can remember, I was born with it. Maybe it is an expression of my telepathic ability and sorcery. For instance, turning into a bat is not the only thing in my arsenal. Still, I feel it is appropriate to point out that I am peaceful and avoid violence as much as possible."

"You're different to the vampires I usually read about in books," I say, still resting my head against the tree trunk behind me.

For a moment, I notice his gaze halting at my throat, but I push the thoughts away. It's probably just my imagination.

"Do you take damage from the sun?" I ask, wiggling my foot thoughtfully.

Sandro raises one eyebrow in surprise.

"The sun's rays make vampires hungrier from travelling in daylight and we are somewhat weaker as our energy drains faster. We take little physical damage as long as we are in good health," he replies, and I see him sweep the tip of his tongue over his fangs. "I feel more at home in the arms of the shadows."

I run one finger over my lower lip while my thoughts circulate. What he says correlates with what I know about some vampires in fiction.

"Interesting," I mutter as I nod thoughtfully. "Do you sleep in a coffin?"

SHADOW DANCE

"I find them to be stuffy and I prefer having an open space around me. Sometimes I like to sleep upside down, like a bat."

The statement makes me grin, before the sound of approaching footsteps makes us raise our heads.

Fuck's sake. Not her, not now.

Anxiety rings in my ears as I catch a glimpse of Ahriele. She has changed from armour to simpler clothes of cotton and linen, her thick golden hair swaying from one side to another in a ponytail. The attire hugs her body and show off her muscles, rather than hiding them.

"It's getting late," she says firmly, crossing her arms over her chest.

I stand up, my legs stiff from sitting down.

"Thanks, but I don't need someone to remind me when it's time to go to bed," I reply, noticing how cold my voice sounds.

I don't want to have an argument tonight. For several days I have avoided talking to her, but now she has taken the step and sought me out. Ahriele frowns disapprovingly as her gaze follows Sandro when he rises to his feet, before turning her attention back to me.

"You look awfully tired and worn out," she continues, tilting her head slightly. "Are you getting enough sleep?"

Your statement rings hollow. And thanks for commenting on my appearance. I'm aware of how hideous I look.

I turn my head away, noticing Sandro has retreated into the shadows with his eyes glowing in the darkness.

I flinch when I feel the weight of Ahriele's hand over my shoulder.

"Falk," she says, making me look at her.

The anxiety has moved from my ears, now clawing deeply in my stomach. Upon steeling myself, I try to breathe normally.

"What do you want?" I ask bluntly, the words hanging in the air for a while.

Her voice is hushed.

"I want to apologise for my previous behaviour. Obviously, you're of importance to my brother, and I should have respected this."

I blink a few times. Her last sentence shouldn't have come as a surprise, but I still get nervous and feel the tingling in my stomach when I hear the confirmation. *I'm important, not just to myself but also to an outsider who isn't part of my closest social circle.* The words I want to say get lost in my throat and after a moment of silence, I pull away from her touch as I take a step to the side, putting distance between us.

"All right," I mutter eventually. "Then that's been established. Now, if you'll excuse me, I'd like to continue my conversation with Sandro."

Ahriele regards me with an immovable expression in her eyes.

"Allow me to be your friend, disregarding my status," she says softly. "Let us start from scratch. I want you to be able to trust me. For Garren's sake."

A frosty smile makes the corners of my mouth twitch as her words find their way into my ears.

"I find it difficult to establish ties of friendship with someone who looks down on others and who judges in advance. As long as we can tolerate each other, then I'm happy," I answer curtly, crossing my arms over my chest.

Slowly she pulls back, shadows wandering across her face.

"My offer stands," she says and gives me a long look. "If you need someone to talk to, I'm at hand."

"Yeah, okay then."

I nod without looking at her and hear the footsteps as she leaves. With one foot, I kick a small stone that disappears somewhere in the grass and take a deep breath. After I make sure the knight isn't eavesdropping nearby, I squint into the darkness and leave a question on the night breeze.

SHADOW DANCE

"Sandro, are you still there?"

My eyes are drawn to my shoes. There's a small three-eyed mouse at my feet. It places its little paws against my sneakers and raises its head, its whiskers trembling. The mouth moves and I can see tiny fangs.

Realising who it is, I squat down and, after a moment's hesitation, cup my hand so he can climb into my palm, all the while focusing on not burning him again. *It works! I can control the power with some effort!* Carefully, I lift my hand and move him next to my ear.

"Her angelic appearance dazzled me and made me shapeshift in pure surprise," I hear Sandro squeak in a thin voice.

I'm taken aback by his statement.

"Ahriele, you mean? She may be beautiful on the outside, but it means nothing if her personality is lacking."

"She radiates strength from within. I could hear it in her heartbeat."

"Seriously? Didn't you notice the condescending look she gave you?" I snort and bring my hand to the ground so he can step down.

In the blink of an eye, I see Sandro rise, now in his usual guise, and I get to my feet as well. He adjusts some of his black curly tresses, the stunning red jewels sparkling in the dim light.

"A judgemental heart is struck with fear and coldness for a reason. But it does not mean there is a lack of room for change and for goodness to take root."

"You remind me more of a pious lamb than a vampire," I blurt out before I can bite my tongue.

A chuckle slips out of Sandro's throat and once again I find myself staring at his fangs. *Pointy, sharp, scary.*

"My tongue has not tasted human blood in a thousand years, which I presume contributes to your impression of me," he responds. "A beast of prey which slumbers indefinitely, disguised as an innocent lamb."

The thought of his fangs penetrating someone's skin makes me shudder.

"Can you shapeshift into any animal?" I ask, in an attempt to change the course of the conversation.

"Many, but not all. Fauna fascinates me and I study them in books and nature, trying to imitate their various forms."

We start heading back towards the camp at a leisurely pace and continue to converse with each other, interspersed with pauses, and I'm feeling comfortable in his company. The moments of silence between us don't feel oppressive and I'm convinced he won't hurt me. He peruses me with an enigmatic expression in his red eyes.

"Human feelings of tenderness remind me of treasures," he says. "Pure, precious gemstones which most people would want in their possession. Something they are afraid to lose once it is in their grasp."

Nervously, I adjust my glasses, and the grip on the lantern in my hand tightens a bit as I step forward. I ask him a question, trying to capture my thoughts swirling around like butterflies in my head.

"Vampires can love someone too, right?"

Turning to face the creature of the night, I see him stopping and glancing at the staff he's holding. He closes his third eye.

"I would assume we are capable of harbouring such emotions," he replies, tilting his head. "To be fair, I do not know what love feels like, nor have I ever been interested in it. My heart has stood still for centuries, unable to send out any frequencies. However, I feel something for my lord. Over the years, I have stood by the side of many royalties, watched them rise and fall, and the loyalty which I feel for Lord Starling is by far the strongest I have experienced. It knows no bounds."

Dark streaks run along his face as the lantern casts its light over his smooth features. My lungs fill with air automatically, without me having to breathe in, when I open my mouth slightly before speaking.

"Do you have feelings for Amarion?" I ask with caution.

"I do not. Perhaps I am so old I have become incapable of feeling anything other than devotion, living in a more or less constant neutral emotional state. Or perhaps I was born this way."

Thoughtfully, I chew my bottom lip for a few seconds.

"When you think of your king, which words come to mind?"

Sandro opens his middle eye to look at me.

"Acceptance. Warmth in an otherwise cold existence."

Warmth. The word causes the image of the holy knight to flash before my eyes and my heartbeat quickens. I notice how Sandro raises an eyebrow at me.

"It sounds like an emotion, though. To be devoted to someone. It doesn't have to be romantic," I say quickly, fixing my fringe and giving him an uncertain smile. *Is he listening to my heart again?*

Sandro sticks his chin in the air.

"My duty is to stand by my lord's side as his advisor, and had I had feelings of such a nature as we are discussing, they would certainly cloud my mind. I cannot remember ever having a romantic interest in anyone, but it does not mean I am not fascinated with the concept itself."

"I understand," I say while nodding. "From my point of view, it's hard to know which ones are genuine feelings and those which are just a fantasy created by longing or loneliness."

A moment of silence passes between us, and I draw an invisible pattern on the ground with one foot. *Kailunn. Maybe he was a shimmering castle in the air, a way to deal with my loneliness back home. But here, there's someone else who lingers longer than the prince in my mind. I just can't stop thinking about those blue eyes. Meanwhile, Kailunn is incredibly graceful, taking my breath away with his mere presence.*

"In your case, I daresay the knight's heartbeat is on the same wavelength as yours," Sandro says. "Perhaps his frequency is even stronger than yours currently."

I part my lips to say something sensible, but find myself getting awkward and staring at the vampire across from me.

"How can you be so sure of it?" The sentence slips out of my throat, and I try not to yawn. *I'm curious, but oh so tired.*

"Everything around us is based on energies and frequencies travelling between us." His eyes seem to smile in amusement when he notices how I stifle a yawn with one hand over my mouth. "You look like you need to rest. I shall stay here at a proper distance from your party and your fires, so the others will not feel uncomfortable by my presence."

"Sorry, Sandro. I'm not getting enough sleep because of Lysander. He finds his way into my head." I run my hand through my hair and shrug. "But you're right. I should probably try to sleep. I thoroughly enjoyed our conversation and would like to talk more with you next time, if you'd be up for it."

I can't help but whimper quietly as Sandro's cold fist grips my hand. I'm surprised by the fact he feels no concern I could do him harm again.

"Do not hesitate to call me if that man shows up," he says, and I notice a predatory glint in his eyes. "I may be inferior on the battlefield since I refuse to drink human blood, but I have other hidden abilities, which may come in handy. Just call my name in your heart and I will find you."

He scares me. I swallow hard, taking a deep breath.

"Okay," I nod, gently withdrawing my hand.

As I wave at him and turn to go back, I hear him speak again in an even lower voice.

"It is rare I speak to humans, and when I do, I am ordinarily met with contempt. But you do not judge me for something out of my control. For this reason, I want to thank you for the conversation and hope to speak to you again, Setareh."

I wince when I hear him say the name. The one I buried in my mind many years ago, one I have tried to disconnect from. It once carried strings of my identity; now it's nothing but an empty shell.

"You're welcome," I stammer, clasping one hand in front of my chest while the other holds the lantern, unsure of how to react. "Let's chat again soon."

How strange that a vampire has behaved more humanely towards me thus far than most other humans, both in this universe and back home.

My eyelids flutter open as I frantically stumble my way out of the heavy fog of fatigue. I have difficulty breathing and when I lift myself up, holding my throat with one hand, I cough weakly. The anxiety ripples deep down in my stomach, making me feel physically sick and cold with fear. *That damned Lysander and his horrible magic.* Even when he doesn't show himself, my dreams are permeated by his suffocating darkness and crawling shadows. I can hardly stand it anymore. *I'm afraid.*

The campfire has since burned out and it's a little chilly to sleep under the open sky. The treetops whisper and sigh in the night breeze and stars peruse us through the grey veils of clouds. I pull the blanket up over my shoulders and grab my glasses atop of a backpack at my side. *I wonder how mum and dad are holding up. And Ambrosia and Remy.*

I shiver slightly as I throw a glance towards one tent further away.

"There's no way I can accept his offer," I mutter to myself, shaking my head.

The situation feels different from when I spent the night at his residence, considering I confessed my feelings to him not long ago. This is by far more intimate and the thought of being so close to him again almost makes my head spin. However, I'm aware I need more sleep to cope with the journey. His aura, lined with light and warmth, will surely give me peace and tranquillity again.

I look around to see if anyone else is awake. Some soldiers have taken the night shift, but they're further away and I don't think they'll notice me. Quietly, I stuff the blanket into the backpack where I keep my few belongings, pull my shoes on, and get to my feet. With quick steps, I make my way towards the tent. Standing outside of it, a sudden awkwardness takes me over. I count my breaths, swallow hard, and clear my throat discreetly before whispering.

"Garren? Are you awake?"

A few seconds of silence pass and in my head, I'm already creating all sorts of chaotic scenarios.

"Saga?"

His low voice, heavy with sleep, says my name and the sound of fabric rustling brings me back to reality, dispersing the chaos. Feeling bad for waking him up, I wonder if I should simply turn around and walk away after apologising to him. But when he opens the tent and my eyes fall on his tousled golden locks, the nightgown with a loose lace around the collar which gives me a glimpse of his pectoral muscles, and a few scars running over his skin, the thought of leaving immediately departs from my mind.

"H-hi," I stutter, feeling a warmth spreading through my chest as a gentle smile dances across his face. "Did I wake you up?"

"Not to worry," he replies softly and gestures for me to get in. "Is there something troubling you, lass?"

"Nightmares," I mumble, tucking a few strands of hair behind my ears as I focus on not tripping over anything. "I know I mentioned I shouldn't sleep here out of duty, but would it be all right if I stay here? I'm exhausted."

"You need not ask."

Garren closes the opening in the tent while I put my backpack away. I sit down, taking my shoes off and leaving my socks on to battle my cold feet. I throw a furtive glance at him and notice him sitting on his knees, fixing the bedding with both hands.

"Sorry again," I say and put my glasses in the backpack. "I didn't mean to wake you."

I'm almost ashamed to have asked to sleep here. What will the others think of me? They're going to get the wrong idea.

"You're a beautiful sight to weary eyes, so there's no need to apologise," he replies, giving me a wide smile. "I've been thinking about you all evening."

With one hand, he lightly pats the blanket and gives me a meaningful nod. I walk over and settle down, the tingling in my stomach making itself known. My eyes follow his movements in the dim setting as he wraps one arm around my waist, pulling me closer to him. My heartbeat is almost deafening as I continue to gawk at him, and he soothingly strokes my back with his fingertips.

"Did you swallow your tongue again?" he asks softly.

A sudden giggle sneaks out of my throat at his statement and I gently rub the tip of my nose against his while wrapping my arms around his neck. *The others can think whatever they want.* I close my eyes as our lips meet, enjoying our energies blending with each other in an invisible dance. The anxiety in my stomach shrinks and an inner calm mixed with an unusual feeling of being ridiculously happy sweeps its comforting blanket over my entire being. I don't remember the last time I felt this way.

"Well, won't you look at that. It seems we found it together," he says with a hushed tone and presses his lips against my forehead in a light kiss.

Something warm blooms in my chest. *I've missed him.* When we lie

C. K. Andersson

down next to each other, and I crawl closer to him, I'm flooded with a feeling of safety. He pulls the blanket up over our shoulders, continues to caress my back and I become submerged in the mists of dreams as he whispers a prayer of stillness in my ear.

CHAPTER THIRTY-ONE

Garren Roseheart

My heart overflows with warmth when I wake up in the morning, with Saga still asleep next to me. Her breath leaves invisible kisses on my skin where she has buried her face close to my neck. My mouth curves into an amused smile when I notice she has been drooling in her sleep and lightly I wipe the corner of her mouth with one thumb. She lets out a faint sound and scrunches up her nose for a second, lost somewhere in the landscape of dreams.

My hand rubs my tired eyes and scratches my beard while I grab my pocket watch. It's early and I'd like to stay here for a while longer, to feel the temperature of her body against mine through layers of fabric. However, there's a long journey ahead of us.

I lift myself up on one elbow and lean over her.

"Saga," I say softly, adjusting her fringe with my fingertips as I caress her forehead.

An indistinct mumble leaves her mouth, and she puts one arm over my waist, sleep holding her in its grip. I bring my face closer to hers, pressing my lips lightly against her eyelid in a kiss.

"It's time to wake up."

"Not now," she sighs, barely audibly.

I nudge her collar to the side a little, placing a kiss on her collarbone.

"Get up, lass," I whisper in her ear when I hear her giggle.

"It tickles."

She slowly opens her eyes, blinking a few times. Her face lights up and a smile plays a warm melody on her lips as she looks up at me. I almost shudder with pleasure when her arms wrap around my neck, and she runs her fingers playfully through my hair. *Her witchcraft is powerful.*

"Morning, Garren."

"Good morning." I let my fingertips trail along her cheek as I absorb the warmth of her skin and inner magic through my pores. "Did you rest well?"

Those dark brown eyes sparkle with the light of a thousand stars, and I find myself being shipwrecked in a storm of emotions. *She's much like a siren.* She pulls me close, pressing a kiss on my lips afore gently rubbing the tip of her nose against mine. A desire to embrace her and, with her consent, allow our magics and our bodies to merge and become one takes over the kingdom of my heart, but I rake in my fantasies. *She's the one who decides if and when that should happen.*

"Yeah, much thanks to you," she says and nods. "I'm still tired, though."

When I get up to a sitting position, Saga reaches for her backpack and rummages around in it. She grabs her glasses, putting them on before pulling her phone out.

"I want to document the sleepy Garren," she grins and lifts the device in front of me.

SHADOW DANCE

"Is it necessary?"

"Yep. Don't move."

I shoot a smile at her with my arm over my leg, which I've pulled up towards my chest and the fingers of one hand between my hair tresses as I lean my head into my palm.

Saga nods contentedly after taking the photo. "Hey, boss," she says in a hushed tone, puts the phone back into her backpack, and looks me straight in the eyes. "It should be illegal to look as handsome as you do."

Laughter almost bursts out of my throat, and I stifle it. With one hand, I hide my satisfied smile as I momentarily avert my gaze.

"Sometimes you surprise me," I admit. "You're unabashed when you choose to be."

"I'm just stating the facts. There should be some sort of warning label attached to you."

One of her hands finds its way up my arm and shoulder, and she brushes my hair behind my ear.

"Garren, let's sleep some more. No one else will be up right now."

"It's out of the question," I retort, chuckling when she glares at me defiantly.

"You're so relentless," she grumbles, rolling her eyes.

I grab her hand, kissing her palm and slender fingers softly. In the increasing light of the dawn, her smile and rosy cheeks brighten my morning. She's gorgeous with her tousled fringe and wild curls which seem to have lives of their own. The strings of my heart tighten. *She truly is the one I wish to spend more of my time with.*

My gaze follows her movements as she adjusts her glasses and stretches her arms over her head while we get up.

"I miss my mattress," she says, massaging her lower back with a mien suggesting she's in pain.

"I'll cure your ailments later."

Her tired face lights up anew like a beautiful spring sun. Clasping her hands behind her back, she tilts her head and smiles widely at me.

"Thank you in advance," she coos, and I try not to be affected by the honeyed voice. "Do you think anyone else is awake right now?"

"Silver Wardens and the Order of the Light are early risers."

Saga groans quietly and runs her fingers through her hair, evidently trying to collect her thoughts. "What if someone sees me coming out of your tent?" she says plaintively.

I wink at her. "Take a deep breath and calm your nerves."

She shakes her head and looks at me with a piercing gaze.

"You don't understand, Garren. Everyone sees me as this stranger who doesn't belong here, and it's true. I'm not from here and I'll probably never fit in. The fact they'll think we have something going on will cause rumours to abound."

Her words sting my heart, and I raise one eyebrow.

"There's no doubt there's something between us and I see no reason to hide it. We're adults, in charge of our own lives and private matters. Gossip doesn't bother me in the slightest."

She turns her head away and murmurs.

"Your professional status. People will talk about us. The recruit who barely understands anything and her boss. They'll think I'm exploiting your status. Ahriele already dislikes me as it is. Oh god, this is such a mess."

Placing my hand over her shoulder, I catch her gaze and lock it into mine.

"Listen to me," I say softly, noting how she presses her lips together tightly. "No one but yourself can stop me from accompanying you. The Light has brought us together in the most peculiar way and this means more to me than what some soldiers blather about. Moreover, it wouldn't surprise me if some of them were to get envious. As far as Ahriele is concerned, she's entitled to her own opinions, but it doesn't mean she's right."

"Hang on—why would the soldiers be envious?" she asks.

"They throw certain looks your way."

I can't help but smile when she rolls her eyes.

"You're exaggerating. I heard two of them from Vincent's brigade talking about me by the campfire. One of them described me as 'about as curvy as a plank of wood'. People who think they may comment on the appearance of other individuals need a crash course on how to behave around others."

Clearly distraught, she shrugs and crosses her arms over her chest.

"I miss my life," she continues. "No one used to notice me, and I was quite comfortable being invisible. Ambrosia is the one everyone sees and wants to hang out with, and I'm perfectly fine with being in the background."

I let the words sink into my consciousness and stroke her upper arms tenderly with both hands. She continues to look at me, clad in a robe of silence. For a moment, her eyes flare in white, the magic in her body reacting to my proximity and her emotional state. Thoughtfully, she fiddles with the pendant around her neck and lowers her gaze.

"I consider myself blessed to have met you and to make you feel something," I say mildly. "For me, you stand in the foreground, and your personality has dazzled me more than once. Even if you think of yourself as a wooden plank, then lass, you're beyond doubt the most stunning one I've ever laid my eyes on."

She chuckles at my last statement.

"You speak with such passion," she mumbles with a shy smile as she raises her eyes to meet mine. "Others warned me and mentioned you're married to your faith, though. The Light being your first love and all that."

I caress her hair, and my other arm finds its way down to her waistline.

"Correct. But I'm fully convinced you've bewitched me, and I've accepted it. You may share the throne along with my faith."

C. K. Andersson

Saga flips her hair and grins.

"You're doing the thing with your eyes again."

I smile wryly at her. "What do you intend to do about it?"

I'm met with silence. Instead, she wraps her arms around my neck, her lips seeking mine as I lift her into my arms with her legs around my waist. The morning preparations can wait a little longer.

CHAPTER THIRTY-TWO

Saga Falk

Shortly after rubbing my tired eyes, I stifle a yawn with the back of my hand. Nature's breath, coated with cold, permeates through layers of chain mail and clothes. Shivering, I pull a shawl draped over my shoulders tighter around me. My mind wanders to the make-out session Garren and I had shared a while ago, my body heating up as I imagine how he had lifted my garment to kiss my stomach. If it hadn't been for Vincent seeking him out, we would have probably stayed in the tent for a while longer.

Now I've done it. I've gone and involved myself with a game character. Come to think of it, perhaps he's not a game character after all, if this place is an alternate version of some sort, eerily reminiscent of *Reign Online*. Whatever it is, it's offline and real. *Moreover, he's good at kissing.*

I scratch my head and swallow a piece of bread. Awkwardness tickles my soul when I think back to hearing Vincent's harsh voice outside. The feeling when I had rushed up in a panic and tried to fix my hair and clothes, before shamefully stepping out of the tent behind Garren, and the warlord giving us both a long look from head to toe, is indescribable in a slightly anxiety-inducing way. *No, I can't focus on it right now.* I'm just going to make myself feel bad when I shouldn't pay attention to what other people think. Garren helps brings out a more light-hearted side of me which I had forgot about.

I'm so preoccupied with my gloomy thoughts, I don't notice the long-eared elf Xanjou has sat down next to me, offering me a piece of dried meat. When I hear his voice, I flinch and turn to him in surprise.

"You look hungry," he says, his seemingly hypnotising light green eyes twinkling.

"We've been travelling together for quite some time, so by now you should know I don't eat that." I shake my head disapprovingly.

When I notice his thigh brushing against mine, I shift a little to the side and wave my hand dismissively as he offers me some of his porridge. My germ phobia makes itself known somewhere in the back of my mind.

"I'm good, thanks."

"I've been trying to get your attention for the past few days," he says, pouting at me.

I shrug, turning my head away to face another direction.

"I'm not very social," I reply dryly and feel my heart beating fast, like a little bird trying to escape from its cage.

Breathe. Don't lose your temper.

"Are you cold? I can keep you warm for a while."

Defiantly, I turn my gaze to him again and scrunch up my nose.

"I don't want to hang out with you," I mumble with irritation in my voice.

Xanjou lowers his head slightly, giving me a friendly look.

"I just want to get to know you better."

"Pay him no attention. He's looking for ladies to chase. The harder they're to catch, the more he enjoys the challenge."

When I look up in surprise, I see Xerxi, Xanjou's twin brother, standing in front of us with his hands at his sides. His long hair is put up in a neat ponytail and the eye, which isn't covered by a patch, oozes frustration. A variety of gold earrings with moss-green gems decorate his ears. *His frosty temperament makes him even more handsome, somehow.* Cináed is standing next to him, his lips curled into an amused smile.

"Thank you for the extended presentation, dear brother," Xanjou grumbles, standing up with a disapproving look directed at Cináed. "I see you still haven't tired of your bearded toy."

Swiftly, I grab my backpack and stand up, almost dropping my shawl in my haste. *I don't want to get in the middle of this.*

"Sorry, but I have to get going," I murmur, hurriedly taking my leave with my eyes lowered to the ground. The men's scrutinising gazes feel like they're burning through my back and drilling into my spine.

I almost trip over a woman, a dwarf I recall being boisterous most of the time, who's kneeling and rummaging around in her pack.

"Sorry! Did you get hurt?"

"Don't worry!" she says with a grin and laughs out loud. "If you knew how often this happens to me!"

I extend my hand and help her to her feet. She's shorter than most other dwarves I've met so far, and judging by the coat of arms, she too belongs to the Order of the Light. Raven-black shoulder-length hair with small, wavy curls, large chestnut eyes, and tanned skin. The freckles on her face give her a cute look and she appears to be around my age.

"Your name's Saga Falk, correct?" she asks. "You're the newest recruit."

"That's right," I nod. "I'm sorry, but I'm not good at remembering names."

"Naira Ironfury," she replies, brushing her trousers with her hands a few times. "I've studied with the Order of the Light for four years."

Out of the corner of my eye, I see a figure dressed in a long black coat, dark red waistcoat, and white shirt with a cravat moving in our direction. When I turn my head, I smile and wave at him.

"Morning, Sandro!" I greet cheerfully.

Naira raises her eyebrows, standing completely still as she looks up at the vampire's face. He stands some distance from us with his staff in one hand.

"Good to see you, and seemingly more rested than yesterday," he replies. When he tilts his head slightly, he gives a cute impression, again in a rather bizarre way. "You need not worry. I do not bite," he continues whilst smiling at Naira.

The woman answers him, although my thoughts are somewhere else, like they've been transported through time and space without me having had a hand in the game. The murmur of voices fades away as a haze settles over my eyes, obscuring my vision. I take a deep breath, swallowing shadows and darkness as I slowly survey the surroundings. Shadowy figures move around me, and fear sends icy little pins down my spine.

"Lysander?" I ask softly and instinctively. One hand travels up my neck. "Is that you?"

A cool breeze against my neck makes me pull the shawl tighter around my shoulders. I close my eyes for a second and when I reopen them; I'm somewhere else. Lysander is seated at an oblong dining table in what appears to be a royal dining room, wearing a crown with raven head-like details; an empty plate and clean cutlery in front of him. He twirls a wineglass between his fingers and draws his piercing gaze towards me.

My heart almost stops when he smiles and bares his two fangs in a silent greeting.

CHAPTER THIRTY-THREE

Lysander Duleon

The feeling of being able to manipulate this woman's mind, to enter the corridors and rooms of her innermost thoughts and telepathically sense the magic within her borders on intoxication. And the smell of her blood; an aroma that, like a thin blanket, broods something marvellous below the armour of the skin. Absolutely outstanding.

Her dark eyes stare at me from the other side of this mental room I have created for us.

"Come closer, dearie," I say, smiling.

"What do you want?"

Her question is uttered in a hushed tone; razor sharp. The dark circles under her eyes tell tales of fatigue and her rapid heartbeat drums playfully in my ears. I fix my gaze on the wine glass in my hand, on the candle's reflections in its iridescent surface—and the lack of my reflection.

"I have missed our conversations," I reply as I put the glass down, placing my palms against the table top. "The thorny rose seems to block the bridge between our senses."

"Rightfully so," I hear her answer, almost tasting the bitter venom in her tone. "You're doing yourself no favours by behaving the way you do. Is it true you've taken over the throne of the vampires by force?"

I blink and draw air into my lungs. Her audacity is palpable. Information about the course of events seems to have travelled unusually quickly between the countries. Has someone crossed the borders and sent a message to the humans of my conquest? *This was not part of my plan.*

"His time as regent was long over and I am the rightful successor," I say.

I straighten my back upon standing up while adjusting the crown on my head. She stares at me, shooting invisible daggers at my throat and chest, no hint of admiration in her features.

"I have personally arranged a gift for you," I continue.

"You don't deserve to be their king," she whispers through gritted teeth, seemingly not paying attention to my statement. "Your actions are atrocious. No one will ever fully respect you. No one."

The way in which she emphasises her words causes a wave of dark anger to wash over me, the structure of my body slowly becoming affected by the black magic and ancient being which have long settled within.

An inner voice drags its claws inside my skull.

"Teach her a lesson."

"Yes, Master."

"Disrespectful girl," I hiss, licking my cold lips as acrimony spreads on the tip of my tongue. "I created a safe environment for us where we may talk, and you thank me with vitriolic outbursts."

The human's heartbeat quickens, her expression contorting in terror as she staggers backwards. A muffled scream stumbles out of her mouth as she catches sight of me appearing behind her. Her shoulders tremble as I grab her by the waist with one arm. Burrowing my face into her neck while digging my fingers into her hair, I pull her head to the side as a whimper escapes her mouth. Tentacles and darkness wrap around her calves and thighs as I paint my lungs with the scent of her sanguine fluid. I want to devour her shadow, lick every drop of her blood, and intoxicate myself on her fear, but I need her alive for now. *Without her, my expansion will take significantly longer.*

"Your fierce temper throws me off balance." I utter the words of warning quietly in her ear, her breaths lined with suppressed sobs.

The stench of the salty tears sitting in her eyes makes me feel sick.

Her slender shoulders are still trembling.

"I get irate when I'm tired," she stammers. "You mentioned something about a gift?"

My ears prick up, and a smile appears on my lips. Slowly releasing my grip on her, I draw air into my lungs yet again with closed eyes, my body returning to its normal guise.

My eyelids wander up. Saga has taken a few steps back, staring at my face. She has wrapped her arms around herself.

"Judging by your reaction, I did not expect you to want it," I say in surprise, the anger vanishing without a trace.

Enthusiastically, I rub my palms together. *This pleases me.*

The woman stands still when I extend my gloved hand to her. I tilt my head, smiling softly. With tightly pressed lips, she lowers her gaze to the floor and hesitantly places her small palm in mine as I lead her towards another mental room.

I squeeze her hand slightly, drinking the warmth from her pale skin seeping through the fabric of my glove, and I wish to catch her fleeting glance, but to no avail. *I need to show patience. She is, after all, a work in progress.*

"You carry yourself in armour with such grace, in particular in this illumination," I comment as we walk up a long flight of stairs with lighted candles at either side of us on the steps.

I want to peel it off your body and feast my eyes on your skin before I drink your blood.

Traces of fury appear on her features, and I note how the skin over her jawbones becomes taut. When she looks up to face me, her eyes burn with disgust, but no sound leaves her lips. *This heavy silence between us is suffocating.*

"Perhaps I became somewhat lyrical, my words sounding more wistful than what is currently considered appropriate," I admit, and squeeze her fingers a little harder. "My apologies."

With the quickness of a deer rushing into the night, she pulls her hand away, throwing me an ice-cold stare without blinking. I cannot expect her to want to be close and bestow her magic on me right away, despite my powerful position. Not as long as the holy knight is in the picture. *Unfortunately for me, patience is not my strongest facet.*

"Where's this gift, then?" she asks, adjusting her glasses with nervous fingertips.

She stands a couple of steps down, watching my face. The stubbornness mixed with fear in her eyes makes me want to dance with her in the shadows, feel her strands of hair caress me, and put my hands around her slender neck. To steal her magically charged breath with my mouth. I must be on my guard, as I do not want the Light to punish me; but if I carefully mix it with my magic, I will conquer and control the strongest of all magics. This is the truth which the Master has been whispering to me about for centuries. *The woman shall be mine.*

"You are being impatient," I smile, gesturing with my hand towards a doorway to the left of us up the stairs. "The impatience of others irks me on normal days, but I am in a rather good mood to have you in my abode for the first time, even if it is merely a mental representation of reality."

I'm met with silence. Saga looks down and walks up the steps with her arms crossed over her chest. When I discreetly approach her as she walks by, she brushes against my arm, causing her to move to the side while still avoiding looking in my direction. My jaws clench. *I require her attention, admiration, and respect, even though she is only a tool for me.*

My gaze fixates hungrily on her as she steps in front of me and heads for the doorway. The scent of her magically laced blood makes me thirstier with each passing minute and I yearn to penetrate her wrist with my teeth, to let my tongue dance over it and lap up every drop of the lifeblood. But I am aware it is safer to use a dagger for this purpose. I get too enthusiastic when biting my prey and usually end up tearing them to pieces in pure euphoria after drinking from them. And I do not wish to kill her—not yet.

Hesitantly, Saga's steps cease in the doorway, and she peers into the dark room, before glancing at me over her shoulder. "I can't see anything."

"Does the dark instil fear in you?" I ask, smiling softly.

"Nope," she replies coldly, and I note the change in tone.

Your lies are as transparent as freshly polished glass.

Her eyes widen as I summon a black candle sitting in a candleholder in one hand and ignite a red flame by staring at the wick briefly. I rarely use fire magic as a part of my black magic due to its danger to my kind. However, I want to leave a lasting impression. *I loathe myself for having a creeping desire to be admired by her.* Her magic is de facto the only thing I need. The rest should be of no importance.

Smiling, I hand her the candle and she hesitantly accepts it.

"Thanks," she murmurs in a low tone.

A magic arrow strikes my still heart as the word slips out from between her lips. *She hides sense and etiquette below her angry surface.*

"Ladies first," I say, gawking at her neck as she takes a deep breath and I see the carotid artery pulse with life beneath the thin skin.

Unaware of my gaze, her steps are slow as she enters the room. "Something feels off," she whispers to herself, halting again.

"Do you like dolls, dearie?" I ask as I close the door to the room and bolt it with the pure power of thought.

The woman turns to face me with a frown. "Why do you ask?"

"It is an attempt to get to know you better."

With my head tilted to the side, I shoot her a gentle smile. She chews on her lower lip.

"I used to play with dolls when I was a kid," she murmurs quietly.

Her gaze moves to the locked door and the hand holding the candle quakes faintly. I take the light source from her and place my palm on her lower back, which causes her to pull away. Carefully, I bring her next to me, and when the light falls on a figure in front of us, chained to a wall further away, she catches her breath loudly.

"Do you like him?" I ask, excitement spreading its roots in my chest. "I took my time with shaping him."

A faint whimpering sound finds its way out of Saga's throat, and she shakes her head slowly.

"What have you done?" she gasps.

"He is alive," I continue, illuminating the figure's face with the candle, close enough for him to make a guttural sound as I almost set his eyelashes on fire. "However, I had to remove some of his limbs. He was being difficult to begin with, and I did not want him to have the nerve to eat you for dinner. Do not worry, his bleeding has subsided, and I have cleaned him so your hands will not get stained should you want to touch him."

Saga hides her face in her hands, taking a staggering step backwards.

"What have you done?" she repeats, her voice slightly louder. "He's mutilated!"

SHADOW DANCE

A gurgling sound is heard from the imprisoned figure as I move closer to the woman again and Saga looks at him through her fingers.

"Is that you, Amarion?" she whispers in a shaky voice, and I sense the foul stench of salty tears.

"He cannot speak," I say, laughing softly. "His former worker cooked a meal using his tongue a few days ago. According to her statement, it tasted absolutely delicious."

"This is inhumane," she says, shaking her head again.

I quickly turn to face her, irritation lacing my thoughts.

"Do not apply human values to me," I threaten. "It was hundreds of years ago I was a half-elf."

Foolish girl. Do you not realise there is no trace of humankind left in me?

"Lysander," she says, her eyes pleading. "Please don't hurt him anymore."

Thoughtfully, I stare at the woman next to me, how she sheds tears and splashes around in a feeble state as the candle casts dancing shadows across her pale face. She has her hands clasped against her chest when she looks at the chained vampire.

"Amarion," she says once more, taking a loud, choppy breath. "I'm so sorry."

As fury draws its mantle over me, I grab the woman's arm, forcing her attention to me.

"Why do you show compassion for this rotter?" I hiss.

"It's entirely my fault he's in this situation," she whispers, an ugly grimace tainting her countenance.

Her beauty shatters; her visage cracks like broken glass when she cries.

"Had it not been for my presence in this universe and the Light in me, which everyone seems to want to exploit, he wouldn't have had to suffer," she whines.

"Do not spout such verbal garbage!"

Rashly, I throw her aside, so she trips and falls in a heap on the floor.

"Don't hurt him!" she shrieks in despair as I take a step towards the other vampire. "Can't you let him grow back his body parts so he can go?"

"Why do you care about him?" I demand to know with a threatening undertone.

"You wanted to take over his throne, and you succeeded. He doesn't need to be tormented. Please, just let him go," she whispers, fixing her gaze on the fallen king.

"Is this how you thank me for bringing you a gift?" I growl, the black magic and my rising anger beginning to blend into one.

"No!" she shouts, looking up at me. "If I accept it, does it mean I get to do whatever I want with him?"

I raise one eyebrow and crouch in front of the woman as I bring the candle closer to her face. She recoils a little, horror playing a symphony in her eyes. *She is trying to strike a deal with me.*

"Do you accept it?" I mutter, twirling one of her soft strands of hair between my fingers.

Her lower lip trembles slightly.

"Yeah. But I want him with me. Not just here, in our mental space."

Our mental space. Us two. Solidarity.

"Then make haste and come to me," I say and cannot help but smile as I let one finger caress her cheek, chin, and down her throat, stopping at the carotid artery.

Oh, how life pulses rhythmically and seductively below my fingertip.

"I will, but I want Amarion with me first. For real." Her words are barely audible; her expression submissive. "I want to ask you to leave him in a safe place where I can find him. Somewhere where he won't be tortured anymore, while I'm on my way." She clasps her hands and looks at me with pleading eyes. "Would you do this for me, Lysander?"

SHADOW DANCE

She closes her eyes quickly and whimpers when I put the candle on the stone floor and pull her head to the side, this time significantly more gently than previously. I burrow my face by her jugular vein, finding myself being seduced by her human scent.

"You smell delicious," I purr in her ear.

Wrapping one arm around her waist, I notice a hint of female form beneath the armour as I hungrily press myself against her body to soak up even more of the aroma, fantasising about her blood on the tip of my tongue. Her muscles stiffen.

"Do we have a deal?" she asks with a shaky voice.

"You will appear on my doorstep with your party, of which a large number are holy knights," I growl weakly, forcing her onto her back on the floor so I straddle her. *Her blood smells even more delicious when she is terrified.* "Are you trying to set a trap for me, my dear?"

"No, I'll be by myself! They're just my temporary travel companions. Without them I'd be lost."

Her words are applied to the air as a muffled exclamation before I lean over her, brushing my fangs against her neck in a warning gesture and placing my hand against her throat. Her hands grab my arm in a tight grip and the symphony of her startled heart causes my still chest to vibrate subtly from deep within, synchronised with her heartbeats.

She dances with the shadowy predator within me, without even being aware of it.

"I promise," she continues, the tears running down her cheeks, glistening in the glow of the red candle. "Let me find Amarion while I'm on my way to you. I'll knock on your door alone and you, in turn, must promise not to take over any more thrones by force. Are we in agreement?"

You foolish girl. So gullible.

My purpose and intentions are based on what the Master advocates and I must make sure everything goes according to their plan. This cretin here means absolutely nothing to me; I lose naught by letting him go if Saga wants her doll so desperately. Even if he were to regain his strength, he could not face me again. I am constantly becoming more powerful, drinking from my Master's cup.

"I shall comply with your wish," I reply, nibbling her lightly with my fangs without scratching or otherwise damaging the skin. "I shall inform you once I have had the rotter delivered to a safe location."

"All right," she stammers next to my ear and when I raise my head to look her in the eyes, I can sense something empty behind the tears and the fear. Her breath sweeps over my lips, and she looks at a point behind my head as she takes quick breaths.

Her eyes catch an intense glow. Instinctively I get to my feet, draping myself with powerful black magic to protect myself from being burned to ashes mentally, and I hear Amarion make a hoarse sound where he is chained to the wall by my magical shackles.

She has grown significantly stronger. I must figure out a way to not be harmed by her when I taste her blood.

Slowly the woman stands up while she glances at me, her palms glowing with the same white glow as her gaze.

"Don't forget about your promise to me," she says quietly, pointing at the other man. "He's mine, so please don't hurt him anymore."

Her eyes dart, and she puts her hands to her temples.

"I want to leave."

The glow in her eyes and palms fade and I hear her counting her breaths discreetly to herself.

I extend my hands in her direction, palms facing the ceiling, and slowly lift them. A dark mist swirls up her calves and thighs in a magical embrace, causing a wide smile to appear on my lips. She quickly draws

SHADOW DANCE

her attention to me, staring with eyes wide open and gasping loudly as my magic suffocates the last of the Light on display outside her body. A hacking cough comes over her lips and she flails around with her arms, trying to shake off the mist finding its way up her hips and waist.

"You are perilous." I chuckle and move around her in a semicircle at a safe distance. "I believe it is time for you to end your association with that knight."

"Let me go," she whispers and wraps her arms around herself as the fog rises over her stomach. "We can talk more next time, when Amarion is with me."

"There is one last thing I must do," I reply, digging my fingers into her curls as I notice the Light in her body is under control.

"No!" she says, and I can almost taste the panic in her voice.

"I will not hurt you, dearie. But I must mark you so that you do not forget who is in charge."

"Stop it!" she screams shrilly and tries to tear herself away, but the fog keeps a steady grip on her.

In the corner of my eye, I notice how Amarion's furious gaze etches itself on me. He opens his mouth and bares his fangs menacingly, but no sound escapes his lips except for a rattling breath. *How ridiculous. I shall pluck his fangs out when Saga has left and crush any remaining pride of his.*

"Don't you dare! I have agreed to a lot, but I won't allow this!" Saga howls and snorts angrily as I sweep the tip of my tongue over her warm neck, thereafter pulling a dagger out of one of my pockets.

"If you do not calm your temper, I might cut you in the wrong place and it will hurt a lot more," I explain.

"No!"

"Do not bother weeping again, dearie."

It unnerves me.

She takes a deep breath and as she parts her lips, a scream erupts out of her throat.

"Garren!"

I notice my telepathic focus shattering due to an underlying, rippling irritation and the tone of her voice reminding me of shards of glass.

"How dare you utter his name in these halls?" I roar. "This is between you and me!"

If she screams too loud, I cannot maintain this illusion. And if she does it repeatedly, she might in fact summon the knight to her side in an awake state and he will likely break our mental connection with his mere presence.

Seething with anger, I pull back the mist which has enveloped her slender figure, letting go of her soft strands of hair.

"Consider our verbal contract annulled," I exclaim, trying to keep my anger in check as best I can.

It takes strength to change shape through the use of black magic, even mentally, and by now I am starving. *I need to replenish my energy.*

"The doll stays here, and you just sealed his fate."

"You promised me, Lysander! The agreement has nothing to do with me not wanting to be touched or marked by you!"

Despite the terror in her voice, she steps towards me, and her hands start to glow anew. She nods at the insides of her hands, then stares at me.

"This is what you want, isn't it?" she says with a low tone.

A lone luminous butterfly flutters up through one of her palms and I stare wildly at it. With clenched jaws, she closes her fingers around it, pressing it so hard her hand shakes and the wings of the creature fall off as it becomes mashed. The magic ceases to pulsate outside her body.

"If I don't get Amarion, then you'll have none of this," she continues. "I'll extinguish every little spark of the Light within me so no one else can take advantage of it."

SHADOW DANCE

I press my lips tightly together, tilting my head to the side.

"What are you insinuating?" I ask softly, realising I have lost a small part of my dominance over her.

"You seem to be a perceptive man, so I'll let you analyse my words using your own frame of reference," she replies. "As you mentioned earlier, Amarion is your gift to me, and he must be alive and well when I find him. Otherwise, you'll never see me again. This I promise you."

Saga's attention turns to the other vampire, her visage veiled with sadness. Amarion's tired gaze regards her as she hesitantly advances to him. Tears fill her eyes and when she turns to face me, there is a fuming anger in the dark depths of them.

"You may scare me, but I can't accept violence caused in my name," she says, her eyes thundering before she screams. "Let me go right now!"

CHAPTER THIRTY-FOUR

Saga Falk

I drink from the cup of darkness, and as I swallow the shadows, they endeavour to suffocate me and drag me down into their negative abyss. A coughing sound leaves my throat and I mentally tell myself I'm wrestling it with the arms of my soul, that a small spark of light somewhere deep inside can make the anguished darkness retreat.

As if from a distance, I feel something against my forehead, hearing low voices mixing with each other making my eardrums vibrate.

My eyelids flutter and a solitary, discreet sigh escapes between my lips as my eyelash curtains rise and the morning light enters my pupils. I blink to try to sharpen my vision. For a second, a panicked feeling washes over me as I notice three red eyes staring intently in my direction and it takes some time before I realise who's holding me upright in his arms.

"Sandro," I mumble unsteadily, wiggling my toes slightly and sensing how I slowly regain control of my body. "What just happened?"

Images flash in front of my eyes and I grimace as the memories fill my mind. One of my hands flies to my mouth and my breath quickens.

"I'm going to be sick," I whisper and balance myself on my feet.

I look around swiftly, noting Sandro has taken me to a calm part of the camp. No one else is nearby, presumably because they don't want to be around a vampire, and most are probably busy preparing for the journey ahead, but their sounds still reach us.

Sinking to the ground on all fours, I crawl to a bush with small yellow flowers before vomiting violently. A terrible taste spreads in my mouth and I wipe my lips with the shawl I have around my shoulders, my body shaking.

Well, that's the end of my breakfast. Out of the corner of my eye, I see Sandro crouching down next to me with his staff laid horizontally across his knees and the weight of his hand on my back.

"Were you contacted by the necromancer?" he asks.

I nod slowly, shutting my eyes tightly and whimpering quietly. *My stomach hurts.*

"Sandro," I say again, my teeth clattering from the trembling and stress. "Where's Naira? The woman I was talking to."

"She got in a scurry when you started slurring and your eyes turned black," he replies. "I am guessing someone higher up in the Order of the Light will show up shortly to question you about what happened, so I would like to ask you to tell me what you saw."

I wipe my mouth and open my eyes slowly. Sandro sits still, his expression immovable while I summarise the course of events, sensing how I'm becoming even more sick to my stomach from his deep perusal. Quickly, I lower my head.

"I asked Lysander to drop Amarion off at a safe place where we can

SHADOW DANCE

find him," I say upon finishing my summary, licking my lips with the tip of my tongue. *It tastes disgusting.* "I think I convinced him, even though he was furious in the end. We can save him, right?"

"Everything has a price, including a life."

I lift my head, meeting his eyes again as his voice finds its way into my ears. This time, the gaze is significantly more penetrating, and I sense something dark behind the red.

"I just want him to be safe," I mumble, taking a deep breath. "There's an understanding between the vampires and the humans. From what I've gathered reading the Order of the Light's writings, Amarion is someone who has honoured the peace agreement." I lift my glasses to wipe my eyes with the back of one hand. "What do you mean when you say everything has a price?" I ask cautiously.

Sandro helps me get to my feet; with no apparent concern I might accidentally burn him a second time. Still holding my hand in his, he squeezes it gently.

"What does the necromancer get in exchange for my lord?"

"Me," I say quietly and hastily withdraw my hand. "And I'll make sure he doesn't hurt anyone else. It's probably why I'm here, instead of back home in Malmö. Because I have to do this."

"What do you assume will happen after he has burrowed his claws into you?" he continues, closing his three eyes. "This vampire destroyed our soldiers and seized my lord's throne. What will he do to you when you are alone, with no protection? What will he accomplish once he gets hold of your magic and learns how to make it his?"

I look at one of my palms and furrow my brows. "I intend to defeat him with the Light," I answer, realising how frivolous it sounds.

I don't even know how to use the magic to its fullest. After all, this isn't a game anymore where I can press practised button combinations via muscle memory.

Sandro blinks with his middle eye slowly, pensive lines appearing by the corners of his other two.

"Your heart brims with compassion for an individual in need, but handing yourself over to the enemy is sheer madness. Your magic will accelerate his conquest of domination."

Frustrated, I touch my fringe and sigh heavily.

"I had no other choice! I couldn't think of anything else at that moment."

The warm morning light caresses Sandro's soft, young features and as a defence mechanism against the increasing anxiety inside, I divert my attention to his long dark eyelashes and the small freckles decorating his face. He's slightly taller than me, unlike Garren, who towers over me.

"How can we save your king?" I ask.

Sandro's gaze crawls along my face, tracing my neck and up to my eyes. His left hand clutches the staff, and the skin tightens over the cheekbones of his round face.

"The only way he could survive and regain his missing limbs is if he drinks blood," he retorts softly, and the underlying strength in his voice makes me think of a jaguar prowling the shadows. "Human blood. Our magical substitute will not heal such severe injuries to the same degree."

"But the vampires have an agreement with the humans that they won't drink their blood," I mutter as I ponder and tuck my hair behind my ears.

"Indeed. Thus, the unofficially legal method for a vampire to drink from one is for the human to allow it—and other humans tend not to take kindly to this."

Sandro turns his head, swiftly moving to the side. I catch sight of Ahriele, who has appeared with Naira in tow, rushing towards us and her eyes glowing in white. *Oh, excellent. Here she is.*

"Commander Ahriele!" I exclaim and step in front of Sandro. "You seem to be in a hurry."

"What has the monster done to you?" she growls, glaring at the vampire as her hand finds its way down to her scabbard.

"Sandro helped me!" I answer firmly, waving my hands in front of me dismissively. "I felt nauseous and couldn't keep my breakfast down. But I feel better now, thanks to him."

The light in Ahriele's eyes fades as she pulls off one of her gauntlets, pressing her palm against my forehead.

"You have a fever," she notes, grimacing disapprovingly. "Such a difficult lass. You're consistently putting spokes in one's wheel."

Saying naught, I purse my lips and cast an eye over my shoulder at Sandro, who has put a distance between us. With a quick gesture from Ahriele's hand, Naira turns around and scurries away.

"I'm fine," I reply quietly and shrug in a nonchalant gesture. "Some fever isn't the end of the world."

"Drop the act," the paladin says with a sharp look and lifts her hand. "The other vampire has been in touch with you again, hasn't he?"

I shrug again, rolling my eyes.

"He's bored," I say in a short tone. "Right, Sandro? You were here when it happened."

"The words of a bloodsucking parasite mean nothing!" she shouts, grabbing my arm. "Do you realise the situation which you're putting us in? The Order of the Light's reputation will be tarnished because of your involvement in black magic and you're becoming more and more affected by it. It's incomprehensible, the reason the Light has chosen you as its vessel."

"It's definitely a mystery," I say and try to keep a cool head. "Clearly, I'd rather be at home right now, sleeping in my bed, instead of having to walk day in and day out."

I shake her hand off my arm. It hurts and I swallow hard, pushing down the anxiety and invisible tears as far as I can into my stomach.

Ahriele glares at me again, leaning closer. Despite the anger, her light brown eyes are gorgeous, and I wonder why she's the way she is, and reacts so fiercely as she does. *Something difficult must have happened to her in life.*

"I've accepted you're important to my brother. Personally, I don't think you belong in our order, and if it was up to me, I'd see to it that you get discharged. I hope Garren comes to his senses before whatever little game you two are playing goes too far."

Frost covers her voice, and I clench my jaws as I glare at her.

"Frankly, you're rather unpleasant from time to time, which is why I didn't take you up on your offer yesterday," I retort, taking a deep breath to restrain myself from swearing at her. "But you're important to Garren. I care about him and respect his feelings, unlike you. You take every chance at hurling hurtful words my way."

Ahriele grabs my arm again, causing the magic inside me to implode. My hands and eyes glow and as I tear myself away from her, I note a strange, steady undertone in my voice which I've not heard previously.

"Leave me alone!"

Luminous butterflies flutter around me on swift wings and Ahriele's eyes widen as she observes me, her mouth open. Out of the corner of my eye, I see Sandro slipping away to a safe distance from us while his gaze jumps from one to the other.

"Ladies," he says with a soothing calmness in his voice. "From what I can gather, there is a certain tension. Perhaps it is better to put the tension and differences aside and focus on more important things at hand."

I take a deep breath, ignoring Sandro's statement.

"You know full well Lysander's intrusion into my thoughts is beyond my control," I mutter, watching Ahriele. "If you'd stop being an ass to me, I might consider accepting your offer and becoming friendly with you at some point. But not right now."

SHADOW DANCE

The surrounding butterflies disappear into thin air. I gasp when Ahriele raises one of her hands. Instinctively, I duck with my face shielded by my arms, but nothing happens. Cautiously, I look up to see Sandro standing between us, despite the imminent risk of being burned by magical energies. His red eyes glow intensely and the stone atop the staff in his hand glistens faintly, hypnotically. Ahriele regards him blankly, staring into his eyes. *She seems to be under a spell.*

"Commander Darby," Sandro says in a silky voice, and she nods slowly at him. "You will return to the cadre and all recollection of what has transpired here will vanish from your memory."

With a slow motion, she turns around and takes her leave, my heart pounding like a hammer. The Light within returns to its slumber once more. One last shimmering butterfly disappears into the embrace of the soft rays of the morning sun, and I feel awkward when the vampire turns his attention to me.

"You seem perplexed," he notes, smiling and exposing his four fangs.

I know a lot about vampires, but not specifically in this universe. Did he use a special spell?

"You're a mystic, I presume," I say, touching my lower lip thoughtfully. "I'm guessing you used glamour on Ahriele."

He adjusts some of his curls, the jewels in his hair sparkling in the sunlight.

"Correct. It is an effortless task to compel her mind, unlike your other half."

My cheeks flush in red and I feel nauseous again, this time in a different way. *My other half?*

I try to shake off the nervous feeling while we walk back, Sandro a couple of steps behind me. Smacking my mouth, I'm disgusted by the thought of having vomited before. My eyes fall on my backpack, and I rummage through it, grabbing a water skin. I take a sip of the lukewarm liquid, hoping

I won't start feeling even worse because of my empty stomach.

"The woman did not mean to harm you," Sandro says, contemplating the stone on his weapon. "Her character is chaotic, despite underlying strength in her personality, but she would never raise her hand against a fellow sister."

"Right," I shrug.

I take another sip of the water, concentrating on the feeling of it running down my oesophagus. The way Ahriele had lifted her hand had caused old memories to appear in front of me and I had tried to protect myself. An old, ingrained defence mechanism from days long lost in the hourglass of time.

"Thanks for handling the situation," I continue after a long moment of silence has passed between us. "How are you feeling after hearing what happened to your lord?"

The vampire looks at a point behind me, radiance flaring up in his eyes again. The intense red glow wanes after a few seconds, as quickly as it appeared. Turning my head, I note it's Naira he has been looking at and realise he has used glamour on her. I open my mouth to say something, but Naira waves at me and smiles before I can get a word out.

"We'll be on our way soon," she says, adjusting the straps of her backpack. "Shall we keep each other company?"

"Sure," I mumble and look in Sandro's direction.

He's gone without a trace. I simply can't stop thinking about how he must be feeling right now. My stomach rumbles unhappily and a silent sigh comes over my lips. *It's going to be a long day.*

CHAPTER THIRTY-FIVE

Saga Falk

The thin mist of drizzle settles like a glistening, damp film over my hair and shoulders. I warm my hands by a flickering campfire we've kept alive in the forest, somewhat sheltered from the weather by the treetops with their proud, overbearing nature. Days and nights have trudged past us as we wandered through forests, villages, and fields, and the only thing which has kept my energy level reasonably high has been Garren's gazes searching for me. Our embraces, edged with secrecy, turning into exploratory kisses when the night draws its cover over us.

My fingers feel stiff, and my nails have taken on a faint purple hue. As it stands right now, I'd happily sell my soul to the devil to sleep in my own warm bed again.

Most of our tents were lost several days ago when it almost blew a gale. We hadn't been close to civilisation, so we sought shelter in a forest, hoping heavy branches wouldn't fall on us. *I'm so tired of having wet socks and sad feet all the time. Tired of being cold.*

Naira sits close to me, rubbing her hands. Normally I would have pulled away a bit, but in the cold, we seek each other's warmth. Sitting beside me on my other side, Vincent Thurston is currently busy gulping down dried meat.

When the warlord had settled down, I was too anxious to move, and I had tried to look as neutral as possible while the nervousness rippled deep down in my stomach. *During cold hours, one cannot be picky about one's company.* Hesitantly, I greeted him, and he nodded in response.

He pokes between his teeth with one of his fingernails before pulling on his long beard and looking at me.

"The more days that pass, the more you remind me of my daughter," I hear him say in a voice edged with subtle softness. "She also has a somewhat rebellious look, similar to the one you display on occasion, when someone asks her to do something she'd rather ignore."

I smile to myself, shyly meeting his gaze. "I hope you don't tell your daughter she's incompetent."

Vincent's boisterous laughter fills the camp, and many turn their attention in our direction, including Garren sitting a little further away and watching me in silence. A feeling of uncertainty grips me, and I don't know what to do with my hands, so I rest them in my lap.

"You sound just like her and are just as good at remembering things which have been said, but aren't true after the first impression has worn off," he says.

The crow's feet by his eyes remind me of Haru. *Kind-hearted Haru.* I steel my heart, telling myself repeatedly not to get sentimental.

"My daughter was furious when I told her I'm travelling to the Highlands," Vincent continues, his lowered eyelashes shimmering faintly in the light of the flames. "She's of the opinion it's time for me to retire after more than half my life in the kingdom's service. I can understand her reasoning. Her mother passed away years ago and we only have each other, Penny and I, and her cat Arthur, who she treats as if he were her own son. She herself is like a cat that usually lands on its paws. Inventive, strong, and stubborn, much like her mother. However, I'm a protector of my realm in heart and soul, and when duty calls, I can't lay my weapon aside. If I take my last breath out on the battlefield when the enemies have fallen, only then can I close my eyes one last time, knowing Penny's safe."

"Your daughter sounds like an incredibly nice person," I smile and nod thoughtfully. "She has a beautiful name, too."

Vincent's mouth curves into a smile, and he taps his knees lightly with his palms a few times. "Have you ever been out on a battlefield, Falk?"

I shake my head in response. "No, never."

Vincent runs his hand through his damp hair. "I should think the lion of Whitekeep won't allow anyone to touch a hair on your head."

"What do you mean?" I ask quietly and blink a few times, feeling the weight of Naira's gaze chaining itself to me.

"Roseheart may be sharp and strict, but his heart is exposed. I've noticed how he looks at you when you're busy with other things. It's the same look I used to give my wife, prior to and after our marriage."

"I think you're mistaken," I mumble and shrug, as if to neutralise the meaning of his words. "He just wants to make sure I'm not causing mischief, since I'm new to the order."

Please don't mention anything about the time when I got out of Garren's tent.

I take off my glasses and wipe them with a piece of cloth, frowning disapprovingly when the moisture spreads around the glass.

"I don't want to fight," I say quietly and put the glasses back over the bridge of my nose. "I think it's more important to focus on being a good person."

Vincent nods at me with tightly pressed lips and puts a heavy hand on my shoulder.

"When violence and atrocities threaten to split peace, security, and love, then you must fight back. If there's one thing I've learned out on the fields, watered with blood, it's that our time's limited. Thus, it's imperative to take every opportunity to surround yourself with your loved ones, and to fight for your survival."

I stare at the older man next to me and open my mouth to say something, unable to shatter my silence. Vincent nods discreetly in Garren's direction and speaks to me in a low tone.

"No one knows when their time is drawing to a close. Keep your chin up and break the chain of worry weighing you down, lassie. Don't hide your heart from the one whose eyes are blind to anyone but you—if your feelings are mutual. Regret is a heavy burden to carry." The hand on my shoulder squeezes it lightly in an almost fatherly gesture. "These same words have been spoken to my daughter over the years and I had a feeling you, too, need to hear them from someone."

"Thank you, sir," I mumble quietly and glance in Garren's direction.

A soldier of high rank has sat down next to him, their thighs touching. She leaves hushed words in his ear, and I see his golden locks, now a darker shade because of the humidity in the air, touching her face. The woman touches his arm in a light motion as she smiles at something he said, and jealousy rears its ugly head at me. I'm well-aware this kind of emotion is often said to be a lack of trust and low self-confidence, but I have no one else here. *Without Garren, I'm left to my own devices.*

Drawing a deep breath, I stand up and pick up the tattered blanket I've been sitting on to keep my buttocks from hurting. I swallow hard and direct my steps towards Garren and the soldier. Kicking her boot on purpose, I force her to look up at my face. Garren, too, looks up and when his bright blue, tired eyes watch me, I feel weak inside.

SHADOW DANCE

"Whoops," I say to the woman, shooting her my cutest smile. "It wasn't my intention to kick you, but you're in the way. I was going to give this blanket to my partner."

My partner. I've uttered the words now, regardless of whether he chooses to express himself in the same way or not.

"What are you saying?" the woman asks, blinking a few times.

She looks like a mediaeval fashion model with her deep green eyes and dark curls. Incredibly charismatic and stunning.

"You heard me. I accompany the grand prior. I would like to ask you to get out of my seat, as I want to sit next to him."

The woman stands up and I notice she's slightly taller than me as she glares at me angrily.

"Do you jest?" she asks, raising a perfectly shaped eyebrow.

Something I've learned from being in this environment is that I have to appear strong, even when I feel weak, cowardly, and don't want to fight at all.

"How would you like to have the piss kicked out of you?" I sneer, taking a step closer so the tip of my nose almost touches hers. "I suggest you don't touch my man again and park your ass somewhere else."

The woman stares at me, then pulls away, taking a seat next to Vincent. Shaking off the feeling of anxiety in my stomach, I carefully unfold the blanket and place it gently over Garren's shoulders as he continues to look at me.

"You look cold," I say quietly while the eyes of the rest of the party shoot curious darts at me. "I know a blanket isn't much comfort in the rain, but maybe it's better than nothing."

When I turn my head, I see Ahriele staring at me with her mouth open. In the distance, Sandro sits curled up in a cart that one horse usually pulls. Two of the eyes are closed and the third in the middle of his forehead seems to smile in my direction. Vincent gives me a curt nod.

I clear my throat silently and lower my gaze as I take my place next to the holy knight. He puts one arm around my waist and pulls me close to him. My cheeks, as well as inside my chest, heat up as he carefully adjusts the blanket with his hands so it lies over both of our shoulders before his arm finds its way down to my waist again. His thumb gently caresses my hip.

"Did you grow tired of having to sneak around at night?" he whispers, smiling with his typical crooked smile and making my heart skip.

"Yeah," I retort in a low voice. "I might as well lay my cards on the table."

"In other words, you've officially marked your territory." Garren chuckles contentedly and winks at me.

"No, that's not what I meant! You can't own another person." I shake my head quickly, wondering how best to express myself. "I have nothing to be ashamed of just because I like someone who's popular."

"It brings me great joy that we finally seem to have ended up on the same page. I've longed to hear these words flourish on your lips."

The dancing warmth in his voice seems to envelop me in an invisible embrace, and I lay my head against his shoulder while letting my eyelids wander down over my pupils. *I'm not as cold anymore.*

While the thoughts slowly walk around in my head, I focus on my breathing to keep the other individuals' negativity and jealousy as far away from us as possible.

CHAPTER THIRTY-SIX

Kailunn Sunseeker

Laifes Vairla, or Sun Hill as our royal castle is called in the tongue of the humans, has opened its gates to the party from Whitekeep. It did not take me many hours to regret my decision. They are dirty—regardless of being offered to wash themselves—loud, and to some extent, shameless in their manners. Their numbers are sparse compared to my army, but despite this, they make such clamour it almost makes my skin crawl.

They have the gall to bring a vampire to my palace. The fanged creature introduced himself by first name only. When my eyes fell on Sandro, it immediately struck me that, much like me, he carries the ability to enter and travel between different dimensions via telepathy. Something powerful slumbers within him, but I cannot determine its nature. The third eye on his forehead had been staring intently, condescendingly, at me as he had bowed with one hand placed on his chest. It is written in the stars neither of us trusts each other.

Ordinarily, my mother would have welcomed the party, but her health has declined severely, and I do not wish to mention this, as it would mean giving them an appearance of weakness. No matter how much magic our healers have fed her, she does not seem to recover. Deep down, I know she does not have much time left and I will soon have to take my place as king, with all its added responsibilities—which, to some extent, I already shoulder in her absence.

My thoughts quickly dispel afore becoming too profound. As my servants bring dinner into the dining room, I do my utmost to drown out the chatter and loud laughter in my ears and concentrate on the young woman with the uncontrolled magic within. She was among the first who had gratefully hurried to wash herself. Her skipping steps had made me raise one eyebrow slightly and Roseheart's gaze had been firmly fixed on her. *Humans are easy to read, much like open books.*

She now sits a distance from me, avoiding eye contact. Sandro has settled down next to her, the gaze from his third eye darting at regular intervals. They are comfortable with each other, though the vampire is clearly on guard. *A budding friendship.*

Out of the corner of my eye, I notice the steely leader of the Order of the Light seated further away from them. Seemingly not too impressed with the table company of the woman, he tries to remain neutral. *It appears the knight's relationship with her has shifted significantly.*

"Do you eat regular food sometimes?" I hear her curious voice ask.

"I dine on foods and drinks for flavour alone," the vampire replies, adjusting a jewelled gold chain in his hair whilst throwing me a wary glance.

I glance towards the warlord's section at the long dining table. Two red-haired twin elves sit on either side of him, telling a story which causes several in the party to burst into a resounding laughter. The short-haired

SHADOW DANCE

twin looks in the woman's direction for a moment. When she catches sight of him, he tilts his head and watches her with an approving expression, resulting in her frowning and turning her face away. Her gaze stumbles, tangles in mine, and her eyes widen. I curve my lips in a curt smile as I nod politely. To my hidden delight, her face lights up with a faint, warm smile. The pale cheeks take on a beautiful, rosy hue which temporarily moves my thoughts to memories of the flowers in our royal garden.

"Hi, Prince Sunseeker. Thank you for your hospitality."

Her whispering voice appears in my mind, performing small pirouettes on the still water surface of my thoughts, before settling in silence on the shore. Fascinated with her ability of making telepathic contact with me, I sip on the sweet wine in my glass, looking at her over the rim of the glass.

"Well met, Saga. You express yourself formally today, unlike the last time we met."

"I apologise if I behaved badly then; it wasn't my intention. Where I come from, we rarely speak formally to each other and very few of us get to meet royalty."

"You need not worry—I am not offended in the least. Your presence is welcome."

The platter of food placed in front of me smells delicious and I inhale the aroma through my nostrils while closing my eyes. I hear soldiers grunt disapprovingly as they notice the dinner is plant-based, causing me to open my eyelids slowly. *Disrespectful knaves.*

"What is the matter?" I say out loud in a crisp voice, making the guests' noises ring out. "Your faces seem somewhat taken with hunger and I welcome you to my home with a warming meal."

My sharp gaze wanders over the group and Saga applauds delightedly.

"It looks good!" she exclaims, her excited outburst causing the atmosphere around the table to lighten.

"I've not seen anyone get thrilled about vegetables," the short-haired elf with fiery hues in his hair utters, gawking at her enthusiastically as his statement makes some of the other soldiers laugh out loud. "Are you amused, you beautiful little flower?"

The elf does not seem to notice Roseheart's slashing gaze, or perhaps it does not bother him.

"In that case, it's your lucky day, Xanjou," mutters his twin brother, poking at the food with his fork. "After all, you have little to brag about, and humour isn't your forte."

"Listen, Flirty-Long-Ears. I only have one thing to say to you," Saga says. She raises one hand, brings it to her forehead and makes a sign with her thumb and forefinger, similar to the letter L in the human alphabet, whilst keeping the rest of the fingers furled.

Xanjou clears his throat and raises one eyebrow. "What does the sign mean?"

Saga sips on a glass of water and a white light flashes in her eyes for a second. With a delighted smile on her face, she puts the drink down and leans back in the chair.

"It means you're acting like a loser. The next time you see me making this sign at you, you know you have some work cut out for you with your behaviour. Consider it a free lesson in common sense and etiquette from my world. I'll be charging for any future lessons!"

The skin over Xanjou's pronounced cheekbones tightens as bursts of laughter spread like rings on the water. Sandro leans into Saga. Whispering something in her ear, she crosses her arms over her chest and grins triumphantly at the red-head. A wry smile decorates Roseheart's lips as he glances at the woman.

To my surprise, I put my hand over my mouth to stifle a chuckle and my guards silently watch me through their visors. *It feels exhilarating to laugh for once, when my soul could crumble into emotional rubble at any moment.*

SHADOW DANCE

Saga turns her head quickly, meeting my gaze and smiling as she nervously adjusts her glasses.

"What a beautiful laugh," her thoughts whisper, blissfully unaware I can hear her inner voice talking to herself. *"He has such gorgeous eye make-up today. I wonder if he does it himself, or if someone else helps him. Probably an employee. I wish I had eyeliner and eye shadow right now, too."*

She gives Xanjou one last teasing glance, afore leaning over the table slightly, palms against the surface of the table, and eyes sparkling with curiosity.

"Are you a vegan?" she asks me, then corrects herself. "Sorry. Do you also mainly eat plant-based foods?"

"Indeed," I reply. "High elves eat only what the sun has touched, grown by its life-giving power. We never take a life to satisfy our hunger."

"I see," she says thoughtfully, closing her eyes after taking the first bite, savouring the meal.

The invisible, ravenous roots within crawl under my skin, desperately reaching for the woman and the magic pulsing from her aura. I tuck a neat strand of white hair behind one ear and give her a long look.

"Yum," she mumbles and looks at the vampire next to her. "I don't know what vegetables they are, but they're scrumptious."

She turns in her chair, surveying a guard. As if reading her mind, Fevienne walks over to her seat. The over two-metre-tall woman, one of my best warriors and my right hand in battle, leans down while directing her silver eyes at the human through the visor.

"If you have the time, could you please let the chef know they're doing an outstanding job?" Saga asks, a smile hidden within her dark eyes. "I've tasted nothing this good in my entire life."

Fevienne speaks to her telepathically out of habit. However, Saga appears confused and cannot navigate her mind to find my bodyguard's inner voice. Fevienne clears her throat quietly and when she answers in a spoken voice, I raise an eyebrow.

"Certainly."

I have never heard her speak with her tongue before, and her hushed voice does not quite seem to match her tall, stately, and, in battle, fearsome stature.

Soon the cheerful voices at the dining table raise once more and the guests return to devouring the meal with no further complaints. I catch Saga glancing at Roseheart furtively. When the knight notices her searching gaze, her face lights up. A thin, sparkling silver chain appears between their hearts, chaining them, and no one, except me and possibly Saga's fanged companion, is aware of their bond.

This individual, once so helplessly captivated and mesmerised by me, has replaced the hesitation in her heart with a fervour which catches flames each time her gaze rests on the lion of Whitekeep.

CHAPTER THIRTY-SEVEN

Saga Falk

"Whoa! This place is beautiful!"

I can't contain my excitement as I step into Garren's chamber. Naira and I share the same room, but it's not as impressive in size and decor as this one, and as soon as I got the chance, I slipped off to spend time with the knight. Two shimmering pillars shift in lavender blue and purple, with white marble on the floor and walls shimmering in a faint purple hue. Climbing plants of various kinds line the walls, and I don't recognise the flowers.

Garren pulls off his dark blue coat with gold thread detailing, fiddling with the pendant around his neck for a second as he watches me with a smile on his face.

"You seem fond of shiny objects," he says, stroking the beard on his chin.

My fingertips touch a flower lightly, and I bring my face closer to smell it.

"Yeah. Things that sparkle catch my eye, but I'm not materialistic," I reply, drawing air into my lungs.

A scent of vanilla forms an invisible sweetness, settling like a thin, quiet blanket over my soul, which is otherwise constantly preoccupied with worrying about Amarion and Lysander. Do these flowers emit some kind of magic?

"Smell this," I say, beckoning the knight to me. "I think it's magical."

"It doesn't surprise me in the least," he replies as he stands next to me, looking at the flower sceptically. "The high elves depend on magic and being able to surround themselves with it in this way only belongs to the upper, well-off strata of their society."

I clasp my hands behind my back, giving him a long look.

"You're probably right. I feel a little strange in the head right now, but rather pleasantly."

My focus falls on the large double bed at the other end of the room and an envious, wheezing sound appears in my throat.

"This is unfair!" I mutter with mock exasperation as I make my way to it, running my hands over the soft, dark purple fabric. "You get to sleep like a king, and I have to share a room with Naira. She keeps snoring at night."

Garren's arms find their way around my waist and shoulders, and he pulls me into a hug from behind.

"Would you grace me with your presence on this night?" He buries his bearded face next to my ear, and the whisper caresses my eardrums playfully, almost teasingly. "After the vagaries of weather destroyed my tent, we've had few opportunities to spend time beyond the reach of prying eyes and ears."

"Yeah, you're right," I say, lightly running my fingertips over his arms holding me.

It has been a while since we spent time together in private.

"The bed is wide enough for the both of us," he continues, and I note the suggestive undertone in his voice, causing my heartbeat to spin.

I close my eyes as he applies a kiss to my neck, and I stifle a snicker as his lips brush against my earlobe.

"I'll have to change first," I smile, feeling utterly calm inside. *Are these flowers working their magic, or is it simply his effect on me?*

Garren gently loosens his grip on me and when I turn to meet his gaze, he puts his hands to my cheeks, thoroughly studying my face.

"It's good to see you standing up for yourself, like you did when you confronted one of the Arrowsong brothers," he says softly.

I stroke the backs of his hands with my thumbs and speak after taking a deep breath.

"Or I never think of the consequences and am too impulsive for my own good."

His gaze attempts to analyse me. "Are you well after seeing Prince Sunseeker again?"

So that's where the shoe pinches. Carefully, I lift his hands from my cheeks, rocking them playfully from side to side.

"Yeah. It's fine he knows stuff about my past—what happened to me isn't my fault. He doesn't make me feel worried these days and behind his sly outer mask there seems to be something else hiding, but it doesn't mean I'm interested in him in the same way as before. My daydreams differed from reality."

Garren cups one hand under my chin, making me look up at his face as he leans over me.

"I'm pleased to hear it."

He strokes my cheek with one thumb and gives me a deep kiss.

"Go on, lass. Go get changed and do what you must do, because soon I won't want to let go of you tonight."

I can feel the weight of the paladin's intense gaze as I stand some distance away in his room, slowly brushing my hair.

Throwing him a few discreet glances when he's looking the other way, I feel nervousness spreading through my body. He says naught and my ears pick up the sound of rustling fabric as he pulls off his shirt and lays it over the back of a chair. The dim lighting in this beautifully designed chamber dances across his body, caressing the contours of his well-defined muscles and setting my heart aflutter.

Carefully, I put the hairbrush down on a dresser further from the bed with the dark purple bedspread, then running my fingertips over the immaculately varnished wooden surface. My other hand fiddles with the hem of my nightgown. As I shift my attention, Garren rises from the bed. His eyes are dripping with honey and the crow's feet at the corners of his eyes fill me with enormous togetherness, melancholy, and anticipation, all at the same time. *Three emotions fighting each other, and I don't know why everything has to be so complicated. Why can't I just feel one distinct emotion?*

When he calls my name in a hushed tone, waves of intense heat wash over me, hitting against the rocks of my soul. For a moment, it seems as if I can't breathe. But the breaths continue automatically, diving into my lungs and climbing out again.

The nervousness makes my fingertips tingle. I don't recall ever enjoying being close to someone else and hardly have any positive memories to fall back on. *Do I remember what I like? I have no sensible frame of reference to lean on.*

Garren's hands gently grab my face, his thumbs slowly caressing my cheeks. *His hands are warm. Safe. Caring. This is real.*

His eyes trace over my face, lingering on my mouth. I part my lips while placing my palms against his chest. Seeing him without his shirt in this context is alien to me; it's different from when we hung out in

SHADOW DANCE

the bathhouse. Shyness grips me and I lift my hands as he lets go of my visage. Grabbing my hands gently, he places them against his chest once more, and his soft smile sets my entire being aflame inside.

"Your touch soothes me," he says in a low tone, and I can't tear my eyes from him.

I open my mouth to retort, but no words come to my lips. There's much I want to tell him; my emotions are overwhelming. They put up barriers and I don't know how to tear them down. *It's hard to talk sometimes.*

"Garren," I finally say after a moment has passed and I've collected the thoughts rushing around inside my skull. "You mean a lot to me."

The words stick to my throat as I analyse the lines of thought and what they're telling me.

This feels right. I must dare to trust my heart, and to believe in myself.

"You think too much," he whispers, caressing my hands with his thumbs. "Listen to your heart rather than the instructions of your mind. You only need to look at me for me to know how you feel. Don't force yourself to speak if it's difficult—just look my way."

Is he reading my mind? Impossible. He doesn't use telepathy. Images from the dinner play before me for a second, and Kailunn's intense silver-grey gaze lingers in my mind.

He had sewn his glance on my soul.

I force the memories away, taking a deep breath and smiling at Garren.

"I'm not used to... well, this. I hardly remember what it feels like to be close to someone."

"I adapt to your wishes," he replies, mirroring my smile.

"Don't get me wrong, I want this. But I'm nervous."

My fingertips trace lightly along the contours of his pectoral muscles, as if I'm trying to get to know a new—and currently foreign—part of him. He gently grabs one of my hands and places it over his heart. Rapid heartbeats vibrate against it and my smile takes on a hint of surprise.

"You're nervous, too," I breathe, feeling a great sense of relief.

He chuckles softly. As he tilts his head to the side, a golden hair tress falls in front of his face, and I gently tuck it behind his ear with my other hand.

"Okay. In that case, we can be nervous together," I continue, moving closer to him. My arms travel up to his neck and he lifts me off the floor in a hug as I rub the tip of my nose against his, then kiss his lips.

Garren's hand finds its way up my thigh under my nightgown, and his experienced touch explores me. For a second, small clouds appear on the sunny sky of my mind, and I wonder how many individuals he has touched in the same way, and if he's telling the truth when saying he only has eyes for me.

He doesn't seem to be a player, despite his popularity. Or is he? No, I need to stop over-analysing. I've established a deep, emotional connection with this man. I have no need for this type of intimacy, but I want to be close to him.

His lips seek mine, and my eyes shut. My playful tongue slips into his mouth and I notice him catching his breath. A soft moan leaves his lips, before his kiss deepens, turning more determined and hungrier. My fingertips dance over his neck and back, and I can feel the somewhat rough surface of the scars against my skin. I think of the bravery it takes to expose himself to another person to this extent, despite the obvious blemishes which tell stories of his difficult and almost shameful past. The realisation causes the cup of my heart to overflow with emotion.

His hand keeps caressing me gently. An intense heat spreads throughout my body, and a fierce longing inundates every part of me. I have wanted no one else to this degree, not even when I was deeply in love with Kailunn's fictional persona. A muffled moan finds its way out of my throat and gets stuck somewhere between our lips and as I let my eyelids drift up slowly, I note my line of sight lined with the glow of the Light. Garren looks back at me with eyes in the same brilliant effect, and he breaks the kiss for a second as his fingers brush away the strands of my hair, so they spread out at the sides of my head on the pillow.

"By the Light, you're ravishing," he whispers devoutly.

"You're staring," I mumble shyly, his words painting my cheeks in red.

"I want to imprint what you look like in my mind, down to the smallest detail."

His words instantly catch me off guard and I watch him with my mouth half-open. Again, I glimpse the halo, the subtle saintly glow, behind his head. One of my hands finds its way to his hair and I run my fingers through it caressingly.

His skin is warm against mine as he leans over me, carrying the faint aroma of the high elven soap. Just like vanilla and roses in a blissful mixture of scents.

When he kisses my neck and reaches for my earlobe, I snicker from his facial hair tickling me and I hear him chuckle in amusement. My hands continue their journey along his back, my heart submerged by desire.

I whisper his name in an exhalation and just about stifle a sound of yearning deep down in my throat. I don't want anyone to hear me, especially not Kailunn, if he passes through the hall outside the room. It almost feels wrong to be doing this in his home when he has opened his doors to us.

"My little butterfly," Garren murmurs softly next to my ear, his words tracing over my skin and mind causing my body to burn. "You've shackled my heart with your bewitching spell and I'm yours to do with as you please."

Golden shimmering butterflies swirl around us, some of them landing in Garren's hair. Laughter lines appear by his eyes as he smiles at me tenderly, making the rider of time stop and everything around us becomes timeless.

I think I'm losing myself in love.

CHAPTER THIRTY-EIGHT

Kailunn Sunseeker

The one person in my life, my only family since the passing of my father over five hundred years ago, has but a few hours left to live. I feel it down to my bone marrow; an internal pain hammering inside my skeleton, my skull, and clawing inside my rib cage with tiny, razor-sharp nails. There are no traces of it on my visage, but inside my soul, I shed spiritual tears as thoughts wander through the chambers and halls of the mind.

My mother, Viessa, is paler than usual. The veins are visible under the skin, most notably at the wrists, arms, and neck. Large pillows protect her frail figure as she sits upright in bed, leaning back. Her grey eyes are half-closed, the colour of her lips slightly faded like wilting petals. Applying gentle, careful strokes, her court lady brushes her long snow-white hair with slow movements, whispering to her soothingly without words. The intricate gold crown with its large magical stones in blue and purple on my mother's head shimmers faintly in the daylight filtering in through the iridescent curtains of the windows, and several subtly pulsating stones of the same type as those on the crown are placed next to her atop the bedspread. Mother has lost weight, and the crown looks far too heavy for her.

I am well-aware it is the presence of black magic in the Highlands having infected our soil, contaminated our crops, and sullied our pure minds. My mother is not the first to be affected; lately, there have been several cases. Not even the purest magical gems, cut ones in addition to uncut, had been able to infuse them with their healing attributes.

In the end, magic starvation alloyed with insanity had invaded them. The most merciful course of action had been to end their lives in a ritual performed by a trained Soul Walker. The Soul Walker uses a magically charged dagger that is sunk into the dying individual's chest. They make use of their spiritual attunement to guide the deceased's energy to the higher dimensions.

"Kailunn," she murmurs in a raspy voice and slowly extends a thin, pale hand in my direction across the covers.

Perhaps my mother is too weak and exhausted to want to use telepathy. I take her hand in mine, gently closing the fingers of my other hand over her fist. Her skin is cold and the emotions which wash over me teetering dangerously close to breaking my neutral countenance.

"*Kyenn,*" I say softly, touching her forehead softly with my index finger and middle finger at the same time; a respectful gesture in our culture. "Do not speak if it consumes your strength."

My gaze seeks the Soul Walker, standing on the other side of the chamber. Their tall, thin figure, dressed in a long-sleeved black robe with a high collar, the attire reaching down to their ankles. On their head, a black wide-brimmed hat, their face covered by a dark thin veil which shimmers faintly in deep blue as the sunlight reflects off the material. The fishnet gloves barely hide their nails, perfectly manicured and painted in a mossy green tone.

Beneath the veil, their eyes twinkle in silver as they reverently peruse me in silence. Their glance is infused with a certain glow, telling tales of having recently smoked, swallowed, or inhaled Shimmer, and I can almost touch the magic they exude, despite the distance between us. They are well-prepared for the difficult ritual, should my mother's energy need to be escorted from this dimension through the gateway to another.

Regardless of their important role, I do not know their name, and this is not unusual. Traditionally, we do not speak to the Soul Walkers, and the few times we do, we need not know a name. It is not imperative for the purpose.

"I can sense a certain magical individual in our home," mother whispers, coughing hard. "She is significantly stronger than yesterday. Largely uncontrolled."

Saga. The woman's name echoes through my mind and the reason she has become more powerful strikes me. My jaws clench and I do my utmost to shake off imaginary images of her wrapped up in the arms of the knight. *Such lack of decorum.*

"Bring me the girl."

The grey eyes watching me are tired.

"We need her for our journey through the Highlands," I reply respectfully as I gently stroke my mother on the back of her hand in a reassuring gesture. "Her energy can help us abolish the black magic which has poisoned our land. She is the key to our continued success."

Her eyes darken, sclerae turning black, and mere seconds later the illusion vanishes without a trace.

"Bring me the girl, *kai*," she repeats in a raspy voice edged with authority. "I am still on the throne and your duty as my son is to do my bidding when I cannot."

My mother slowly withdraws her hand from my grasp and the invisible chasm between us drives yet another wedge in my soul. It is something I have been aware of for many years and tried to bridge; all my attempts unsuccessful.

Most of the guests are still in the dining room, consuming the first meal of the day. They seem much more sympathetic to the vegetables, fruit, and nuts served, unlike their disapproving banter during yesterday's dinner. Earlier in the morning, I had excused myself and made my way to my mother's chamber and as such, I have not yet had time to dine. As I settle down and reach for a small bowl of fruit salad which has been prepared for me, I notice Roseheart sitting next to Saga with one arm over the back of her chair, watching every move she makes. On her other side, Sandro is clearly sceptical as he stares into a bowl of porridge whilst playing with a chain in his hair.

Saga's smiling gaze finds its way to me, and she wipes her mouth with a napkin before speaking to me with a cheerful mien.

"Good morning, Prince Kailunn. Thanks for the breakfast."

"Thank you for your hospitality," says the knight, and I can sense genuine sincerity in his tone. "The meal is outstanding and leaves nothing else to desire."

"The youngster beside Falk seems to be of a differing opinion," I say mildly and glance at the vampire, who has just put a spoonful of porridge in his mouth.

Sandro swallows the bite and runs the tip of his tongue over his teeth, as if to make sure food does not hide between them.

"I expected a greater taste sensation. Besides, I am considerably older than you, lad."

"Sandro! You can't speak to royalty like that!" Saga whispers to him, causing him to shrug.

"I may look young, but I most definitely am not," he replies. "The elfling appears to clothe himself with words which are too big for his young tongue."

His eyes fix on me once more, his mouth curved in a smile displaying his four fangs, and I feel my heart becoming encased in a thin layer of ice.

An abominable creature—dark as the blackest nights, a monster which seems like it could devour the stars in the sky—with writhing, leech-like tentacles decorated with what appear to be hundreds of eyes and a slimy secretion mixed with blood dripping from their mouths. It creeps behind his chair, growing in size to tower over him. Sandro's third eye glows intensely in red with a blackened sclera, and the creature lurking behind and above him keeps a respectful distance from the other two individuals in his table company.

"Be careful when you peer down into the abyss, little elf. You might lose your footing."

A telepathic voice tries to invade my theatre of thoughts, and with the help of my sharp determination, I close the gate to my mind. The voice lacks the vampire's characteristic features, appearing to belong to someone else. Something more monstrous than this particular blood-drinking creature. Within the blink of an eye, the illusion has departed, and Sandro is about to take another bite of the porridge. *He carries an infection.*

My thoughts scatter when Saga makes a sound of approval after sipping the contents of a cup. My shoulders relax, my heart slowly beginning to thaw from the vile sight I have witnessed.

Now is not the time to speculate about the infected monster at the dinner table or paying attention to his sheer disrespect. Had he wanted to stir trouble, he would have done so by now, and my guards would have reacted accordingly. Mother's declining health should be my number-one priority, as it is directly connected to the journey ahead.

"You have tea here! I haven't had it since I left Malmö!"

She holds the cup in both hands, as if warming them, sinking back into her chair contentedly. Roseheart moves his arm and rests it around her shoulders.

"It's delicious," she continues, closing her eyes briefly as she takes another sip. "Sandro, you might like it, too."

"I have not had it served to me, as it is a common misconception that vampires drink nothing but blood," he says, a curious mien on his features as Saga opens her eyes to look at him. "May I please have a little taste?"

The perplexed expression on her face testifies to hundreds of thoughts rushing through her head.

"Sorry, but I don't know where your mouth has been," she mumbles with reddened cheeks. "Maybe you drank rat blood last night."

"No one should drink from someone else's cup, in particular a bloodsucker," the knight interjects gruffly, staring the vampire down. "You have a functioning tongue in your possession. Use it to request your own drink."

"The saliva of a vampire is significantly cleaner than human saliva," Sandro responds, clearly ignoring Roseheart's gibe.

He catches Saga's gaze once more, rubbing his palms together and closing two of his eyes while the third watches her sweetly. The knight grunts as he pulls his arm back from Saga's shoulders, mildly annoyed.

What a reprehensible, bizarre creature. Why is he so keen on tasting the woman's saliva? Is it something to do with the infection, or is he trying to ingest small amounts of her magic so he can build up a resistance to the Light?

"I'm weird," she says, adjusting her glasses. "I can't even share food and drink with my friend, who I've known since we were little."

Taking a few quick sips, she wipes her mouth with the back of her hand before handing the cup to Sandro.

"Here. I've saved half of it for you."

"Many thanks, little star," he says cheerfully, directing his attention elsewhere as Roseheart shoots him a murderous glare.

My appetite is nowhere to be found and with determination, I push the bowl of fruit away from me. Resting my elbows against the surface of the table, I lean forward.

"Falk," I say. "I would like to have a word with you in private."

Raking the fingers of one hand through his golden tousled curls, Roseheart leans back in his chair and crosses his arms over his chest.

"What's occurring, Prince Sunseeker? Are you taking my recruit aside without talking to me about it?"

"Soon the girl will need permission to breathe outside of your company."

I am aware of my hushed tone teetering close to that of anger, and I do my utmost to calm myself by smoothing the fabric of one sleeve. *Mother's health is altering my psyche more than I would like to admit to myself.*

"It's fine!" Saga waves her hands quickly in front of her as if attempting to defuse the situation.

Out of the corner of my eye, I notice the vampire hiding an amused smile with one hand. The knight's temper softens as she turns to face him, placing one hand over his arm.

"Don't worry," she says softly and smiles at him, her visage bright like the sun. "Lysander won't try anything, not right now. I'm sure of it."

Roseheart's eyes follow her movements as she rises from the chair. She struggles to ignore the rest of the party whose curious looks—some perhaps even judgemental—shoot invisible arrows at her. Tucking her hair behind her ears, she speaks to me with a lowered gaze.

"Of course, we can talk privately, Prince Kailunn," she says in a steady voice, but her nervous thoughts create a cacophony that echoes too loudly for me to disregard them completely.

The woman nervously touches her blouse sleeve as we walk side by side through the lighted corridors leading us in the direction of my mother's chamber. Shyly, she glances at me, running the tip of her tongue over her lips as if to moisten them before speaking, but naught leaves her throat.

"You seem apprehensive," I say to break the silence between us as I thoughtfully twist a ring on one of my thumbs with my other hand.

"And you always seem to carry yourself with a great deal of self-confidence," she replies and quickly falls silent while her cheeks flush with colour. "I'm sorry. I didn't mean to speak to you in a casual manner."

Shaking her head, a few strands of dark brown hair cascade over her shoulders and chest and she tucks them behind her ears. For the first time, I see her wearing sparkling white stones in each earlobe. The stones, while glistening pleasantly, do not look to be precious.

"You are apprehensive, despite your heart having made a conscious choice," I say, and my feet cease their movements in the middle of the hall, my hands clasped behind my back.

Saga, too, stops walking, and she draws a pattern on the carpet with one foot whilst gathering her thoughts.

"It is what it is," she replies and grimaces apologetically. "I'm probably nervous since it wasn't that long ago that I was… well, emotionally invested in your fictional self. It's strange for me to meet you like this and know you exist outside of my mind's palace."

SHADOW DANCE

"The robe fits him so well. The way it hugs his body, without it being too tight. Is it wrong of me to think like this when I'm dating Garren? My gaze draws constantly to this man's beauty and radiance. Damnit, Saga, pack it in already."

Her thoughts reach me unconsciously, drawing my full attention to them, swirling around me like invisible, intensely coloured autumn leaves dancing in the wind. I want to catch them with my hands, listen to what else is on her mind, but it would be immoral of me to do so without her consent. I run my palm lightly over my attire, as if preventing wrinkles from appearing on the fine, exclusive fabric. In reality, I simply wish to see her reaction. When she turns her head away, blushing for gawking at me, I smirk in delight. She is quite entertaining; able to dispel the clouds of worry about my now gloomy existence, caused by my mother's health, even if merely for a few minutes.

"Are you familiar with any of our customs, Saga?"

I taste her name, painting the tip of my tongue with each letter. Judging by Saga's mien, she notices it as she tries her utmost to appear collected.

"It depends," she answers curtly and sticks her chin in the air as she looks up at me. "Is there a specific one you have in mind?"

"*Amar.*" To subdue her confusion, I translate my statement, thereafter continuing. "Yes. In this case, it is a soul migration ritual."

Saga watches me with a perusing expression and a moment of quiet settles between us whilst she ponders. After a while, a deep breath nestles in her lungs, and she adjusts her glasses.

"It's about your mother," she exhales softly. "And to answer your question: yes. I vaguely know how the ritual works."

I clasp my hands behind my back once more, turning away as I step up to a family portrait in oil decorating a wall. Bearing an invisible, yet heavy mantle of reflective silence on my shoulders, I let my eyes wander over it, fixating on my father's figure. It seems like yesterday we were talking to each other, and not over five hundred years ago. I am aware of the rumours that abounded, claiming he did not die on an expedition in search of magical sources, but instead was poisoned by a slow-acting magical overdose administered by my mother before his departure. *Absurd words.* There is no reason my mother would have extinguished the life of the king, her beloved husband. There may be an emotional chasm between the two of us, but I never noticed any such thing between my parents.

My ears pick up the sound of Saga's footsteps as she stands next to me, looking up at the oil painting.

"How old is this portrait?" she asks.

"It was painted a little over six hundred years ago. Some years prior to my father's passing."

"Oh, I'm sorry. My condolences."

She tiptoes, trying to get a better view.

"The two of you look alike. And you look the same in the painting as you do now."

"High elves reach a certain age afore the wheel of time no longer changes our appearances," I explain, perusing the woman beside me.

Despite her young age, grey strands of hair scatter in her fringe, and I notice fine wrinkles at the corners of the mouth and under the eyes. Ageing has always fascinated me, even though I rarely have the opportunity—or a strong desire—to spend time with the humans. They are born, grow up, and leave this dimension in the mere blink of an eye, whilst I continue to wander through the ages at the same old, leisurely pace. Diseases do not strike us, provided they do not correlate to contaminated magical sources. *A striking resemblance to my mother's current state. Perhaps Saga's pure magic can cleanse the dark sorcery which has lodged itself in her heart.*

"I need your help," I say, bending my back so our eyes are level.

SHADOW DANCE

Concern spreads on her features, and her shoulders stiffen. "With what?" Nervously, she tucks hair tresses behind her ears and takes a deep breath.

"My mother is not well. In recent months, she has deteriorated significantly."

Carefully, I place my hands over the human's shoulders. She flinches but does not pull away. Avoiding letting my inner thirst for magic affect my mind, I pierce my perusing gaze into hers.

"Black magic has tainted her soul," I continue in a hushed voice, bringing my face closer. "I would like to ask you to use the Light to cure her. Time is of the essence, and she does not have long left."

"I hardly know what I'm doing." Saga's gentle voice borders on panic, and she slowly shakes her head. "Can't Garren or the priests in the party help? They know more than I do."

"Unlike the others, physical and mental boundaries do not restrain your power. Your magic has increased—this I noticed as soon as I caught sight of you this morning."

A deep shade of embarrassment paints her cheeks as she lowers her gaze to the floor. *She sees through the thin veil of my polite words.* Her lips part and the words seem to wander in silence, and thus I continue speaking to her via telepathy.

"It would mean a lot to me if you were willing to use your healing touch. My mother is the only family I have left, and I do not feel ready to take over her throne. If there is a small possibility that she may live a little longer, then I wish to capture it. If you lend me a hand, you will receive ample recompense."

My jaws clench. *These unbridled emotions bubbling up from the depths! I have said too much.*

Giving no sign of my state of mind, I lift my hands from the woman's shoulders, sensing her body heat on my palms as I clasp my hands behind my now straightened back. Saga's fingertips sneak to my upper arms, and I survey her, unblinking. Her eyes glow intensely, and I hold my breath for a moment as the magic of her soul flows into my body. *Her shift in magical power from one day to another is remarkable.*

"I promise to do my best, but I can't guarantee the result you're seeking. And please don't mention compensation. I'm doing this because I want to help."

Her whispering inner voice lays its thin silk blanket over my thoughts and the euphoric feeling of the Light dancing under my skin washes over me in warm, soothing waves.

"*The promise of your best effort is good enough for me, Saga.*"

At this point, I have no choice but to ask an individual from an alien universe for a favour. Under any other circumstance, I would have resented the notion, but her magic is intoxicating, making me swallow my pride.

Royal guards let us enter my mother's chamber while taking a long look at Saga, the hunger for magic playing in their eyes. She seems oblivious to their glances when she steps into the room in front of me, before respectfully stepping aside so I can approach the bed while she watches us from a distance.

"*Kyenn,*" I call to her softly in my native tongue as I sit down on the edge of the bed, gently touching her forehead with two fingertips. "Mother," I translate when I notice the baffled expression on Saga's countenance. "We are here."

Mother's eyelids flutter, slowly drifting up, and a weary look meets me.

"You brought her," she says hoarsely and coughs.

For a second, darkness seems to appear in her expression, thereafter leaving without a trace. I glance over to my side, nodding for the human to come closer.

Saga fiddles nervously with her necklace and stands next to me.

"Good morning, Your Majesty," she greets, bowing her head.

"Wow, she looks gorgeous, despite her illness. She radiates such beauty."

Saga shakes her head quickly, as if coming to the realisation I can hear her thoughts.

"Take a seat, *unie las*."

Mother gestures for her to sit on the edge of the bed on her other side. A faint smile plays on her pale lips, and she offers the girl her hand. Temporary confusion sneaks across Saga's face, afore taking mother's hand and closing her slender fingers around it.

"You're cold," she murmurs, rubbing it with both palms gently, as if to warm her. "Would you like me to get you some delicious tea?"

My mother looks at her intently, slowly shaking her head. The woman speaks again.

"Thank you for welcoming us into your home. It was truly indescribable to eat a proper meal and rest on a soft seat after travelling for what seemed to be an eternity."

Her eyes begin to shine, and an unexpected gasp leaves my mother's lips. Glowing butterflies flutter in the room, one of them landing on my arm. As if brimming with hunger, my body devours the magical being. I turn my head away swiftly and close my eyes briefly, affected by the pleasurable, magically satiating sensation pulsing in harmony with my heartbeat.

The Soul Walker stands on the other side of the room, immovable, while the rest of the servants fidget. It is obvious they want to catch the butterflies and imbibe them, just like I have done. *Disrespectful individuals who try to take advantage of the situation.* When I shoot them a stern look, they bow their heads in respect before quietly leaving the room.

"Do not move until you have my permission."

My unspoken, strict command reaches the Soul Walker, and they give me an obedient nod. I move my gaze from them, placing my focus back on Saga. She smiles as the magical shimmer travels up my mother's arm, her body absorbing it just above the elbow.

"I can heal better now!"

The joy of her thoughts rubs off on me and I find myself half-smiling as I watch her. Mother closes her eyes, drawing a deep breath into her lungs. She squeezes Saga's hand gently with her own and coughs.

"Tell me about your family," she says softly, sinking further back into the pillows.

"My family?" Saga blinks in surprise a few times, following one of the fluttering butterflies with her gaze across the room. "There isn't much to tell. My parents live outside Malmö, and I grew up in the suburbs. I have an older sister, but we don't spend time together."

Carefully, she pulls her hand out of the grip, her breathing a little ragged. The butterflies quickly disappear with a thinning shimmer in the air.

"I'm sorry, Your Majesty, but I need a break," she says apologetically. "I'm new to healing."

Uncertainly, she glances at me, and I nod reassuringly. She already looks somewhat tired, her cheeks slightly rosy from the effort. With the back of her hand, she wipes her forehead. When I look at my mother, I can see she is still as pale as before. *Is there a possibility she will make it?*

Her hand searches for Saga's knee, touching it and half-opens her eyes.

"Do tell more," she whispers hoarsely.

And just like the sun rises in the morning, it dawns on me. *False kindness.* The same procedure which she has engaged in over the years to get magical beings to gain trust, to open up to her as she drains their power and leaves behind an empty, lifeless shell.

To deceive one's mind, heart, and soul.

I am well-aware this is not morally right; it goes against our traditions. Ever since my father passed away, she has done everything in her power to

SHADOW DANCE

strengthen herself magically. In truth, she did this when he was alive, too, despite him being opposed to using living beings. I can vividly remember how my mother argued with father when he intervened and forced her to release the creatures.

After he left us, it had fallen on my shoulders to find sources of magic to bring to mother, whether it be mystical powders, gems, plants and mushrooms I would set in our garden to later harvest—or capturing living beings.

"*Kyenn*," I utter before Saga has time to speak again and caress my mother on the shoulder. "Do not do this."

Despite her physically weak state, my mother slaps my hand away, giving me a look, which could have killed me on the spot had she had the ability.

"Do not act like your father," she says coldly.

With a confused expression, Saga tries to stand up, but my mother narrows her eyes at her. I realise that mother has saved the last of her energy for a moment like this. Using telepathy, she has stepped into Saga's mind and locked the human in a firm grip, keeping her in place. Not many high elves possess this ability, but she has always been exceptionally powerful.

"*Kyenn, elurru,*" I say, a hint of a pleading tone in my voice. "Please. We need her alive."

"You have always been troublesome, just like your *firenn*. A replica of your father's moral values. Do not force my hand to dispose of you, too."

I stare at her, unblinking. *Are the rumours of my father's passing true? Have I been blind to the truth?* She avoids looking at me, focusing entirely on draining the magic from Saga's body through the touch of her hand. The human's face gradually grows paler, her eyes empty.

"Did you poison my *firenn*?" I ask, attempting to catch my mother's gaze.

Her silence ripples at me. Saga's one hand slowly finds its way up to her chest while she breathes heavily, her face contorted in pain. The roses on the pendant hanging around her neck sparkle in the daylight and conflicting feelings of deep sadness and irascibility invade my heart.

"Illasa's spirit was distressed," my mother says, the tone of her voice devoid of emotions. "He believed my actions drove him into the arms of depression. He claimed he truly loved me, but that I loved magic more than him. My hunger, too deep-seated. But he was mistaken—I never loved him. Our merger was a political stance, to strengthen Laifes Vairla's position, and he knew this the day he agreed to take my hand in marriage. When you were born, I could not overlook the fact that you looked just like him. You grew up to possess the same sense of duty, visual resemblance, and the same fear of hurting anyone, much like your father. As you got air under your wings, you, too, became a dreamer. You overlaid my soul with disappointment when you followed in his footsteps."

She catches her breath before continuing.

"Did you believe I would not find out? You deliberately left creatures behind during your expeditions, instead bringing home stones, ones which have nowhere near the strength of a magical, beating heart. You refused to break ancient traditions, despite my commanding you repeatedly. Both of us know that creating new customs would strengthen our people, making us superior to the other realms."

My bones are cold. My mother is a stranger and not the same woman who carried me in her womb and gave me life. Out of the corner of my eye, I notice Saga's blank gaze being fixed on me, and I turn my head away from them both.

The daylight is blinding as it slips across the white marble floor, the atmosphere carrying the beautiful song of a distant bird. The melody shatters in my ears as the sound crashes against my eardrums. Fabric curtains make the light dance across my mother's face as I look at her once more and for the first time in my life, I am struck by a pain in my chest. Our kingdom's historically most humble king was taken from us because of an individual's selfishness and hunger for more magic. *My goodbyes to firenn were taken from me.*

"Prince Kailunn." Saga coughs in a strained manner as she collapses next to my mother, unable to remove herself from her touch. "I can tell you're a good person and your father would have been proud of you. That much I can say without knowing all the details."

She gasps for air and her eyes have sunk into their eye sockets. I see how she clenches one hand around her necklace as tears make their way down her cheeks.

"I'm so glad I got to meet you. The real you." She forces herself to smile, but it looks painful. "And Garren. And everyone else. I always felt alone at home, but here, I've got to meet so many individuals and I've learned to dare to speak up. I've learned to trust again, and that being alone doesn't always strengthen you."

Her words cause something of a foreign nature to break free deep inside. It pains me immensely, and I want to shake off the remaining heavy, invisible shackles. My mother's eyes are as dark as a night sky, devoid of stars, and I can sense something vile in her being as she absorbs the young one's magic.

Kyenn, this cannot go on. You are beyond my limit, and I cannot reach you.

The string of my thoughts is barely finished before the Soul Walker steps to my side. In silence, they hand me a black dagger with small, magical purple gemstones set on the handle. Daylight licks the dark blade, seemingly to be swallowed by the depth of its darkness somewhere along the way towards the tip of the knife.

"Is this the right decision?"

My question feels redundant, but still, I must ask it.

"The time has come. The irreversible state of confusion is spreading."

"I cannot guide my mother's soul. That is your task."

Slender fingers close around my hand holding the weapon. Through the veil, they look at me, and the stillness which radiates from their gaze gives me inner strength.

"I will always follow you, my prince. You are the rightful leader of our people and only you can continue to maintain peace between the realms. It is time for our majestic queen to rest. Let us help her together."

Thin, cracked shards of birdsong in my ears. A fresh breeze from outside. Curtains swaying slowly, dancing. A sense of loneliness spills invisibly over the marble floor and splatters the walls and ceiling. A deep breath finds its way into my lungs, and I try to catch my mother's blackened gaze, but she does not look in my direction. She is too occupied with mercilessly draining the human of magical life force.

"Farewell, kyenn. We shall meet in the next dimension when my time has come."

Her eyes widen as I drive the dagger through her heart. The Soul Walker's fingers caress the backs of my hands reassuringly and I hear a muffled, anguished sound leave my lips. I can see my mother is screaming, but I hear nothing. All other sounds except the one born in my own throat are drowned out. My eyes land on her attire, intensely painted with blood, and something warm journeys down one of my cheeks. *This is the right choice.*

The sounds come back to me as the Soul Walker speaks softly, performing the ritual in our native language. I want to let go of the dagger, but they keep cupping their hands over mine. I turn my head away. Even in death's grip, her hair looks smooth, just like when her court lady had brushed it.

An eternity passes, and my mother takes her last ragged breath. The Soul Walker touches her forehead with two fingers, afterwards turning to meet my gaze.

SHADOW DANCE

"Viessa Vairmilenne has found peace in a higher dimension. May her path forward be lit by the sun's warming rays and bordered by joy and serenity."

Respectfully, they lift the crown from my mother, place it on my head, and touch my forehead with their fingertips.

"I am eternally bound to you, *Illennehe* Vairmilenne," they say in a low tone, kneeling before me. "At your hand I shall serve."

Illennehe Vairmilenne. King Sunseeker. The words echo in my empty heart.

"His surname. The high elves rarely mention it in their own language in front of a human due to it being sacred to them."

I look down at my open palms, closing my eyes, and pushing Saga's surprised thought as well as the nausea in my stomach away.

"What is your name?" I ask monotonously.

I am met by their silence. The one thing being heard is Saga's breathing. My eyelids open as her blouse rustles when she gets up from the bed, pressing her back against a wall and staring at us with bloodshot eyes. She seems to have recovered enough to move around.

"My name, Your Grace?" The Soul Walker exhales in bewilderment after a while. "It is Winterbloom. Mertena Winterbloom."

The crown atop my head appears to be incredibly heavy for a reason unbeknownst to me. My mother's body heat still lingers in the metal, soon mixing with my own. I continue to look down at my open palms resting on my thighs, noting how a warm tear drips down and stains my clothing with moisture.

There is always a first time for everything, including shedding tears in grief.

CHAPTER THIRTY-NINE

Saga Falk

The queen almost killed me!

The individual who has been in the room all this time is trying to force me out of the chamber. Perhaps I should go with them, instead of staying in a place where a person was executed in a bizarre ritual. My strength seems to have recovered, but inside, my chest feels heavy, and the aftereffects of the pain are still present.

When I see the grieving son's slumped shoulders, drooping ears, and tears streaming down his smooth, expressionless face, the only thing which comes to mind is I must stay with him a little longer. I can't leave him like this, despite feeling sick to the stomach from seeing someone's life snuffed out before my eyes.

"Don't touch me!" I snarl at the tall high elf, tearing myself out of their grasp.

I rush over to Kailunn, sitting on the edge of the bed with his hands in his lap. Mertena grabs my arm unkindly, pulling me backwards.

"Leave me alone! I want to speak to him!" I scream at them.

I fall silent when Kailunn raises his gaze and directs it at the roused Soul Walker. Judging by the atmosphere between them, they seem to converse with each other in silence. Angrily, I glare at Mertena and feel a little relieved when they finally turn the other way and take a leave.

The door creaks softly as it closes and I take a deep breath before shifting my gaze to the other high elf again, whilst trying to avoid looking at the dead woman in the bed.

Kailunn watches me in silence. The light from the window drifts across his features and his grey eyes seem to have a shimmering film of silver over them. Despite the tears, he's so preternaturally beautiful my heart almost stops.

"Listen. I'm going to put official titles aside for a while, because I want to speak to you as an equal," I say quietly, swallowing hard.

As if affected by a sudden fever, my cheeks feel warm, and I'm flustered. The blushing spreads down to my neck and I'm hit by nervousness, making me even more nauseous.

"I've also lost someone whom I loved dearly. My grandmother. She always offered home-made pie when my mother and I used to visit her on the weekends, about once every two months. Sometimes my aunt and uncle also showed up, and then it got lively, but it was nice to have a small part of my family tree gathered in one place. I always felt safe at granny's house."

My gaze moves along the walls of the room stealthily until I see a beautifully carved dressing table. With slow steps, I walk over to it, my back to the bed and Kailunn, and steel myself. A small box adorned with jewels, much like the one the former prince has in his possession, lies next to the large oval mirror belonging to the piece of furniture, on which a hairbrush with intricate details also rests. A few snow-white hairs protrude from the brush.

"My favourite pastime at granny's was her telling fortunes in coffee. She didn't like being nagged about it, so I tried to be discreet. I helped her set out the cups, made the coffee, and then quietly waited for her to settle down. I used to drink a small amount, even though I disliked the taste of it, and she would tell my fortune by looking into the bottom of the cup. It was exciting."

A faint smile spreads across my lips.

"She used to say I'd meet a king one day. I thought she was mistaken because she was getting older, but she was right—you're a king now."

My voice wanes for a moment, a sigh stumbling from between my lips.

"One day, granny suffered a stroke. It paralysed her, causing her to end up in the hospital. Mum and I were the ones who didn't cry openly in front of her so she wouldn't feel worse, and after ten days, her body gave up. Only then did I allow myself to cry. At that point, I was twelve years old."

My eyes sting. Discreetly, I lift my glasses to wipe away some warm tears with the back of my hand.

"You know what the absolute worst thing is, Kailunn? The fact I no longer remember what she sounded like when she laughed, or her voice. What I remember is most likely figments which my brain has created in order to fill a void. I have very few photos of us together. Our technology wasn't as advanced back then."

My voice cracks and my hands clench at my sides. I teeter dangerously close to vomiting from talking about my memories.

"Please forgive me for talking about myself," I say with tense jaws. "I don't want to take the focus away from you. But I want to let you know I can relate to your grief, and if you need someone to talk to, then I'm here for you. You don't have to feel that you're alone. Being able to put difficult things into words is proof of your inner strength; exposing your feelings isn't a weakness."

Turning around, I take a quick breath and swiftly wipe my eyes. Kailunn meets my gaze, standing before me. *He must have moved as quietly as a cat.*

"Speak no more," he says with a low tone.

I swallow hard and stare at him, wide-eyed. His long, dark eyelashes are damp, sticking together. Despite the tears, his eye make-up hasn't run at all.

"S-sorry if I upset you," I stammer nervously, clumsily stumbling over the words and starting to sweat.

What have I done? I need to get away from here. I can't…

"Do not speak with your tongue."

His arms wrap around me, and he embraces me gently, as if I'm fragile and could break at any moment, arching his back to match my short stature.

"Thank you for your honesty. It sounds like your grandmother was an exemplary individual. The fact we can share similar sorrows somewhat lightens the weight on my shoulders."

His telepathic voice pierces my nervousness, which has so far kept most of my emotions in check, and I sigh weakly as I'm overwhelmed by a torrent of emotions. I hug him a little tighter than I should, focusing on trying to reach him with my inner voice.

"I'm sorry for your loss. And I'm sorry my strength wasn't enough to help your mother."

"Deep down, I knew this was my mother's last day in this dimension. I was selfish; black magic had tainted her for a long time. After that display, I knew she would not recover. I did not mean for you to get hurt."

His embrace tightens as well, and he buries his face against my neck. I steel myself as he sobs quietly, his damp eyelashes and cheek brushing against my skin. Not sure what to do with my hands, I stroke his back comfortingly, if hesitantly. *I mustn't let myself be affected. I mustn't start crying.*

"I never got to say goodbye to my father," he whispers, barely audibly. "That is the reason I did not shed any tears for him. His existence was erased, his remains vanished. And now, with the information I have learned from my mother regarding her role in his disappearance, and her own final moments…"

"An estranged son, with a mother incapable of loving her own flesh and blood!"

For the first time, his telepathic speech sounds significantly louder, stronger, and nowhere as soft as before, much like a hurricane threatening everything in its path.

I'm terrified.

My inner voice gets lost and the words I want to say get stuck in my throat instead.

"D-don't think like that," I stutter after a while. "She wasn't feeling well, and probably didn't mean what she said."

Kailunn slowly pushes me away, breaking the embrace. His hands still rest on my shoulders, and he stretches his back, so I have to crane my head in order to look up at him.

"Desperately, you cling to any thread of optimism you find in the misery." His statement exudes a chill, making me shiver.

"Well, what else is there to do?" I reply quietly, trying hard not to burst into tears. "Should one lie down and just give up? Trust me, I've done it before and it's not a pleasant situation to be in. It's far better to try to find something positive to cling to in the darkness, and maybe then the shadows will eventually dissipate."

A moment of reflective silence has our tongues chained to our own thoughts, and yet, I can't help but be distracted by my heartbeat echoing in my chest and the blood rushing in my ears.

"I can glimpse what I presume Roseheart sees in you as well,"

Kailunn finally says in a discreet exhale. "My assumption was that you were naïve, but it was a mistake on my part."

Something else, something alien, has replaced the previous coldness in the tone of his voice. It finds its way into my mind, causing an earthquake in my mental space. My hands fly up to my temples and I flinch as he lifts his grip from my shoulders. I narrow my eyes tightly, noticing his hands cupping over mine.

"It hurts!" I gasp.

"I do not wish to hurt you—I wish to help you find a moment of peace, as you have helped me today. Hold on a little while longer."

The hammering pain slowly fades away and when my eyes fly open, I find myself in my room at home. My heart jumps in my chest and I spin around in confusion.

"This can't be," I stammer, my pulse increasing.

I rush to the window, pulling aside the dark blue curtains and watching the city of Malmö spread out in the night. Turning Torso stretches towards the sky in the distance and the stars sparkle like diamonds, when they're not playing hide and seek behind the rain-heavy cloud veils that patchily decorate the sky. With a slight tremble in my breath, I suck air into my lungs and my shoulders drop a little.

Slowly, I turn around and sit down on the edge of the bed. Lightly, I stroke the duvet with the tips of my fingers. It's familiar and soft, smelling like it's straight from the launderette around the corner. As I lie down with my head on the pillow and look at my hands and arms, keeping them outstretched before me, I notice I'm wearing my favourite hoodie, puffy pyjama pants, and thick socks. I wiggle my toes as I close my eyes and let my arms rest at my sides.

"Malmö, I'm back," I say, savouring the words. "I've missed you so much."

Something heavy rests on my chest and without opening my eyes, I run my fingers over it. The gold chain with the pendant. His family heirloom.

I don't want to go back to Sun Hill. But I don't want to leave him, either.

I chew my bottom lip as my thoughts swirl around and open my eyes slightly to squint. The eyelashes create a visual grid in front of them and I reflect on what Garren looked like the first time my eyes fell on him at the inn. Even then, my heart had somersaulted, all whilst clinging to the fictional image of Kailunn. His grip around my hand when I had glued myself to him in the church in sheer terror. How he watched over me when I had nightmares and the feeling of waking up and silently registering every feature of his face while he slept. Those deep worry lines and the scar on his cheek that give him character. His safe arms which hold me. A man without ulterior motives, who I slept next to and who respects me—and thus, I had allowed him to paint my heart with the brushstrokes of love.

I recall his smouldering gaze caressing me, his searing kisses and the intense moments we had shared the previous night. Two similar energies in two different bodies, merged into one.

He sees past my outer shell.

The rain patters against the window in a dull, drumming melody, and I close my eyes again. The jewellery is warmed by my palm and the fingers closed around it. *There we have it, the familiar feeling in the deepest chamber of my soul. Melancholy.*

"I don't want to leave him."

I hear my voice as I speak out loud; I'm a little surprised by how determined I sound. What will happen to my parents if I don't come back? To my job, my life, everything I'm used to?

A sigh finds its way out of my throat and an icy lump of anxiety forms in my stomach. *I don't know.*

Seconds stretch into minutes. I'm about to fall asleep when I hear a silky voice next to my ear.

"Saga, it is time to return."

"I want to rest," I mumble, rubbing my closed eyes.

"You cannot stay here any longer, or you might never find your way out."

I exhale with a faint sighing sound and blink a few times. My head feels heavy and I'm trying to get used to the light stinging my eyes. My pulse quickens as I realise Kailunn is holding my hand, leading me down a long corridor, towards the door to the chamber where I would have slept last night had I not spent it with Garren.

"Welcome back," says the high elf, his voice holding an unexpected gentleness. "I hope you found a moment of peace in an environment familiar to you."

I rub one eye again with my free hand and almost trip.

"What's going on?" I murmur tiredly.

"You need a change of clothes," he replies, glancing over his shoulder as he walks a couple of steps ahead of me. "Otherwise, you might receive unwelcome questions."

I look down at my blouse. Blood stains from his mother.

"Oh, gosh. You're right."

I swallow hard and follow him with my eyes as he lets go of my hand and stands by the door frame.

"One of my servants will wash them for you. Be sure to place them in a neat pile on the right side of the door preceding leaving the room."

"Thanks, but I can wash them myself. I don't want to trouble them," I smile, fiddling with my blouse sleeve nervously.

"You should focus on resting, rather than engaging in chores which others get compensated for," he announces curtly, putting the fingers of his hands together in front of him. "It has been an eventful day, and I must take my leave to attend to family matters."

His facial expression is icy, making me reminisce about a beautiful winter landscape. It's hard to imagine this is the same man who, a while ago, had buried his face in my neck and allowed himself to grieve openly.

"Kailunn," I say quickly and shake my head. "I mean, Your Majesty."

He looks away, his eyes half-closed.

"You need not be so formal with me, Saga. I foresee many hours of talking with each other, and in soulful conversations, complications will arise if one has an ever-present position of power over the other. So, I want to ask you to call me by my first name."

The sentence he has just uttered sounds like a command disguised as a polite phrase.

"What if someone else hears me call you by your name?" I gasp.

Kailunn's silvery eyes remind me of a snake. Beautiful, enigmatic, cunning. *Dangerous?*

"Are you worried about what others might think in regard to you conversing in a casual manner with a king?"

The question makes me halt my train of thought and focus. How will I be able to explain to the others why I've become bonded with the king of the high elves? I'd rather not have to tell them about our brutal time together in the other chamber.

"No," I utter and shrug.

That day, that sorrow. There's no point in making myself get worked up unnecessarily. There's already too much on my plate as it currently stands.

"What were you going to tell me earlier, Saga?"

Nervously, I rub my hands together as I look up at his face, moments of silence passing between us. My gaze flits over his eyes, cheekbones, and lips. An unknown feeling takes root inside me, and I sense a strange affinity with him.

"Thank you for taking me back to my home," I mumble. "It means the world to me."

He did it for me. I didn't ask for it, and yet he did it. Before I allow myself more time to think, I cup my hands over his, feeling the Light seep from my pores into his skin. I want to share my magic with him, perhaps as consolation for the misery he's going through. *I feel something... something between us. Something familiar.* A hunger settles in his gaze, but he masks it by blinking, before pulling away from me and breaking our touch. *Doesn't he want my magic? Is it because I'm just a lowly human to him?*

"You should rest," he says with a cool tone in his voice and nods to the side of the door frame. "Put your clothes there so they may be washed. We shall leave tomorrow."

Somewhat baffled due to him pulling away from me, I attempt to focus on his words instead.

"We? Will you be joining us?"

The question hangs in the air for a while, and my gaze flutters over his fancy regalia. The blue-purple stones sparkle almost hypnotically and the daylight from the window a short distance away kisses the gold, making it glisten. He looks good in it; a true king.

As he tilts his head, one of the long white strands of hair falls over his shoulder and cascades down to his chest.

"A magical leak in the Highlands has caused deaths among my people and in my family. Today I cremate my mother," he says, and the coldness of his facial expression makes me shudder. "And now it falls to me to seek the person causing it in order to extinguish their spark."

After I had changed into clean clothes, I fell into a deep, dreamless sleep. Something warm caresses my cheek and hair as I lie on my stomach with my hands under the pillows, supporting my head. Indistinct words stumble over my lips, and my eyelids flutter before I open them slowly. For a moment, I'm unsure of where I am, but soon the memories return.

"Hey," I say, smiling sleepily when I realise who it is that's sitting on the edge of the bed and stroking my back.

I reach one hand in his direction and run my fingers through soft, golden locks of hair.

"Good evening, lass."

When I turn over, he leans over me, kissing my lips as a pleasant warmth spreads in my chest.

"Wait, what?" I mumble in between the kisses. "Is it evening?"

Garren smiles, some hair tresses in front of his eyes. Gently, I tuck them back behind his ears as I rise to a sitting position, leaning my back against the headboard.

"Yes," he replies, stroking the beard on his chin thoughtfully. "Earlier in the day, I stopped by to see where you were and noticed that pesky vampire hanging upside down next to the door of your chamber. He had wrapped himself in his cloak, resembling a slumbering human-sized bat."

He grimaces disapprovingly, furrowing his brow.

"I put my hand on the doorknob to enter the chamber. His third eye opened and stared at me so intently, I almost drew my sword. He had the gall to announce you were asleep and no one, not even I, was to disturb you."

"Looks like I've got a bodyguard," I grin. "One which even made you stay away. Now that's a feat."

"I don't find it particularly humorous," Garren says grimly. "Do you not want my company?"

"I'm teasing you," I chuckle, placing my palms against his face. "Please don't get annoyed with Sandro. He and I have become good friends."

"Something's not quite right about him, aside from the fact he's a blood-sucking parasite, that is," Garren continues, the hardness of his gaze softening as I caress his forehead and bottom lip with my fingertips.

"He's a good friend," I repeat, bringing my face closer to his. "Don't you think it's terrible to call him by such words when he can't help having to drink blood to survive? He doesn't jump on people."

While gently stroking Garren's neck with my fingernails, I brush my lips against his.

"You're better than that," I whisper, pulling back teasingly as he leans in to kiss me. "Be kind to him, and I'll be kind to you."

Garren's bright blue eyes penetrate my soul, and I do my utmost not to blush when he shoots me a wry smile.

"You don't have to be meek with me, lass," he says softly. "I can handle being treated roughly by your hands."

One of his hands finds its way into my thick hair, cupping behind my head as he winks.

My words stumble over each other. "That's not a sacred thing to say!"

"You don't look upset. Rather surprised and a little curious."

"You tease," I mutter, hiding a smile by diverting my attention elsewhere momentarily.

My previously dirty clothes are clean, neatly folded, and piled at the end of the bed. One of the royal servants must have brought them here while I was sleeping. I give whoever it was who took care of them a grateful thought, before shifting my focus back to the holy knight.

"Garren," I say thoughtfully, watching him intently. "Did you meet with Kailunn today?"

He tilts his head to the side slightly as he caresses my neck.

"I saw him together with his guards and two advisors. They were silent, and I assumed they were conversing the way high elves do as they strode down the corridor. He gave me a polite nod, wearing the royal crown atop his head."

"How did he look?" I ask, realising how awkward it sounds. "What I mean by that is: was he visibly distressed?"

With a surprised eyebrow raise, Garren watches me enigmatically.

"Haughty and cunning," he replies. "Judging by the crown, I conclude his mother has passed away, and he has stepped on the throne. No one was permitted near her chamber and there was a pyre outside in the castle yard."

I adjust my fringe while I collect my thoughts. As far as I know, the high elves don't have grand rituals when crowning their next monarch, and I'm guessing Mertena—and possibly me, despite not being a part of their culture—were the only witnesses needed for the change of power to go through on a statutory basis.

I swallow hard, feeling anxiety creeping around inside the skin on the soles of my feet and an icy lump sloshing around in my stomach.

"It's true that she's dead. I was there when it happened," I say hollowly.

I close my eyes, but they fly open again. The image of Viessa Sunseeker, lying motionless and bloodied in bed, appears to have etched itself onto the back of my eyelids. The sight of Kailunn violently driving the dagger into her chest sends small, cold drops of worry running down my spine.

Garren's arms find their way around my body, and he pulls me into his arms. His hands stroke my hair and back and he gives me a tender, comforting kiss on my neck.

"I presumed something had happened since you slept for so long, and the changing of your clothes to elvish attire," he murmurs next to my ear, and I feel his warm breath caress me. "Do you wish to talk about it?"

I burrow my face against Garren's collarbone and neck, silently inhaling his scent through my nostrils. *His aura calms me.* My stomach rumbles from having been without food since this morning and I try my utmost to sharpen my focus.

"That would be nice," I sigh softly and force myself to close my eyes again.

With great difficulty, I push away the image of Queen Sunseeker and listen to my heartbeat. Garren's hands heal me through the warm touch on my back and neck. When we lie down next to each other and he holds me in his arms, I tell him about the day in whispered words, resting my head against his chest, and mixing the cadence of my heart with his heartbeat in my ears.

CHAPTER FORTY

Saga Falk

Ever since we left Sun Hill a week ago, I've had a strange feeling of uneasiness under my skin. It creeps up through my stomach, spreads along my shoulders, and then slides down my arms, all the way to my fingertips. It makes me feel tired, even though I've been sleeping next to Garren for the past few days, and his aura usually calms me down and energises me. Something heavy rests in the air, an invisible threat which constantly makes me wince and throw glances over my shoulder.

At first, we had travelled with horses, both our own and creatures similar to unicorns belonging to the high elves, but the more we had journeyed through the land, the more tired they had become. There's obviously something not quite right around these parts. The animals had fallen ill quickly, and I had desperately tried to heal a unicorn who had been breathing with great difficulty. Powerful waves of despair had washed over me as its eyes had rolled back into their eye sockets and it had taken one last breath.

The black magic also seems to affect the rest of us, as our steps seem more tired than usual, and I have noticed something dark in the high elves' eyes at times.

"Naira," I say under my breath as we wander through a deep forest, snapping twigs where we put our feet. "Don't you think the forest is unusually quiet? There's only the sounds of our footsteps."

She nods and surveys the surroundings as she plucks pine needles from her hair.

"The Light is with us," she replies, waving an insect away in front of her face. "It will protect us from evil."

"Sure," I say, trying not to roll my eyes. "But the fact is something's wrong. I can feel it. I neither can nor want to rely on an outside source for protection. We must protect ourselves and act methodically and cautiously, don't you think?"

She waves her hand at me whilst muttering something about having the right faith, taking a few quick strides so she's walking next to another knight instead. I can't help but feel down about being rejected by someone I consider a friend.

My gaze seeks the high elves. They move much more quietly and nimbly than the rest of us, comparable to felines, and appear to feel at home in the forest's embrace. Helmets cover their heads and faces. Kailunn's armour is white and purple, shimmering in silver, set with several magical stones which glisten in purple and blue. It's visually obvious he's royalty, and he doesn't hide it, nor camouflage himself either, for that matter. He, too, has his face and head completely covered. The cover reminds me of a death mask, a cast of someone's face after their last breath has left their body, and it makes me a little unnerved. For being a peaceful people, they look significantly more intimidating than the soldiers with their banners, heavy armour, and powerful weapons.

Sandro skulks in the gloom nearby, casting no shadows, and I feel safe knowing he's monitoring me. Garren and Vincent walk at the front of the line, and they've asked me to stay in the background in case something happens. I know fully well why they had put it that way—I still can't handle my sword properly and I have little physical strength to boast of. The Light in me is still capricious, and I'm not sure if I'll ever learn to fully manage it.

In a low voice, I call Sandro's name and within a few seconds he walks beside me, between the crowd of soldiers and holy knights, staff held in his left hand. *He's brave to be in the middle of magic, which could burn him to ashes within seconds.*

He smiles at me with his fangs showing, blinking all three eyelids at the same time.

"Twinkling little star," he says, and I mirror his smile when I hear his nickname for me. "How are you faring? Tiredness veils your visage."

I nod and push my glasses up the bridge of my nose.

"Yeah, I'm exhausted. It's tiring to walk around with armour."

I sigh discreetly. He offers me his arm and we walk together.

"I, too, feel my strength waning," he admits, leaning in close to my ear so his curls and hair jewellery touch my cheek. "I have not eaten in days and have run out of synthetic blood."

"No way!" I almost shout in surprise, smiling apologetically when Xerxi's scrutinising gaze is directed at me where he walks a few metres away from us.

I lower my voice and whisper in his ear.

"I haven't seen a single animal here, except some insects. Not even a bird, other than a white raven I saw in the corner of my eye, but when I looked for it, it had vanished. It doesn't seem normal to me."

He shakes his head and closes two of his eyes while the third squints at me.

"I need nourishment soon," he murmurs. "Without access to animals or magical blood substitutes, the situation is going to be less than ideal."

The thoughts race around in my head and a twig snaps under one of my shoes as I step over a dark green, moss-covered rock. The wind whispers and sighs in the treetops above us and the visibility is about to deteriorate, fog finding its way into the hiding places of the forest. I can't remember visiting this location in *Reign Online*. It must belong to a completely new area which the players didn't have access to.

I stop for a moment, realising I'm still thinking of this as an MMORPG. *Girl, you know fully well this isn't fictional.* I turn to Sandro as his glance fleets over me and I whisper again.

"How much blood do you need to drink to regain your strength?"

"It depends entirely on who, or what, I'm drinking from," he replies softly, adjusting some long, coily strands of hair over one shoulder.

I swallow hard and notice how my heartbeat increases in pace.

"What would happen if I pricked my finger, and you were to lick the wound?" I ask, barely audibly, scratching the back of my neck nervously.

"I do not drink from people!"

The fierce whisper is applied to a thin, chilly breeze and creeps into my ears.

"I know," I grumble and pout at him sourly while we follow the others into a tunnel in a rock face. "But I can't think of any other solution, and I don't think anyone else here would let you get near them with your fangs. You're my friend, and I want to help you."

"Nip that thought of yours in the bud," he retorts firmly.

He lets go of our arm hook and runs his fingers across a wall. Deep creases furrow his brow, and I try to make out what it is he's looking at

SHADOW DANCE

in the light from the torches which some of the party members carry as we march forward.

"What is it?" I mumble and feel a thin film of worry settle over me.

Sandro glances at me and it looks like beads of sweat have broken out on his usually smooth forehead.

"We must leave this place," he says quickly, twisting around while waving his hands and shouting. "Fall back!"

"What's occurring back there?" I hear Garren call in the distance.

"The parasite is giving orders," Vincent bellows and makes a beeline for us through the party.

"Sandro?" I whisper anxiously. "The warlord looks pissed as hell."

"There is no time to waste," Sandro continues hurriedly, and a rebellious hint flashes in his eyes. "Listen to me, and I will explain everything once we are safe!"

"We're not going anywhere until you speak your mind, beast!"

Vincent shoves Ahriele, too slow in moving out of his way, unkindly with one shoulder, forcing her to step aside.

Garren's gruff voice echoes in the tunnel as he rushes after the warlord.

"Thurston!"

The voices form a cacophony in my ears, and I put my hands to my temples. The sounds from the party merge and fade away, as if in a distance. I squeeze my eyes shut tightly, counting my breaths to three. When I let my eyelids drift up, the others have become transparent. I can still see them moving slowly, but I can't make out any distinct shapes.

"Hello, dearie."

His voice. It cuts through me like a sharp knife, reaches the bone marrow, and I lose my breath as one hand flies up to my chest. My knees shake and my feet feel like lead.

"You." I force my words through gritted teeth and lift my head slightly.

I see him in the tunnel, floating in the air on a throne made of vile tentacles and hundreds of erratically darting eyes. Despite the distance, the voice is menacingly close, his features clearly visible. A furious expression is settled on his face, and he's holding something in his arms, but I can't make out what it is.

"Have you forgotten my name amidst your love frenzy?" the voice hisses, as if he were next to my ear. "Last time we saw each other, I mentioned the relationship you and the knight have established must be terminated; it affects what you and I share. I assumed you would be his disciple, and possibly a short-term pleasure, and thus your magical power would increase. But you have broken your promise to me and are bringing with you a larger band of soldiers than previously—and what I have established from your actions is you have no plans of ceasing your amorous pleasures."

Lysander draws in a deep breath through his nostrils, and his red eyes are glassy.

"Saga. Do you know what I do with those who misbehave?" he asks.

I swallow hard, my heart wanting to burst out of my chest, but I dare not speak. Lysander's fangs grow longer, and his eyes turn black.

"Let me teach you."

Lifting the heavy object in his arms, he juggles it between his hands a few times and tosses it in my direction. It rolls on the ground with a thud and stops when it hits one of my feet. Only then does it strike me what it is.

Even through the deformity of the badly beaten face, it's impossible to mistake whose severed head it is staring up at me with red, lifeless eyes. My throat wants to scream out loud, but no sound departs my lips. My mouth feels dry, my heart beating violently against the rib cage. *I want to cry. That poor man.*

"We had an agreement." My words sound weak and pathetic once they hit the air. "You promised me Amarion would live if I came to you.

And I'm on my way; you see that, right?"

"You are on your way, not solely with your bedmate, but a retinue, including the high elves. It is clear you have no plans to leave your travelling companions."

"And why would I have to come to you, anyway?" I retort. "If you wanted to get hold of me, why didn't you seek me out in person? Surely, it would have been much easier, given I don't know your areas well?"

"Shut your mouth!" he barks. "You know nothing!"

Lysander opens his arms, and his cloak unfurls into a pair of wings. Nimbly, he floats down from the hideous throne and lands with a barely audible sound some distance from me.

"I am immensely disappointed." The voice claws its way into my ears and when he lifts one hand, I end up falling to my knees, unable to fight back. "Your magic belongs to me. I was the one who saw your potential in the first place, through the dimensional curtains between our worlds. Not that nettlesome knight and his paltry order."

He takes long, determined strides in my direction. The transparent figures around us move in slow motion, as if in battle, but he and I are unaffected by it. In pure desperation, I try to pull away from the severed head touching my thigh, noticing the foul taste of acid regurgitation in my throat. *I don't want to throw up in front of him.*

A frustrated squealing sound stumbles out from between my lips as Lysander crouches down in front of me. I'm unable to move away. His gaze softens, and the anger subsides, replaced by melancholy. The vampire's features are even clearer now, and I can see every little detail, down to pores on the skin. The black eyes slowly return to their normal colour and a shrill sound is born in my throat as he places his armoured hands against my cheeks. *This feels different from when he usually touches me. It seems... real. In a real, awake state, outside mental figments.*

"By the gods," he says softly, gently pushing my neck back a bit as he moves in closer. "You smell even better in reality. Blood and magic. A wonderful sensation."

I breathe out the words and find myself sweating in panic. "In reality?"

"Your beautiful neck is slender and vulnerable. I have to be careful not to accidentally break it," he smiles mildly, a puzzled twinkle appearing in his eyes as my shoulders start to shake.

"Please don't hurt me," I whisper in terror and take a deep, trembling breath so as not to lose myself in the fear. "I don't understand why you're after me. I'm a nobody and there are others who also have the same magic as me and they know what they're doing with it."

It feels like my heart will stop at any moment. *He's unhinged. Be careful.*

"We do not have much time for long harangues," he replies, stroking my forehead as if to adjust my fringe. "The others are busy battling my creatures, and this magical curtain, hiding us from them, will not last for long."

He digs his fingers into Amarion's hair, dirty with dried blood, giving the head a cold stare and casting it aside before turning back to me.

"The reason I need you is that your power is different. Your energy is good, but in a chaotic, unbridled state. I wish to control the Light for various reasons, and you are my key to it."

"But you're a vampire," I whisper and narrow my eyes as he brings his face closer to mine. *I dare not look him straight in the eyes.* "You can't use the Light, can you?"

"You are mistaken, dearie."

He lightly sniffs my neck, and a low, almost purring sound finds its way out of his throat.

"As long as I ingest small amounts of the Light from you, I will build up a certain resistance, whilst also becoming more powerful."

Panic is slaloming inside me. I need to get away from him. He's like a hungry predator, ready to tear me apart. *Why can't I use my magic to defend myself? Why am I so useless at everything?*

"Calm your little panicked sparrow heart," I hear him mutter as he straightens his back so he's face to face with me.

One hand finds its way to a hidden pocket and the blood in my veins freezes as he pulls out a dagger, black as the deepest, darkest of winter nights. *I've seen it before.*

"Please," I whisper, my words clad in desperation. "Please, Lysander. Don't hurt me. No, no, no."

I squirm in pure panic as he grabs my arm, pulls off my glove, and exposes my wrist. My courage and inner strength have completely vanished.

"This time I need to be careful," he explains as he puts the edge of the ice-cold blade against my skin. "Damage inflicted via telepathy is usually considerably less, compared to what could happen right now if you flinch and I cut a blood vessel, or if I were to be affected by my state of mind and stab you in anger."

He puts a finger to his lips, urging me to be quiet, and smiles gently, tilting his head to the side.

"Your fear is intoxicating," he breathes out, his predatory gaze devouring me. "Finally, I have you right where I want you, all to myself."

As the blade of the dagger kisses my flesh, painting my wrist in a blood-red hue of pain, a shrill scream explodes from my throat and my mind shatters into a thousand pieces.

CHAPTER FORTY-ONE

Sandro Oyemi

They had refused to heed my warning.

I press my back against one of the rock faces, my staff in my left hand at high alert, as I attempt to remain unharmed by the holy knights' spells. Three monstrous creatures, looking like large mutated demonic lizards with razor-sharp claws and teeth, pounce on Roseheart. A blinding light surrounds him for a second and a dark roar erupts from his throat as he shakes them off, violently counterattacking. Blood and body parts fly in different directions. His face, with eyes glowing intensely, contorts with rage as he decapitates a creature and crushes the skull of another with his sabaton. The sound of bones crashing cuts in my ears and the smell of monster blood mixed with black magic stings my nose.

Ahriele is standing behind him, her hands glowing and her mouth uttering a prayer. She heals him by casting spells and temporarily protects him with a thin, magical shield while he goes berserk. Now and then, she reaches for her weapon and slashes at the creatures.

"Where's Saga?" he roars, cleaving one that is climbing the rock wall towards me, and I watch the vile guts spill out onto the ground as it collapses.

"I do not know!" I shout, not sure who he is talking to.

Something hisses next to me, and I turn to face it just as an arrow hits the monster between the eyes. A red-haired elf with long hair and a bow in hand rushes by, using the wall to take a quick acrobatic air leap and raining arrows down on a number of enemies. His brother uses two battle axes to assist Thurston and Cináed in slaying a massive spider with long, spiny legs and a skeleton-like body partially covered in loose, decaying skin.

It is not just the enemies who took damage. Soldiers have fallen, among them many high elves. Perhaps it is the black sorcery of the Highlands, which is affecting their minds and weakening them. Their king still fights as valiantly as when the first wave of enemies had appeared from several rifts in the atmosphere. He moves through clusters of monsters while performing a synchronised sword dance with a pair of tall female elvish soldiers close at his side. No sounds escape their lips—they are as silent as the shadows in the night. Somehow, they stay clean, despite the amount of blood spill, and dirt does not seem to stick to them. I presume they use cleanliness magic to keep themselves from getting soiled, no matter the situation.

"Where are you, Saga?" I hear Roseheart call out in a voice which is cracked at the edges. Incipient panic coursing through his mind.

"I don't see her anywhere!" someone shouts in response.

I close two of my eyes and look around with the third. A powerful individual is hiding somewhere in the middle of the battle, and the staff in my hand begins to shimmer like the night sky as I focus my energy on trying to locate it.

SHADOW DANCE

Something dark, hidden deep within my stomach, begins to beckon me, tantalising me to harness its raw strength, but I push the feeling away as far as it will go. *The time has not come yet—go back to your slumber.*

As if from behind a magic curtain, I can even feel Saga's terrified heartbeat and the trembling frequencies she sends out.

"Roseheart!" I shout, hearing him grunt as he decapitates another monster.

When he looks up at me, his face and hair are painted with splatters of blood, and his shining eyes burn with fighting power. *I have seen the same expression on his ancestors' faces hundreds of years ago.*

"I have located her," I continue in a loud voice, ducking nimbly as an arrow flies over my head. "I will go get her!"

There is no time to await an answer. Despite not needing to breathe, I draw air into my lungs, chanting a spell while the air slowly leaves my body. I must break through the barrier of black magic immediately.

A gasp leaves my lips as I finally make it through the magical curtain, and transparent figures slowly move in different directions around me. They go straight through my body, and I realise it is my party. Time barely moves in this magical sphere.

In the distance, I see Saga and a figure dressed in dark armour holding her arm. I hear her thin voice and the suppressed sobs having settled in her throat.

"You don't have to do this," she stammers, her shoulders trembling. "Please, Lysander. It's not too late for you to change your ways."

The figure crouched in front of her seems so preoccupied with studying her wrist that he does not notice my intrusion. An intense scent of hot blood tickles my nostrils and I recognise it all too well after having spent much time with her. In one hand, he holds a dagger and I exhale briefly. He has used the weapon rather than biting her, meaning the two will not have the same physical and mental connection to each other, which a bite mark would have built between them.

There is no time for speculation.

My hand holding the staff tightens its grip and I tell myself I must not summon the entity—the one that rests as a small component of its eldritch wholeness in a soul shard in my stomach—no matter what happens. I am well-aware I lack fighting skills, but the ancient deity will whisper to me with tempting promises if I allow it to gain control. Eventually, it could invade my thoughts, actions, and my sanity. *Its power and strength are not worth the risk.*

Out of the corner of my eye, I catch sight of a severed head. Momentarily, I see his smirking face before me, with his crown resting proudly atop his head and his beloved white raven on his arm. *My lord. This is not a fate you deserve.*

I, who usually stays relatively calm and neutral, am feeling the dangerous waves of anger rippling within.

"Hold your tongue, dearie," says the man, caressing her cheek.

Her terrified shriek cuts through the air as he fiercely pushes his lips against the bleeding wound, sucking on it. *Something needs to be done!*

I hear him murmur indistinctly as he lifts his mouth from her wrist, his face twisted in pain. When he speaks again, his voice is hoarse.

"You have indeed become stronger, and it may take longer for me to handle your magic. But no matter. Once I have you with me, we will have all the time in the world to get used to each other. Get up."

His gaze quickly shifts in my direction, pain turning into surprise. My jaws clench and I charge at him. I deliver a powerful blow to his face with the stone on my staff, causing him to stagger backwards. Saga rises

SHADOW DANCE

with her uninjured hand against her bleeding wrist, staring wildly at me.

"Help me, Sandro!" she screams shrilly, throwing herself straight into my arms.

The smell of blood catches me off guard and a quiet growl appears in my throat, but I swallow it before it escapes and fix my eyes on Lysander, who is rising to his feet.

"So, you are Sandro," he hisses and wipes the corner of his mouth with the back of his hand; his cheek which received the blow being angrily red. "Amarion's old mongrel. I was wondering where you were hiding."

His eyes travel down my body, fixating on my stomach. I straighten my back and stand firmly in front of Saga.

"I see," he says, his face lighting up like the moon. "So, the rumours about you hiding a dark secret are true. Truly exhilarating."

"Silence," I threaten him, tapping the end of the staff on the ground a few times.

I can tell he is significantly younger than me. Nonetheless, I am not sure how powerful he is, should he decide to use his full force, and in order to break through this magical barrier, I have to use intimidation to keep a distance between us. My vampiric age matters not in terms of power, as I actively avoid drinking human blood and do not dabble in black magic anymore.

The other vampire smiles darkly, making a straight line for us. I bare my fangs and when I speak, it is another tone which does not belong to me. It has woven itself into my voice.

"Aye, come here, lad. Come closer so I can dismember you!"

"Did I not ask you to slumber?"

My garbled voice causes Lysander's feet to stop moving and Saga to take a shaky breath. He adjusts the monocle over the bridge of his nose and tilts his head to the side.

"The mongrel knows how to bark," he says between gritted teeth.

I continue to tap the end of the staff on the ground rhythmically, focusing the energy within on a silent spell in my head. Saga's hands grip my clothing convulsively, and I hear her faint, anguished sounds. I sincerely hope the Light will remain slumbering in her as long as she is close. With one last pained look at the severed head that once belonged to my lord, I gather my energy, creating an orb inside my chest and my eyes glowing intensely.

"Know your place," I say in a breath, my voice dominated by the being inside that nimbly climbs up my spine, bounces around in my cranium, and chatters loudly in my ears.

I raise the staff and as I slam it into the ground even harder, a bellowing roar erupts out of my mouth. The invisible curtain cracks and the sounds from outside seep into the magical sphere.

Taking a couple of steps back, Lysander surveys me, his face emotionless. I presume he is planning his next move. Does he have the strength to face the entire party? Will he wipe us out and take Saga? *I am bereft of my lord, and I cannot lose the only friend I have left. I will not let him take her away.*

"Insolent, three-eyed swive!" he sneers, and I see the hand holding the dagger tighten its grip. "You dare to intervene? The woman is mine!"

"Saga belongs to no one but herself!" I shout. "Touch her again and I shall strip the flesh from your bones!"

The ancient god inside the soul shard in my stomach plays the chords of the vampire's inner voice in my head while chanting ominously.

"I may have misjudged the situation and thought I could easily get my hands on Saga, but greed got the best of me. Seduced by her blood, I became greedy enough for this degenerate vampire to show up and ruin my plans. At least I had a little taste. I know what to do next time."

A shimmering rift of black and dark purple—normally an invisible curtain between time and space—unfolds behind him, and he stares at Saga as he slowly takes a step back. He calls to her and her hands gripping my clothes tremble.

"Dearie, you should review your actions and how you plan to act the next time we meet. Because we will meet again, be sure of it. And you, whelp!" He points the dagger at me. "Enjoy your fragile friendship with the human while you still have the chance. In the near future, I shall cut you open and claim ownership of your soul shard."

In the blink of an eye, he turns and disappears into the rift, sealing it behind him. The magic barrier cracks violently, and as it crashes, there is a loud sound reminding me of glass being thrown against a wall.

A muffled scream leaves Saga's lips. Her arms desperately hug my waist, and she hides her face against my back. For a moment, I am taken aback. *Her hands clasp over the soul shard.* The injured wrist has smeared blood on my attire. The monsters let out shrill howls that would have frozen the blood in my veins if I were a human, and collapse in lifeless heaps.

"Saga!"

The leader of the Order of the Light rushes towards us. Reflexively, I back away as the knight's tall figure towers over me. Using my free hand not holding the staff, I bring my arm behind me and wrap it around the woman in a reassuring gesture.

"You are safe now," I whisper to her calmly and see out of the corner of my eye how Sunseeker stands next to the knight, along with Naira and others from the retinue.

Some of them look tired. Others are injured and many appear to have fallen. Roseheart wipes his face with the inside of his cloak, but I can still see sanguine fluid staining his golden hair and armour.

"Saga," he says again, this time in a hushed tone, and I notice how she slowly loosens her grip on my waist.

I turn to face her. She opens her mouth, but the words seem to get stuck in her throat. The wounded wrist trembles violently, despite the bleeding having been mostly stopped by Lysander's saliva, and when Roseheart catches sight of the injury, he shouts.

"Is there a cleric alive?"

Carefully, he takes hold of her arm, gently stroking her across it while caressing her cheek with his other hand. Sunseeker moves behind Saga with soundless steps, placing a slender-fingered palm on her shoulder. I can see the rings of sparkling purple jewels on his fingers, and he still wears the full-face helmet. My guess is he is speaking to her telepathically, and the touch of his hand is a way for him to more easily cut through her chaotic state of mind.

For some strange reason, I want to chase these individuals away and take Saga with me to a location where she does not have to have the eyes of others on her; a place where she can deal with the experience at her own pace. Fear has nestled itself in her heart, and I wish to help her, as she has helped me realise the value of friendship. *My friend.*

One of the surviving priests begins the process of healing Saga. I note how Roseheart gives Sunseeker a sharp look when he notices the elf is still resting his hand on her. The king shoots him a cold glance, his eyes glittering in silver behind the mask.

"Thank you, Sandro," Saga mumbles and shifts focus from her wrist to me.

She looks unusually pale. Her other hand finds its way to mine, and she squeezes it lightly in a comforting gesture.

"About Amarion. I'm sorry…"

Her voice cracks and she shakes her head, before pulling her hand back and wiping one eye with the back of it. The expression on her face is dejected as her gaze slips over injured travelling companions and lifeless bodies.

"The wound isn't healing," the priest notes pensively, drops of sweat glistening on his forehead.

"Step aside!"

Roseheart shoves him with an annoyed grunt, pulling off one of his gauntlets. His palm shines with an intense glow over Saga's arm and I take a swift long jump to the side. The searing power licks my skin, despite me putting some distance between us, and I cover myself with my cloak—along with a film of invisible magic—and feeling how my skin cools down almost instantly.

"Your efforts are in vain," I say out loud, taking a few steps back and the paladin gives me the side eye as I peek out from behind the fold of fabric. "Lysander's dagger is laced with black magic, as is his entire being. He is powerful and your magic will not heal that kind of wound, at least not as quickly as you wish."

"And what does the parasite suggest we do instead?"

Vincent steps towards me and I turn away with the gaze from two of my eyes, while the third stares at him rebelliously. The distance is enough for the Light not to burn me any longer. I pull the cloak away in front of me, tightening my grip on my staff in my left hand.

"The black magic resides mainly around the opening of the wound, just below the surface. It must get sucked out, and only someone who does not take damage from it can do so, someone who has dabbled in black arts. Moreover, a wound inflicted by a vampire can only get sealed with vampire saliva. Subsequently, another person may heal the superficial mark."

Cináed cleans the blades of his daggers carefully against his pant legs, and a dark smile splits the long, thick beard.

"It sure sounds like the vampire is looking for a tasty morsel."

"A preposterous accusation!" I sneer and notice how my voice is shrill at the edges. "I am merely trying to explain—"

My voice falls silent as Xerxi draws his bow, aiming the arrow at my third eye.

"You don't have to explain anything," he utters coldly, and the eye which isn't covered by an eye patch burns with disgust. "Your intentions are obvious."

"Have you hit your heads so hard in battle you cannot use proper reasoning? You seem to have not noticed she and I spend much time together, and I have had abundant opportunities to use her for my own needs, but I am not garbage just because I am not a human anymore!"

My words hang in the air, and I am beginning to lose my temper from being frowned upon. Roseheart's hand stops glowing, and he leans down so his gaze is level with Saga's. His hands cup her face and his thumbs slowly run across her cheeks gently while Sunseeker releases his grip on her shoulder, standing aside.

"Do you trust him?" the knight asks softly, the perusing gaze softening as she gently leans her forehead against his and closes her eyes.

"Yeah," she replies, barely audible. "But I don't want everyone to look at us so strangely. I can't take it right now. None of you, except me and Sandro, were there, and therefore, it's wrong of you to judge in advance. None of you have met Lysander face to face yet and you have no right to call Sandro a parasite when you don't even know him like I do. He saved me."

Intertwining his fingers in her uninjured hand, Roseheart straightens his back.

"We shall be back anon," he says, glancing at the warlord.

Thurston nods and gives Saga a long look.

"You must be careful, lassie. You're no longer at home where you can sit back and enjoy the comforts of life. If you notice you're feeling unwell or something strange is happening around you, you must inform us. Speak out loud instead of thinking. We're not mind readers."

Upon hearing the statement, two high elves, who have taken off their helmets, give each other an ironic smile.

"I'm doing the best I can, but sometimes things happen in an instant and I can't keep up," she answers timidly, mere moments from bursting into tears.

"I mentioned something was amiss, but no one listened to me," I say, growling the words out. "Do not push her anymore. Our attention should be on the recovery of the remaining retinue and the care of our fallen comrades."

"Sandro! Let's go."

Roseheart's gruff voice cuts a deep crack in my thoughts, stunning me momentarily. *It is the first time he has mentioned me by my name.*

CHAPTER FORTY-TWO

Saga Falk

The forest grove some distance from the cleft in the mountain is eerily quiet. The fog is getting denser and out of the corner of my eye, I see shadows moving and whispering indistinctly. A scent of rain lurks in the atmosphere and I'm cold. The bleeding has slowed, but the long wound from the dagger is still furiously open, and the throbbing pain is increasing in intensity with each passing minute.

We've settled on a fallen tree trunk and the moisture from the moss growing on it seeps through my trousers where the armour plate doesn't fully cover the fabric.

Garren holds me close, whispering a prayer to the Light in my ear as he strokes my hair. Too distressed to focus on the words flowing from his honeyed tongue, I stare at Sandro kneeling in front of me with his hands over my kneecaps.

"Do not be afraid," he says in his angelic, youthful voice. "I truly do not wish to do this to you, but there is no other way."

"What was it Lysander mentioned about a soul shard in you?" I blurt out.

A veil of melancholy settles over the vampire's red eyes, and I can't stop staring at the gold chains and jewels in his beautiful hair. Distracting thoughts wander inside my head and my right leg shakes nervously.

"What kind of soul shard?" Garren asks, his voice overlaid with rising suspicion.

"It does not affect me," Sandro explains quickly and puts his chin in the air. "I have lived with it inside me for over two thousand years and am fully confident in handling it."

"But what is it?" I whimper, noticing how anxious I sound. "We're friends. Close friends. Aren't we supposed to be honest with each other?"

A moment of silence passes, and I try not to panic and yell at him to hurry with the explanation.

"You are right, Saga."

Sandro sighs quietly, touching his fangs thoughtfully with the tip of his tongue before speaking.

"In the ancient times, the veils of the various dimensions thinned, and the influences of the ancient deities increased significantly. Their sometimes invisible tentacles could reach important people of various walks of life and control their minds. These individuals then became their heralds, powerful individuals who fed on the gods' black magic for performing their deeds, spreading their words and visions to those who were receptive."

He shakes his head slowly.

"Realising the true nature of the ancient deities, the armies of the various kingdoms joined forces to kill them. The strongest herald had been so severely infected by several gods, his insides had crystallised. As they had slain him, his crystallised soul burst, and the shards spread over the lands and seas. Some shards can still be found, sought after by those who turn to black magic and wish to amplify their wizardry."

A wistful smile plays on his full lips, and he looks up at my face with such sadness in his features, I feel like offering him a hug.

"I grew up with only a father. He found me in the woods, abandoned by my actual parents. To make a long story short—after pursuing magical studies for many months, I came back to our home. A pack of werewolves had slaughtered him. I watched them leave the cabin, shifting back into their human forms and mocking my old man. They butchered him for enjoyment. Out of a furious desire to avenge my father, I allowed myself to be turned into a creature of the night, thereafter searching for and finding a soul shard. I consumed it without a second thought."

I cover my mouth with my uninjured hand, eyes wide.

"Are you like Lysander?" I ask with a trembling voice.

An almost offended look settles on Sandro's visage, and he scrunches up his nose angrily.

"Most certainly not! I have not delved into black arts for a long time, nor do I allow myself to be influenced by the being within."

Garren's grip on me tightens slightly and noisily he draws air into his lungs.

"I should kill you here and now, Sandro," he growls. "However, the Light tells me to be patient. At this point, your task is to help Saga, and I must accept this and send prayers to the Mother of the Light to cleanse us of our sins. But listen to me carefully: if you make a single wrong move, I'll cut your heart out."

"I am well-aware of it," the vampire replies, avoiding looking at the knight. "Brutality in the name of the Light is close at hand in your family, Roseheart. You are the spitting image of your ancestors, and in battle, you fight precisely like them."

Cold shivers run down my spine. *What did I miss when I was inside the magic barrier?*

"The pain is increasing and I'm cold," I say, trying to steer the conversation onto a new track before the discussion turns into a heated argument.

"Come here, lass," Garren whispers, proceeding to pull me into an embrace so I'm sitting on his lap, wrapping his arms around me as he buries his face next to my neck. "Close your eyes."

I take a deep breath and shut the windows to my soul. Sandro's cold hands grab my wrist, and I close my eyes even tighter. Worriedly, I fidget, desperately trying to swallow the lump of anxiety being stuck in my throat.

"I am the one who should be struck with fear," I hear Sandro say, as if he has noticed my anxiety, and judging by the tone of his voice, I can imagine him smiling in his strangely bizarre, yet cute way. "You have the ability to destroy me."

"You're strong and incredibly brave," Garren mumbles next to my ear. "Do you remember when you tried to hit me the first time we met?"

I can't help but snicker and nod.

"You threw me over your shoulder," I murmur. "I was furious."

I wince as Sandro's razor-sharp upper fangs penetrate my wrist. "Ouch!"

I thought he was going to lick the wound, not bite me...?

"Forgive me," he murmurs in a hoarse voice. "I must take my time—the magic in your blood is akin to tasting fire. I apologise in advance for what may be a somewhat lengthy process."

The feeling of him gently sucking and licking my wrist clean has me almost pass out, but Garren holds me and whispers soothingly in my ear. I hear the vampire spit repeatedly as he mutters about Lysander's vile witchcraft. In my mind, I picture myself lying on the couch at home with a bowl of crisps and watching TV, my legs resting on Garren's thighs as he sits next to me, massaging my feet.

SHADOW DANCE

The sadness inside weighs me down and sometimes I find it hard to breathe. The group, including Garren, had been gathering up the fallen and digging graves, and after I had swept my gaze over the pile of bodies, I had scuttled away and vomited in a bush.

My wrist feels much better now that Sandro and Garren have taken care of me; the pain has mostly subsided. I sit huddled on the ground with my back to a large, cold boulder a distance away and the sounds of the party reach me. Maybe I'm perceived as weak and a burden, someone who doesn't help pull their own weight, but I've never seen so much death in my life and it's making me feel sick.

The mark from the dagger's sharp kiss on my wrist is almost gone, thanks to the Light. Running a finger lightly over it, I'm unable to get the image of Lysander out of my head as he cut me in an almost caring way. He had seemed indifferent to my screams, and when I desperately tried to get him to see the error of his ways, he had sharply ordered me to be quiet.

I take a deep breath, count to three, and exhale slowly. Terror claws at me at the thought of having to see him again.

My ears prick up when I hear quiet footsteps approaching, and I turn my head to the sound. Somehow, I know it's Sandro, even before his figure appears.

"How are you, little star?"

His youthful voice finds its way into my tired ears, and I wrap my arms around my legs, pulling my knees up to my chest. His clothes have my bloodstains on them, and his hair looks dishevelled, but he appears to be more alert. *Maybe he's less hungry now.*

"I'm hiding from the others," I answer with a wistful smile on my face.

"They look at me so strangely. Stranger than usual, that is."

"They judge not only me, but also you."

He settles down, and I move a little closer to him. Ever since he cleansed my wound of Lysander's magic several hours ago and sealed it with his own saliva, I feel our friendly connection has further strengthened. It's like spending time with Ambrosia, but without all the fuss that comes with it from her being headstrong.

"Sandro," I say, looking at him analytically. "Why does it feel as if you're about to become my best friend when I already have close friends where I'm from?"

He shrugs and smiles to himself as he closes his eyes.

"The first time I laid eyes on you, I knew I would find a friend. My first one," he replies.

"I'm sorry to hear about your father," I whisper. "I can't fathom the pain you went through."

"Thank you, but please do not feel bad for me."

For a second, we look each other in the eyes, and I wrap my arms around him in an embrace. He says naught, squeezing me tightly prior to breaking the hug. We hook our arms together, staring at a distant point in the forest for a while.

"Lysander strikes my heart with fear," I murmur, breaking the thin veil of silence between us. "Surely, it's idiotic? Me, a grown woman, who's paralysed with terror just because he looks at me."

"It is not idiotic at all," says Sandro, opening his eye in the middle of his forehead. "I, too, am afraid, yet for a different reason."

"What are you afraid of?" I ask, puzzled.

"I fear what Roseheart is capable of if something were to happen to you, and he believes it was me and my soul shard who caused you harm."

My cheeks blush fiercely as I let his statement sink into my consciousness.

"He may be intense sometimes, but I don't think he'd hurt you. You're peaceful and you don't let yourself become influenced by... that thing."

I point to his chest, but he shakes his head and pats his stomach.

"Here," he says. "I cannot wear skin-tight attire without attracting people's attention. It surprised me you did not notice the shard when you were holding on to me earlier."

"I was probably too busy with all the chaos to give it any deeper thought," I admit quietly.

Thoughts race through my head as I desperately try to rake them in. This dark concept, with soul shards from ancient gods, is something that's foreign to me and nothing I remember from either game notes or as something already established in *Reign Online*.

I'm thinking like that again. These two aren't the same thing at all—I can't compare these two universes to each other, despite the similarities.

"This means Lysander has one, too," I say in a breath, scratching my chin. "Which means we have to get it out, but how do we do it?"

"One who has swallowed a soul shard cannot get rid of it," the vampire replies, adjusting some locks of hair over his shoulders. "Someone else has to cut it out, causing the host to perish."

"What?" I mumble while putting one hand to my forehead. "I thought we could solve it with a more peaceful method."

"Your optimism is ever fascinating."

I gasp in surprise when catching sight of Kailunn emerging out of the shadows with a slim pipe in his hand and Sandro unhooks our arms as he slowly stands up. He grins with his fangs peeking out, putting his chin into the air as he looks up at the elf's features.

"An eavesdropping elven lad. It is the first time I have come across one," he says, and I can pick up on the teasing, almost condescending tone in his voice.

"The fanged creature appears to remember what humour is, even though he is ancient." The smoke slowly exhaled after taking a deep puff from the pipe swirls in the air and Kailunn gives him a forced, chilling smile back. "I am here to see how the girl is faring and have a private conversation with her."

The height difference between Sandro and Kailunn looks rather hilarious, and amidst the personal misery I'm going through, I can't stop myself from chuckling.

"Sorry, I don't know what has got into me," I giggle with my hand over my mouth and wave one hand apologetically in front of me.

Either I'm losing my mind, or I've already lost it.

Sandro's ears twitch and he stares intently at Kailunn with all his eyes at the same time. His gaze moves to his chest, then he lifts it again and tilts his head.

"I know what you are up to, lad."

Kailunn takes another puff from the pipe, eyes as cold as a midwinter night. "What are you insinuating?"

Sandro takes a step closer to the high elven king.

"Do not even think about it," he says in a low tone. "I can hear your intentions in your heartbeat. You have no right to drive a wedge between them."

"Sheathe your tongue and disappear from my sight at once, *ayis*," Kailunn responds sharply. "I have no patience for you and your ilk today."

The men stare each other down for a while as a weighty silence sweeps over us.

"What's going on?" I mumble nervously as I get up on my feet.

"Nothing, little star. I will return later," says Sandro quickly, giving me a long look. "Do not get yourself into trouble while I am gone."

In a flash, the grove swallows the vampire with its shadows. I massage the backs of my thighs with my hands and grimace. They hurt from sitting on the ground for so long. *I wonder why he talked so strangely to us. I'll ask him about it later.*

"Are you all right?" I ask, scratching the back of my neck before leaning my back against the large boulder. "You lost quite a few soldiers. I'm sorry for your loss, Kailunn."

"Losses are always difficult and weigh heavy on one's heart."

I nod at his statement, feeling even more miserable. Kailunn stands next to me—he, too, with his back leaning against the stone—and hands me his pipe.

"This may help with calming your nerves."

I stare at it. A scent of vanilla wafts from it, causing hunger to stir in my stomach.

"Thanks for the offer, but I must decline. I don't do drugs," I answer with a nervous smile and blush. "Sorry, I didn't mean to say you use drugs. I was just thinking about what Garren said last time when I was about to take the magic powder on my tongue."

Frustrated, I put my hands to my temples and massage them. *Why do I constantly make myself sound like a dumbass?*

Kailunn watches me without averting his gaze, his lips slowly curving into a smile.

"Your description is accurate. This works like a magic drug. It allows me to recover my life force; to live. Magic is essential for me on a daily basis. In your case, a drag could help you reduce your worry and anxiety. The choice is yours."

I can't stop looking at the pipe; his slender fingers with the perfectly trimmed nails holding it and the way his bejewelled rings sparkle. The image of Lysander with his harsh gaze as he cut me with the dagger has been etched into my head, and not even Garren has made me break this thought pattern so far.

Shyly, I look up at Kailunn's smooth face.

"What if I grow addicted to it?" I ask in a low voice. "I don't want to become dependent on anything."

"In general, people who do not have a desire for magic tend not to become addicted, especially when used in small amounts. I would not fret."

Just do it. It might help and prevent me from being a nervous wreck in front of Garren.

Carefully, I grab the pipe and study it. It has beautiful, intricate details on the wood. The head around the chamber is carved like several flower petals. For a moment, I think back to my woodworking classes in school and chuckle at the memory of trying to make a spoon, which ended up not looking particularly useful.

My gaze lingers on the bite, and I hesitate briefly. *He's clean and seems healthy—perhaps bacteria and viruses from high elves work differently from humans?*

"You don't have a cold, do you?" I ask, cursing myself inwardly as I hear how stupid it sounds.

"My people do not develop diseases the same way as humans," he explains, smiling politely. "I daresay you run a greater risk of catching a cold from your relations with Roseheart."

"I see," I mutter, annoyed with myself for getting embarrassed.

Okay, Saga—it's make or break time. Do it now before he makes more embarrassing comments.

I close my lips around the pipe and take a puff. Nothing happens.

Confused, I stare at it and then at the elf. He takes it from me, tapping the chamber a few times with one finger.

"Patience," he urges in his typical silky voice.

From a hidden pocket, he pulls out a beige handkerchief with gold edges, carefully wiping the bite before putting the pipe into his own mouth. After taking a deep puff with his eyes closed, he looks at me again, his eyes glistening like ocean waves with silver foam on top.

Something's happening.

A heat rushes down my trachea and into my lungs, where it builds a little nest and curls up like a purring cat. The magic of the Light is brought to life by the sensation and glowing butterflies swirl around us. A sudden calm settles in my head and Lysander's smooth, cruel face blurs out. Instead, I see sunny summer days on the beach together with Ambrosia, the feeling of warm sand between my toes, and when we built sandcastles together.

Kailunn clasps his hands behind his neck as he leans back against the stone, following the light phenomena with his eyes. The pipe protrudes boldly from the corner of his mouth, and he seems mesmerised by the butterflies.

As the two magical energies mingle within me, I remember the concerts I used to attend, both at home and abroad, with Ambrosia. Notes of forgotten songs play in my head, and I hum a melody that seems both foreign and familiar at the same time. My feet tap lightly on the ground, and I close my eyes. Hands and arms move in the air, synchronised to the internal music. Before I know it, I'm dancing, still with my eyelids closed. I don't feel any worry about tripping up—the notes take over my mind and I let myself become one with them.

I don't know how long I've been dancing for, but after a while a pleasant weariness creeps over me—which I assume is the magic from the pipe wearing off—and I sink to the ground in a sitting position, panting. As my eyelids open, Kailunn watches me enigmatically, and some of my magical butterflies seem to have landed on his armour. Embarrassment washes over me and I put my hands to my cheeks.

"I'm not sure what happened," I whisper, shaking my head slightly to adjust my messy fringe.

"You allowed yourself to be free from the shackles of worry and fear," he replies quietly, and when he takes a step towards me, the butterflies seem to melt into his armour and disappear without a trace. "I have seen no one move like you do."

"It's nothing special," I answer shyly. "At home I used to attend dance classes and I miss being able to dance in the living room, to music I'm used to hearing, when I need to unwind."

I grimace in surprise as he offers me his hand. With a grateful smile on my lips, I take it and stand up.

"I, too, appreciate being moved by music," he says, smiling to himself, his gaze fixed on one of the magical purple stones on his gauntlet.

Once more he takes out the handkerchief, which he moistens lightly with the tip of his tongue, before gently polishing the stone, and I ogle him. His eyes shift in my direction as he tucks the piece of cloth back in the pocket and clasps his hands behind his back.

"The next time I train with my soldiers, I welcome you to watch the training session. Perhaps you would appreciate our traditional martial arts interwoven with dance."

"That would be amazing, thank you!" I exclaim enthusiastically.

Maybe I can learn something new from them.

"Kailunn," I begin, gathering my thoughts for a moment. "Thank you for taking my mind off my worries for a while. This is the second time you've helped me."

Again, I lean my back against the rock, and we stand next to each other in silence for a while. As Kailunn's thoughts slowly find their way to me and twist around mine, I hold my breath and allow them to enter my mind. *Confusion, curiosity.* They polish away some of the anxiety in the dark recesses of my brain. I dare not look at the high elf. It feels as if his energy wraps around me like a snake, and I tell myself I should break the spiritual connection between us. Instead, I stand there. Completely still, smiling in surprise as his inner voice touches my soul like a soft feather, playfully tickling me in a way I've never experienced previously. I... I like it.

When I finally pluck up the courage to glance at him, I see he's looking at me with such penetrating intensity I forget where I am momentarily. I watch him questioningly as he positions himself in front of me with both his palms placed at the sides of my head against the stone. I open my mouth, but he interrupts me silently.

"Let your tongue rest."

I grimace in confusion as he removes my glasses with one hand. Slowly, he brings his face closer, placing his forehead against mine. *Warm skin, ice-cold eyes.* He doesn't avert his gaze for a second.

"Anxiety has closed its petals around you," he whispers telepathically. *"Your people cannot handle it properly, allowing it to build up barriers. Even the Light cannot illuminate your path more than a few steps in your present state."*

It feels like it crackles where our foreheads touch; completely painless. A chilly, pleasant sensation and an unusual stillness spread, starting in the middle of my chest.

"I don't know what to do to get rid of it," I answer him in my inner voice.

"Let me help you, as you helped me when I lost a loved one. Open the gates of your innermost self and allow me inside."

"But I don't know how to do it. And you've already helped me once today—I don't want to trouble you."

I blink again, and he holds my gaze firmly in his. He's close enough, our breaths mingling, and nervous thoughts race my head in a panic. *What if Garren sees us and gets the wrong idea?*

"Saga. Would you like me to help you?"

I sense the familiar feeling once more; the same one I experienced when I tried to give him some of my magic. *It's like my soul wants to pull him to me. I'm confused.*

"Saga."

"Yes. Please."

"Very well. It is just like a dance. Shut your eyes and follow my steps."

As I close my eyes, I'm transported somewhere else. *It's the beech forest in Torup!* Autumn leaves crackle intensely in yellow, red, and orange hues during the golden hour before nightfall, and a scent of faintly damp moss tickles my nostrils playfully. Time and space seem to have stopped, and yet, I can hear the sounds of the forest's inhabitants, the occasional chirping of birds, and the whispering rustling of the wind in the treetops.

A smile spreads across my lips as I bend down and pick up colourful leaves in my arms and toss them into the air, just like when I was younger, and my soul was not so gripped by melancholy. As the leaves fall, I notice Kailunn is standing some distance away, watching me with steady eyes. A pair of black pants, boots, and a dark purple semi-sheer shirt reaching down past his hips have replaced his armour. The shirt appears to have no buttons, held together by a wide red sash. The long white hair softly cascades over his shoulders, chest, and back. I can make out what he looks like under the garment, and immediately my mind drifts to Garren and memories of his bare skin against mine, despite the man in front me looking entirely different physically.

"Will you let me guide you?" he asks.

I look down to check myself out. I'm wearing my black and pink dancing shoes, black leggings, and a long-sleeved, light grey jumper. My hair is in a messy ponytail.

"Yeah," I answer and nod at him.

When Kailunn takes a couple of feather-light steps in my direction and begins to dance, I can't take my eyes off him. The movements are soft,

SHADOW DANCE

confident, and fluid. I'm almost hypnotised. Something powerful flashes between our palms as his long, slender fingers close around one of my hands. Parts of our energies are winding around each other, outside of us, as I let him lead me.

Never have I felt so carefree. It's a feeling of weightlessness similar to the one I experience when Garren heals me, but stronger and much more profound. Yes, this feeling transcends the physical body with its limitations and transforms into something completely different. Something indescribably soothing and satisfying.

The rays of the golden hour filter through the foliage as our bodies and energies move in synchronised harmony, and I wish I could share this feeling with Garren. The light makes Kailunn's hair shimmer and his jewelled rings and earrings sparkle. *He's so captivating.*

His grip around my hand is soft, and as he leans me back in mid-dance and grabs my hips to keep me from falling, his energy seems to seep into my body and dance with my own. Discreetly, I catch my breath and look him straight in the eyes. This feels different and not at all like when I'm healed by the Light. The hidden recesses of my soul lie bared before him. *What we share right now is tender, intimate, and closer than anything else I've ever experienced. Almost sensual.* I get a little anxious when I realise that I enjoy it.

"Tear down your inner barriers," he urges in a hushed voice. "Do not let worry and negativity weigh you down. Allow yourself to walk as if on clouds."

Kailunn lifts me up so I'm upright and puts his hands to my temples. Our energies are fully intertwined. His is significantly stronger, guiding me through inner labyrinths where I usually get lost. His frequencies penetrate deeper and deeper until it feels like we are no longer two distinct energy fields; my mind blossoming into a thousand roses with such intensity, causing a gasp to leave my lips. I grow drowsy, and the petals of anxious thoughts are carried away on a breeze as he rests his forehead against mine once more.

Calmness.

My hands hesitantly cup the backs of his hands and I close my eyes as I sigh shyly, and sentences echo in my mind.

"No one has ever walked where you have left your powerful, confident imprint on my soul and I'm so grateful for your help. But I can't stay for much longer. I'm tired and I need to go back to the man who has chained my heart to him."

CHAPTER FORTY-THREE

Garren Roseheart

The thought of Lysander hiding Saga from my sight and hurting her has seated a rage within me, but I mask my fury with a calm and composed mien. My temples throb and the headache spreads. A number of our brothers and sisters were buried tonight, and the mood is low as we eat and rest in an abandoned cabin by a wide-open field. The field, which is now barren and withered, was probably fertile once upon a time.

Somewhere in the distance, thunder rumbles ominously as it shakes the firmament, its sound reaching my ears in invisible waves. Heavy raindrops patter against the roof of the cottage and some of them seep in through a small hole in the roof, causing Thurston to move and curses to be muttered under his breath.

Saga sits close to me, with one hand tucked under my arm, on a bench, with Sandro on her left. She seems deep in her own thoughts while playing with her phone. The warm glow from the fireplace causes shadows to wander across her face, and the circles under her eyes appear darker and deeper. A discreet sigh squeezes itself past her lips.

On the screen there's a photo depicting Saga together with Ambrosia posing next to a group of men. Saga looks incredibly captivating, dressed in a sparkly green dress and her long hair in wavy curls cascading down over her bosom. *She radiates an exuberance of happiness.*

The same arm she's holding finds its way to her leg and I stroke her thigh with my hand, thereafter giving her a light squeeze. She looks up for a moment, treasuring me with a warm smile and making me want to lean in and kiss her, but now is not the time. Sandro glances at the screen and when he makes a sound of surprise, I glimpse his four sharp fangs on the top row of his teeth.

"Curls in your hair suit you nicely," he notes with an approving expression in his red eyes.

"Thank you," she replies, leaving her gaze from me to the vampire. "Ambrosia helped me fix them, and it took about an hour. I don't know how to do it myself without burning myself on the curling iron."

"Judging by your clothes and shoes, you must have had plenty of riches where you come from. In my culture, only the wealthy ones wear high heels."

She shakes her head. "Gosh, no. I found both the shoes and the dress for cheap at a thrift store."

She tucks strands of hair behind one ear, and I notice she smiles to herself.

"Who are they?" I ask, nodding towards the men in the photo.

One of them has his arm around her waist, arching his back slightly and pressing her to his chest so her cheek rests against his as they smile.

"They're a boy band Ambrosia and I like," she explains. "They're not young anymore, but their music still makes me happy. The one holding me is my favourite member ever since I was a little girl. I was beyond ecstatic when I finally got to meet him in person."

SHADOW DANCE

She leans against the wooden wall behind us as she puts her phone in her pocket, takes off her glasses, and rubs her face with her hand. An eyelash falls onto her cheek, and I reach towards her and gently pluck it away with one fingertip. A wistful smile plays on her lips, and she rests her head on my shoulder after putting her glasses back on.

"Garren," she says in a low voice.

"What's on your mind?"

A moment of weighty silence follows; the way she lifts her head to look at me leaves me feeling discouraged.

"I miss my life. Everything was a lot simpler at home, even though it didn't feel like it at the time."

The words make my chest sting, a razor-sharp needle of pain penetrating my heart. In my mind, I say a prayer to the Light to forgive me for my sinful thoughts—it's only natural she would miss where she belongs and the environment here isn't what she's accustomed to. My thoughts dip into the gloom. *Will she leave me and keep the memories of our moments together if the opportunity presents itself? I neither can, nor want, to forget her.*

"I know, lass," I answer quietly, and my hand reaches for her small fist.

She grabs it gently and I stroke her reassuringly over the back of her hand with my thumb. A hushed, foreign language causes most people's attention to shift to the high elves. It's unusual to hear them conversing with each other in Qyarallin outside their invisible walls of telepathy. They've removed their helmets, and grimly, I admit to myself that these elves possess a mysterious, almost magical beauty which is hard to resist, in particular Sunseeker.

"*A vair via riaye a linki,*" Saga mumbles to herself and smiles doubtfully. "It's the only sentence I know by heart, and I suspect I've got the pronunciation wrong, too."

With a swift, slight movement of his head, Sunseeker throws a glance in Saga's direction and captures her attention. My headache intensifies as I notice his normally icy silver gaze dripping with honey.

"The sun shines brighter than the moon," he translates, a smile spreading across his lips. "What delightful pronunciation. It is as if your tongue was made for our magic speech."

Gloomily, I see a fierce blush spreading across her cheeks, but she answers him with no more than a curt nod. *Look my way instead, Saga. Don't you realise what you've done to my heart?*

"What made you study Qyarallin?"

One of his female soldiers, Fevienne, interrupts my thoughts as she asks the question, and I detect an impressed tone in her thin voice. Long, spiky black hair, silver eyes with long, curved lashes, and dark skin. Her stature is slender and tall, slightly taller than Sunseeker, and it's clear as day she possesses enormous physical strength. Her radiating beauty almost stings my eyes and I resolutely avert my gaze from her.

Saga shrugs.

"I like languages," she answers quickly, and a few strands of hair fall in front of her face.

"If you wish to delve further, seek me out," Fevienne continues. "I am proud to belong to my people and am happy to teach our rich language to those who have a genuine interest in their soul for it."

Xanjou, standing with his arms crossed over his chest, leaning against one wall and glancing out the window now and then, turns his attention to her.

"You're welcome to teach me all you know," he says enthusiastically, winking at her, while Ahriele and Naira snort disapprovingly from across the room.

Fevienne gives him a cool smile, but says naught.

Rising to his feet, Sandro's ears twitch.

"Be quiet," he says and closes two of his eyes. The third glows intensely red and darts across the room.

Saga's gaze glows in white, and a third eye in gold appears on her forehead.

"I can see them," she whispers in my ear. "They're tormented, and our weapons can't touch them."

The additional eye vanishes, and I hear them. The eerie, creeping sound of a woman's crying, whining nearby, and a chilling scream in the distance. My hand instinctively finds its way to my sword which is leaned against the wall. The vampire growls quietly like a predator, baring his fangs as he turns around at supernatural speed, glaring at us.

"Lie down immediately and do not make a sound!" he whispers. "Otherwise, we will all die!"

I pull Saga down on the floor, protecting her with my body.

"There's something you should know," she whispers as she clings to me, and I notice the panic in her voice.

The grip on my sword tightens, and she buries her face against my neck as I evaluate the situation and what our group's next move should be. Sandro's words echo in my head. *Be quiet.*

"Garren, I love you."

The trembling whisper sets my heart on fire, and I fill my lungs with air. Carefully, she lifts her head, and our eyes quickly lock into each other in an intense moment which merely lasts for a few seconds.

You're the song of my heart. I'll protect you until the last breath has left me.

Once again, the white glow appears in her gaze, as well as the third eye on her forehead. Surrounded by a crown of light, she rises and a glittering, magical shield pulses around her. As I reach for her hands, the shield blocks me from reaching them. With wide eyes, I see a tender smile spread across her lips.

"There's something I must do," she says, taking a couple of steps back so she puts distance between us.

Her voice has an undertone which is unknown to me.

"Lie down, Falk!" Ahriele hisses from across the room.

Sandro pushes himself against a wall whilst hiding behind his black cloak as he stares at her over the arm that he's holding in front of him.

I ignore the vampire's earlier words of warning. Swiftly I get to my feet and reach for Saga once more, but I'm pulled to my knees by glowing, magical chains around my legs, wrists, and chest. Frustrated, I try to tear myself away. *Her magic has become uncontrollable beyond my wildest imagination.*

"Saga, listen to me!" I say in a low voice. "Your chains may hold me, but I can't let you leave the cabin. You don't know what's waiting out there."

I can't protect you if you leave my side.

Golden butterflies flutter through the room on shimmering wings and she continues to smile. I see her feet lift slightly from the ground and when some of the high elves fly up from the floor like agile felines, they, too, find themselves chained and pulled back down. The magic from her aura seems to be so powerful, their bodies cannot fully absorb it.

"Stay here," Saga commands in a crystal-clear voice.

The gaze sweeps across the room and settles on Sunseeker, who's staring intently at her with silver shimmering eyes, protected by Fevienne and another one of his bodyguards. She raises her hands slightly with her palms pointing to the ceiling, causing chains to wrap around him and the rest of the party, except for Sandro, who has shapeshifted into a spider and climbed the wall to keep his distance.

Before I can open my mouth again, Saga whirls around in the air, thereafter bursting through the door to the cabin with a loud bang. A roar erupts from my throat as I call for her, furiously fighting against the chains' firm grip on my body.

SHADOW DANCE

"Sandro!" I hear Sunseeker utter in an icy voice. "You are the only one not being held down. Follow the girl and make sure she does not get herself killed!"

Sandro flings himself across the room and when he lands on the other side, a safe distance from the magical chains, he has shifted himself into his normal stature.

"I was already on my way, lad!" he exclaims, fangs bared, rushing out the doorway and his cloak flapping wildly behind him.

CHAPTER FORTY-FOUR

Sandro Oyemi

"Saga!" I shout, quickly shielding myself with my cloak and flinging myself to the side as a magical, searing breeze sweeps past me. "Your body cannot handle the magic!"

Saga is standing on the ground now, some distance from the cabin, and has attracted the attention of a large group of creatures lunging at the shield that surrounds her. The creatures are tall, thin, and twisted by black magic which has largely taken over their bodies, giving them monstrous physical attributes and immense strength. Hollow eyes stare wildly at her, and screeching sounds erupt from their mouths as the Light burns them. *They keep being drawn to her magic repeatedly, as if they are addicted.*

"Saga!" I exclaim again. "Listen to me!"

In the distance, I can hear Roseheart calling her from inside the cabin. The intense glow from her palms spreads up her arms and engulfs the rest of her body until she takes on the guise of a living light phenomenon. The crown of light behind her head transforms into shimmering daggers, thrusting violently into a number of the creatures.

Like a shining whirlwind of light and heat, she sweeps through the rest of the monstrosities, hurling glowing bodies around her as if they weigh nothing. Swiftly, I shapeshift into a raven and take to the sky before I get hit.

The glow around Saga fades as she staggers. From above, I watch her collapse on the ground, hearing how the air leaves her lungs. I dive down, almost crashing next to her in my usual guise. Placing my staff beside me, I gently grasp her head with my hands as a strange feeling of emptiness takes root within me. My ears prick up with the sounds of running footsteps and panting, panicked breaths.

The cadence of her heart flickers like a dying light and extinguishes, leaving nothing but the vivid memories of a lively young woman who had her whole life ahead of her just mere moments ago.

CHAPTER FORTY-FIVE

Kailunn Sunseeker

I shut all sounds out of my mind as I stand to the side, watching Roseheart clinging to Saga's lifeless body and trying to instil a spark of life in her. A few clerics have gathered around to offer their healing touch, and judging by the look on the knight's face, I can tell he is yelling at them. Saga's features look peaceful, in a way I have not seen afore. *In the silent embrace of death, she has found the peace she so desperately sought.*

"When your heart breaks, mine cries together with you."

My gaze lifts as the notes of the whispering, telepathic voice reach me. Her figure shimmers in a blue-violet shade where she stands behind Roseheart, her eyelids lowered. Between her slender fingers she spins a thin, sparkling web which she places over the knight's shoulders, before attaching the end of one thread to the centre of her own chest.

"I wanted to protect you, just as you have looked after me."

Her thin arms embrace him, and he seems oblivious to what is happening on this spiritual plane as she places her cheek against the back of his neck.

"Saga."

I call to her with my inner voice, and her shimmering eyelids wander up. The energy field rises, smiling wistfully at me.

"Come back."

"It hurts my soul when I'm in my physical shell, Kailunn."

A deep breath fills my lungs.

"Let me help you, like the time we danced together. I can ease your pain. He needs you. We need you."

I bow my head slightly as the caresses of her shimmering hands find their way across my forehead and cheeks, like an invisible dance of jewelled words lost in time and space.

"Saga. I need you, more than you know."

A soothing, chilly breath of air sweeps through my body as she attaches a thread from the sparkling net to my chest.

I notice several shimmering figures appearing in the distance, silently surveying us. Floating over to Roseheart yet again, she tugs at the net over his shoulders, causing him to lift his head up. Wrapping her arms around his neck, she leans down to kiss his mouth. The knight catches his breath as raindrops journey down his face, masking his tears.

"Garren. My love for you couldn't be conveyed in mere words. It was as if we knew each other from another lifetime."

The unspoken words make me reminisce about the arrival of winter over Laifes Vairla; glittering snow falling slowly, silently, in the nights.

Her eyes seek mine and as the shimmering figures move in closer to us, she dances around Roseheart in fluid movements, wrapping the thread attached to her chest tightly around his body. Slowly he looks

SHADOW DANCE

down at Saga's still face, tracing her cheeks with his hands, and in this moment, the proud lion of Whitekeep becomes a broken man.

Her energy whirls around, tugging at the string attached to me, and I find myself unable to move. I can sense fingertips touching my visage, a chill breeze pulling my eyelids down and making me hold my breath.

"Thank you for helping me and giving me solace when I needed it the most."

Invisible arms embrace me, filling my heart with a song from another dimension, and an ache which almost causes me to fall to my knees.

When my eyes fly open, I catch sight of the energies as they dissipate together. She has left us.

No, your tale must not end here. I cannot let you leave!

Glossary

Qyarallin ('Magic Speech')	English
A Illenneihe	The Great Queen
A lirenri Illenneihe	The most beautiful Queen
Amar	Yes
A vair via riaye a linki	The sun shines brighter than the moon
Ayis	Monster
Elurru	Please
Fevienne	Doer of good deeds, also used as a proper noun
Firenn	Father
Illasa	Worthy or able to correct, also used as a proper noun
Illennehe	King
Kai	Son
Kailunn	Resplendent son, also used as a proper noun
Kyenn	Mother
Laifes Vairla	Sun Hill
Mertena	Worthy or able to encourage, also used as a proper noun
Sulsair	Knight
Unie las	Young one
Vairmilenne	Sunseeker

Acknowledgments

Thank you to my family. To my father, who taught me how to be true to myself and not let anyone beat me down. To my mother, one of the strongest women I know, who took me to the library when I was young and inspired me to be a dreamer and a conjurer of written worlds. You both raised me with so much love and made me see my own worth.

James. Thank you from the bottom of my heart for your unending support, all the cups of coffee and all the love and laughter you have given me over the years.

A heartfelt thank you to my beta readers, whom I trusted with my first, second and third drafts. Your words lifted me and pushed me forward. Special thanks to Mariam and Inger, who made the solitary process of writing a book a little less solitary by keeping me company on the phone.

Massive thanks to Shade of Stars, who illustrated my book cover and breathed life into my characters with each brushstroke. I cannot convey in words how much it means to me to see my lifelong, fictional friends as stunning, visual beings.

To you, my reader. Thank you for exploring a fragment of Theadrath, a world which I worked on and built for over twenty-two years. I have poured my life, heart and soul into writing this book, and I hope my words made you experience something.

This is just the beginning of a great adventure, and I hope you will join Garren and the others in the forthcoming sequel to Shadow Dance.

About the Author

C. K. Andersson is an author raised in Sweden. Since 2017, she resides in England together with her partner, their rescue dog and two rescue cats.

She is inspired by the small things in life such as the aroma of coffee in the morning, the rain drumming against the window, and the warmth of the sunlight caressing her cheeks. Her happy place is Tokyo, where she has spent countless hours looking up at the stars.

Website: https://www.ckandersson.com/
Links: https://linktr.ee/ckandersson
Twitter: @ChrisKAndersson
TikTok: @ckandersson
Hive Social: ckandersson